Of Gods

&

Globes II

— EDITED BY —

LANCELOT SCHAUBERT

— STORIES FROM —

Kaaron Warren • Howard Andrew Jones
Tracey Baptiste • Vonnie Winslow Crist
Ken Altabef • J.T. Glover • F.C. Shultz
Brandon McNulty • Brandon Ketchum
Anthony G. Cirilla • Alex Sirkman
Andrea Obaez • Emily Munro
Carole McDonnell
&
Lancelot Schaubert

This is a work of fiction. Names, characters, places, and incidents either are the product of the author's imagination or are used fictitiously, and any resemblance to actual persons, living or dead, business establishments, events, or locales by name or by likeness is entirely coincidental.

Schaubert, Lancelot

Of Gods and Globes 2 / Lancelot Schaubert

ISBN-13: 978-1-949547-05-4

1. FICTION / Fantasy / Dragons & Mythical Creatures/ FIC009120
2. FICTION / Science Fiction / Hard Science Fiction/ FIC028020
3. FICTION / Fairy Tales, Folk Tales, Legends & Mythology/ FIC010000

I. North America
II. Oceana

Printed in the United States of America

The Music of the Spheres:

Of Gods & Globes II

Lancelot Schaubert

Once more, my friends and colleagues and I have banded together to compose literature connecting astronomy and mythology: to write *Of Gods & Globes II.* Each one of us chose a name that connected astronomy (science fiction) and mythology (fantasy) such as "Janus" and wrote forth.

But why on Earth — or off Earth — would we do such a thing?

Well for starters, in his introduction to Bernard Silvestrus's *Cosmographia*, Winthrop Wetherbee III (which, let's be honest, is a *doozy* of a name but PERFECT for anyone destined to study and teach Latin) said that the thinkers of the classical and middle ages offered up:

The idea the events of earthly life were governed and predetermined by the orderly disposition and activity of the heavenly bodies and could, in part, be foreknown through the careful analysis of celestial phenomena... Adelhard of Bath, in the De eodem et diverso, *extols the power of the Arts to guide the soul in its earthly journey; they teach her to recognize her special relation to the rest of creation, to know the nature and intuit the divine pattern of the universe. For the soul's basic affinity is with the divine* rationes *of things...*

Man, like the universe, lives and moves through the interplay of rational and irrational forces... **which evokes preoccupation with the archetypal implications of myth and the themes of classic literature.**

We had such a successful launch last time that we decided to come together and write even more stories around this theme. We have continuations on a couple of new universes, hilarious new additions, heartbreaking horror stories, and flirtatious little romps.

In the spirit of drawing on themes of myth and classic literature and of the tidal influence of the constellations, I rounded up sci-fi and fantasy writers to write about cosmic influence. The fantasy writers took a more mythological approach, speaking of the symbolic (or perhaps godly) Mercury and Mars and Neptune. The sci-fi writers tell you what it's like to live on Jupiter and Uranus. All of them, though, speak of the influence of what one writer called "the music of the spheres." These are stories *Of Gods and Globes*. They're quite the ride: I enjoy each of these stories differently. They made me laugh and cry and chilled me to the bone with terror and one of them made me long for a home that… well for a home I don't think I've ever been to before.

Come fly with us. Let's fly. Let's fly away.

Or, if you prefer, to appeal from Sinatra to Sinatra:

Fly me to the moon
Let me play among the stars.
Let me see what spring is like
On Jupiter and Mars…
Fill my heart with song
And let me sing forevermore
You are all I long for
All I worship and adore…

— Lancelot Schaubert
Brooklyn, New York
2020

. . . and to my listening ears
all nature sings and round me rings
the music of the spheres.

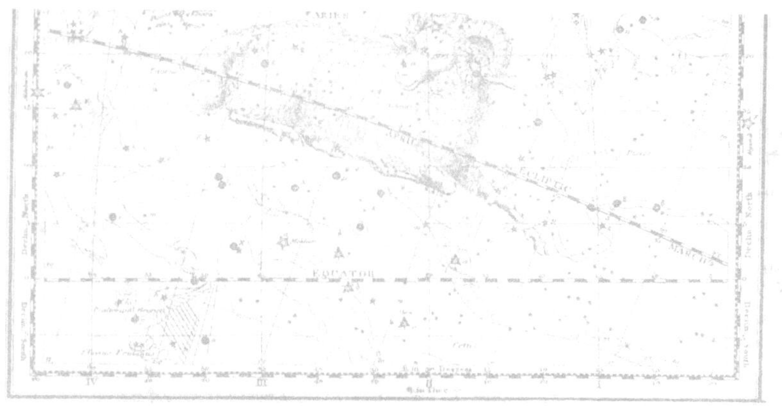

TEN-YEAR PHOTO

Brandon McNulty

Never should've clicked on Ten-Year Photo. We first came across it a decade ago, back in '09 when I shared a ratty college apartment with my bandmates Tony and Shane. I was head bitch of our metal group, and while Tony was a reliable bassist, Shane usually ignored his drums and hit computer keys instead. Big mistake. The habit led him to Ten-Year Photo and its simple three-step concept: upload a photo, click submit, and see your future. If you had one.

Our first upload was Tony's ex-girlfriend. She was your typical Pre-Law babe wrapped in preppy clothes and drenched in sunny-blonde highlights. Heavy makeup, lots of jewelry—the type that scrunched her nose at my white-girl dreadlocks, my tattoos, my Megadeth tank tops. Shane and I couldn't stand her, so we found a picture of her and hit UPLOAD.

Then we waited.

A yellow loading bar inched across the screen. Beneath it was a logo. It depicted a man's head with two faces looking in opposite directions. Next to it were the words POWERED BY JANUS.

"This gonna take all night?" I asked. Shane's room always gave me headaches for one reason or another. Tonight, it was the smell of burnt popcorn in the trash and the neon-green blaze of the Rolling Rock sign hanging above his computer. That, plus the fact that he didn't have his gear ready for rehearsal.

"Little patience, okay?"

"Sorry, none left," I said. "At least not for this goddamned joke site."

"It's not a joke, Ash. You weren't listening." Shane swiveled in his chair, sending his tie into a pendulum-like swing across his shirt. He was fresh off a job interview (which he bombed) and his unruly red hair was gelled down hard. He drummed his fingers over a briefcase in his lap. "This site is Deep Web shit. Supposedly, it takes any photo and shows what the person will look like in ten years. With spot-on accuracy."

I groaned.

"Admit it, Ash. You want to see what 2021 holds for you. Maybe your music career will finally rise from the shitter."

I scowled. "You want to eat your keyboard?"

He yelled for Tony as the loading bar hit 100%. For a moment the screen froze, then up popped a picture of Tony's ex, only this time her flawless face was a tug-o-war battle between wrinkles and laugh lines.

"Recognize her, Tony?" Shane asked.

Tony hunched forward and squinted, his long rocker hair swishing over his cheeks. His smooth face was more boy-band than metal-band, but one look at the screen had his eyes burning like black fire. "That supposed to be Lindsay? Seriously? Piss off, Shane."

Shane explained the site's concept to him and said, "Don't you guys think Lindsay'll look like this in 2021? I mean, she burns through like sixty Camel Lights a day. And plus—"

Tony left. He didn't want to hear it and I didn't blame him.

"Shane," I said, "grab your drums and quit acting like a fucking twelve-year-old."

"There's an idea, Ash. Get me a picture of yourself from when you were twelve. Then we can test—"

I slammed the door on my way out.

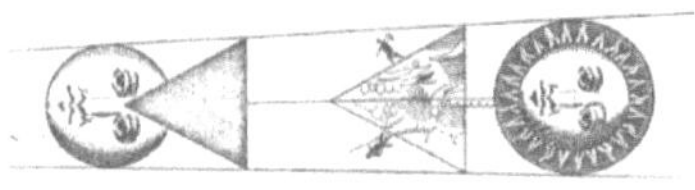

Since our music was too loud for the neighbors' sanity, we had to rehearse between the damp walls of the apartment basement. Or at least when all three of us showed, we did. That night I spent twenty minutes alone with my Gibson Les Paul, taking out my frustration on the fretboard and sending up a series of howling notes before anyone joined me.

Tony eventually came down and snuck a bite from my half-eaten cheeseburger sitting atop one of the washers. When I called him out on it, he stammered through an apology until I tore open the Burger King bag and tossed him a fresh double-cheddar.

"Take it. Got it for free anyway."

Tony snorted. "You 'forgot' to pay again?"

"Nah. Some zit-nosed cashier called me a Joan Jett wannabe, so I went and bitched to the manager. Told her 'sorry' wasn't enough of an apology."

"That's our girl."

"Nobody's girl."

Minutes rounded the basement clock. I shredded through warm-up riffs while watching for Shane in the stairwell. My fingers stampeded down the frets while my pick-hand chopped at the strings until one of them snapped.

Then I snapped. I flung my Gibson onto a dryer, filling the basement with a gong-like echo accompanied by a six-string twangy dissonance, and went for the stairwell. Tony cut me off and we got into a shoving contest that ended with his cheek scraping the cinder block wall.

"Jesus, Ash," he said, wiping the blood with the collar of his Slayer t-shirt. "What's your deal? Shane's always late?"

"Never this late." I licked my thumb and wiped a red smear off his cheek. "He's pulling this shit to piss me off."

"It's probably the interview," Tony said. "Case you lost count, that's the eighth-straight one he's bombed. Cut him a break, will ya?"

Back upstairs, the apartment was pitch-dark aside from a neon-green line beneath Shane's door. A gloomy Nine Inch Nails song screeched inside. I tried the knob. It spun, but the door was stuck. One hit from my shoulder knocked it loose.

Shane jumped at the sight of us. He shut his briefcase and tossed it in the corner near a Christmas tree decorated with crushed beer cans. On his desk was a baggie of coke that he stuffed into a drawer.

"Grab you drums," I said.

"In a bit."

"Now."

Shane sank into his computer chair and nodded at his screen. "Still waiting on that picture of you from ten years ago."

"Cut the shit," I said. "We got a gig tomorrow."

"Why the hell should I care?"

"Come on, man," Tony said. "Ash needs us and we need money."

"You think we matter to her?" Shane asked, as if I wasn't there. "Then why'd she run off and fuck the lead singer of Under Ice?"

Tony glanced at me.

"That was a mistake," I said through gritted teeth. "I was blind drunk that weekend."

"Not blind enough to miss that post on their website about needing a guitarist. Way to cheat on our band."

"Fuck off. I'm too talented to screw my way into a band. Grab your drums."

"I'll grab my drums when you grab me that photo."

"Goddammit, Shane! Enough with—"

Tony stepped between us. "Chill, both of you. I got an old photo album under my bed. Ash, come give me a hand."

Tony's room was somehow messier than Shane's, with Ozzy posters peeling off the walls, a mini Christmas Tree sprouting out of a desk drawer, and Snickers wrappers swamping the carpet. We squatted near the bed, and, fuck, did it reek hard of cigarettes. He dug out old music mags, chipped bongs, and a stack of LSAT books with yellowed pages. I asked him when he was re-taking the LSATs and he ignored me. Among his findings was a dust-caked guitar case with a gold Fender logo branded into the lid.

"Since when do you own a Fender?"

Tony shrugged as if it were no big deal. I couldn't understand why he'd keep it stashed while slaying away at that cheapo one he'd had since sophomore year.

The excavation ended in success. Tony flipped open a leather photo album to the Christmas photos. He slid one loose: a picture of his cute, boy-band face at age twelve, wearing a white button-down and a reindeer-patterned tie.

"Always an ugly bastard, even then," I said with a grin.

Tony snorted. "Pack my junk up while I run this to Shane."

Instead of packing, I flipped through his photos and saw one of an older guy, maybe forty-ish, playing a Fender bass onstage at what looked like a church bazaar. I eyed the guitar case near the bed.

Tony was still jawing with Shane in the other room, so I popped open the guitar case. The Fender gave off an eerie black shine beneath the ceiling light. Two tattered Led Zeppelin decals were peeling near the pickups. The base of the guitar was smudged with grimy fingerprints. I lifted the bottom of my tanktop to wipe them.

"Don't."

I jumped.

Tony stood in the doorway, glaring at me as if I'd tried to rob him.

"Killer bass," I said.

"It was my dad's."

My mouth turned to cotton.

Tony shut the case, glaring at me.

I tried to explain when Shane blurted from down the hall. "Guys, hurry!"

The loading bar was at 98% when Tony and I swung in.

Shane poked a pipe between his lips and hit it. He exhaled a warm, sweet cloud. "Moment of truth, right here."

The loading bar disappeared. The screen went black. Everything froze. Even the mouse wouldn't budge. Shane threw up his hands in frustration.

Then the screen flashed.

Black to white.

From the top-down an image loaded, and into view came shaggy dark hair. Tony's face appeared, looking almost exactly as he did now. It even showed the scrape on his cheek.

Tony and Shane lowered their jaws, shocked.

"Right," I said. "Real funny, guys."

Shane blinked. "This is funny to you?"

I pushed Tony's hair aside and revealed the scrape on his cheek. "You took that picture just now while I was in his room." I turned to Tony and jabbed him in the ribs. "The future-lawyer falsifying evidence. They should disbar your ass."

"Ash." Tony shook his head. "We didn't."

Then the loading finished. It left me speechless. At the bottom, his neck was hulking through the collar of the kiddie shirt. The top button had torn loose and his reindeer tie hung askew.

Tony had grown. His clothes hadn't.

Rehearsal went nowhere. Shane swatted drums, Tony thumbed his bass. The more distant they grew, the more I second-guessed my skepticism about that website.

Ten-Year Photo.
POWERED BY JANUS.
A decade in one click.

While there was image-alteration software readily available, no way could Shane doctor Tony's shirt and tie like that. Not in three minutes. But if they weren't pranking me, what did that say about the website? And what was Janus—a person? A company? Some hush-hush government group?

We ended up back in Shane's room, the popcorn stench fading as Shane toked his pipe. Tony agreed to upload a picture of his mom from that same Christmas collection. In it, Photo-Mom wore a tight, candy-cane sweater and looked awfully thin—much thinner than the globby, hammock-chinned woman Tony introduced me to during homecoming week.

The three of us mauled a six-pack of Coors while Photo-Mom loaded. Shane downed his beer seemingly in one gulp and reached for a second. Tony leaned in when the loading bar hit 100%. Once again it froze, this time longer than the last. Part of me prayed that Janus ran out of power.

The screen flashed. Tony's mom appeared, brow wrinkled and cheeks ballooning. She looked as plump as her current self, but what shocked us was the sweater. That candy-cane sweater fit Photo-Mom fine, but now her chunky arms stretched the fabric like fishnets, with her suffocating pink skin poking through.

Maybe it was the booze, but I started laughing. I had to. I needed to believe it was a joke. Shane joined in, the two of us howling.

Tony, not so much. "Shane," he said, scratching at the label of his bottle. "Upload my dad next."

Shane and I traded a look. The humor slid off our faces.

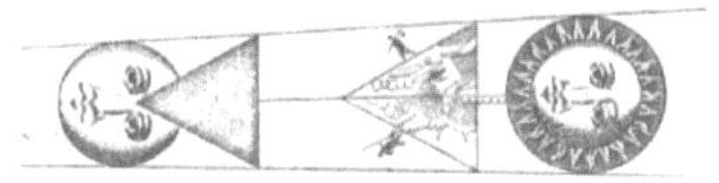

Tony told me about his dad one night when he was drunk and I was pretending to be. The last time he saw his old man, the guy was in a hospital bed, a thin blanket covering his bumpy ribs and jagged knees. Worse yet, with all the IV stands and monitors around, Tony couldn't give his old man a goodbye hug. For a brief moment his dad stirred, noticed him, and lifted a scrawny hand above the bed railing. Tony reached out, and right before their fingers brushed, his dad's arm fell short and hung there.

Right now, Tony's eyes held the same glossy stare as when he told me that story. Except this time there was a sick, wistful hope in them. No doubt he was cycling through what-if scenarios: What if his dad beat the cancer? What if he regained weight? What if he were here now?

The loading bar hit 99%.

Tony's throat hiked in his neck.

I knew I had to get him out of the room, away from the computer. Seeing it would tear him apart. I pinched his elbow, but he shook me off and leaned over the monitor.

The loading finished. The screen froze for several minutes. Nothing happened.

Nothing, nothing, nothing.

I cleared my throat to say something. But when my mouth opened, no words fell out.

The screen flashed. Black to white.

And back to black.

There was no picture.

Just one word: "Error."

The bottle went frigid in my grasp. A numbness spread up my arm. I knew I was supposed to say something, but I was never the consoling type. And now seemed an impossible time to start.

Shane finally broke the silence. "Want me to re-upload?"

Tony left the room.

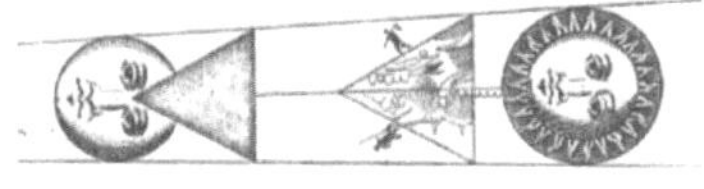

Water flushed non-stop from the bathroom sink. I listened with my ear pressed to the door. Never had Tony needed a moment alone more, but I couldn't trust him with total solitude. The look on his face when that Error message hit was something out of hell, and while us rockers were headed there, it wouldn't be tonight.

There came a final splash of water and the slap of a towel. He coughed a few times and the bathroom tiles creaked. He was leaving. He was okay. Thank Christ.

I hurried away to the kitchen and grabbed another six-pack. When he started down the hall, I stepped out all casual, bottles rattling at my side. He tried ignoring me on his way to the front door, but I stopped him.

"So," I said. "Shane's ideas can be shitty sometimes, huh?"

He didn't reply. Just swallowed. He smelled of sweat and soap, his hair shining wet in the light from the kitchen. His eyelids were swollen and red.

Before I could stop myself, I snared him in a hug. The bottles clinked behind him as I squeezed tight.

He trembled, his cheek moist against my forehead. It took him a second to register what was going on, then his hands slid across my back, bumping my bra as his palm meshed against my spine.

We pulled back, still in each other's grasp. I wiped a wet clump of hair from his face. He brushed a couple stray dreadlocks from mine. I froze. His lips plunged toward mine.

I shrank away. "Let's not turn this into *Days of Our Lives*, okay?"

He stammered something about heading out to the bar, but I couldn't let him leave. Not with that broken look in his eyes. I steered him by the shoulders back toward Shane's room. Maybe not the best therapy, but not the worst either.

"Shane's uploading me next," I said. "You don't want to miss this, not if I burn-out and end up looking like some knocked-up Pat Benatar."

The loading bar shot across the months, the seasons, the years. I wasn't doing this for Tony. Not entirely. Sure, it was an excuse to keep him home, but the truth was I needed to know where I was headed. I'd been dragging my fingers down guitar strings since kindergarten, and every time I closed my eyes I saw myself on-stage in front of assloads of loyal fans. If that life was coming, it'd be written all over my future-self's face.

At 100% I nudged Tony. He was staring at a crack in the wall, still mixed-up about his dad and our non-kiss. Another nudge broke his trance.

The screen flashed.

I braced myself for the big moment.

It flashed again and I saw a stranger. A bald, baggy-eyed stranger with shriveled tattoos webbing her neck and shoulders. The tough metal chick was gone, replaced by a heroin-thin banshee who probably hadn't slept in a decade. Shane threw his head back laughing and Tony snorted into his sleeve. I leaned over the keyboard, my mouth tasting of dust. How could I go bald at thirty-two?

Tony went next, apparently loosened up enough by my shitty outcome. When his future arrived, I forced myself to laugh. Somewhere before his thirty-second birthday, he got himself a crewcut and went gray in the process. I joked about the long hours of lawyering in his future. He didn't laugh.

Afterwards, Shane clicked out of the program.

"The fuck, Shane? If we can look like dogshit, so can you."

"Tomorrow, maybe. Let's hit the bar."

I looked to Tony. "Grab him."

Tony pinned Shane to his chair and rolled him away from the keyboard. Shane whined and moaned, his voice growing childishly desperate as I uploaded a recent picture of him. The loading bar chugged along while the guys slammed each other into a bookcase crammed with PS3 games and Tom Clancy paperbacks. They thrashed around until Shane landed on his stomach and tried crawling toward the computer. I took a seat on his back and stamped him against the floor.

"Ash, please," he croaked under my weight. "I don't want to see it."

When the loading bar struck 100%, I climbed off. He scrambled to his feet, diving after the computer. His hand bumped the mouse and knocked it back behind the monitor. He fumbled for it, spazzing like I'd never seen him. By the time he wrestled the mouse back down, everything flashed.

Black to white.

And back to black.

Error.

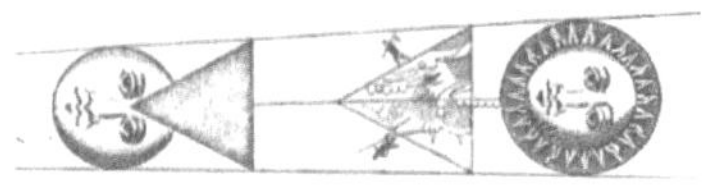

The kitchen felt like the only place left on earth. I don't know why we picked the kitchen after Shane threw us out of his room, but we did. Tony and I sat with our backs to the fridge, its stainless-steel sending chills through my tank top. The floor was sticky from old soda. A wet stench of used coffee grounds hung in the air. Now and then, the light above the sink flickered and the faucet dripped. Everything else seemed hollow and motionless.

We started drinking and a small forest of empty bottles arose between us. We kept going till the last beer.

"Want to split it?" I asked.

Tony lumbered to his feet. "Think I'll go check on Shane."

"Don't," I said. "He's gotta be winding down. There's only like eighty photos on his computer."

"What, you take an inventory?"

I snorted.

Tony sat back down. He squeezed the lid off the last Coors and offered it to me. "What about you? You all right?"

I scratched at my dreadlocks to make sure they were still there. I'd been twirling them like a circus act ever since we sat down. Any minute now, I expected them to pop loose and slither away. Tony was no better. I caught him checking his reflection in the chrome door handle, probably afraid the color would leak from his hair any second.

"I was pretty goddamn bald in that photo," I said.

Tony shrugged.

"Who knows," I said. "Maybe I'll get sick of my dreads and shave them. Try a new look. Go all punk."

"Yeah, maybe."

"My head didn't look shaved though."

Tony frowned. "Does anyone in your fam—uh, never mind."

"What?" When he looked away, I shoved him. "Go on, say it."

There was a long pause. Only the faint rumble of the fridge and the buzz of the light sounded. He frowned and said, "I was going to ask if anyone in your family had, you know… cancer."

Hearing it sobered the night's booze right out of me. I took his Coors off him and knocked it back. The beer hit my throat like a blessing. I handed it back and told him about my Aunt Kay.

"You mentioned her one night when you were wasted," he said. "Something about her and your Gibson."

"My Gibson was hers originally. She babysat me a lot, gave me guitar lessons. Then when I was seven the lessons stopped. My dad said she had to go on tour. I was thrilled for her, I thought she joined Metallica or something." I swallowed. "But it wasn't that kind of tour."

Tony set his hand on mine.

I didn't budge. His hand, its warmth—it felt like it needed to be there. "Last time I saw her, she was lying in her apartment bed. Soon as I walked in, she told me her Gibson was mine now. I ran to hug her, all excited, but when I threw myself over her chest, something wasn't right."

He raised an eyebrow.

"See, Aunt Kay had these huge boobs. I expected them to be there." I shook my head. Sighed. "She had a double mastectomy. Not that it saved her."

Tony brushed the back of my hand with his thumb.

I reached for the beer as an excuse to free myself up.

He cleared his throat. "Nobody in my family went gray until their fifties."

"Nobody in your family stresses out like you. Every time I see you with those LSAT books I want to pelt you with Xanax." I made a throwing motion with my wrist and we laughed.

"Sounds like I should pull the plug on law school."

"Fuck no," I said. "I'll need a good lawyer when I start touring. Remember, I'm good for a stage riot or thirty."

We laughed until our tired heads thumped against the fridge door. We stared back at one another, our beer-soaked breaths collecting on the stainless steel. Tony shifted toward me, his eyes fixing on mine. Our breaths overlapped on the door. He leaned in.

I roadblocked him with my hand. "You can do better," I said. "I might go bald tomorrow."

"I might go gray." He folded my hand down into his and I felt his breath, warm and boozy on my nose. I closed my eyes and bent toward him.

A crash sounded down the hall.

Tony and I stared at each other wide-eyed. We wobbled to our feet in a reckless hurry, stumbling into chairs and walls on our way to Shane's room. Tony beat me to the door and tried the knob. Locked. He pounded and yelled.

His urgency sent me into a drunken run and I stumbled into him from behind. The force popped the door open, dumping us onto stacks of CDs and textbooks. Everything clattered and avalanched around us.

When I twisted loose, I screamed.

Shane lay on the floor at the foot of his chair, his face impossibly pale in the green neon. His elbow was knotted tight with his tie from the job interview. Nearby, his briefcase was butterflied open, a spoon and plastic bag lying inside. I crawled over and my knee crunched something. A used syringe.

"Tony! Hurry—get him into the shower!"

Tony took Shane by the armpits while I got his legs. We dumped him in the shower and threw the water on full blast. Cold spray soaked his shirt, spreading through it like a shadow. He should've twitched by now, but he simply lay there blocking the drain.

I felt powerless, useless. It was my Aunt Kay all over again.

Tony stammered through a 911 call. He opened his mouth to say something but couldn't. He slumped against the wall, sliding to the floor as the operator's tinny voice chirped through the receiver. He shook his head.

No. That website had to be wrong.

I climbed inside the shower and pumped my hands against Shane's stomach over and over. I slapped his face, pinched his ear lobes. No response, nothing. I went back to pumping.

Tony yelled at me to keep at it, not to give up.

I didn't intend to.

I only stopped when the cold got to me. That was when I realized that it hadn't gotten to Shane.

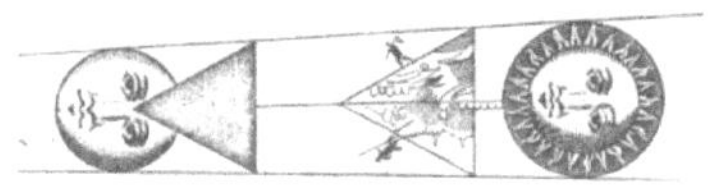

Today marked the ten-year anniversary of that night. I celebrated with a routine trip to the oncology ward, where a nurse donned a C-list actress' smile and led me to the chemo room. It was bright inside, the sunlight warming the leather chairs, the air tingling with fake-lilac freshener. What could've been a halfway-peaceful visit turned hectic when I saw who was sitting inside.

"Nurse," I said, "can I have a minute alone? Let my stomach settle?"

The second she left, I squatted next to the man sitting by the window. I couldn't believe it.

"Tony?"

No response. His arm slid off the armrest and dangled there, the IV tube swinging in rhythm. He smelled of sweat and worry. Probably his first chemo session—he still had his hair, after all, gray as it was.

"Tony, remember me? From the old apartment?"

He stared ahead, his breath leaking out. Somewhere in my mind I could smell warm beer and undercooked burgers, could feel his palm against my spine.

"Who?" he asked.

"Ash. Ten years ago we—"

"The website."

"Yeah. The website." I took his hand. "You'll laugh, but I became kind of addicted to it. I upload my photo every day now. But get this—I'll survive my cancer. And my hair's supposed to grow back. Guess it'll be powered by Janus." I laughed stupidly. "Did you know Janus was a Roman god? The god of time, beginnings, doorways, and—"

He moaned.

"Yeah, yeah, I know it's silly." I squeezed his hand. "What about you, Tony? Have you been uploading yourself?"

"No."

My skin prickled at his tone. It was unfair. Here was the only guy on earth who understood the website. Janus' power. My addiction. Maybe Tony didn't want to know if he'd be around in 2031, but I did.

I snapped a picture of him and booted up Ten-Year Photo on my phone. My thumb hovered over the UPLOAD button.

"Ash… don't."

"Why not? Why wouldn't you want to know?"

"What if…" He dozed off, his breath warm on my face. Warm as it had been in front of the fridge ten years ago. Before everything became predictable. Before everything went to shit.

I checked my phone. My thumb hovered over the word UPLOAD.

Instead I hit CANCEL.

Then I took his hand and waited.

THE CALENTURE

Kaaron Warren

The city is cold, full of echoes, empty of people in the chill night. All of them warm inside, windows double-glazed so they can watch the spectacle of the geysers at any time, moonlight permitting. Long term residents claimed they never got tired of it. Gary watched from his hotel room, looking out over a series of mud pools and if he concentrated, he thought he could hear them bubbling. Certainly from where he stood he could see them, the incessant boiling thickness. He was tempted, as always, to dip a toe in, to plunge in, to somehow climb over the protective walls (and some of them laughable meagre) and dive. At sea they called it calenture, the desperate desire to sink beneath the waves. A dive in that hot mud would stop his heart.

Gary drove into the parking lot of the enormous Rotorua Palladium Convention Centre, pulling right up near the entry. He hoped for a Disabled spot there, but they were full, something he should have been prepared for. Unlike others, he could walk if he had to, although every step brought him pain.

He parked his car, pulling forward as he always did because turning his head hurt too much and at times brought on minor seizures. He didn't regret coming alone, though: he didn't want any helpers for this. He wanted to meet Athena on his own, without anyone whispering in his ear, telling him he was foolish, he should save his money, this was a waste of time.

Those who didn't suffer chronic pain had no understanding, none, of those who did. The carpark was well-lit, at least. Needed on this dark night.

As he approached the massive metal doors, they opened towards him. Others were headed there, too, and in his haste to beat them through the door (he hated to wait for others) he elbowed a young woman, who sucked her breath in and held it.

"Sorry," he muttered.

She held her elbow as if he'd drawn blood and he felt a moment of irritation at her.

The foyer was full, thriving with people, and he stood for a moment, planning out his pathway. He could see the others who'd entered alongside him doing the same thing, all of them looking for the easiest way towards the hall, the one that would cause the least interruption and pain. He stepped aside to give himself time to think, pausing by a massive statue. There was one on either side of the doorway. One was Pallas Athena, with shield, weapon and a piercing, intelligent gaze. One was Pallas, whose statue had kept Troy safe and who stood now, stooping, considerate, protective. Both looked powerful, strong, healthy. Quotes beneath the statues said, "As we guard, so shall we protect, as you protect us."

The foyer was lined with tables covered with merchandise: bottles of Rotorua mud, packets of Epsom salts, and balms. There were symbolic items in the name of Athena: small owl statuettes, decorative weapons, tiny, shiny rocks of palladium, which seemed to glow, examples of local crafts, olive oils, serving platters in the shape of her shield. There were craft objects, too: knitted tea cozies, small cardigans, baby clothes, scarves. A soundtrack of owl call comforted him, but he didn't like the beautiful bird caged in the corner. He had a glimpse of himself acting out a moment of great heroism, letting the bird free, but he looked at the low hanging chandeliers, the tightly closed doors, and could see at once it wouldn't go well.

On the walls were posters; blissful depictions of people free from pain in contrast to those racked with it, anxious and cringing from the world.

Around him, people clustered around the doorways as if was nearly time to go in. Conversations began amongst strangers, all of them with something in common. He could hear them, sharing their stories, about what bit hurt and how long it had hurt for and what the doctor, who didn't believe them, had said.

They all had the same story and he was tired of hearing about it. He was tired of telling it.

That's why they were all here.

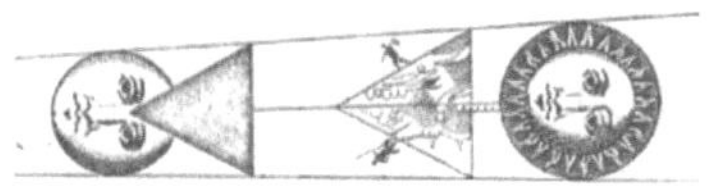

The call went out that the session would begin soon. "Have your tickets ready!" staff called out. They were all dressed in impossibly green t-shirts and were tall, healthy, strong. They moved through the foyer effortlessly, helping others negotiate the obstacles. "Tickets ready!" they called. Gary had his. It had cost him the better part of two-hundred bucks and he checked his pocket periodically to make sure it was still there.

Then they were inside. It was a smaller venue than Athena usually played, only five-hundred seats. Gary hoped this wouldn't affect the way she treated them. Sometimes, people would play small venues as if they were doing you a favor. He didn't think Athena would be this way. He'd seen her in Sydney, and in Auckland. He'd watched her a thousand times online. She'd never been anything but magnificent.

They took their seats. He was four rows from the front, right in the middle, but the seats were further apart than usual so there was little difficulty getting through. People smiled at each other, they touched hands, they made room. He took his seat next to a woman in her forties, great bags under her eyes but those eyes were clear, blue, beautiful.

"Gemma," she said.

"Gary." They nodded at each other, but he was not keen on conversation. He wanted to immerse himself, be ready.

The lights dimmed. The crowd hushed: any time someone spoke, the rest would shush them and people would laugh. Gary laughed along with them. There was a sense of camaraderie here he had not felt since his school days, when the football team would play and everybody would come out in support. Some knitted or crocheted, wanting to keep their hands active. Others sat still. In the silence, the clicking of needles was strangely comforting.

Music played, the owl-sounds from the foyer. Then a spotlight on stage, and Athena was carried in, sitting cross-legged on her shield. Her porters were enormous, wearing skin-tight shirts that shimmered like silver. Rumor had it the shield was covered in skins, although stories differed as to where the skin was from. He'd heard the skin of a giant she'd killed, or that of a best friend killed in a terrible accident. He'd heard she used the foreskins of lovers, many, many lovers. All of it fanciful, of course: this was not the real goddess, but simply a wonderful woman who played the part to perfection.

On stage behind her was projected the asteroid, Pallas, her spiritual guide, her link, her influence. Silverish, beautiful, almost magnetic.

The porters turned her so she faced the audience, and placed the shield on a sturdy plinth. She unfurled her legs and crossed one over another like a glamorous actress. She was so close, Gary could look straight into her steel-grey eyes and his insides turned to liquid.

"Welcome to Rotorua, land of hot steam, hotter mud, healing. Welcome to your salvation. Welcome to the war on pain."

The room erupted. Gary forgot his pain, and Gemma jumped to her feet, wincing slightly but carrying on, her arms in the air, cheering.

"We're going to take your pain away," Athena said. "Because we believe that pain exists. We know it's there."

The man next to Gary began to cry out. "Oh god," he said. "Oh god, oh thank you."

"She hasn't done anything yet," someone called out, the tone clearly joking, and the audience laughed.

"Look beside you, in front of you. These are your people. You can lean on each other. You will help each other. Beside me are my uncle and my cousins, who will help you to rest, to be calm."

The audience cheered, waved their fingers in the air. Some clapped.

"We are family. We are all family. All bonded under Pallas."

Behind her, a beautiful slide show began, of the asteroid Pallas, silvery, magnetic, and its orbit. "Pallas provides an influence on us, those of us who matter, every 1686 days. Think about it."

Dates scrolled through, every 1686 days for the last 60 years. "Not everyone will experience this. If you haven't, if you can't look at these dates and definitively tell me that something occurred for you on each of them, then this treatment might not work for you. You may not remember, but each of these days were good days. Less pain, less sorrow, more of all the good stuff."

They spent time calling out events of their lives and after an hour or so, most people in the room felt they belonged. Some left (*"You will have a full refund," Athena told them*), but most stayed.

Athena began to dance, using weapons and her shield, creating something beautiful and yet war-like. Watching her made Gary feel dizzy, hypnotized: he couldn't take his eyes off her. She sang as well, sometimes with music, sometimes without, and Gary felt no pain for many, many hours.

When the lights went up sometime after midnight, he blinked, almost blinded. He hadn't felt his body in all that time, so transported had he been.

"Oh my god," Gemma murmured, and she reached over and took his hand.

He took the hand of his other neighbor, whose name was Jim, and they sat there, not wanting to leave, until the green-shirted staff members began herding them all back outside. They were subdued, slow to go, lingering at the doorway to stare back inside. No one wanted it to be over. They were each given a small box containing a piece of Palladium, labelled "Pallas Athena's Metal."

When the invitation came a week later for a reunion at the Waitangi Soda Springs, Gary didn't hesitate. Transport was part of the arrangement, usually something of an issue, and, with an upfront payment, a picnic lunch would be provided, and as much assistance as required.

On the hour-long ride in the large bus, the conversation turned to pain, as it often did, each person waiting for their turn to tell their story, all of the stories sounding the same by the end. Gary felt drained by it, by the need for sympathy and the boredom of listening to them talk, so he tucked himself up and gazed out the window, shoulders turned away from his seat companion.

"Will Athena be there?" someone asked.

"No, she's helping people who are on the next step from you. It's a progression, you know. A slow climb."

Gary knew he wanted to be there, at the top of the stairs with Athena, looking down at the others.

They had their picnic lunch first, olives, quiche, elderflower cordial, chunky salad sandwiches, oatmeal cookies.

The pool was enormous, room for all, and as they changed into their swimwear, they laughed and joked. Gary was one of the first in the water, desperate to feel the healing warmth around him, and he sank into it up to his chin. The sulphur smell was strong but not unbearable, and he could feel it in his lungs, doing him good. The temperature of the water was hot but easily bearable and he wished he could stay there forever.

After thirty minutes or so, though, he began to feel tired, as if his blood had reached the temperature of the water and he now WAS the water, ebbing and flowing, light but heavy. He closed his eyes.

There was a tap on his shoulder. "Time to get out, Gary. We need to head back before it gets dark." This was Gemma. Her hair was damp around her reddened face and he thought she looked incredibly beautiful. He didn't know if he could say anything, but on the bus, when they were dry and dressed, she slipped her hand into his and squeezed it, and laid her head on his shoulder.

They listened to Athena over the speakers on the way home. Gary closed his eyes and fell into a semi sleep, with her words in his ears. "Under my wing you will get protection and safety. You will sink into a state of comfort and you will be well. You will need to make the sacrifices of the millennia, the same sacrifices we have been making forever. But these will make you a better person. They will make you well. They will help you win the war on pain." She told them to seek out Pallas, and how to do so. How to find that bright asteroid, the one that would draw out the pain-giving metals in their bodies and help them live simpler, more comfortable lives.

The next time, there were fewer people. Hotter water. They covered themselves in mud first, let it dry, then sank into the water. The mud helped them acclimatize. By the time it washed off, they were used to the heat. Simply putting a toe in without the mud would be unbearable.

Gary had spent some time living rough on the street, back when his mother died and he hadn't yet learned to look after himself. Even now, with his job at the supermarket, he was never sure from day to day if he'd have a place to live. So he liked to be clean. Bathing was an integral part of his well-being. When he had access to a shower, even if he could wash his face, he felt far better than if he was dirty.

Athena's uncle spoke, his voice slow, sleepy, calming. "Have you ever had that feeling that you wanted to throw yourself off a building? In front of a train? Off the boat into the deep blue sea? They call that Calenture. We call it the desire for wellness."

Gary and Gemma sat together, every time, in progressively hotter waters. Progressively thicker mud. Pallas would pass over in another three months: they had to be ready.

"I like to have a celebration," Athena said in a video link.

Gary and Gemma sat on her couch together, watching it through her laptop.

Athena was on the other side of the planet on a retreat (and Gary would have given anything to be there with her). Everybody needed to hear her words, everyone needed to be healed by her.

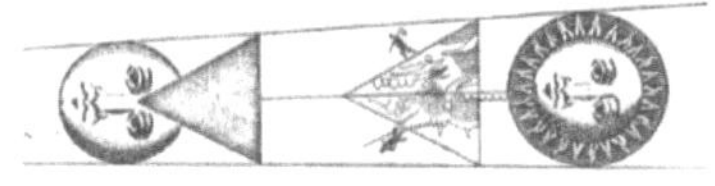

And then, oh glorious day, Athena came to them again. "There are always enemies, even when you think they're not. They present as friends, supporters, and then they call for your blood. This is why we have so many engagements. So many levels before you reach the ultimate."

She took individual interviews, with each of them. "You're taking painkillers again," she said to Gemma. "I can see it in your face. Don't surrender to that, Gemma. Stay with me. Stay with me." Athena looked paler, weaker, her eyes a less livid brown. "The old gods are fighting against the new reality. No one believes in the old gods but we are here. We haven't left. Our influence is everywhere but so much weaker. And weakening by the day."

There were ten of them left from the original group. Gary felt proud to be one of him. He was without doubt, without any concerns.

Gary couldn't stop staring at Athena. He didn't want to be aroused by her but he couldn't help it. Every time she moved, her whole body seemed to shiver. Her clothing clung to her like skin. He wanted to gaze at her without thinking, to hear every word, but he found himself thinking about her naked, covered with mud, with him slowly swabbing the mud from her using hot water, and her skin emerging, reddened, sensitive, available.

The other men were the same.

Some of the women, too, and the rest focused on the knitting and hearing her words.

He put his arm around Gemma. They had kissed, but she was so nervous of it, so terrified, he hadn't tried any harder.

She told them all about her father, and how he'd ruined her for love, she said, and while she didn't say how he'd ruined her, it didn't take much to guess. Her mother had killed him and not gone to jail for it, that's how bad he was.

Athena said, "The body is a tomb. Titanically evil on the outside, divine on the inside. We need to free the soul from the body. We need to free you from the confines of your painful surrounds."

Her uncle and her cousins hummed rhythmically, making Gary feel so sleepy he could barely keep his eyes open. He didn't want to miss a single word: he wished they'd be quiet.

She said, "Just as I had Cadmus bury dragon's teeth to produce soldiers, so shall you become soldiers. With the influence of Pallas, you will be changed forever. You will not be who or what you are now. You will be soldiers in my army."

A great roar at that, a great excitement.

"Why is she pretending to be weak?" Gemma whispered to Gary.

He looked at her, aghast. "You can't say that! She gives us everything!"

The others in the room rose in anger, furious. "Why are you here?" they shouted at Gemma, pushing her, poking her, wanting her gone.

Gary wanted her gone, too, although she had made him the happiest he had been in a long time. He hesitated, then finally joined them in pushing Gemma away.

"Thank you for your fury," Athena said. "We need that. But you can calm it, now. We have removed the last one. We are down to the best. The strongest. The good men and women, my dear, dear soldiers. I will protect you, the heroes," she said. "In any battle, there are heroes. But you have to win in order to be one. There are no heroes on the losing side. Follow through. Following through is heroic. Standing up for yourself, beating that pain, rising above it. Hercules fell into a coma too late, after he'd already killed his wife and child. Perhaps I am saving some of you from the same mortal sin, the same terrible violence you might have otherwise committed. Who knows? People so driven by pain and sorrow; who knows? I do not see the future."

They fell to the floor in a form of ecstasy.

Gary lay on his back beside the mud pool that was so hot every breath was painful. He gazed up at the star-filled sky. Pallas was there, so bright he had no difficulty picking it out. It was beautiful, so beautiful he cried.

"You've sent your messages?" Athena's Uncle asked. "You've told people you are going on retreat? You need to be in a medically induced coma to withstand the heat and there will be some time of recovery afterwards."

"I have," Gary said, and the others, too.

Athena called out their names, making it sound like an epic poem. "For all those before, and for you," she called, hundreds of names, Gary thought, so many of them.

Her Uncle moved amongst them, injecting them gently.

"No more pain, no more pain," Athena sang. "My magnificent dragon's teeth. Cross the river with me, cross over, cross over. The body is a tomb."

"See you when I wake up," Gary said. He wondered if she would love him when he awoke from this coma, once the mud was washed off and he was new and brave, strong and magnificent.

She said, "There is only a thin casing for the soul. It can stretch into a new body. The greater the soul, the greater the new body."

But she winked.

She winked.

"Rise, my dragon's teeth," Athena said.

Pallas, shiny, silvery, bright, passed close by as it did every 4.6 years, drawing out metals, drawing the soldiers out of the mud and to their feet.

The soldier rose, feeling no pain.

Feeling nothing.

Coated in mud, shining and silvery, a second skin.

Where flesh was, metal was now, layer by layer, under the influence of Pallas.

They began to march, palladium army, pure instinct or memory of movement led by Athena, their goddess, their commander.

It wouldn't hurt a bit.

That Tiny Little Section of Human Life

Carole McDonnell

At a distance the flickering water hinted at a struggle; Hannah imagined that one of the countless herrings in the herring run was trapped against a pebble. A fellow onlooker –an old-timer eating a Big Mac-- had given her the unasked-for advice: *Human interference goes against the natural order of things. We're not supposed to help them. It's like helping chicks get out of their eggs. It harms them in the long run.*

Hannah was not one to harm anything. Which was one of the things that had just stopped her from telling off her mother-in-law. Being a minister's grand-daughter, she was by nurture "repressed" but the stress of that unrelieved adrenalin was causing her body to shake. Even now, a whole hour after the usual in-law nastiness, a sob lodged in Hannah's throat, the latest in a queue of immobile sobs. "I'm so damned locked in," Hannah said to herself now that the old-timer was gone and only she and her disabled son were around. She listed the emotions that weighed her down. "Grief, anger, shame, abandonment, humiliation, and profound regret." Then repeated her mantra. "Forgive. Forgive. Forgive." She glanced downward at her pendulous breasts, her sagging forearms, and her hammock thighs covered up in bright blue leggings. "This being overweight is totally the result of me being weighed down by grief. And now age has plunged me into fat cronehood."

Her husband, Farr, was nothing more or less than a well-trained robot she could never reprogram or divorce. He would bring her to an early but oft-wished for grave. "Why was I so blind when we dated? His weirdness was right there in front of me. What the heck was wrong with me?"

Hannah watched as herring struggled upstream, flopped, and dashed against rocks, pebbles. *Okay, Hannah, just enjoy the peace while you're here.* Then she broke her self-talk to urge Dane, her disabled twenty-nine-year-old son to "Look, look at the herring. They're trying to make it upstream. Because it's what they have to do." She wasn't sure if he understood what she said but it was a useful discipline to hope and believe that he did. *Yes, yes, hope is a discipline.*

The bubbling pocket of water in the middle of the stream called Hannah to tread on the slippery stones past the herring rush and she walked into the middle of the stream for closer inspection. What she saw unsettled her; certain sights one cannot unsee. There, struggling in the water, was a tiny six-inch long creature with two human heads and torsos that merged into one fish tail. Hannah had not only happened upon a mermaid but a two-headed one.

Hannah was no stranger to strange things. Over the years, she had seen cruel comments manifest as invisible spirit arrows, demonic lances, and cruel darts that pierced the hearts and brains of the walking wounded. It was strange walking around and seeing people with demonic lances piercing their bodies. But she had gotten used to that, and because of that she was always kind, always forgiving. She saw other things as well. Months before she married, she had seen invisible snakes slithering in her then-boyfriend-now-husband's art studio. Not that she had understood or heeded that warning. So, a mermaid wasn't particularly strange. But a two-headed one did give her some pause. *Would two-headedness be considered a disability?* she wondered. She peered deeper, looked lower into the gently flowing tide. *It's odd. To see a mythic little creature gone all wrong.*

Dane lingered near the water's edge making the ASL sign for "cookies." Hannah vehemently replied, "No! No cookies." Dane muttered his non-verbal resentment of his mother and Hannah gave him a warning look. *Dammit, I wish Farr would at least try to break him of this habit! The kid is eating nothing but rice, spaghetti, cereal, milk, and Oreos.*

She turned to study the mermaid again, and soon footsteps approached behind her. Thinking her son had followed her into the stream, she turned but her gaze met that of a twenty-something young man of fragile delicate beauty. He seemed of mixed Caucasian and Asian ancestry.

The stranger smiled from beneath his beige bucket hat, then peered past Hannah at the stream. "What're you looking at?" he asked in a Japanese accent.

Hannah moved to block the stranger's view of the two-headed green-haired pale-skinned mermaid. "Nothing."

"You're looking pretty intensely for someone looking at nothing," the stranger said and walked past her. "The name's Aleksu." He focused on the spot where Hannah had been gazing.

"Ah! How strange!" he said to himself then glanced at Hannah, his face flushed with delight. "Is that what I think it is?" He turned to the stream again, bent, peered closer.

"She's very pretty. Well, both of them are. I guess we should think of them as two different people, shouldn't we? Very dainty."

"Ah," Hannah said, and luxuriated in his delight. She hadn't realized how much she missed seeing that kind of delighted joy. "Yes, they are."

Aleksu stared at the mermaid, the index and middle-finger of his right hand on his right cheek. "We have a sickly mermaid on our hands. What're we gonna do?"

Hannah's chest tightened with worry. "You aren't planning on taking it…her…them… back with you?"

"Like put them in a jar or something?" He shook his head. "Nah! And it's not like I could take her back to Japan with me."

"Japan? That where you're from?"

A grin, a nod. "I don't look it, but I am."

Hannah smiled. He was quite beautiful, with straight shoulder-length hair like someone out of an anime or video game. "You *do* look it."

"My fellow countrymen don't think so." Aleksu bent, peered closer at the mermaid. "Pretty homogeneous that culture. They can spot the slightest deviation."

"Your English is pretty good for a Japanese national." Hannah looked behind her at Dane pacing back and forth on the stream's muddy bank.

"My dad's a Canadian," Aleksu replied. "He sent me to an English International School in Tokyo when the bullying got bad."

"So, what're you doing here in Massachusetts?"

"Vacation. Meeting my father's family. Saw Niagara Falls, then decided to see Cape Cod on my way to New York City. And now I'm apparently attending the last moments of a dying mermaid. And you?"

This is so like the guys I'd fall for when I was younger, Hannah thought, but what she said was, "My husband's extended family has a wedding. Irish-Catholic, so ya know… large family reunion. They took over the entire hotel and more keep coming."

"You still haven't told me your name."

Shyness mixed with cockiness in his voice. Woundedness, too. Hannah always liked the shy and damaged ones. "Hannah. Hannah's my name."

"And you're down here at the stream because your hubby's family is too stressful?"

"Something like that."

"I understand. I've got my issues too. Family issues and otherwise."

Hannah was suddenly in the middle of a conversation and because of this, her heart leaped. Mundane as the conversation was, it was like water poured on dry ground because she normally had so little conversation with anyone. *Could someone truly thirst for conversation?* she wondered and almost burst into tears of joy and self-pity.

An old memory suddenly pushed itself into Hannah's mind. Except for the occasional pain on her right sole, she did not usually think about that childhood incident. A seven-year-old child, barefoot, she had stepped into the shore of the Caribbean Sea and onto a broken glass bottle. Blood gushed forth and pain startled her. Screaming, she fled the water and ran to her mother who took her back home and covered the wound with oils and ointments. A year or two later, when her mother dragged her to an old obeah man with the complaint, "My daughter is having bad dreams," the old shaman told her that the gash in her leg had been a blood sacrifice to the marine spirits and that she had acquired a spirit husband, the same one all the women in her family had been married to.

"That evil spirit will never let you go," the old man, who smelled of lust, dirt, and strange-smelling oils, said to Hannah. "And if you don't allow him to take you, he will make all your love affairs sorrowful."

Hannah grew up in a Jamaican household that used fear to control the younger generations, and she distrusted the old man's pronouncements fearing the old shaman and her mother had been in cahoots to keep her unmarried and trapped under her mother's willful hand. That night, however, a stranger came to her in a dream. Her breath caught. She had never seen a man so beautiful. He seemed to have all the beauty of all human races within his face, and all its kindness and power.

"Are you worrying," the stranger asked, and stroked her face, "if the old obeah man said that because your mother told him to?"

In the dream, Hannah chuckled. Because the stranger spoke so kindly and showed a loving familiarity, as if they had known each other for eons.

"Your mother doesn't know about this," the stranger went on. "In her generation, she wasn't the one whom the spirit married. That honor was your aunt's."

"My crazy aunt Kathleen?"

The spirit nodded. "And before that, it was your grandmother's sister. The one who died unmarried. The one whom all the parish feared because of her power."

"So… the shaman was telling the truth? I am to be his?"

"Yes. Mine."

"For how long?"

"For as long as you live."

"Does our marriage begin now?" Hannah asked.

"I will come again," the stranger said. "And I will receive you unto myself. Only do not marry anyone. You are my bride. Mine alone."

"Will you be human? Are you a human spirit?"

"No."

"But I don't want a spirit husband."

"It is not what you want, but what I want. My desire is all that matters."

"But what if I fall in love with someone human, someone other than you?"

"You will live to regret it. And even then, I will come when you're old and take you away from him."

Why the wound incident, the obeah man's words, and the dream conversation suddenly came to mind at that moment, Hannah did not know. But the sudden memory was so powerful that goosebumps trailed up and down her arms, colder than the stream pouring over her feet.

"Something flooding up from your stream of consciousness?" Aleksu asked.

Suddenly uncomfortable, Hannah began walking to the stream's banks. "My son and I've been here too long." She called to Dane. "Come here! Let's go see Daddy."

Aleksu pointed toward the trail's exit. "I'll drive you."

"It's okay. Walking is good for me."

"Don't trust me? All those true crime programs have affected your mind. You should trust strangers more."

Hannah stammered, "True enough. For all I know you're a cold-blooded murderer who'll take us lord-knows-where and rape and murder us." She hurried to her son and grasped his hand. "Thanks for the offer, though. It was good meeting you."

"I'm kinda pissed at you honestly," Aleksu shouted playfully as she raced away. "You made me see this. Now

I'm gonna have nightmares. If I hadn't seen you standing here, well…bending. And peering down---"

Hannah laughed and defended herself. "Is it my fault you were curious?"

"Yes, it is!" He pulled his meticulously-crafted linen jacket closer about his neck then zipped it. "It's not like one can unsee the numinous." He winked at her. "And you are beautiful, do you know that? Numinously so."

The compliment seeped into her like champagne. Her husband didn't understand the necessity of words, let alone a compliment. She turned away from the stranger whose frail, feminine masculinity was intriguing her and knew she would be thinking of him all night. Nevertheless, she forced her body to stiffen. "Excuse me, I have to go."

She walked away, briskly. Or as briskly as one could when one is fighting the urge to stay. At the exit to the park, she turned back to look at him but he was peering down into the stream where the two-headed mermaid lay floating in stasis.

On their way back, she held her son's hand tightly, firmly. He spotted a deli. Finding delis and mom-n-pop stores was not one of his disabilities. He could sniff out sugar and processed foods no matter where they drove. She resisted his tugging. Next, he yanked her toward a bodega then a mini-mart. Again, she held her own against his yelling and fuming, which was something her husband would not, could not, do. Dragging and screaming, they made it back to the hotel room.

Hannah closed the hotel room and raced toward a bag of goodies on the hotel's chest of drawers. She resisted the urge to ask her husband why all that deli crap was in their room and to crush his kindle that he was always so focused on. "Farr, everyone's in the park across the street. Playing touch football."

He looked up at her. "I know."

She grasped the cookies from Dane's hand. "You're not joining them?"

A shrug.

"You should, though. It's not like you see them every day. Or even every year."

No answer.

"I saw a mermaid."

Farr raised an eyebrow but said nothing.

"Unhuh. A disabled one."

A smile but no response.

Seriously, it's like talking to a brick wall! "I didn't think mermaids existed."

She walked to the mini-fridge in the hotel room. "I hope she's okay. She seemed to be struggling."

No response.

"Where's Jude?" Hannah asked about their older son, who really should have been with them in their room instead of hanging out with his creepy grandmother.

"With his cousins," Farr said, then, "I've never heard of mermaids struggling."

"Her disability was very obvious."

Hannah remained silent when her husband brought out a carton of milk from the fridge, but she did wonder when Dane and Farr managed to buy it. The doctor had warned them for two decades that milk caused blood to appear in Dane's urine. But Farr, a slave to routine, could not change. Worse, his neuro-atypicality made him a know-it-all who thought doctors, educators, nurses, building contractors, etc didn't know what they were talking about. Only he, Farr, knew best. Hannah had given up arguing because there was no use arguing against stasis and neuro-atypicality.

She walked into the hotel bedroom. "Maybe she learned to deal with that two-heads, two-torsos thing. To acclimate herself, you know. Still, she seemed to have a hard time moving. All the herring kept bouncing into her."

Farr stared at her for several seconds, then chuckled. "I would imagine they would."

Hannah was grateful he was in a good mood and had not dragged the numinous down into the mundane. She was pretty much burned out by his tendency to solve all arguments by dictionaries and scientific semantical statements.

Hannah grabbed the milk from Dane and immediately poured it into the sink, but after returning from the bathroom, she saw Dane sitting on the bed eating cookies.

Grieved, stressed, she went to bed. Milk got Dane so congested that he kept her up nights with his coughing and moans. And this night was the same. Farr, who could never admit to being the cause of his son's sickness or his wife's emotional, physical, and spiritual fatigue, slept soundly. But having met Aleksu, Hannah fantasized about the young biracial young man who seemed so familiar that he might have stepped out of one of her daydreams.

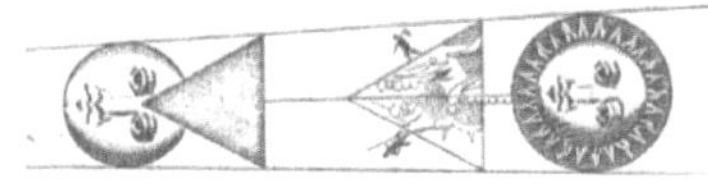

The next day started with Uncle Jay emceeing. At 85, and despite four bypass surgeries, he was the loving active center of the entire clan. He and Aunt Helen had been the first in the extended family to accept Hannah. Watching him at the projector exhibited the clan photos made Hannah wish she had married into his branch of the family instead of the crappy limb to which Farr's father belonged.

She focused on the photo montages, avoiding Farr's mother who sat two chairs away from her. Only when ninety-three-year-old Uncle Jay tapped her on the shoulder and—gesturing wildly—said, "I love to see all the cousins playing together," did she realize she had been holding her breath.

Uncle Jay's kindness cheered Hannah momentarily but after he moved on to another table, she fell back into isolation. She decided to go to the food tables. As she approached, she saw Jude talking to Amy, her niece-in-law. Amy was Julia's daughter, after all. Julia, Farr's sister, had been the first in the family to meet Hannah forty years before. Hannah had believed the meeting went well, only to be greeted with disdain from her future mother-in-law when she met her at the family's homestead. Julia's gossip against her had been the one to start that family hate-ball running.

Hannah approached slowly and eavesdropped. She didn't have to wait long before she heard Amy say, "Grandma doesn't like your mother and Grandma likes everyone."

Hannah thought, *This is bullshit. Okay then, I have decided from now on to indulge my oversensitive side. From now on, I shall affirm and indulge my paranoia and suspicions. I will give no benefit of the doubt and I will restrain my morbid introspection and sense of fair play. I shall withdraw from possibly dangerous situations and people without giving them a chance to explain themselves or to hurt me further. Sometimes you have to be conceited just enough to survive. It is what it is.*

But great decisions need the opportunity to be acted upon and there was no way Hannah could escape the room or the event for the whole weekend. She headed toward the lasagna and the corned beef and cabbage, thinking, I've *turned into my mother. Overeating and watching Asian dramas will be the only joys left in my life.*

"A lot going on," a male voice said behind her. She turned to see a thirty-something priest with sandy brown hair standing behind her.

"Sure is," she said and smiled.

"Those photos of Uncle Jay's of all those family vacations at the beach. They make me want to go to the ocean. Maybe we could drive down to Truro and check out the dunes. Or, a stream, maybe?"

Hannah detected an accent. "I didn't know there were priests in the family."

"A relative of a relative," the priest answered. "But aren't we all?" He gestured toward a large jug of apple juice. "You seem down. You okay?"

"I'm okay."

"Occupational hazard," the priest went on. "I can spot a depressed person a mile away and as soon as I see them I want to help."

Hannah thought but did not say, *You're looking a little depressed yourself. That's why you can see it in me.*

The priest extended his right hand. "Josef's the name."

Hannah took the hand and shook it, but Josef squeezed her palm gently, and his right index finger played along the back of her hand. Time seemed to stand still as she peered into his pale blue eyes. Need was there. Loneliness, too. A sexuality desperate to break forth. Hannah saw all this and at fifty-nine, she should not have been pondering responding favorably to it. But Josef seemed familiar. Like someone she already knew. Like someone she had met in her dreams or had conjured up in a sexual fantasy.

"People say I have a good sense of humor. You'd be doing me a favor, and I'd enjoy the company. A walk maybe?"

The hotel stood on top of a hill. Any kind of walk would mean a downhill trek which would, of course, be bookended by a return journey up the rough side of that mountainous hill. Remembering her previous journey to the stream, the idea of a walk loomed in Hannah's mind like the Boston Marathon. Besides, a walk wasn't what he really wanted. "Let's just walk around, Father Josef," Hannah said and thought, *Hannah, go gently into the good night of Black cronehood and haggery. You were cute once. You are perhaps somewhat cute even now. But it's time now for you to put away that need to be attractive to men. Attraction is useful if one wants to marry or if one wants to escape marriage and needs a crutch. It's important for only a tiny sliver of life and then...death, heaven, Gloryland.*

Josef was smiling at her, his eyes admiring her, all too obviously and there was no missing the flirtation in his seductive voice. "You will forgive me if I say this but you're quite pretty."

"Thank you."

"I don't talk like this often. I suppose...it's a momentary flight of fancy."

"The downside of being celibate," Hannah responded.

"Forgive me. It should subside soon. If you...wish it to."

Hannah looked down at her hand to hint that perhaps she would want her hand back. Perhaps. It had been a crazy weekend with guys hitting on her. Were family reunions, like weddings, events that made people leak pheromones right and left? Were non-relatives hooking up in hotel rooms over the course of the four days?

They stood there staring into each other's eyes, right hands seemingly locked forever.

Josef reminded Hannah of a character in one of her longest-running daydreams: a lovely and celibate priest had been so caught up with desire for her that he took her to his room. In the "Farr side of the room," her husband's siblings were giving Dane ice cream. Hannah thought, *Compassion means the ability to understand someone's pain and the willingness to free them from that pain. That's what the dictionary says, Farr. Why can't you just stand against the kid bullying you into eating ice cream? He's supposed to listen to you, not you to him. But no, I have a husband who has allowed his autistic son to train him to go to delis. Jesus, please help me not to kill this man!*

Some years ago, when his father died, Farr returned from the funeral and as they lay in bed he made the following comment: "I always thought our marriage was wrong but when I saw how Jude cheered up our family, I thought our marriage couldn't be a mistake if we created this kid." That very night Hannah dreamed that one of the snakes in their bedroom died and crumbled to nothing on their mattress, and she began to understand that the snakes were the many lies Farr believed. He was entangled and constricted by them and there was no way for her to hack through so many entangled snakes to unbound him. She simply had to endure. Besides, she didn't want to deal with Farr's sarcasm. The guy was nasty when he felt cornered.

So, Hannah let it go. She took her hand back from Josef and stuffed her face with lasagna, pierogis, and stuffed shells. That night, holding her breath waiting to exhale, hands clenched, eyes focused on the ceiling in the dark bedroom, she endured but questioned. What other lies bounded her husband? What lies and snakes constricted her? Where did his neuro-atypicality end and his own weird family issues begin? Why did his family blame everything Farr did on his illness? Surely the guy had some agency and some responsibility for his behavior? Were people with extreme spectrum disorders completely unable to sin? Hannah lay in her bed hating her life and hating her marriage. Why did she insist on remaining married to Farr? Was it because he had made her so physically ill that she now believed no one else would have her if she were divorced? Was it because she was old and black and was nothing more than a mammy figure, devoid of sexuality? Was it because she feared jumping from the frying pan into the fire? Was it because she feared that their older son, Jude, would hate her if she divorced his father? Why was divorce even out of the question just because she was a good little Pentecostal married to a good Irish Catholic? Why imagine or want passion this late in life? Was it even right for a woman as old as she to want love and passion? Wasn't passion only a thing reserved for a tiny, tiny speck of human life? Hannah thought of the Samaritan Woman at the Well and the Seventh Man who was that Samaritan woman's truest husband. *And yet...* Hannah wanted a human hug. No, she craved it. *Flesh hunger*, her mother had called it.

The *flesh hunger* had grown larger and deeper over the years and-- with the wedding and family reunion-- the need for affection now had her almost on the verge of tears. She wondered where the priest's room was and if his momentary flight of fancy had subsided or was still in operation. Would he be able to give up a kingdom, or at least his parish family for her?

"I need a hug," she told her husband, and he stroked her back mechanically, dutifully, as he had done for all the years of their marriage. How kind and willing he was to comfort her, and yet how utterly incapable he was of comprehending what affection truly was. She had to admit that on the whole, Farr was a good husband. He made her breakfast every morning, took their son out for long two-hour-long drives every day, would never fantasize or daydream about sex with younger women. Her friends envied her.

But Hannah needed sleep and the one proven way to get even fifteen minutes of sleep was to fantasize about affectionate lovers. Sex with Farr never lived up to the passion her fantasized lovers gave her. Was she the only one who had dream lovers from day one of her marriage? *From day one.* She wanted to cry but couldn't. Because no one had ever been there to comfort her. Farr often eyed her suspiciously whenever she cried. Once he even accused her of manipulating him when she fell apart with worry that he was killing their younger son.

Hannah stared outside the dark night and thought of the great-might've-beens, of ex-boyfriends who had nuclear families that loved her, of might've been hookups, of affectionate future husbands with loving children who would take her into their hearts and give her the loving normal family she wanted and needed. Then she remembered the mermaid and thought of how cold the night was. She thought of the poor little disabled anomaly suffering alone with no one praying for her. Then she thought about how much time she had spent imagining fantasy lovers and how little she had spent on imagining what Dane's life would be like if he were healed. It was all too much—life, her wrong use of her mind, her misuse of hope. Couldn't she have used her imagination better and for better things?

Awaiting sleep, she turned on the hotel television and watched several episodes of "Investigation Discovery." The lonely deaths of widows looking for love in all the wrong places only added to Hannah's hopelessness. Living far from Jude and having no extended family nearby, she figured her future would be one of continued diminishment and she had accepted that. She and her husband would live until one of them died, and the other would be left alone in New York to take care of Dane because Jude was busy with his own life in California. If the parental survivor was Farr, he would survive in the isolation. If, however, Hannah were the survivor, she would be a friendless lonely old hermit with a sickly kid. And what would happen after she died? She imagined the day of her sudden death with Dane walking around the house looking for cereal, her decaying dead body unfound, uncared for, unloved. Would Dane die of starvation inside the house? Or would he open the door and walk to the deli for cookies every day until someone reported it to the cops and they came and found her decomposed body?

On the other bed in the hotel room, Dane was crying. The milk and cookies Farr had given him were upsetting his stomach. As usual, Farr slept on, immune to the trouble he routinely caused.

Dane could only be comforted at night by Hannah's singing. She had a veritable songbook of old-fashioned Episcopalian hymns and Vacation Bible School kid songs. She went through the songs now as she usually did. But now, because they were in a hotel, her voice was lowered. "There is a Name I Love to Hear." "Leaning on the Everlasting Arms." "There is power in the blood." "Hallelujah, sing to Jesus." "Down by the riverside." She sang for two hours straight, and Dane fell quiet. Not exactly asleep, but calmed. Hannah, however, did not sleep. Years of marriage to Farr had stolen sleep from her.

***

Hannah was late for lunch the next morning. She had to be. Staying in bed for four hours each morning was necessary or she would feel faint and weak throughout the day. Farr and Dane had walked to a local deli and they had brought back milk and cookies for Dane and a buttered roll for her. Now, she walked toward the table assigned to her immediate in-laws where her mother-in-law, Farr, and Farr's twin brother sat and she hoped for a good meal with zero drama.

But then Farr's twin brother had glared at her. The one who had told her on her wedding day, "I hate that my brother married you." Hannah immediately lost her appetite but muttered under her breath. Forgive, forgive, forgive.

"You're awfully late," the mother-in-law said. "But you never had any respect for people, did you?"

Hannah waited for Farr to defend her. He didn't. He just looked at his kindle at some news article he was reading. Farr was always about information.

From day one, Hannah thought. *Dammit, Farr defend me! Even if you hate talking, open your mouth to defend me!*

A hand touched her arm and she looked up to see an impeccably-dressed dark-haired middle-aged man who oozed power and machismo. He wore a diamond pinky ring and seemed every ounce the kind of "made man" she had seen in gangster movies.

"You got nothing better to do than to insult your daughter-in-law?" he directed his question to Farr's mother. "You insult her one more time and I will personally knock your teeth in." He directed his next comment to Farr. "What are you? A pussy? You let your Mama do your wife like this?"

Farr didn't answer, but of course he wouldn't. Words were strange creatures to him.

The stranger directed Hannah toward the door. "You're too good a woman to let that family jump all over you, Hannah."

She sensed an invitation. Of sorts. But true crime TV shows had convinced her that if she ever left her husband, she would be jumping from the frying pan into the fire. Hannah pondered the beauty of violence and the ugliness of weak men who couldn't stand up to their children or their mothers. "Thank you," she said and lowered her head, flirting.

The stranger put his arm around her, squeezed her shoulder gently, whispered, "If I had a good woman like you, I would let everyone around me treat her like a queen. What do you care what these assholes think of you?"

Not being regularly complimented Hannah nodded and walked over to the piles of aluminum baking pans, cold and hot salads, preferring to chat with relatives of relatives rather than veer back to her mother-in-law's table or to dash out of the room with the "made man" who would treat her as a queen.

Hannah's macho rescuer kissed her hand then walked through the door leaving Hannah feeling both guilty and unprotected. Several minutes after he left and while Hannah was stuffing sorrow and hurt down her throat by way of a cinnamon bun, a hand touched hers. She turned to see Aleksu with a paper plate of paprika-sprinkled potato salad and fried chicken.

"Aleksu?" Her voice gave her away: not only surprise but something akin to joy.

He kissed her forehead. "The one and only."

She eyed him nervously. "What're you doing here?"

"Should I tell you that I'm a part of the tribe?"

Hannah giggled. "Only if it's true."

"Okay, then. I won't." A grin.

She wondered if he had stalked her, but her girlish glee at seeing him prevented full-blown fear. "So... you don't belong here?"

He bit into a chicken breast. "Not really. You're beautiful! How old are you?"

"Why do you want to know?"

"I suspect you know why," was Aleksu's answer.

Hannah studied his face and thought, *Beauty as a commodity is highly prized...especially the beauty of young women. There are those who see others as prey; they look upon the belongings of others as if those belongings -- gold, houses, a woman's body, beauty, whatever-- is seen as something that already belongs to the predator to own, to ravage, to destroy, as he sees fit. Not that the ugly are necessarily safe but those whose beauty exists within a tiny, tiny, section of human life -- younger than 30 years of age, perhaps-- are seen as highly prized possessions. The aged, the ugly, the morbidly-obese, while not safe from predators, are not highly prized. And I have long ago stopped being beautiful. You are odd, Young Man, or burdened with a fetish for old women, or even for Aunt Jemima.*

The thoughts were hers, she figured. Or maybe she had heard them on a true crime documentary. Or maybe God was warning her. Goosebumps trailed along Hannah's arms. The sinking feeling at the pit of her stomach took away her appetite. She had given a perfect stranger enough information about herself for him to track her to her hotel. *I'm being a ridiculous old woman,* she thought. *I've entered cronehood and am past the time when a cute kid like this would like me. What kind of desperate delusion am I falling into?* She put down her plate of cinnamon buns, lasagna, macaroni salad, and girlishness. "I suggest you leave, Aleksu. This is a family of Irish cops and firemen. Just so you know."

"I know." A wink. "I'm not worried."

In a far corner near the wall, her husband was feeding Dane a cookie. The kid would be up all night. Hannah tried not to fume. "Why are you here anyway, Aleksu?"

"Are you saying you didn't feel a connection between us back there at the stream? Your heart called out to me. I'm here for you."

Hannah raised her eyebrows. "Why would it cry out for you exactly?" In the back of the room, Dane was now drinking milk.

Aleksu put a heaping spoonful of mac and cheese in his mouth. "You didn't ask what I do for a living, by the way."

Hannah aimed the anger at her husband at Aleksu. "I didn't ask because I didn't care."

"I'm a male prostitute. Licensed. Studied. Took the exam. Passed."

This husband of mine will be the death of me and of my son, Hannah thought, but said, "I don't like your sense of humor, Aleksu."

His face darkened. With hurt? With rejection? Or was it anger? Hannah wasn't sure. "In Japan we're licensed. We're taught how to see a woman's sorrow and how to alleviate it. I saw you and I thought...she's got issues and I've got issues. We're perfect for each other."

True, there was a joy, a bond, in sharing issues. Farr had issues but he would never share them with her.

"Okay, Aleksu, you've got to go." Hannah then turned toward her husband and Dane who immediately hid the milk when he saw her. "Dane! Come here! Have some real food!"

Dane was at her side looking at the spread but nothing on the table interested him. Not the chocolate cake, the chicken nuggets, the sauce-covered spaghetti, the meatballs, hotdogs, or teriyaki chicken.

"Not willing to try?" Aleksu mouthed as Hannah turned to look at him.

Hannah thought, *Not really. I told you I've lived a long time. I've seen other women try. And what did they get out of it? Humiliation. Pain. Death and disease. Out of the frying pan and into the fire.*

Aleksu burst out laughing… as if he had heard her thoughts.

Hannah walked over to Aleksu, dragging Dane with her.

"Do you think what I thought was so funny?" she asked. Somehow the question and the familiarity both seemed right.

"Admit it. It was," Aleksu replied with the same familiarity.

"I'll have you know, Aleksu, that I have seen quite a few stories about sad old women who went off with their dream men, young men whom they deemed beautiful and otherworldly—who ended up killing them, leaving them nude, hacked to pieces and humiliated in death. This sudden sexual attraction I am feeling toward this smiling twenty-something in front of me is nothing more than a demonic choreography of evil, created to ruin my life and my immortal soul. Therefore, please stop bothering me."

Aleksu smirked. "Your immortal soul? I see you are very upfront about your worship of Zeus Pater?"

"Zeus Pater? Who is Zeus…oh, Jupiter?"

"Well, you would call him 'Deus Pater,'" he said. "Father God."

"Whatever." Hannah felt the familiarity again. "Have I met you before?"

"In dreams, yes. And that god you worship is my great enemy."

Hannah took a minute to take that in. "When you say you are enemies, are you saying that he hates you or that you hate him? Because my God – Deus Pater-- hates no one."

A shrug. "He hates us." Aleksu took a bit of his mac and cheese. "He created the lake of fire for us, did he not?"

Hannah wrinkled her brow. "So, you're saying you're a demon? Or are you a Satan worshipper?" She poured some juice for Dane who was trying to drag her toward the exit of the hotel conference room. "Son," she pleaded, "drink this!"

"I am that spirit that came to you in night visions." Aleksu extended the hand that was not busy holding the plate. "Typhon is the name."

Hannah raised her hand to her husband who was sitting at a table with some of his cousins and holding a can of beer to his chest like a shield. "You left my dream before I got a chance to tell you that I didn't want to marry you."

"That hardly matters," Typhon pooh-poohed her response. "Heaven and hell are privy to the darkest thoughts of you humans."

Hannah paused in the conversation to hand-off Dane to Farr who had come immediately at her bidding. As both her silent men dashed through the door, she got back to the conversation with Aleksu. "So? I did not vow to be yours. A fantasy is not an inner or outer vow, is it?"

Typhon poured himself some ginger ale. "Can you not see how much I love you? I can be anything and any kind of lover you need."

"I'd rather not get into a relationship with a demon. I have read the verse, 'Hell was created for the devil and his angels.'"

"I know the place well. It's an eternal prison made to eternally cage beings who are spirit and eternal."

"Exactly. Since there is no chance for even spirit beings to escape it, how can I –a mere human woman—escape it?"

"It's not certain that you will end up there."

Hannah laughed. "Should I risk my immortal soul just for love and sex? With a demon no less? I would probably die in the middle of adulterous sinful sex with you. How humiliating to suddenly be thrust into death for all on earth, heaven, and hell to see!"

"Dear me! You certainly overthink things."

"It's safest that way. So, stop bothering me, okay? Take this as my official refusal and divorce from you, Spirit Husband."

Typhon placed his plate beside the ambrosia container and walked out the door, leaving Hannah trembling and shaky but not surprised at her supernatural encounter.

She spent the night listening to Dane coughing and giving him gluten-aid, dairy-aid, anti-gas meds, and anti-constipation meds. Then she marathoned episodes of ghostly encounters then watched YouTube videos of people's near-death experiences in hell. She reminded herself that being married to the wrong person entailed continual daily forgiveness and she forced herself to forgive Farr for being who he was, and to forgive herself for not being loving enough. Then she grieved for all the missing women, diseased children, and murder victims because life and earth were filled with sorrows and human life was a vale of tears. Sometime during all that, she managed a prayer.

Heavenly Father, it's hard to get old. Especially as a fat Black woman in America. But others have done it gracefully. Help me to do it. Death is the Last Enemy, right? Can you kill me now, though? Take me from this world. I'm depressed. And if you don't, then help me make it up the rough side of the mountain gracefully and holily. Amen.

She trusted that He was near and had heard her.

After Dane finally fell asleep, she googled Typhon. The illustrations showed him as many-headed and wrapped about with snakes. The search for Typhon also led her to Python, his counterpart. *Many heads*, she wondered. *Many guises.* In bed, fantasies rushed at her. Old imaginary lovers she had created, beautiful men of all ages, status, and races who had comforted her in times past. *Were they all Typhon? Was it he who created those fantasies in my mind? Or was it me? Dammit, life is confusing.*

Would this need for human touch not be the death of her body and soul? Then the thought came to her: *Typhon has choreographed all this*. She looked at her husband. *The neuro-atypicality, aside, has Typhon also created hubby's entanglement and lies? All those snakes! All those pythons that constrict the soul!*

She was pissed at Typhon now; she steeled her mind against the flesh's need for intimacy and commanded all seductive spirits and demonic snakes entangled in her life to leave.

***

Because the bride had specified that children were not allowed in the church during the wedding, and Dane was considered a child, Hannah was spending the wedding in one of the hotel suites babysitting. Little Irish-Italian, Irish-Polish, Irish-Hispanic, etc, kids – all born within the decade, were treating her like some aged nanny or grand-aunt. She had fallen into crone-hood without ever having had a fun middle age.

Hannah imagined the bride walking down the aisle, adored, head held high; The bride probably looked ravishing, as brides often do. Hannah had lived her entire life feeling unadored, unadorned. The marriage had only deepened her feelings of rejection and abandonment. But Hannah was now committed to hoping.

Sitting with the children – ages ten and under—Hannah listened to the younger ones chattering away or attempting to chatter. Her non-verbal son was moaning to himself in a corner. *What would his voice sound like?* she wondered. Even now she still got weepy when she heard toddlers speaking. She walked to the window and peered down toward the little stream where the herring struggled to perpetuate life. Was the mermaid already dead? Or had she managed to get herself out of her rut? Life was about struggle but Hannah was tired of fighting. *She must be dead then. They. They must be dead, our little mermaids. Or maybe they made it over those pebbles. Or maybe someone – another mermaid? A human? -- came to help. Or maybe God freed her from her misery.*

The door opened and, a tall blonde guy, in a cowboy hat and denim jeans was looking at her through squinty eyes. She rose and approached him. "Excuse me? Can I help you?"

He pointed to his outfit. "Would you believe my sister forgot to pack a suitable outfit for this-here damn wedding?"

He had an accent. Texas, Louisiana, Oklahoma – Hannah wasn't sure. All she knew was that he was square of jaw and was everything she imagined a manly confident forty-something cowboy would be. Just as Aleksu was what she imagined a wounded Japanese outcast might be.

"Are you…one of the relatives?" she asked him.

"Yes, Ma'am," the cowboy said and looked around the room. "We're a big clan, aren't we?" He extended his hand. "Rich Lukov." He paused, grinned. "Joan's daughter who died on that airplane gave me up for adoption before she died. Took a while for me and everyone to get acquainted and comfortable with each other but it's all good now. Well, almost all good."

"Not everything's perfect?"

"Well, I was raised in the Bible Belt. Or maybe a little underneath it's belt. So…I'm Pentecostal. And a minister to boot. It took 'em a while to get used to."

Hannah was already suspicious of him. "A lot of interesting family relationships turning up at this reunion."

"I hear ya. And you?"

"Hannah. Eugene's son's wife."

Rich whistled. "Ah, I heard of you." He winked at a little girl who had brought a dinosaur book to Hannah. "Hey, you want to be read to?"

The little girl – Farr's second cousin once removed, if Hannah remembered correctly—nodded. The result was that Hannah and her second cousin-in-law were regaled with what was simply the most Americana cowboy voice ever.

Hannah had missed the male voice. A non-verbal younger son, an older son who preferred the company of his buddies, and a laconic husband made her house silent. She listened to him and thought Rich was the kind of guy who would make a great father. Kind but authoritative, gently communicative, affectionate and witty without being sarcastic. He was the kind of guy she would love to sleep beside. She wondered if he were Typhon or if he were human. Not that his true identity mattered. She had decided to endure Farr.

They talked for about two hours until one of the older female cousins walked in, tears flowing. "Oh my God!" She squealed in her Long Island accent. "It was a beautiful wedding! So beautiful!" She wiped her nose with a richly-embroidered handkerchiefs then extended her hand to one of her many grandkids. "You guys hungry?"

A collective scream of "Yes!" was answered with, "Reception's ready! Now don't get all grabby. There's more than enough. Oh my gosh! The spread's amazing." She directed them to the door. "Come on now. Follow me. Family photo time!"

Within minutes the room was emptied of all but Rich, Dane, and Hannah.

"You ready to indulge your gluttony?" the cowboy asked, but his eyes hinted that he would be willing to hang out with Hannah for a while.

"I'm cool." Hannah pointed at Dane. "Crowds freak him out sometimes. We'll wait 'til everyone's settled down."

"Yeah, sometimes you need to get away from the clan."

Hannah looked toward the stream and the herring run. "Yep."

"You don't love your husband, do you?" the cowboy asked.

Hannah turned to look into the cowboy's soulful eyes. "How'd you…?"

"It's obvious. I've lived long enough to know when a woman doesn't like her man. Why not divorce him?" the cowboy asked.

"It's not his fault he has a disability," Hannah apologized for her husband. "His parents should have taught him better. Or they should have prepared me better. Or...maybe I simply shouldn't have married him. Do you know…at church there is this prophetess friend of mine. Cassandra. Well, she believes she's a prophetess and she does kinda know weird stuff sometimes but you know…."

"All these little storefront churches have prophetesses galore," the cowboy said and Hannah laughed.

"How did you know it was a storefront church?" Hannah asked.

The cowboy grinned. "I figured."

"Ah. Well, she warned me against marrying him. 'You two don't match,' she said. 'That isn't peace you see in him. It's impenetrability.' But I married him anyway. Because I didn't want his mother triumphing over me."

A knowing smirk. "Your weakness? So, love and willfulness created your marriage? Quite an entanglement. That's what they call a Pyrrhic victory. You won the battle but lost the war."

"I'm cold-hearted, I think. I should be more patient. That's what they tell us at the support group. To change ourselves. But it gets tiring." She was crying now, which was strange because she rarely cried. "When you've married someone who isn't right for you, and when his own odd habits are hurting your child, and when you try to be a good Christian woman…you just end up having to forgive continually."

"Just divorce him."

"I can't divorce him. He and his stupid family have made me so sick over the years, that I can't function on my own. No one else would want me. I'm kinda stuck with my oppressor. And who would take care of me?"

A slight pause, then the cowboy said, "I would." He stroked her forehead. "Be my old lady."

Hannah almost melted into the cowboy's touch. But she caught herself and thanked her lucky stars that she was no longer young and enslaved to her affections. After thirty-four years of marriage to Farr, she had learned a hard lesson about being enslaved to anger, love, and willfulness. She began walking toward the door. "Ready for more macaroni salad and ambrosia?"

"I mean it, Hannah."

Hannah smiled, thanked him for the compliment.

"Do you really want to go to the reception or should we escape the family for the nonce?" the cowboy asked.

"The Herring Run," Hannah said. "There's something I have to see. Can you take me and Dane there?"

The cowboy nodded. "Sure enough, Little Lady."

"Is the human heart made to pretend to love so many people, I wonder?" Hannah asked.

"I suppose humans have many sides so love is possible with everyone," Rich said. "Or our many sides help us to accommodate the many sides of a single lover."

"Funny thing," Hannah said. "It's not marriage that I have a problem with. It's attraction that's the scary untrustworthy thing. At least, in my experience. So many people have destroyed their entire life because of some feeling that overtakes them in their youth, that tiny, tiny section of our immortal life."

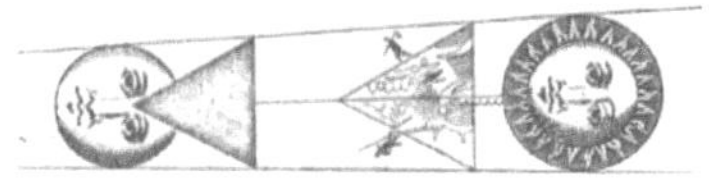

Inside the stream, herring – healthy or bruised, fast-flying or floundering—swam. The ancient biological edict had to be obeyed. Procreate, lay eggs, and all else be damned. Hannah walked into the stream toward that little area of stasis. The mermaid was still there, struggling, breathing her last breath.

Even now, even after all these years, even after all I've seen… I still find it strange to believe that the world is magical.

Rich chuckled.

"You're Typhon, aren't you?" Hannah said. "The many-headed one?"

"See, you did recognize me."

Hannah held her son's hand tightly. "You do have something of a personality. How could you not know that I recognized you? If you were human, I wouldn't have trusted you to come here with me. Even if it's a handsome cowboy. Humans are scary people." She pointed at the mermaid. "She's expecting something from us. Do you think she – they-- want us to help them?"

Evening was approaching. Silence now, except for the din of herring and water. Rich returned to his Aleksu form and Hannah wondered if he did this because that bi-racial Japanese man was actually her truest type. Was Typhon still intending to seduce her?

"Help them with what?" Typhon asked. "Mercy killing, you mean? Do you think she got trapped here as she journeyed to somewhere else?"

"She probably got swept up in the rush. You're a spirit being. You have some power, don't you? Ask her where she wants to be and take her there. I don't think she wants to die. I think she came here to live."

"Why wouldn't she not want to die?" Typhon asked. "Just look at her. She has two heads! Surely she desires relief from such a disability."

"I'm not going to assume that two-headed mermaids are an anomaly," Hannah said.

"This is the only mermaid you've ever met, right? Maybe dying is her only relief."

Silence again, and Aleksu touched Hannah's arm. Hannah thought of the snakes and false truths that entangled her husband then of the false truths that also entangled her. She tried to see clear. Deus Pater had been silent and often he seemed far away and unloving. Why had he left a little-two-headed mermaid to stasis and death? Hadn't the mermaid grown wearied with spiritual and physical fatigue?

She stooped and tried to feel the answer in the mermaids' eyes. When Hannah spoke again, she made a sweeping gesture that indicated all the struggling herring.

"No," she said, "Let her alone. Let the struggle continue. She knows she may die if she continues here. But that's what she wants. Perhaps the search for relief is the false dream. I reckon the struggles here cannot in any way compare to the joy we will receive in the future, human, mer, abled, or disabled." Hannah rubbed her forehead, shrugged and grasped her son's hand. "Don't come to me anymore. Not in dreams or in fantasies." She turned toward the exit, and began to climb the rough side of the mountainous hill. Although she held her son's hand she was not leaning on her son. She was leaning on the Everlasting Arms.

The Touch of Lethe

J. T. Glover

From across the parking lot, the mural looked unfinished. Up close we could see care in the brushwork, tendrils painted in intricate knots almost too small to see. Paige traced one finger along a morning glory vine's strangling length, and I took some snaps to get the scale. Then I realized what I was seeing and lowered my camera.

"Wow, is that..." I said, trailing off.

"Yeah," Paige said. "That wasn't done with a mural brush."

"Why would anyone do this? I mean—look at that wall. It's, like, mortar and stones, not even brick."

"Dunno," Paige said.

Friends since we'd started at RISD last year, we were both in sophomore photo seminar and had decided to do our street photography assignment together. I don't usually like photographing artwork, but a four-story toddler studying giant vines while floating in a group of... asteroids?

It was legit cute, and we'd both been drawn to it the moment we turned up Clemence and saw it framed by the deepening sky. There was a quiet sense of wonder unfolding that I didn't quite understand, but which satisfied me somewhere deep inside. In the last of Providence's purple twilight, the streetlamps just coming on, the mural would have been easy to miss.

"It's so intricate," I said. "Like the world's biggest miniature."

"I know! That took time. Had to be someone local."

"Yeah. How long, you think? We should have, you know, seen this before, when it was going up."

"How do you mean?"

"This didn't take a week to paint," I said. "Or even a month. We're downtown once a week for Korean food alone, and we'd have seen people coming and going."

I stepped up to the wall, swinging the camera aside to protect the lens, and leaned in. The closer I looked, the more detail became visible. It was now dark enough that the work vanished at a certain level, but by day? With a magnifying glass? I wondered how the swirling greenery might resolve, what the light might uncover.

"Come ooooon, Samantha," Paige said, grabbing my arm and tugging me back toward the street. "This is cool, but we got photos to take, and there's a party at Emily's tonight."

"Yeah, yeah."

I glanced back as we headed up the street, and the mural seemed faded by the glare of the streetlights between us and it. The detail that had so puzzled me was invisible, of course, but now the whole thing appeared flat, barely a silhouette. How would it look tomorrow when I was editing my shots? Then Paige started in about the boy she'd dated for a second back in June who just wouldn't stop texting her. I listened dutifully, but my heart wasn't in it.

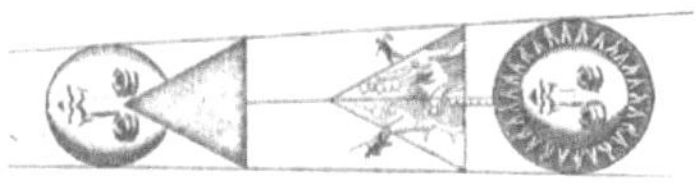

What appeared onscreen the next morning was fuzzy no matter what I tried—spinning the mouse wheel, adjusting this, leveling that. My Nikon D850 was the best rig that mom's money could buy, did amazing things, but somehow it hadn't captured any detail? I scowled and leaned back, wondering what I was going to say to Forney. Our prof for this class was encouraging, but she was firmly in favor of using gear you could make work, talking about how only shitty artists blamed their materials.

I took my camera back into the main room, where I studied the lens in the light streaming from the front windows, filtered through the lindens outside my Benefit Street apartment. A few flecks of dust, a little schmutz. Otherwise it looked good as new. I snapped a few quick shots—dishes in the sink, the Rodchenko bridge photo by the door—and then zoomed in on the mums I'd neglected to death, still sitting on the coffee table.

Back in my bedroom, surrounded by the chaos of piled underwear and jeans, I pulled the new shots up on my MacBook. They were fine. Nothing amazing, but fine, with all the detail you'd expect. I stretched and yawned, thinking vaguely about shooting the mural again, wondering if there was time before class. It wouldn't be a night shoot, but—

My phone squawked, and I saw a message from Paige: "Hey, you look at last night's photos?"

"Yeah," I replied. "Class is tonight! Those mural photos, tho…"

"Mine were fine, just blah. Yours."

Huh. So, why...? "P, were yours a little fuzzy?"

"Nope. Just, yknow, banal."

I frowned as I stared at the screen, thinking about scenes from horror movies. When I was old enough to beg off my parents's annual pilgrimage to Aspen, I'd stay with my mom's sister, Tansy. We'd sit up all night in her cluttered den, where we gorged on popcorn and watched Freddy, *Scream*, *The Ring*, all that old shit. I didn't believe in any of that stuff in real life, but it was odd that the rest of my snaps were fine, and only the mural ones had gone wrong.

"Want to get lunch at Mokban?" I texted. "Just a few blocks from the mural, and we could check it out afterward."

She didn't respond quickly, so I started scrolling through my photos again. I had enough good shots—verticals of a dumpster, a woman awkwardly adjusting one shoe outside a club, homeless guy sleeping in a doorway. I quickly put them into a slideshow on our course page and was just wondering if I should text again when—

"Sure. Be there soon. Just gotta say goodbye to my date…"

I smiled as I texted back and started getting my stuff to head out the door. So that was why she'd been slow to answer. The party the night before had turned out to be a little bigger than I wanted on a weeknight, but when I left she'd been talking with a couple people I knew and seemed all right, so we'd just said our goodbyes.

After a year of college, I'd proved to myself that I could do more than loaf on my trust fund, but I'd also come to appreciate how it pushed me into meeting different people.

I rented in a College Hill house with more lineage than all of Paige's family, and I spent her food budget for a semester in one month of rent, but we both loved photography, and had fallen together easily. A couple months back we'd even gone on a whirlwind road trip to do Fourth of July with her folks back in Iowa, complete with cherry pie, a parade, and fireworks. It was like nothing I remembered from childhood, but I'd seen enough movies to play along.

Even with RISD being what it was, Paige fit in almost seamlessly, making friends and dating with ease. I went out sometimes, but the guys I met at RISD were... well, they were mostly boys. Paige, who had spent most of her life a hundred feet from a cornfield, had found whole new worlds to explore in the big city.

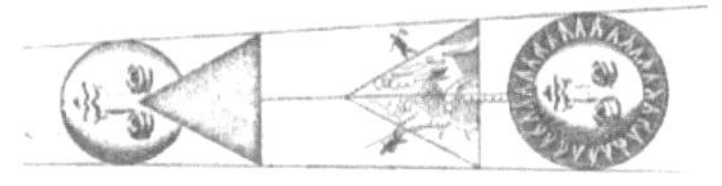

We were ambling along after lunch when we made a turn and I stopped dead at the edge of a familiar parking lot. The heat radiating up from the concrete made me feel half-baked, sense vanishing with my cool.

Paige kept walking another ten feet before she noticed.

"What the fuck," I said.

"Huh?" Paige said, looking back at me quizzically. "Oh yeah, let's... Wait."

In broad daylight, the mural we'd photographed looked almost entirely unlike what I remembered. As if exposed to a giant flashbulb, it had been burned to almost nothing, like a ghost sign advertising some bygone brand of soda or motor oil. The honk of passing cars on the street just a few feet away seemed unreal, like news from another planet.

"Come on," I muttered, "let's take a look."

Up close, there was no mistaking it. The toddler and the vines were clearly aging, weakened by years of sun and rain, crying out to be painted over. And the detail that had so fascinated us? Vanished entirely.

"Huh. Sam, what do you think?"

"I… This was different. It was a *lot* different last night."

"Maybe," she said, frowning, "but we weren't exactly sober, were we?"

"Yeah," I said, "but I still remember…"

"Okay," Paige said, gesturing. "We got enough pictures for class, anyway, even without this." She had clearly lost interest, playing with her phone while I continued to study the mural. There was a puzzle here, but there were also movies to watch, assignments to finish.

I started to turn away, and then did a double-take.

Was it actually *paler* than it had been a few minutes ago?

My stomach lurched, the kimchi roiling uneasily. Time hadn't stopped, though, and it was less than an hour until class, so we took off.

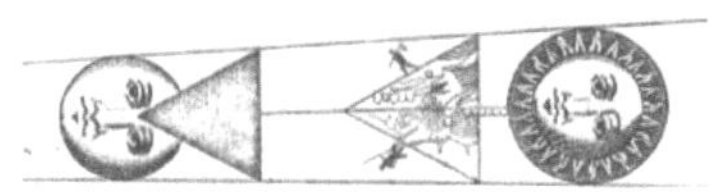

Group crit went well for me, and I even learned a thing or two. Forney commented favorably on my grouping, even musing about similarities to some of Atget's earliest work, and gave advice about avoiding blown-out highlights. Most everybody seemed happy to leave it there, even if I caught a couple side-eyes, but Brandon laid into me, the fat little hack trying to show off his knowledge about focal distance, processing, all that. Paige fared worse, stone-faced to avoid crying. Her crit lasted forever, twice as long as anyone else's. People kept taking turns with the sneering compliments and fake-apologetic insults, all the while Forney nodded sagely and checked her phone. It was ugly.

Walking out into the early evening, I didn't say anything about class, just kept pace with Paige, thinking that I was hungry, hoping that she would be okay. This wasn't the first time my friend had gotten savaged during a crit. She worked hard and had an abundance of natural talent to justify the full-tuition scholarship, which made some of our classmates hate her. It had taken a call from my dad to the RISD development office to get my half-assed portfolio over the bar, but I didn't begrudge my friend her talent. She'd be earning her way as a photographer soon enough, but I had options if my career fell through.

"What the fuck is her problem!" she finally said.

"Teachers gonna teach," I said, shrugging.

"I know, but motherfucking *dammit.* Sometimes this whole thing just seems like so much ego..."

I didn't look over as she wiped at the corners of her eyes. Eventually she stopped, took a shuddering breath. We'd paused at the monument down by the canal, the bronze figure turned a warm almost-red as evening light came on, and we looked over at downtown silently. I was thinking about the mural, I realized guiltily, but—

"God," Paige said, "how am I supposed to go to work like this? Ugh."

I put an arm around her shoulder and squeezed gently.

She smiled, and we headed for one of the bridges. Soon we were coming up on Emiliano's and said our seeyas. I quickened my pace, and before long, I was walking up Clemence again, telling myself I was only curious, even as my heart pounded. Why did I care about this? Surely, we'd just had too much to drink and mistakenly thought we'd seen something we hadn't? And then I came to the lot in the middle of that block, surrounded by now-familiar worn bricks and rusty fire escapes.

The wall we'd twice studied was covered from eye level down by wheat paste posters. Higher up—nothing, not even the ghost of a ghost.

Up close, the posters looked like they'd been there for months. I goggled at it, dimly aware my mouth was hanging open. I started to pull out my camera, but something caught my eye. Most of the band names meant nothing to me ("Gunchugger Returns!" read one, "Raindogs at Last Call" another), and the fight fliers meant less, but then there was this, faded and scratched: "INXS/KICK World Tour! Great Woods Amphitheater!" And just under it, peeking out, I could see a red, white, and blue flier with a "-kakis" and "Bentsen."

My vision doubled, shimmered, and then eased back together. Nothing had changed in front of me, or behind me, but briefly I caught an odor of... paint? Jasmine? The air seemed to vibrate around me, rippling with heat from the wall, and I took out my camera, looking at it through the viewfinder. I couldn't see anything, just an efflorescence of colors that mingled and wavered in and out of each other.

What the fuck? First fuzzy pictures, now a fuzzy viewfinder?

I knew it didn't make sense, but none of it did. It was getting late, I still had homework, and this thing wasn't going to solve itself. The colors, though, somehow they reminded me of... the aurora borealis? Yeah, my sweet sixteen trip to Sweden. As I walked, dodging groups of leering boys and a tour group, an idea started to come together. I searched on my phone, one eye on the traffic, trying to figure out what I'd need.

Soft chime and hum of the Lumineers in the background, accompaniment to the pounding of my heart. For the last couple hours, I'd been crouched at an improvised observation station, panning my binoculars-and-camera rig around what I could see of the city from my window. The beer on the sill had gone flat, my stomach clenching and unclenching like I was about to take my fourth trip to the toilet in the middle of a long night of stomach flu. My homework was... well, not a distant memory, but it seemed abstract, irrelevant.

I was seeing colors that shouldn't have been. Through the binoculars alone, nothing. Put the camera up to one lens, though? Parts of the city were hazier than others, like the buildings weren't quite all there. And the spot where I'd seen that mural? It was like a light show: flares and streamers of color jetting into the air.

"What the hell," I whispered.

Once I'd gotten home, I looked online and confirmed that, yes, the posters I'd seen on that wall were wrong. They were from 1988, and surely nobody, however clever or funny, had taken time to recreate a 1980s wall in downtown Providence. A couple halfhearted searches confirmed no movies filming nearby, nor big new guerilla installations. I had no real idea of what was going on, just a memory of my stomach churning when I was at the wall, the scent of strange things.

Sitting there earlier, I'd finally started to wonder about aliens, time travel, and all that *X-Files* crap. But... really? I'd never believed in conspiracies before, and I wasn't about to without hard evidence. It was at moments like this that I wished I had a brother or sister, that my parents hadn't been so cold. My family wasn't terrible, just not really, well, family-like, and even with boarding and prep schools, I had few close friends. Paige was the closest I had to a BFF, and she was busy tonight. So there I sat, wondering if I was going crazy.

I looked into the viewfinder again, and this time it was no flicker, but a corona lighting the sky from a spot... south on the other side of the canal? Further? I wasn't sure, but I took a few reference snaps that looked fine onscreen, threw on my coat, and left.

College Hill was virtually silent this long after midnight, the Colonial roofs and mullioned windows looking out on more peace than any American window deserved these days. I hustled down Angell Street, past the jaundiced baroque façade of the Fleur de Lys house and into downtown.

Before long I was standing in—big surprise—the entrance to another alley, this one-off Mathewson. I'd passed by the plush Haven Brothers trailer on Dorrance, smelling the burgers cooking and listening to the drunks's happy chatter, feeling distant from and envious of their self-absorption, even as my brain throbbed inside my skull.

I looked through the viewfinder again, and unlike last night, I could see the colors flaring and flickering. The cobbles dug into the soles of my Chucks, and I slowed as I approached the corner that opened onto the middle of the block.

Non-descript walls. Nothing strange in the slightest. I didn't even see any...

Wait.

There, in one corner, something plastered. Slowly I walked over, studied the sober-faced man on the poster. I wouldn't have recognized him, but the big letters spelling out "Roosevelt" were plain as day. I ran my fingertips over the image, felt the subtle rise and fall of offset printing, like no one had used for years on fliers like this. Up close, I felt that same thrum and tickle, that *off* scent. This time it was like exhaust and garbage and summer-piss all rolled into one, not quite like anything I ever smelled walking around town. It was an echo of something else that wasn't supposed to be here anymore.

"...and that was just the once," someone said from behind me with a laugh that cut off abruptly.

I turned, and two plain-looking men in coveralls had just rounded the corner and were looking at me.

"Well, hello there, missy," said one of them, a tall, young-looking guy with the lightest-colored eyebrows I'd ever seen. "Can we help you with something?"

"Yeah. You see that?" I said, pointing at the poster.

The two of them looked at each other, then at me.

"What have we got here?" said his partner, a short, dark-skinned man with a pencil-thin moustache and a cast eye.

They came over and looked at it, the tall guy sounding out the syllables silently, brow bunched in concentration.

"Huh," said the short one. "Somebody likes Etsy, I guess. Am I right, Colin?"

"Yeah. People do anything for a laugh, huh-huh-huh."

I looked back and forth between the two of them, thinking that it was three in the morning, but I could see both of them clearly, their skin almost sparkling. For some reason I wasn't afraid, though I probably should have been.

"That isn't a reproduction," I said, as confidently as I could. "And this doesn't make sense. Why are you guys here, anyway?"

"Night cleaning crew," the short one said promptly.

"Okay. Where are your buckets? Your cart? Your tools?"

This time he said nothing, just looked at me.

"Don't know what you're on about, missy," the tall one said at last, frowning. "Now, if you don't mind, we got work to do, *including* getting our gear," he said, pointing to a leaning shack in one corner that I somehow hadn't noticed, but which looked like any old building. Common, the sort of thing you see every day, and it damned well hadn't been there a minute ago.

Was I losing my mind? Here I stood, arguing with two janitors who probably were about a second from calling 911 about the batty chick… Wait. I raised my camera again and looked at the viewfinder. Crazy, fuzzy colors were flickering wildly as I pointed it at the wall, and it was impossible to see the poster at all for the… efflorescence? radiation? My stomach pitched again. I lowered the camera and looked at the two guys, eyebrow raised.

The short one sighed. "Look," he said quietly. "We're the night crew, okay? We clean things up. All sorts of things. I don't know what you think you're seeing, but you aren't seeing it, okay?"

"Fuck that," I shot back. "I know very fucking well what I'm seeing."

"It's the camera," the tall one said, voice gone flat and strange, nothing like the high, dumb voice he'd spoken in earlier. "Something wrong with it. You never know what happens with those things lately."

"Dammit," the short one said, breathing out slowly. "Look, I hate to do this, but I have to ask for that camera."

"What? Why? I'm getting the story of the—"

"You're getting nothing," he said, sounding less patient. "I'm sorry, but things like this happen from time to time. You aren't seeing anything new, just using a new tool.

People like us come through to make sure everything's 'tidy.' Memory's a tricky thing, and it doesn't always take care of itself, either the remembering *or* the forgetting.

"People been telling stories like this forever. We maybe leave a mess, people get worried. Always been that way. Knowing this stuff isn't making you happier, is it?"

I stood there, looking at these two… Were they just wackos? Was this… I looked around, wondering if there was a camera in sight somewhere, but nothing I could see. Not that this proved anything, but he didn't sound fake.

"This is crazy," I said flatly. "How do you even—"

"Look," the short one said. "You know basic physics, right?"

"Of course."

"Humans dream up ghosts, demons, everything under the sun to explain what they don't understand, and they don't understand very much. People really only figured out quantum mechanics recently, right? But it was happening all along, and yet—all that other stuff got the name or the blame. What makes you think there aren't other rules, other modes of existence, as unknown to you as the quantum was to Newton or Euclid? You remember, you forget, and both are a blessing."

I looked them over again. Two perfectly nondescript men with no distinguishing marks, wearing dingy old coveralls. Who would even...

Who would remember them?

I closed my eyes, and I tried to think of their faces, and there was a curious blank spot in my mind's eye, barely even man-shaped. I opened my eyes, and in the vague, yellow glow leaching in from the streetlights, for a moment I thought I saw two swirling things, clouds with ribbons of light and dark running through them. And then that was gone, and I was looking once more at two average guys. The tall one's smile was thin. I reached for my camera, wanting to capture it, but there was no strap around my neck, no bag on my shoulder.

"Nothing is ever what it seems," the short one said. "There's going to be a new camera waiting at home for you, and sadly your pictures from last night failed to save properly. Soon enough you'll forget this. Some people try to remember, write stories or paint pictures, but they never quite get it, and their lives are strained and short, the ones who try. Once upon a time, they might become the favored of the gods, but people don't leave much room for that these days."

"What are you?" I whispered, rubbing one cheek, dry hand rasping against sweaty flesh, feeling as alive and present as I ever did anywhere

"Night crew," he said, smiling faintly—eyes shining and maybe, just maybe, glowing. "Nobody important, just part of machinery that was set in motion long ago. The day crew you mostly don't see either—they help you remember. We clean things up, help people forget, otherwise you'd go mad, remembering everything that ever was. Now, don't you...?"

"Guess I should be going," I mumbled, trying to wrap my now-aching head around it all. Strange, but I couldn't remember why I'd left my camera at home. I started walking toward the street and away from the two men who were now retrieving cleaning supplies from the shed in the corner. One was muttering, the other whistling, as they set to work over by one of the walls, scraping and scrubbing.

Nobody out walking tonight but me, and I thought wistfully of my Canon 5D, sitting back on my desk. Empty streets, hazy yellow with the glow of streetlights. I held up my hands, squared up a few shots, but for some reason it didn't feel quite right. I looked around restlessly, thinking about how things felt *off* for some reason I couldn't divine. It was the kind of aesthetic that people like Gregory Crewdson or David Lynch created, fantasias as far from street photography as you could get and still use a camera. It made me wonder just what kinds of scenarios I could dream up, the worlds I might be able to uncover, if only I remembered them on waking.

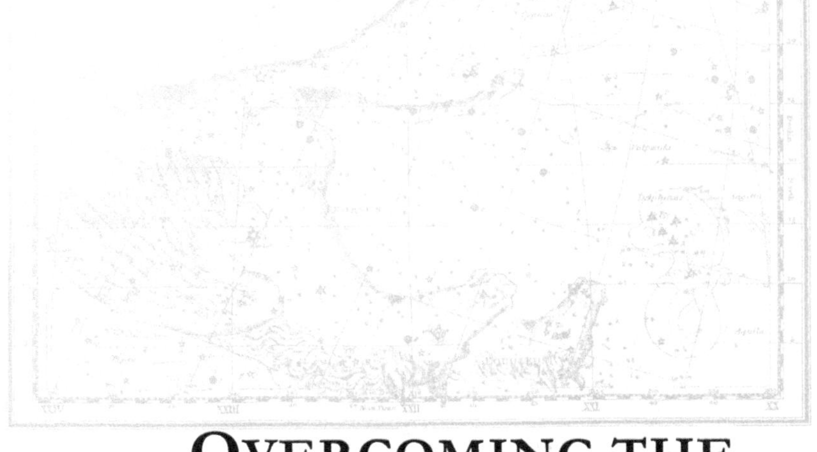

OVERCOMING THE EARTH

Anthony G. Cirilla

"He who sings prays twice."
— Augustine

Entry 1: Laying Bare the Wound

My kid sister is a musicologist, and she says the best therapy for grief is writing. I went into law because I think the best therapy for grief is nailing the perp's ass to the wall, but I guess that approach doesn't always work. But she dates an organist so maybe her judgment isn't the best either. Anyway, weird stuff happened, so I think I'll start writing some of it down. Hopefully if I keep track, I'll piece everything together in the end. Then throw the whole notepad in the fire.

It was a quiet sunny afternoon, and I'd had enough drama already that I didn't expect it to be a good day. The smell of hospital rooms haunted me like stubborn perfume.

I hated the quiet, peaceful atmosphere of the street – the way the road curved away from the main street and gave the neighborhood a sound barrier from the traffic felt like a cul-de-sac. I bet men were on the golf course on the other side of the trees that lined our back yard, congratulating each other on their objectively pathetic swings. The blue house looked sad with the stump in the front yard as my AirDrone touched down on the pavement. I stepped out and the AI offered a melodic thank you for your business we hope to see you again dear friend, and I ignored it as I remembered when that stump used to be a majestic blue spruce. Mom told us stories it was home to fairies when we were little, that Santa Claus himself would get workers for his shop from the fairy village hidden in its lanky branches. I liked the story but never believed it. Laura believed it, and probably still wants to.

She had her ugly little electric car parked near the garage door, charging it on the station. I don't understand people who still drive – misplaced nostalgia or something, I don't know. I guess they like the feeling that user error could result in death at any moment. Well hey, accidents still give me business, so I appreciate the job security.

The wooden railing had seen better days — cracked and weathered, Dad would be outside repairing it were he still around. That was all he seemed to do in the last days before the cancer incapacitated him — tinker around the outside of the house with pointless projects a professional could have finished in half the time. The screen door squeaked with surprise as I opened it and I let it slam shut behind me as I stepped into the mudroom. It was absurd that dad's boots were still sitting there, like he might come out and change into them so that he could go out and clomp around in his dinky little garden. As soon as I opened the front door I could hear Laura playing her music.

"What is *that*?" I shouted in protest. "Are you playing music with actual Latin words, you big nerd?"

Laura didn't reply. I let that door slam behind me too, just to annoy dad's spirit. Why he had the compression on those doors so tightly pressured, I have no idea. We used to joke that he was trying to turn it into his own Temple of Doom, and that any of us could lose a hand if we didn't get out of the way in time. I stood in the hall and looked at the ugly flowered furniture in the living room – furniture that was old fashioned even when it was made and straight up old even when dad had bought it. Dear old cheapskate.

Laura had some old movie playing on the HoloVision – one made for flatscreen TVs so if you weren't in the right spot the side or back of the characters distorted. Some superhero movie from the teens. It didn't look all that bad if you looked at it straight on, but you could tell it wasn't made to be viewed in 4D holo, with bits of the superhero stretching weirdly as his metallic suit snapped into place over a head that bulged weirdly, creating a comic effect that wasn't meant for the movie. Stupidly, tears welled up. I wiped them away.

I looked into the kitchen, where Laura had her archaic tunes blasting out of her phone, filling the house with the eerie sound of some intentionally anachronistic Gregorian chanter singing on top of pathetic strings. *"Clara tenebris iustusque tulit crimen iniqui,"* I thought I heard. My Latin was rusty but that was close enough to my wheelhouse for me to pick it out — something about the just bearing the iniquities of criminals and light being hidden by shadow. No kidding. I hit the pause button and the whiny medieval timbre was gone. "That's much better," I said, intentionally loud.

"Hey!" I heard from upstairs. "That's Boethius you just shut off!"

"What in the heck is bow ethers? Painkillers you can shoot?" I shouted back, looking up the stairs. I had read Boethius as an undergrad in philosophy, but she didn't know that.

Her blond hair stream through the door way and she looked at me with strangely emotional eyes. "Sis, I've been waiting for you. You have to come look at this."

I groaned. "I do not want to go through some nostalgic sobfest with you right now. Mom is doing awful today you know."

"She's been doing awful for a while now."

I felt a knot of irritation swell up in my chest. "Yes, obviously. That's my point. I don't need to get all sentimental over whatever random memory of when dad and mom were together today. I can't handle it. We're just trying to go through things efficiently today. Then I come in here and you've got some medieval Gone with the Wind stuff blasting."

She rolled her eyes and came into the hallway. "Listen. I found something that is seriously weird. I've been reading it all day, and…"

"Wait, seriously? You have been here reading?" I suppressed the urge to swear. "Laura, we don't have time to walk through memory lane every ten minutes, reading some diary entry about the first-time dad talked to a girl with his mouth. We need to take care of stuff, you know. Mom needs it."

Her cherub face darkened with a petulant cloud. "Listen to me, Lizzie. I know that. I don't need to be told that. But this is seriously important. You need to read it." She came down the stairs and shoved a notebook into my hand. It had *Saturn Files* written on it in my dad's terse penmanship.

"We've all looked through dad's pictures from Saturn and his press tour, sis," I said, confused. "I thought you said you didn't need to be told now isn't the time for a trip to memory lane."

She grunted with irritation and stormed past me into the kitchen, grabbing my hand. I trailed and followed suit as she sat down with a box of cereal. She pulled bowls out of the cupboard and I took milk out from my seat next to the refrigerator door.

"Lucky Charms?" I scoffed. "Seriously? We're going to die from diabetes before Mom dies from cancer."

She smirked at me. "You are such a bitch today. You obviously need to eat before you get any hangrier."

I couldn't deny that.

She poured me a generous bowl and then did the same for herself.

As I lifted the spoon to my mouth for the first bite, she flipped open the notebook, revealing a pouch in the back. Some loose-leaf paper had been tucked inside the pouch.

She pulled out the stack of loose-leaf paper and unfolded it. "I spent the morning cleaning until I found this – knocked it out by accident. Read it."

I looked down at Dad's Ernest Hemingway scrawls and quirked an eyebrow. "Dad's secret last Dear Diary?"

She nodded, but didn't share my lighthearted smirk. "You have no idea. It's weird, and it'll blow your mind. You *have* to read it."

So I started to, at first half-heartedly between bites of Lucky Charms. The way the cereal rubbed the roof of my mouth raw was oddly pleasant, reminding me of eating breakfast with Laura when we were kids. Within minutes, though, the cereal was forgotten as I read my dad's bizarre account.

"I have dreams of Saturn I don't remember," I quoted incredulously. "I'm not sure that sentence makes grammatical or logical sense."

"I know what he's trying to say, though," said Laura, somewhat defensively.

"But how can he write about the dreams if he doesn't remember them?" I said with a snort.

"No, he means, like, he remembers the dreams as *dreams*, but they contradict what he remembers when he's awake," she said, the frustration roiling in her voice.

"Yeah yeah I get it, it's just a weird sentence. Anyway." I went back to reading. The way he characterized Maro was how I remembered – the easily spooked graduate student, obviously intelligent and gifted, whose life was lost in the fight with space pirates. Freebooters, they were called in the news, and Frank Ocelot, the criminal who had been brought in by Dad and that stock shark Alice Wolffe.

I could feel Laura staring at me, waiting for whatever reaction she was expecting. I tried to ignore it but finally it became distracting. "Would you stop?" I snapped. "I can't think with you ogling me like some college dude."

She laughed. "Fine. I'll go watch my movie."

"Or you could do something useful."

"Using my imagination is useful," she said, slipping off her chair and going into the other room. Calling back she said, "And usefulness is the worst possible metric for the success or value of any act or thought."

I heard the volume go up on the HoloVision, where someone was having an argument about a giant rabbit.

"Could you turn that trash down?" I pleaded.

I heard her offended squeak (she loved dad's old superhero movies) and chuckled in self-satisfaction. But then I went back to the story, and as my sister predicted, it was getting weird. Instead of just waking up in a crash and helping Alice to get Frank Ocelot restrained, they were slapping into the surface of Saturn – scientifically absurd of course – and then being saved by some wind fairies. Dad making references to Pascale's Wager and Lewis Carroll seemed too true to form – he didn't really like fantasy or theology, but he loved to pepper in references that made him feel smart. So now he's writing about how they have some magical song that heals them of the toxins from Saturn's outer atmosphere, but how this will force them to make the difficult decision of staying on the planet with the wind fairies or leaving and having their memories of this orgasmic song stripped from their memories. My eyes widened as I read Dad imagining himself cuddling with that Alice Wolffe chick to comfort each other over. Uh huh. I felt a sense of betrayal flash over me, so that my hands felt hot as I held the paper. I fought it down and finished the story, though I was getting a sense of what all of this really was about. So Maro and that kid Dice stay on the planet while he goes back to the real world with Alice and Ocelot. Nice.

I slapped the paper down, sublimating my anger and disappointment. "Well, that was as weird as you said it would be, Laura."

The HoloVision went quiet and she came bounding into the kitchen and perched on the edge of her chair. "So… what do you think?"

"What do you mean what do I think? It's obvious."

She twisted her mouth skeptically. "Obvious?"

"Yeah. Dad had an affair with that Alice bitch and couldn't bring himself to confess it openly so he wrote some stupid fantasy story about a magical sex song." I waved my hand, trying to keep my voice cynical and calm and not let the rage boil over too much. "And he is dealing with the guilt over Maro and Dice dying by pretending they're living on some Utopia. Oh, excuse me, *Chronotopia.* Even he pointed out how dumb that name is."

She looked stunned. "I hadn't thought of it that way."

"Well, what did you think it was? What, Dad really went to a magical colony of humans on Saturn who turned themselves into wind fairies?" I eyed her with the sort of contempt only sisters can have for each other.

She turned a little red and grunted. "No, I'm not an idiot Lizzie."

"Are you still sad that the fairies in the Blue Spruce all died after Dad cut it down because of the wood rot?" I couldn't help but push the teasing a little further.

She rolled her eyes. "Look. Why did Dad write this? You say it's about sex, but the whole thing is, they *didn't* have sex, they just cuddled. And I think it's pretty stupid to say that the Saturnalia song is about sex! They have this cosmic vision of how beautiful Saturn is, how beautiful the world is."

"Yeah, exactly the kind of sleazy rhetoric guys use when they're trying to get girls to sleep with them," I retorted.

"Does Alice really seem like the kind of person who would be fooled by that? She's a no-nonsense businesswoman who makes a point of being able to play rough with the boys, and she's older than Dad. You really think he's confessing an affair here? Mom and Dad were divorced before he died and he still never said anything about it then. Come on."

She had a point there, but I couldn't bring myself to admit it. "Okay. Well maybe it's not about him trying to keep it secret from Mom or us. Maybe he's just ashamed of it himself. And it would still hurt his relationship with us if we knew about it."

She shook her head. "I don't think that's what it is, Lizzie. Look, do you remember that music dad used to listen to over and over again while he was sick? The same songs? He used to say that it made him feel like he could remember things he never experienced."

I nodded. "But Dad hated fantasy. He liked Batman and Iron Man specifically because they used science – and he thought those Harry Potter type movies were dorky because they used magic when it was science that made the special effects happen. Why would he write a fantasy about wind fairies?"

She smiled that annoying smile that meant she had a good point. "But that's just it – they're not *really* wind fairies, are they? They're humans, and it was the science of Rosicrucia that made possible what they did when they transformed their bodies."

"Okay? So Dad writes a science fantasy and doesn't tell anybody about it because… what? Why does he write it and stick it in the back of this folder in a spot where it might never be seen?"

Laura raised an eyebrow. "But it was seen. I found it. Dad probably expected us to. I mean, he mentions it right at the end."

I nodded. "That part was nice. I admit it." I paused, and suddenly felt as if a trick was being played on me. "Wait. It sounds like you are arguing that it's true. You think it happened?"

Laura pressed her hand against her lips thoughtfully. "Well. I don't know."

I blanched. "You don't *know*? What the… What do you *mean*, you don't know? I know as sure as I'm sitting here, as sure as I have two hands, that this did not happen."

Her eyes got that academic twinkle, and I guessed the sentence by the first word. "Depends on what you mean by *happen*," we both said at the same time.

I rolled my eyes. "What, are you going psychoanalytical on me?"

"Well, did Clara's story in the Nutcracker *happen*? Yes and no. Does Wagner's *Der Ring des Nibelungen* happen? Yes and no. Music happens, it's there in the math, and the music is the meaning of the story."

"Okay, so Dad had some meaningful experience, and he wrote it down in the form of a science fantasy to express what he was seeing in his dreams."

"Exactly."

I thought about it. Dad did have a sentimental streak, despite his gruff bluster – after all, he had worked to buy his childhood home specifically so he could have us grow up on Spearhead Lane with the Blue Spruce in the front yard and the big backyard with a golf course in the distance. But he was also an incorrigible braggart and could never keep secret something he had done that he thought was even mildly accomplished – even if it was just a particularly loud belch. "No, it doesn't add up. Maybe what you're saying is true, but it doesn't account for why he kept it hidden. Look, he cuddles with Alice before they enter the song, and then they don't cuddle again after it. That means they had sex, and then he decided he didn't want to live that way anymore and they broke it off. He remembered where he'd come from, what he had back home. He felt bad about it. As he started to die, the guilt was coming back in the form of dreams, but he couldn't bring himself to face the shame of confessing it openly. So he wrote this story. And it can still be true that he felt something more beautiful than just lust – maybe he really had some part of him where the universe opened up and he saw beauty he hadn't before. Maybe that's why he broke it off with Alice in the end. But I don't think he just wanted to tell a story about wind fairies."

She nodded, then glanced at the clock. "We probably should get some work done before dinner, and we should go see Mom again tonight. It's not like we can just settle this question, but I want to talk about this some more before we tell Mom anything about it."

I nodded. Then a thought hit me, like the cliché lightning bolt they talk about in stories. "Just a minute now. We can settle this question."

She looked at me curiously. "What do you mean?"

I grinned. "We can look up Alice Wolffe."

Entry 2: The Music of Our Household

I indulged Laura by letting her drive us to Niagara Falls. It was different than I remembered from my childhood, much better kept up – at least along the main drags. Dad used to talk about what it was like before the United States of Canada was formed, when Niagara Falls was split between two borders, north and south – it was worse, though he missed it for some reason. Huge potholes, shut-down factories and run-down cockroach motels were what the town was known for, until the union of the American and Canadian sides. Of course, poverty was just pushed around, but on the face of it, the place did look better. AirDrones whizzed above us, electric cars zipping around to pass us.

"You're the slowest driver," I moaned.

"I'm a safe driver," she replied. "And at least I take my destiny into my own hands, unlike you."

"I'm letting you drive me – I would call that taking destiny into my own hands."

AirDrones helped to lessen the traffic in most places, but even here there were plenty of people still driving. Dad said he remembered when self-driving cars were banned, but because of some loophole they couldn't stop autopiloted drones. Truck drivers were protected by the measure but taxi services found it harder to stay in business, except for the ones who actually owned the drones. It wouldn't last, of course – people were working even in my law firm on moving against the self-driving car ban, and eventually we would be in a world of fully automated transportation. It made sense to me – I could never understand why people would want something that dangerous to be left in the hands of error-prone humans.

As if to confirm my thoughts, Laura hit a pothole and swore. "AirDrones never hit potholes," I reminded her. "You're so annoying," she replied without looking at me.

"Demarcation Avenue," I said, reading the name of the street we were turning on that ran parallel to the tiny local highway. "That is a stupid name."

"You think everything is stupid," Laura said. "If we took that word away from you, you wouldn't have much left to say."

"There wouldn't *be* much left to say," I said. "Is that the street?"

The streets had been renumbered, so the street signs had been repainted several times. It wasn't exactly a good look. On 1097th off of Demarcation Avenue, right near the tiny highway, crowded by too many houses on too little street, was the biggest house in the area. It looked distinctly out of place, a floor higher than any of the surrounding homes, with a meticulously kept lawn and deep blue siding. Laura parked in the street and stared up at the three-story house. "This is it?"

"It has to be."

Wolf statues kept watch on either side of the sidewalk leading up to the door, which was lined by a row of flowers, and bushes nestled up against the side of the house. On the somewhat overly ornate door was a giant wolf's head with a knocker in its mouth.

"She's really playing up her last name, isn't she?" I asked.

Laura shrugged. "Maybe it was her husband. You know how men are."

Boy don't I, I thought, but didn't say anything. We stood there idly for a few minutes, looking at the paneling and the fancy ironwork on the porch fence. It looked like someone with more money than belonged in the area lived here, but not quite enough money to get out and go somewhere else.

"Knock," Laura said.

"Why me? Why don't you knock?"

"This was your big idea. Go confront the big, bad Wolffe." She looked at me askance. "What, are you chickening out?"

I rolled my eyes. "Nothing to chicken out over. It's just an old lady." I lifted the knocker and rapped it sturdily on the door three times, then two more times. As I stood there I became aware that something was on inside, maybe a

HoloVision, with music and voices drifting out in a disembodied pattern that didn't fit regular conversation.

"Nobody home," I said with a shrug.

Laura started to speak, then the sound of a deadbolt unloosening stopped her. The door scraped in its frame as it opened, and there in the darkness of the threshold was an aged face, stubbornly beautiful in spite of the weight of years and disappointment. Her hair was an almost metallic gray, and something like hatred burned in her intelligent eyes. The sound from the speakers inside became more discernable – someone was talking, something about composition techniques and stylistic flair.

"What do you want? I'm in the middle of an episode," she snapped.

"I'm sorry, ma'am, I just, we're sorry, but we…" Laura stammered, her people-pleasing instincts going haywire with this unexpected hostility. Oh gee, we're just here to accuse her of adultery, I thought, don't be so nervous.

"Good afternoon, Mrs. Wolffe," I said, standing straight, and letting my most lawyerly tone come out, not giving Alice a chance to interrupt. "We are the daughters of Gerald Portinari, this is Laura and I am Lizzie. I'm sure you recall us from your acquaintance with our father. Our mother is ill and as we work to get their old house in order, we're just hoping you could talk with us a bit to find some closure."

Her face soured. "Ah, Jerry Dirt's girls. What a nice surprise," she said, not bothering to mask her sarcasm. "I don't see what closure I can provide. Your dad died a while ago now and I never knew your mother."

I saw Laura stiffen at her callous manner out of the corner of my eye, but I just smiled. "We found some old notes of his about his trip to Saturn, the same expedition where he first met you. There were some odd details here that we were hoping you could help us to understand. It would mean a lot to us to know what exactly went on up there, and to our Mom too." As I spoke I suddenly felt idiotic, as if this whole expedition didn't make sense. So what if Dad had an affair in outer space? What exactly were we even here to accomplish? I guess it was just my prosecutor's instinct that wanted to know all the evidence before I could make a judgment about something so odd.

She looked at me carefully, her intelligent eyes telling me that she knew I was dissembling about something. It was just like dad said in his story – in her presence, I felt like I wasn't part of the inner ring. She would send us away and we wouldn't know anything more.

"Fine, come in. Jerry Dirt wasn't all that bad, and you girls should know whatever you want to know."

Laura and I exchanged surprised smiles as we followed her into her house. The architects had done all they could to make the house look fancy, with smooth, curving bannisters, arched doorways and almost Victorian paneling, but it was clear that it was nothing more than a done-up example of suburban sprawl. Faded oriental rugs protected stained wood floors, and paintings of wolves and war generals adorned the walls. One was a portrait of a more contemporary man.

"Mr. Wolffe?" I guessed.

She looked up at the painting. "Oh, oh yeah. Sorry, not much of a tour guide. Here, have a seat."

We sat at a heavy round table made of dark wood. It had damascened patterns carved into the top and sides. She had just made some tea and was setting out two more cups.

One of those corny, ostentatious pieces of classical music announced itself from her radio. I almost guffawed that she was listening to a radio.

"The Orpheus in the Underworld overture, Jacques Offenbach," said Laura. "Nice."

Alice smiled, seeming genuinely pleased. "Yes, that's right. Good ear. This is the episode I mentioned. It's one of those shows where they play the music and talk about its composer its historical significance and all that. I never much cared for posh culture, but I guess in my old age I feel like I missed out on some of that stuff. Did you know he wrote about 100 operas? Here I used to associate his music with cartoons." As she spoke, she turned the dial down a bit so we could hear each other more easily.

"I'm studying musicology at Cornell," Laura replied, lighting up.

"Oh, wow, so you already know all about Offenbach. Who do you think the greatest composer is? Tchaikovsky? Mozart? Beethoven? Chopin?"

Laura smiled. "I don't know if you can quantify best at that level of talent. Beethoven probably, although it's Wagner who always gets to me for some reason. But I'm a medievalist, so the Romantic era isn't really my area of expertise – though we all have to know the greats, you know. They're all mandatory."

"That's right, I like that. Mandatory." Alice leaned back with her tea. "You know, I was—"

"I am sorry," I intervened, feeling the conversation spiraling into a musical nerdfest. "I don't mean to interrupt. But you know, I don't want to take up your whole day talking about musical history, as interesting as it is." I ignored a glare from Laura. "Here's the thing." I took out the papers from my purse, and Laura stifled a gasp, probably upset that I had taken the precious papers out of the house. I put them on the table. "Do you know what this is?"

Alice looked at the papers. "Last Entry: The Bells are Ringing," she read aloud. "No, of course not."

I nodded. "Dad wrote this, apparently near the end. Jerry Dirt, as you called him. Do you know what he said happened in Saturn here?"

She looked at me, puzzled but sensing that she should be on guard. She knew I was prepping to make some kind of accusation.

"In this story, Dad says that you and the rest of the crew on the rockhopper didn't just crash into a moon after a firefight with the Freebooters. Maro and Dice didn't die in an explosion. Instead, it says that all of you crashed into Saturn's surface, and you were saved by humans who had used some kind of magic to turn themselves into another race. A race that you called wind fairies in the story. So, we just want to know what really happened."

It seemed like hours passed while she stared at me, her eyes gone gimlet and hard. As her face darkened I was expecting her to burst into rage and throw us out. Her chin quivered.

Then she laughed, laughed until tears came out of her wizened eyes. "Yeah, that sounds like Jerry Dirt. Bullshit artist to the end. Communications Specialist, my foot. I'd almost be offended that he made up a story like that, in the wake of such a tragedy. That Maro and Dice, you know, they were good kids. *Good* kids. Smart, capable. But that's Jerry. No wonder Frank Ocelot didn't know what to do with him."

Laura looked at me smugly.

I shook my head. "Listen, I don't mean to come here and make accusations, I was just—"

She straightened up and the tears of laughter dried away quickly. "Accusations? What are you talking about, kid?"

I felt shaky, so I took a steadying breath. "Okay, so, here's the context. In the story, you and Dad have to decide whether you're going to stay on Saturn or come home. You've sort of partnered up by this point. Look at what happens."

I had her read the section, and her eyes went big with amusement.

"Me and Jerry cuddle? Fat chance! He had a rich fantasy life, I'll tell you what!" She laughed.

I let out a frustrated sigh. I wanted to keep a hold on my courtroom patience, but it was too personal to keep a cool. "Don't you see that this suggests that you and my father had a more personal connection than we were aware of? Why would he fabricate a fantasy where the two of you were intimate in this way?"

Her amused grin snapped away at the word intimate, and she stood up and glowered down at me. "Intimate? What the hell are you suggesting?"

"I just…"

"You just thought you'd pay a senior citizen a call and accuse her of being a little too close to your idiot father because of some crazed fantasy he wrote when he was on chemo? Don't you see what you're saying here?"

"You're being awfully defensive," Laura tried to point out helpfully.

At that point barking had broken out in the back yard, big rugged thunderclaps of anger from something big that was slamming itself against the back door.

"Dammit," spat Alice, and she swung around her chair and opened the screen door. "Pigsty, shut your mouth and go lay down," she commanded in a fierce growl. The barking stopped and the banging on the door went quiet.

I felt nervous suddenly. She had a big dog in the back yard, and then I recalled the shotgun hanging over the mantlepiece. Hopefully she wasn't too unstable when she got angry.

She turned and looked at me, walking over to the table like a prosecutor approaching a witness. "Do you in fact mean to suggest that you are here to accuse me of committing adultery with your half-witted father?"

Stunned, I looked up at her feeling like a child who had just been reprimanded for stealing from the countertop. "Yes," I managed to say. "But I didn't, I was…"

Her glower reduced me to silence again. The seconds ticked by, and then, like some miracle, she began to laugh. She sat down. "Listen, I don't know why Jerry wrote this thing. I really don't. But I have to tell you, Lizzie, this was not the best way to meet you." Her face softened as she continued to look at both of us. "Listen. Your father isn't the hero the press made him out to be, but he's still a hero. He was braver in the face of Ocelot's betrayal than I would have guessed. He was a good man, and he talked about both of you and your mother all the time. He couldn't wait to get back to you."

I nodded, grateful for kind words that she was certainly not beholden to offer, especially under the circumstances.

"I will say this, though. Your dad had a way with words, and if he wanted to be with a woman, he could probably have gotten his way. But he was a gentleman. Kept his hands to himself. Not only did he never make a move on me, I don't think he'd ever have betrayed your mother like that."

Laura's eyes were glossy and I had a feeling she was going to cry.

"That's kind of you to say, Mrs. Wolffe. Thank you for being so understanding. I'm sorry about this whole thing."

She shook her head. "No surprise your dad would have one more joke to play on me. Mind if I read this whole thing? I would like to see how the whole crazy story fits together in your dad's creepy mind."

I nodded, and looked at Laura, trying to find a way to lighten the mood. "Laura was listening to some crazy song the other day, some kind of classical piece, right?"

She smiled and managed to keep her eyes from spilling over. "Yeah, it's a reconstruction that was put together a number of years ago. I can't remember how long, back before dad died anyway. But it's not classical, it was actually medieval. Music written in the 900s, and the poem itself in the early sixth century."

Alice's eyes widened, and she nodded, impressed. She turned off her radio. "Could you play it for me?"

Laura's grin was obnoxiously happy as she brought out her phone and started looking through her files. "That was O stelliferi conditor orbis I had playing," she explained, "But this one is even better. See, the context is that Boethius, a Roman philosopher and politician, had been imprisoned on false charges, and he was basically writing this book, *The Consolation of Philosophy*, to comfort himself. He actually wrote a textbook on music, too, which is what my dissertation is on – er, is going to be on, I mean. Anyway. He wrote this song near the end of the *Consolation*, when Lady Philosophy's consolation is starting to work. It's called *Bella bis quinis*."

Alice was charmed by my sister's enchanted adoration for her subject matter, even if not quite so enamored of it herself. But for whatever reason, in spite of the unpleasant introduction, she seemed to be in an obliging mood. "Play it, Miss Portinari. That would be lovely."

She did. The music started, and it sounded at first intolerably primitive to me. The man's voice was annoyingly falsetto, a poor male attempt at sounding effeminate, and the strings of the lyre made me feel like I was listening to something out of an archaic Dungeons and Dragons videogame. I tried to share a sarcastic look with Alice, like, "Who would listen to that?" But her eyes were closed and her head back. I guess she really had become an amateur music lover, not something I would have guessed from her profile as Dad had cut it. I looked at Laura and she was doing the same thing. So I decided to close my eyes too.

Suddenly the words began to appear before my mind's eye, and the Latin started to sound less foreign and more intimate. I felt like I could see, of all things, the rings of Saturn, spinning the way dad had described them, and then I could see the wind fairies surrounding him and Alice as they sang and danced and laughed. I could see the politicians laughing and the talking heads furrowing their brows and the heartbreaking war to just be heard, to lift above the noise. Somehow, I actually heard the last line, clear as day: "Superata tellus, sidera donat." I even was able to interpret it: Overcome the earth, and you will be given the stars. The music was over.

Laura was looking at Alice. I looked at her too, and Alice was looking up at the ceiling, her eyes brimming with tears. "Oh," she said. "Oh my. I have, I don't understand it, but I have never quite felt that way. It isn't my style exactly, but…" She choked up with emotion for a moment. "But it makes me feel like some of the great music does, you know." Her voice descended to a whisper. "It makes me feel like I have dreams of something I don't remember."

I felt as if someone had slapped me across the face. She hadn't read the opening lines of the story – I had showed her where to read. She had no idea that Dad talked about dreams in his story. Why did she say it that way? She didn't know… I snatched the paper from her. "Thank you, Alice. Thank you so much for visiting with us and for being so understanding. I'm sorry about what I asked you, I didn't mean to hurt you or offend you."

She looked puzzled. "Oh no, I suppose I get why you'd get to that conclusion. I think I do. But I thought you said…"

"I know, but I don't think I can let you keep the story. I'll make a copy of it and send it to you. I'm sorry."

She nodded, then she looked around. "Hey, why don't you wait a minute. I want to give you something." Alice stood and walked out of the room for a few minutes. When she came back, she was holding a pouch that was closed with a drawstring. She put it in my hand.

I looked down at it. "What is this?"

She smiled. "Those are the dice that Dice was named after. Loaded, it turns out. Your dad found them in the wreckage and gave them to me to remember her by. But you know, after all this time, I don't think I need them anymore. I think you should have them. They should remind you that your dad looked out for me – he did me no wrong, and he did your mother and you two no wrong."

I didn't know what to say. We took our turns embracing, and she walked us to her front door. We stood there, looking at her, feeling like we should say something but not knowing what.

"Hey, don't look so glum. I'd love to have you back, Laura, to talk about music sometime. I don't guess I'd like to have you back to make wild accusations against me,

Lizzie, but if you can hold that back, I guess you can come again sometime. Not any time too soon though," she added with a wink.

I laughed, and we embraced again, and then we went to the car.

Once strapped in, Laura looked at me, her eyes wide. "Did you hear what she said, when I played that song?"

I nodded. "I did."

"What does it mean?"

I shook my head. "I don't know. I guess maybe it means nothing."

She was quiet for a moment, looking down at her hands with her keys in her lap. Then she looked out the driver's window and murmured something.

"What? I can't hear you when you mumble like that," I said, cringing at how much I sounded like Mom.

"I said," she repeated, turning her head to look out the dash window, "that there is someone else we could talk to, if you have more questions."

I furrowed my brow trying to think of who she could mean. "What are you talking about?"

She looked at me. "We are not that far, you know. It's on the way back."

"What's on the way back?"

"Attica. We could go see him, you know. If he'd even talk to us."

I felt startled for a moment as I realized what she was suggesting. "You mean, we should go see Frank Ocelot?"

She looked at me and nodded, her eyes brimming with strange fire. "I want to know why she said that. I don't think she knows herself."

I could feel a creeping sense of foreboding, a warning that if we went to go see Frank Ocelot, something would change. I stared at the drawstring pouch in my hands. "I don't know if that's a good idea."

She smiled fiercely. "That's what I thought you'd say. But unfortunately for you, you're not the one who's driving."

The electric car hummed to life, and we turned back to Demarcation Avenue and headed for the highway.

Entry 3: Weaving a Labyrinth

The grey entrance into Attica Correctional Facility looked like some strange amalgamation of a medieval castle and a warehouse. I had been here before, of course, for a number of reasons – sometimes as defense or as prosecution. But I had never made a personal trip. We had just about enough time to stand in line and fill out our visitation request before processing was stopped at two. Some girl behind us had been waiting to see her boyfriend and nearly got herself escorted away when the clerk told her processing was closed.

Eventually we were called back. It was unpleasant, moreso for Laura who had never experienced anything like it – we were stripped of our possessions and patted down like criminals. Then we were led unceremoniously to the meeting room. It was surreal seeing him for the first time – it felt like some kind of minous music should have been playing in the background or something. He looked like he was just trying on the orange jumpsuit, sitting on the other side of the glass as if he was a visitor pretending to be an inmate. His bald head made the heavy, blackish grey eyebrows look huge, and his mustache reminded me of a portrait I had seen of Friedreich Nietzsche. Something in the dark intelligence of his eyes reminded me of Alice, but there was a frightening gleam in his stare that she didn't have. His grizzled mouth tightened with apprehension when he saw us.

We sat down at the behest of the guard. Ocelot took the phone off the hook and held it carelessly beside his ear.

I held our phone between us, so that we could both hear.

"Hello, Mr. Ocelot," I said, before Laura could speak.

"Miss Portinari," he said mildly. "You can imagine my surprise. Hope my butler here has made you comfortable."

I allowed myself a small smile. "I know this is probably a strange visit. You probably don't want to talk to us."

He shrugged, and let his eyes wander places that weren't polite.

I frowned but didn't say anything.

"No problem there. Most of my conversation partners around here aren't so sweet as you ladies."

In spite of the bullet proof glass between us, I felt my skin crawl. "Okay, listen Mr. Ocelot, we aren't here to upset you. We are just a little confused about the accounts our father left surrounding your arrest. We'd like to get some things squared away."

His eyes narrowed as he studied me carefully. "You don't talk like some ditzy blonde, girl. What are you, a lawyer? Something in your voice says bloodsucker."

"Oh well thanks, yes, Syracuse University actually," I said, not allowing him to get to me. "I'm glad my training shows off so naturally. Listen, I know you probably harbor some animosity towards my father for his involvement in your arraignment, but we are not here to harass you in any fashion. You're paying your dues as the State of New Amsterdam sees fit. We're just trying to understand exactly what happened to our father. I realize this may not be meaningful to you, but our mother is sick, and having things clarified would give all of us some peace."

He sat back slowly and eyed us. An unsettling notion that he knew why we were there crept into my mind. It wasn't possible, and yet he seemed too unsurprised by the visit. Something weird was going on, and I was starting to think this visit was a bad idea. "I don't have to talk about anything without *my* lawyer present," he said slyly.

"Of course not. This is off the record. It's not about you, we aren't looking to press any further charges or anything like that. We just want to know—"

"Your dad wrote some goofy notebook, didn't he? Some diary entry where things happened that weren't the way you all know the story?" He pulled on his mustache thoughtfully as he spoke.

"Yes," said Laura before I could cut her off. I wanted to smack her. "Dad wrote a sort of science fiction version about your encounter with your Freebooter friends, but instead things happening the way we heard about it, your rockhopper hit the surface of Saturn and was kidnapped by wind fairies. They played some music that healed you all of Saturn's poison, and then put you under some forgetting spell. We're trying to understand why he made this up – why he fabricated this fantasy. Did something happen that we don't understand?"

He grinned and leaned towards her. "That isn't what you want to know, Miss Portinari. Maybe your uptight sister," he said, dismissing me with a wave of his hand. "But not you. You don't want some clarification to know why he wrote this weird little Dear Diary. You want to know if it's true."

We shared a look, and I leaned away from the window. "Maybe this was a mistake," I said, my hand brushing over Laura's.

"No." She pushed my hand away. "I want to know. I want to know what you think."

He leaned back again, his grin at once ferocious and smug. "Oh, it's all true. The whole thing. Wind fairies, the song, all of it."

"But wait," I said. "Why can you remember while Alice can't?"

He laughed. "Alice? Seriously? What exactly do you think that bitch believes in? Oh, spare me your shock over language. I'm in prison. Don't expect your prim and proper elocution here. I'm not your dirt father. No damn communications specialist. Yeah, it's all true. The memory spell or whatever, however their science works, it lasted for a while. Then I started to have weird dreams. And here's the thing, your dad, Alice, they had lives to live. They had the cloud of life helping them to forget. But all I had was time to think about whatever my mind threw at me. So I started to think about my dreams, and ran over my memories. At first I thought I just had some weird subconscious thing going on, maybe guilt over what I'd done or something. But then the dreams started to make me think about inconsistencies in the story as I remembered it. Little things that didn't quite make sense that only someone who'd been in the situation could notice. I mean I guess Sherlock Holmes could figure it out, but there isn't much time for careful detective work out there. So yeah, eventually I started thinking it was the dreams, not my memories, that were real. And then it happened. I remembered something Jerry did, while I was awake. He saved me from the death penalty on Saturn, so that I could be stuck in this prison. I could have died and gotten free from all this shit, but he sentenced me to a life of remembering the fact that I had once tasted music built into the fabric of the universe. That screwy mouthed fool, who even gave me something to be grateful for while giving me something to hate him for. And once I felt how real my hatred for him was, it all came back – I remember everything now. So here's what I want to know." He had inched closer and closer to the glass, and his voice was careful and low but filled with an insistent, murky anger. His limpid eyes were hypnotic in their intensity. "What exactly happened? Something happened. You went to Alice and she said something. You wouldn't come here if you'd seen Alice and she'd just told you she didn't remember. Of course she didn't. She's greedy like every wolf of Wall Street, but she lacks the vision to know what it takes to really grasp hold on the golden goose. So something in her must be slipping, something happened to suggest that she is waking up too. What was it?"

Laura gave me a blatantly uncomfortable look, and I felt frustration and fear welling up in my sternum. There was something about this I didn't like. He was talking too much and trying to get information from us. A convicted criminal. Somehow, I didn't think telling him was a good idea. What did it matter if he was playing along?

"Well," said Laura, "before we left her house…"

"Alice said she couldn't bear to think about Jerry," I interrupted her quickly, thinking he shouldn't know what happened, though I didn't know why. "I guess prison has left you with nothing better to do than lie to grieving children. You pointed out yourself that my dad didn't let you die in space — no nonsense about space fairies need apply for that to be true. Maybe this was God's last chance to let you do something right, to help us come to peace with things and instead you make up a bunch of nonsense."

He laughed. "You're a smooth talker, Miss Portinari, but I have been lying a lot longer than you have, so I know you're bullshitting me just like your dear old Dad would. Well listen. Let me read this story your dad wrote, and I can tell you just how accurate it was."

"I don't think so," I said. "We apologize for troubling you, but…"

"Now hang on a minute," he said, standing up angrily, forgetting to keep the phone up to his face. But his raised voice made it clear enough what he was saying. "I didn't have to come see you. I could refuse this visit. Your ass-hat father stuck me in this shithole, and the least you can do is tell me what exactly happened at Alice's place. Did she give you something? *Did she give you something?*"

"It's three o'clock, visiting hours are over," announced an officer as he stepped into Ocelot's side of the room.

"Wait, hang on," Ocelot sputtered. "We're in the middle of something important here."

"They can come back tomorrow," said the guard coldly.

Our escort was indicating we should follow him.

"Listen to me, you Portinari bitches," Ocelot was practically shouting as he was being taken away. "You came here and brought this up to me. If you want answers, come back here tomorrow, or I won't tell you one more damn thing. And you better tell me everything."

Shaken up by the experience, we left the facility hastily and didn't speak to each other until Laura pulled into the parking lot of the first coffee shop she saw, her hands shaking. We went in, and she got a decaf tea and I got the blackest cup of robust coffee they had available. We sat in the corner, away from everyone, at a little table made of black metal.

She looked at me finally. "That was… seriously freaky."

I looked at her and nodded once. "It was. But you told him too much. He's an angry old man in prison – he's messing with us. Now I don't think we'll be able to get a straight answer out of him."

Laura shook her head. "I don't think so, Lizzie. I think that *was* his straight answer. Come on. You've worked with your share of liars in the courtroom. You can't tell me you thought he was lying."

I fought down the panic that was slowly growing in my stomach. "Well, he *has* to be. Categorically. He can't be telling the truth."

Laura smiled, but it wasn't smug. It was more sad than anything. "He said something that I didn't. Something that was in the story — that Dad saved him from the death penalty on Saturn. How could he have known that?"

I felt dizzy for a moment, as if the floor was one of those tilt-a-whirl things at an amusement park. I breathed in and took a sobering gulp of the hot coffee. "No. Look, he's a con artist. He lied for a living working for Richards. He was actually apprehended by Dad and Dad actually stopped him from dying out in space so that he could be charged with his crimes. It's just a logical extension of what really happened."

She looked out the window, and my gaze followed suit. In the distance, we could see the anachronistic turret of Attica Correctional gazing at us.

Absurdly, I felt like Ocelot was watching us from the tower, laughing at the situation we were in. "Let's just go back to the house," I said finally, after a long period of silence. "There's nothing more we can do to chase this thing down, and there's no way I am coming back to talk to Ocelot. I don't know what he's after, but giving information to someone who is known to have been in league with an interplanetary crime syndicate is not a good idea."

Laura looked at me curiously. "It's a maximum security prison. The Son of Sam became a Christian there. Do you really think that he can cause us harm from inside?"

I raised an eyebrow. "It's also the site of one of the worst riots in American history before the split. I'm the lawyer here, don't spout obscure legal history facts at me. I don't know, probably not. But it's playing with fire. Besides, we can't go tell mom that we've been investigating into whether Dad was losing his mind or if he really met space fairies or something. Let's go do some actual work."

Entry 4: Every Kind of Fortune is Good

The car ride was spent in uncomfortable silence, until Laura decided to put on some music. Thankfully it wasn't anything weird, just some old tunes Dad liked to listen to. I let my eyes scan the horizon and filter everything I saw through the music, giving myself some time to calm down after the disturbing conversation with Frank Ocelot. We were on Spearhead Lane before I knew it, and a pregnant silence followed when Laura turned off the car and the music went silent with it. I followed her up the deck and into the front door, but she went into the kitchen and I sat myself down in the wingback chair in the living room. Reacting to my presence, the HoloVision shot up a menu with recently viewed movies and other suggestions, but I ignored it and looked at the pouch in my hand.

"I know we should get some sorting done," said Laura, "but I'm just not ready for that. Do you mind if I make some dinner and then we get to it?"

It occurred to me just then that it was strange, how we had been living in a house where neither of our parents had really lived for years. It felt like home, but it also felt like a strange land, and I probably could never reconcile those two feelings. I decided then that we should sell the house instead of trying to keep it in the family.

"Hello?" she said, popping her head into the living room. "Did you want dinner?"

I looked at her and nodded. "Dinner sounds good."

I opened the drawstring on the pouch and rolled the contents into my hand. Five blue dice with white circles to indicate the values of their sides looked up at me expectantly. It was subtle, but I could feel something was off with them – in the weighting or in the texture, something about them wouldn't allow for a fair throw. But maybe I could only tell because I knew they were loaded – or maybe it was a projection entirely. It was hard to tell.

"Let me put on my Boethius," said Laura. "Helps me to focus while I cook." Her phone was sitting on an end table across from me. She walked over, and put on the song she had played for Alice. Ordinarily I would have protested, but at this point I just didn't have the energy.

Bella bis quinis operates annis…

My right hand suddenly started to burn, and I looked down and saw in shock that the blue dice were glowing. Startled, I tossed them away from me before I knew what was happening. The dice flung into the air and then slowed, and instead of falling to the ground they hung in the air as if caught in orbit. The music seemed to grow heavier, as if I could see the strings and the words and the voices streaming from Laura's phone and into the middle of the living room. Something sparked and the HoloVision went dark. There, over the carpet, the dice hovered and sparked, and in their center a blue film seemed to emerge. I looked at Laura, who was staring with her mouth actually agape – I realized then that I had been doing the same thing. I closed my mouth, but I looked back at the impossible event transpiring before me.

At first, I saw flashes of images from the song — a Greek warrior king buying the wind with blood, cutting the throat of his own daughter, and another, a man of twists and turns hiding in a roughhewn cave as stalked over him a threatening, one-eyed giant thirsting for the taste of his blood. Another man, as godly as he was human, battled Centaurs and lions and stole from dragons and chained a giant three-headed, shaggy wolf beast, wrestled rivers and fought a many-headed serpent. His labors finished, he stood, and seeming to make eye contact with me for a moment that lasted intolerably long, he turned and stood straight, and the blood of monsters burned away, and he walked to a high mountain and then into the very clouds and then his hands reached up to the heavens and tore them asunder. His body began to burn so brightly it was hard to look upon him, but as he rose past the moon and began to take his place among the stars, he cast out his hand and the vision spun away from his figure. Like some cosmic camera, the vision moved first to Mars, and it seemed as though in the dark red planet I could see some ancient Viking surrounded by winged women playing a great drum, and then again to Jupiter, and the planet's red eye seemed to fill with lightening and for a moment I thought I could see a bearded man in a chariot of fire wearing a flaming toga and wielding the lightning in his hand with mighty joy.

And then the vision spanned across the stars again and set upon the browned-yellows and blue-burnt orange of Saturn's ringed face. The room seemed to disappear as we were drawn into that vision and the planet grew, and then we seemed to plunge into its surface and, although a vision, we could feel the winds and rains and storms and it seemed that we could hear the happy laughter of an ancient, hurricane-like voice. Then the clouds broke and we saw, on the hard and dark core of Saturn's surface, beneath the hexagonal storm above it, an amphitheatrical city, six sided at its base, cruciform in its center and rising up with an almost roselike shape in its ivory walls. But miles from the city, upon the precipice of a mountain stood a woman, her eyes seeming to burn with an everlasting passion. Her hair was dark and her form seemed strange, at once squat and tough and yet beginning to grow translucent, as if her whole body was changing from an earthen vessel to a creature of wind and rain.

"Dice," I said with realization, and her face was before us, looking down on us in the darkness of the room from her place atop the Saturnine mountain.

Her eyes shimmered with a sadness but not without some measure of kindness as well. "Yes, once I was called Dice. I am thankful to you, Lizzie, for releasing the talismans, and to you, Laura, for playing the song, so that I could reach out to you in this manner."

"Talismans?" I echoed. "The dice?"

The half-alien woman nodded. "Because they had been touched by me after I had participated in Saturnalia, they bore my essence. Because you are in your father's house and because they were in proximity with an ancient song of the deep harmony, I was able to use them as a conduit to appear before you as I am now. I have waited in case that might be so, and watched you as closely as I can from afar."

I was reeling. I didn't know what to say.

"Why have you been watching us?" asked Laura.

"Not only you, but also the Wolffe and the Ocelot. We monitor them, as well as your father while he was still on Earth, because we knew that the songs which held at bay their memories might disintegrate over time. That it has done so — and to this degree — is of great concern to us."

I remembered that the Chronotopians had forced my dad and his companions to make a choice: they had to stay on Saturn and lose touch with the outside world or be sent away and be forced to forget the cosmic vision which Saturnalia provided.

"You are worried that we are going to give away your secret," I said.

Dice looked to me. "I realize, Elizabeth Portinari, that you are not an individual of ill will. You must understand how dire this is. Division and hatred tears apart your people. If Earth's inhabitants were to know of Chronotopia, our way of life would be jeopardized. You must cease looking into the matter of your father's visit here. You must *not* meet with the Ocelot again. He is dangerous and his connections are more troubling than you realize. I ask that you destroy your father's diary and do not speak of this experience to anyone."

I shook my head. "Dice, I understand what you're saying, but this doesn't seem right. You say 'your people' as if we're something fundamentally different from you, but we're not. I mean, you were just as human as I am not long ago. As I understand it from dad's account, you can't even become a full Chronotopian because you were born a human – that can only happen to your children. We *are* your people. You have technology that could make a difference, could cure sickness like my Dad had. You could have saved…" I felt myself choke up as I realized the enormity of what I was saying.

She looked at me with sadness. "It is not as simple as it seems. The balance which the children of Rosicrucia struck here is precarious. It expends resources to bring anyone to the surface of Saturn. There are more factors than I could explain in this discussion — even bridging this harmony so that we could communicate is more costly than you realize. We could not have saved your father. He understood that when he left."

One thing I certainly couldn't argue with was her assertion that I didn't understand everything. I looked at Laura helplessly.

Laura looked at Dice with a mixture of wonder and anger. "Dice, our mother is dying now. We're too young not to have parents. So many people are suffering the way we are. Why shouldn't we try to get access to the same privileges you have?"

Dice sighed. "I have thought of this too, Laura Portinari. The same music that moves your heart moves mine. But we have peace here on Chronotopia, peace which would be utterly destroyed if the humans found a way to touch down on our surface. Even now it is all we can do to protect Saturn's rings. Imagine if they could get to our city – the resources of the Saturnalia would be used up and then no one would benefit from it. And there are other matters, about which I cannot speak, which make it imperative that our society remain a secret. Even now, your own country has rumors of war. How can we justify ruining our peace when it would not create peace in your own communities?"

I looked at Laura, then back to Dice. "In the story our father wrote, he said that your song could have cured his cancer if he had stayed. Could you cure my mother, now that the talismans have opened this gateway?"

Dice paused to consider. Then she shook her head. "It comes with too great a risk."

I frowned. "You appear to us in this time and space splitting vision just to tell us to forget about you? You want us to keep you a secret, but the secret is out already. Ocelot knows about you, and if you know what we do, then you know that Alice probably will start remembering too. I understand why Chronotopia wants to keep itself secret, but I think you should at least do us a favor for doing so."

Dice considered me. "So you would threaten us with exposure if I do not comply?"

Laura looked at me, her face conflicted.

I thought about it. I wanted to. I could hear that lawyer's tenacious argumentative streak coming out in the back of my head, the one Dad loved to tease out so much. Why not drive a bargain if it could help Mom? But I looked at Laura and the wonder in her eyes as she looked over the landscape of Saturn and its city of humans become alien, and I knew it wasn't the right path.

"No. I promise to keep your secret. It's what Dad would have wanted. It's what he said he wanted, and my professional and personal inclination is to respect the wishes of the departed. But I am asking you to take a risk. To help me and my sister keep what remains of our family. You had the power to cure our father and you didn't." I held up a hand when Dice began to protest. "I am not blaming you. I know there are reasons. But I have a feeling that now that this gateway can be opened, you can help Mom. You didn't say it wasn't possible, just that it was risky. Well, I am acting in good faith towards you. If you tell me no, I will take Dad's story and bury it away and no one will know about any of this. But if you tell me yes, I'll burn his story and my own notes about this adventure and no one will be able to find out. That's my promise."

Dice smiled, her eyes glistening. "Elizabeth Portinari, you are a woman of character. I can see your father in you. Although the elders of Chronotopia will not be pleased, I think your request ought to be honored. This time tomorrow, bring the dice to your mother's room and place them upon her, and then play the song which holds the ancient harmony. I will enact the healing as you ask. Be at peace, sisters."

There was a blue flash, and the apparition of Dice and her gloaming utopia was gone.

Entry 5: Chance is Nothing at All

Fading sunlight cast somber shadows in the stillness of the muted colors of the hospital room. Mom was sleeping heavily, her face shadowed with a pained expression that suggested the battle required to extract rest from slumber. The periodic, haunting noises of the machines punctuated the quiet. It was hard to look at her with the wires and bandages, to see her look so helpless and unfamiliar in the hospital gown. Laura sat on one of the chairs on her right side, and I stood beside her on the left.

Laura had her phone out with the song ready to play. Her glossy eyes connected with mine.

"Do you think this will actually heal her?"

I nodded, and felt my throat constrict with emotion. "There's no denying it now. Dad was on Saturn, and they have science that works like magic there."

Gently, I set the dice at mom's stomach, my hands trembling slightly.

"You can play it now," I said.

The strings and the voice began to play. The dice glowed and floated into the air as if gravity had been cancelled out. Like a HoloVision, a projection of Saturn flashed between them, though there was the unsettling feeling that the air had grown thin, as if a little more pressure could cause the sheet of space to rip and tumble us all out into the void if whatever controlled the connection were mismanaged. Saturn's glow covered the room in its burnt-bluish orange and yellow hues, and then the surface of the planet rushed up to us and seemed to swallow the room entirely. All was dark – the light from the hospital window was gone, the plain colors gone. It seemed as though we were hovering in the moment before light was spoken over the surface of the deep.

And then a spot of light began to glow, like a small fairy creature, which as it grew became Dice, and she hovered over us, translucent. She began to sing, her voice at once small and gentle and feminine, while also vast and invincible and rugged, like slight sheets of wind that struck melodies on the edges of mountains in the dark and happy heart of Saturn. Her song enveloped us all in a warm light, and poured most of all over Mom, whose form was for a moment changed and she seemed in that instant regal and proud, a queen of ages and angels rather than the person I had known my whole life. Then the song was ended, and Dice hovered there in the center of the room, still and silent.

Mother's breathing went from anguished and struggling to steady and profound.

"Thank you," I said, and Laura echoed me. "Thank you so much."

Dice looked at us both in turn. "Sisters Portinari, I wish you well. Your mom will sleep deeply until the morning, and then she will be in good health. Realize, however, that as with your father, we cannot remove the biological disposition to this disease if the individual does not dwell with us on Chronotopia. Even if she should fall ill again, I ask that you honor your commitment. Burn all accounts of this day, and hide the dice where they can never be found. Their power will be lessened after this second usage so that they will not be able to make a connection this strong again, although they are still bound to Saturn." She paused. "I do not expect we will meet again, know that the souls of Chronotopia look over you with love and good will."

"And we will look up to the heavens with the same," said Laura.

Dice smiled to her, and then to me, and then, without flash or fury, her apparition was gone and we were alone with our mother.

I walked around the bed and sat on the flat top of the heater beside my sister's chair, and patted her on the shoulder.

"Something about it all doesn't make sense," Laura said quietly.

"What do you mean?" I asked.

"Well, now that we know it's all real, that means that Rosicrucia really discovered a way to live on Saturn and transform his companions's bodies to become suitable to the planet there, right?"

I nodded, and looked at her with expectation. She didn't say anything, so I prompted, "So?"

"So, it seems by implication that Dad and his companions were saved when their ship hit Saturn's surface by the wind fairies. That's what I gather from it anyway, given that they were monitoring and even interacting with the rings and the operations on Saturn's moons."

"Hmm, that's a good point." I thought for a minute, then I realized what she was getting at. "But there were no wind fairies when Rosicrucia's ship crashed into Saturn's surface. It's one thing to say he used the Harmonic Theorem to save his people once there, but how did his ship make it? The wind fairies weren't there already like they were when Dad's ship crashed."

Laura nodded, smiling. "Exactly. So there must be something else going on."

"Something else occurred to me, but it had nothing to do with that," I said, scooping up the dice and putting them into the pouch, which I then deposited into my purse. I looked at mom's peacefully sleeping face. "Remember how Dad said that he had to make a choice between living on Saturn or coming home to us?"

I looked at Laura, and she met my gaze silently. Her head nodded slightly but she didn't say anything.

"Well, he knew he was going to get cancer. He knew he would die." I felt a lump of emotion constricting my throat. "He came home so he could be with us, knowing that."

She nodded, and in spite of her best effort tears were starting to slip out from her heavy lower eyelids. "He could have been happy on Saturn, with Alice, singing in the depths of Saturn, but he came back home instead."

I slipped off of the heater and Laura stood, and we embraced tightly. "And now we have mom back," Laura whispered.

We couldn't bear to leave, so we stayed in the room, propping ourselves up in the uncomfortable chairs. After a while I fell asleep. When I woke again, Laura was still sleeping. Darkness had come into the room. I went into the bathroom, and I could hear Laura yawn and stir as if she had woken up. "I'm going to order us some food," I heard her say.

"What did you decide on for dinner?" I asked after I came out of the bathroom. But she didn't reply.

Laura was frozen in shock, her eyes glued to the screen of her phone.

"What's wrong?" I asked quietly.

Her eyes raised to meet mine, and she shook her head slowly, then looked back at her phone. "You have to see this," she managed to say.

I walked over and sat next to her. My mind reeled when I saw the headline.

DANGEROUS CRIMINAL FRANK OCELOT HAS ESCAPED FROM ATTICA CORRECTIONAL FACILITY.

"What do you think that means?" I asked slowly. "Did Dice take him?"

Laura shook her head. "No, it doesn't seem like it." She scrolled through the story. "It looks like it was a real escape – broken bars, damage done to the inside and outside of the cell. It does seem like he had help, but it doesn't seem like the magic song variety."

I looked at her, a sense of dread welling up inside. "Do you think he'll come after us?"

Her eyes were blank with fear for a moment, then started to process the question. "Why would he do that?"

"Well, we're the daughters of the man who helped put him away, for one thing. And he seemed interested to know if we got anything from Alice. He might know about the dice."

"But they don't work anymore."

"He doesn't know that. And it's not exactly that they don't work anymore – they don't work as strongly. There might be something he wants to use them for."

She shifted uncomfortably. "Maybe we should call someone, the cops, you know. Let them know about the connection, that we could be in danger."

"Maybe. You could call that boy. He was a cop, wasn't he?"

"Was, yeah. I don't know." Her phone buzzed. "That's Tony now. He says he's coming by the house to drop off the shop vac we needed for the basement."

I stood up with a start. "Tony's going to Dad's house? I bet Ocelot could figure out where that is easily. He might already know."

She regarded me quietly. "What should we do?"

"Tell him to get out of there. To stay away."

She punched a button on the text message app and the phone started ringing. It rang, and then went to voicemail.

"Why isn't he answering?"

"He probably got out of the car, left his phone on the dash mount, and is setting up the shop vac. Knowing him, he won't even look at his phone. He's expecting me back – I honestly forgot. A lot has been going on lately, you know."

I nodded, looking at mom. "You need to get over there and tell him to leave. Keep calling him on the way – if he answers, tell him to come to the hospital and don't go over there yourself. I am going to stay with mom in case she wakes up."

Laura walked to the door, then stopped. She turned back to me. "Lizzie, what exactly are we afraid of? We don't know what Ocelot would do."

"We don't," I agreed, "but we have to take precautions. If he had help escaping, he probably has dangerous friends."

She said something I couldn't quite hear and was gone. I went over and took the pouch of dice out of my purse. I thought about calling the cops, thinking I could ask for surveillance. Feeling the dice in my hands, though, I had a sense that we had walked into something bigger than dad's secret past. Things weren't piecing together; they were coming apart. Saturn might want to be left alone, but Ocelot had other plans, and that meant both me and my sister were going to be caught up in the influence of his madness.

I looked at my mom sleeping peacefully, and at the dice, and decided then that it didn't matter. Just like Dad had asked, we'd keep Saturn secret, and we'd keep each other safe.

PHAETHON'S GRACE

Brandon Ketchum

Phaethon brushed through kelp curtains into his mom's foyer. The seaweed floated away from his touch. Glowing plankton filtered through a crystalline ceiling to light the room. Bubbles streamed in ebbs and flows of breath. Dazzling colors shimmered in his watery vision. Phaethon's sandals settled mutely on mother-of-pearl tiling.

The foyer went dry, including his tunic, water banished beyond the room's invisible boundaries. Mom descended a coral staircase, a driftwood tiara, shark-tooth necklace, and aragonite bracelets and anklets her only clothing or ornamentation. Her skin was a light green, unlike his own tan complexion, inherited from his absent father. A long-lived Oceanid, Mom nevertheless looked younger than him.

She stopped before Phaethon and grasped his shoulders. "Ready for the big day?"

"Ready for decades. When will Helios...*Father* arrive?"

"He won't." His mom led him to a whale-bone couch. "You would think a god with a penchant for Oceanids would be willing to pop in under the sea, but no. That damnably charming man claims he's too busy tending his chariot team to come."

"So much for my boon."

"Go to him."

"How? Stables are on Mount Olympus."

She clucked her tongue. "You're finally recognized as a demi-god. Blink there like any other immortal."

"I can *blink* there? Huh." He stroked his smooth chin, contemplating. "How?"

"I'm not sure. Close your eyes, picture the stable, and imagine yourself there?"

"Imagine myself to a place I've never been," he said deadpan.

"Picture a stable and think of Mount Olympus. It only has one."

"That…might work. I'll go, then." Phaethon stood.

"Wait." She rose and grasped his wrist. "Decide on a boon now so as not to embarrass yourself the—"

"—first time I meet my father."

"You could ask him for a tour of the palace." Mom set to pacing.

"I'll have my own chambers soon enough."

"A trip to the Pillars of Hercules, then."

"Nothing there but more water."

"Sip ambrosia with Ares."

"Drink with that crazed killer? No thanks."

"How about—"

"Mom."

"—you ask him to—"

"Mom!"

At last she stopped. "What is it?"

"I've already decided on my boon. I'm going to drive the chariot today."

"What? When did you come up with *that* idea?"

"Yesterday. As the sun dipped below the horizon, spilling its last light, I lay upon the sea shore. The boon, and what I might ask for, drove me crazy. About to slip into sleep, I heard an exquisite sound. A flock of swans floated nearby, singing to the heavens. Felt like all the wisdom of the world was in their music. Lulled me into a restful sleep, plunging me into dreams of stars and light, of fiery horses and golden chariots. Those swans brought a clarity nothing else could.

"So, I'm driving the chariot today."

"Don't be ridiculous, darling. You'd never be able to wrangle the team into place, let alone drive the sun across the sky for a full day. Never fear, we'll think up something appropriate."

Phaethon had pondered his swan dream upon waking. If he was to take his place on Olympus as a demi-god, he must test his capabilities. As Helios's son, he was born to this duty. In risking all, he would prove to his father and to Zeus he was worthy to live amongst them.

"Appropriate or not, that's the boon I'll ask for."

"He'd never let you," she warned, then contradicted, "except he *has* to. Helios never could break an oath, that lovely, stubborn man. Listen to me. If you lose control, the results will be dire: death, famine, drought, frozen deserts, desiccated forests, never mind what Zeus will do to *you*. Oh, promise to be careful, and follow your father's instructions to the letter."

He creased his features with a smile. "I promise."

Blinking to the Olympian stables didn't work out quite as well as Phaethon had hoped. After picturing the *inside* of a hay-filled stall he and Icarus had fallen asleep in after a drinking bout, Phaethon felt a tug at his stomach, a sudden vertigo, and appeared *outside* an enormous set of open double-doors. And he was ten feet above the ground. With the ease of a swan, as comfortable in the air as in the water, he settled to the ground.

Up close, he couldn't see Mount Olympus beyond the massive stable. To house horses powerful enough to transport the sun across the sky, Phaethon supposed Helios—Father—had to build big. There wasn't much else to see, but he smelled plenty: hay, manure, leather, manure, urine, manure, and manure. "Comes with the territory," he muttered.

Father, a man with a bronzed complexion in a simple tunic and sandals, worked inside, grooming a golden horse twice as tall as he was. Phaethon wondered how many hands high that would make the great beast. Too few to carry Helios's ego, to hear his mom speak of him, though she smiled serenely whenever she did.

Three identical horses, untethered, waited meek as lambs for their turn. Light struck their coats, reflecting blinding beams. Phaethon stood back, sheltered his eyes, and watched his father brush the horse until its coat gleamed, then repeat the process three times, speaking to the horses under his breath. His sandals never left the floor, but he finished, unhurried, in an impossible couple of minutes. Being a god came with perks.

"Son," came Helios's voice. Phaethon had expected deep bass. Father's warm tenor caught him unawares. "Come in."

Phaethon did, marveling at the supernatural animals as they loomed ever higher.

"I won't apologize for not acknowledging you until now," Helios said.

Their eyes met. Looking into his orbs was gazing at the sun.

"I have mortal friends, and Mom raised me right."

"Clymene. Oh, I remember her. What a glorious Oceanid. My little swan." Phaethon stared at him. "She never withheld my name voluntarily. I compelled her to, lest all the Oceanids think to trap me into fathering a child with them. As you're grown, I must now do my duty and acknowledge you. For burdening you to life without a father, and for denying your rights as a demi-god these decades, I am prepared to offer you a boon."

Pompous much? If Phaethon hadn't observed the god's unbridled enjoyment with his team, he would have thought his father as stuffy as Zeus was reputed to be. And Phaethon *had* a father, of sorts, in Daedalus, Icarus's dad. "Mom told me."

"Have you given thought to what you might wish?"

"I'll be driving your chariot today," Phaethon said.

"Impossible. Son, not even Zeus is strong enough to handle my team."

"He's the strongest god of all, the King of the Gods!"

"The mightiest of us, but not the strongest. A subtle distinction. Why would you even want to undertake this dangerous duty?"

"Because I'm your son. Because if the son of Helios can't shepherd the sun, I'm not worthy enough to assume my place on Olympus."

"There are other ways to prove yourself. Should you fail in this, the consequences—"

"Mom's covered those: death, famine, drought, Zeus's wrath and all."

"Zeus will *kill* you. Not a mortal death, either. Death is as final for demi-gods as it is for gods."

"Anything to put me off, Father?"

His golden visage cracked into a frown. "No. I've given my word, and I'll honor it. You're a strapping lad, so maybe, maybe you can handle them." Tone and features both expressed doubt. "Come here and meet the team. Bronte, hold steady, girl." He laid a hand on her neck.

Phaethon approached her, trying to radiate a calm and certainty he didn't feel. Normal animals could sense fear, and these majestic creatures were anything but normal.

"Her name means 'Thunder,' and it's earned. Bronte is a yoke-bearer and pulls on the inside left. She's the strongest, and proudest. Come, stroke her mane."

Phaethon did so without conscious thought. Muscles bunched beneath his touch, muscles covered in silky golden strands. She snorted, her breath hot on his cheek. Without Father's steadying hand, Bronte would not have tolerated him. Belatedly Phaethon knew he was both standing on the floor and stroking her mane. An impossibility for a mortal but not for gods, nor, it seemed, for demi-gods.

Father introduced the rest in turn: Sterope, or "Lightning," the other yoke-bearer, and the male trace horses Eous, "He Who Turns the Sky" and Pyrois, "Fiery One."

"Stay here with them and introduce yourself around. I'll prepare the chariot. Behave for Phaethon, now," Father finished, with a hint of pleading.

Later Father led the team out into the courtyard. He walked through the double-doors and they stepped obediently after. Father hitched the team in place.

"Where's the sun?" Phaethon inquired. "It must be housed nearby, but where?"

Father grinned. "Once you're under way, you'll feel the tension of the sun dragged behind. Also, you can't look back. The chariot's enchantment repels the heat, but not even I can glance at the sun up close."

"But you're the sun god!"

"Even gods have their limits. Now listen, Phaethon, because there are three parts of the journey, and each one presents its own challenges. The beginning is easiest, for the going is uphill and steep. At dawn, my fresh horses can hardly climb the track into the heavens. Do not allow the team to lull you into false confidence."

"I won't."

"Once in the heavens you will be at a dizzying height without comparison in the mortal world. *I* tremble to behold the world as a pebble, the sea a blue pinprick upon it. The team will strain in the traces. You must not let them rush you."

Phaethon imagined balancing upon the heavenly vantage and trembled.

"The last leg of the journey tests my mettle and skills in a different manner each day. Tethys, who receives me into her submissive waves at day's end, always fears a headlong dive into the sea, despite my strength and experience. The churning sky spins upon its own axis, oblivious of the world's forces. Stars whip in all directions, dancing in their terrible brilliance. The threats lurking in and around them are too many to number. Would that I could give you clearer warnings!

"Then the team will truly test you. Rein them as best you can, opposite the sky's orbit, and perhaps you will bring the sun to Tethys's embrace without incident."

"I'll heed every warning as if reciting the laws of Olympus."

The sun god in a blinding moment shone brighter than any mortal could, then Father grunted his doubt, though he didn't voice it. "Until nightfall, then. The chariot is yours."

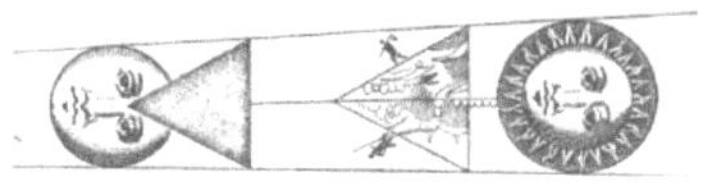

Heart clouting his chest, Phaethon watched as the world fell away. Clouds brushed his brow, condensation streaking his face. His clothes soaked through and water puddled in the chariot. In a moment of will, Phaethon drew from the soft heat at his back and eliminated the moisture, like his mom cleared water from a room.

How the sun illuminated the world below while the team dragged it from the atmosphere, Phaethon couldn't fathom. Though darker, it was not *dark* up there. The stars raced, in anticipation of his arrival or in their own pattern, he couldn't say. Other heavenly bodies twinkled in the distance.

The team, hooves clawing at the air, heaved breath and strained to gain the heights Father had warned him about. Phaethon held the reins in a firm, gentle grip. Tight enough to keep a bird from flying away without crushing it, a balance of demi-godly strength and a mortal touch. The chariot reached heaven's pinnacle, the zenith of creation, and rolled to a stop. The horses trembled with fatigue: they would need recovery time to continue. Phaethon's attention began to drift to the wonders splayed about him.

Barely had the chariot come to a halt before the team shot away, yanking him forward. Sawing at the reins to wrest control made the team slew sideways, tipping the chariot on a dangerous angle. Sensing disbalance, the team surged, changing directions precipitously. With all his might Phaethon worked the reins, heaving one moment, lightly flicking them another, once even giving the team their head. Just when the chariot eased into its descent, Phaethon's universe tilted. Though his eyes showed them hurtling ever closer to the globe below, his inner ear cried out in panic, proclaiming the heavens spinning madly about him. This discombobulation threatened to break his newfound concentration. Phaethon drew in a deep breath, blocking up his ears. The spinning sensation eased without going away altogether. Remembering Father's words, he imagined which way the sky's orbit wished him to turn and, locking it in his mind, guided the team in the opposite direction. The chariot should have plummeted into calamity, yet somehow stayed the course.

The team settled, testing him on occasion, otherwise churning along docilely enough. He whooped, ignoring the sights around him to revel in the warmth at his back and the pure joy of controlling the chariot. Who could blame Father for his hesitance? Phaethon had questioned his own sanity when considering this boon but had wanted to test his mettle. He was *born* to this!

Light particles danced at the edges of his vision as the heavens whirled. Luminous pinwheels celebrated his accomplishment, heralding him as Helios's successor. Closer they reeled, the brilliant blurs growing larger, great fiery balls that suddenly shot at the chariot like tuff exploding from a volcano, or rogue meteors. They *could* be meteors! No, he realized as he guided the team through this flurry of heavenly fury, they must be the stars. Well, fast as the stars came, *he* was faster. They couldn't bring him and his team down.

An arrow of energy sizzled overhead. Phaethon banked left, causing another arrow to fly higher above. Sagittarius must have been crouching in ambush, but he had no time to search for the archer. Around a star ahead came a charging animal composed of hundreds of balls of burning fire, twin points of stars surmounting horns aimed at the chariot. Taurus the bull stampeded straight up the track, head lowered. The track was not a visible nor physical thing, only a path in the sense that Phaethon instinctually knew it was there, and so did the team. Yet as Taurus charged, star sparks exploded from the track beneath his hooves. The team whinnied their distress as a collision loomed. *So Taurus wants to run on the track*? Phaethon urged the team up and above. To his delight they obeyed, surmounting the celestial bull with feet to spare, dropping nimbly onto the track behind him.

Taurus snorted frustration; hooves clambered behind the chariot.

Bronte thundered, leading her brethren on at a mad dash. Flaming breath puffed out through the horses' mouths and nostrils. Pyrois was then indeed a fiery one. Sterope moved in the traces like her namesake lightning, while Eous, well, he had already helped "turn the sky" against its counterintuitive orbit. Phaethon ruled them with a respectful hand upon the reins, allowing the team a measure of freedom under his calm control. The heavens faded, replaced with natural, clear light. The sun was in its element. The sky was crisp and clear, the day in full bloom.

Standing out against the shimmering azure sea, a giant bird flapped ponderously. The creature rose a hundred feet, paused and sank a bit, then leapt higher with the next flap. Its long, white-feathered appendages didn't match the body, which should have been at least boulder sized, given the wingspan. Nor were there thin legs or clawed feet or a jutting beak. The slender figure between the wings was decidedly humanoid in shape.

"Icarus! That crazy, glorious fool has done it!" Joy for his friend, who was like a brother, suffused him. His vicarious triumph proved short-lived.

Icarus rose closer to the chariot while the team dragged the sun closer to him. With his demi-godly sight Phaethon watched a single feather drift from the inventor's homemade wing. Then several fell from the other side. Soon dozens of downy bits drifted on the air current, blown from the wings with increasing magnitude.

"That idiot didn't use wax, did he?" Phaethon groaned, knowing in his heart of hearts his friend had. "Wax melts in the sun, Icarus!"

Icarus never heard him, scrambling to remain aloft as he was. The more he flapped the more feathers fell out, and the more feathers fell out, the more altitude he lost. He would plummet into the sea and crack like an egg against the surface from such a height. Could he blink to Icarus, catch him, and blink back into the chariot? No, his powers were underdeveloped, and he couldn't chance releasing the reins even for a second. The gods could only guess where the team would take the sun if he did.

Phaethon had no time for lengthy consideration, for Icarus would shortly impact upon the sea. A flick of the reins ordered the team to swoop beneath Icarus. They hesitated, uncertain of leaving the track, but he insisted. With a perfection even his father may have found difficult, Phaethon positioned the chariot below Icarus precisely before the team passed him by. Feathers clouded the air, provoking a cough.

"Icarus," he choked out. "What in Tartarus are you playing at?"

"Nice catch," the other mumbled, shrugging out of a leather harness and wire frame creation. The chariot rocked under the extra movement. "Helios actually agreed to it, huh?"

"Hold still, will you?"

"One second." Icarus heaved the getup over the side of the chariot, then fell back into Phaethon.

"Watch it, I said!"

"Phaethon, the sun." Icarus shook his shoulder and pointed.

"What about it?"

"Look!"

"I can't, or I'll go blind. You too. What are you—oh."

Icarus hadn't gone blind because the sun wasn't behind them. The chariot flew so low the team's hooves nearly skimmed the sea, and the sun, the sun sent up geysers of steam as it dragged beneath the waves.

The team juddered in their traces to compensate for the drag. Shrugging off his friend's hand, Phaethon bent to the task of righting the chariot. Sweat mingled with flecks of salt water on his brow as he strained with effort. Golden foam stood out on the horses' flanks. They were exhausted, and he was asking them to climb the sky again. It took a Herculean effort to coax them up, but up they went, winding in a ragged spiral, for there was no track here to follow. Finally, a thousand feet up, he settled the chariot into its invisible groove, from there to descend properly to the sea.

A crack, and lightning plunged from the clear sky into the sea, sizzling mere feet from the chariot. Icarus cupped hands around his eyes and gazed skyward, but Phaethon had no doubt as to the bolt's origins.

"Gods, Zeus is trying to destroy us! The vengeful fool will explode the sun, too!" Too late Phaethon saw the irony in invoking the pantheon whose ruler sought to punish him, and the world in the balance.

"I haven't failed in my duties," he shouted, guiding the team around another bolt and back onto the track.

A third bolt glanced off the golden chariot, cutting through half the traces.

The impact flung Icarus out.

Phaethon called out to the lead horse. "Guide them home, Bronte!"

He tossed the reins aside and, with a swan's grace, dove from the chariot.

Icarus flailed, like he still wore his wings and might fly to safety. Phaethon tucked arms to his side and angled for his friend. His compact form fell faster, but Icarus was too far below to reach in time. Phaethon imagined Icarus thrashing in mid-air and blinked to him. A thud of impact, and he wrapped Icarus in his embrace. The sea, though, the sea was right there. Sand and trees flashed past his vision, then Phaethon saw no more.

MOLLA & MANUELLA

F.C. Shultz

The shouting woke her up. The sun hung just over the horizon as Molla sat up in the grey hollowed bed. Limbs cracked and popped. Her fur matted. Shouting continued outside the home just as it had the morning before. And, the morning before that.

Riots.

Protests.

Mustellut did well to keep up the distractions. He read aloud from the histories and even replaced the lanterns in the entire oglaa—which Molla had been asking him to do for six cycles.

But, as he slept next to her, silent in his carved bed, the rising voices from outside crept through the walls of their home; through Molla's coarse outer layer, through her undercoat, and into her heart.

She stood and walked to the window, careful not to wake Mustellut. As she peered around the pulled curtain, flashing signs and furled brows filled her vision.

LET THEM DIE!

KEEP US PURE!

WHERE IS SCIENCE?!?

"Molla?"

She pulled away from the window.

"Leave them be."

"They've doubled since yesterday."

"They won't change our mind." He sat up in his bed and arched his slender, furry spine. An arpeggio of pops followed. "Let's have breakfast."

She nodded.

"It's a good day, Molla."

She wanted to believe him. The rock-sized hole in the sitting room window convinced her otherwise. Mustellut had patched it two days before with the ground-clay, but Charon's cold wind whistled through a crack and reminded her of the vandal who thought the residents traitors.

Maybe the vandal is right, she thought.

"Did you sleep?" Mustellut asked as he cracked an abalone over the heated cooking table.

"Some."

"Some is good," he replied. "Do you want one or two omelets?"

"One is fine." Her gaze had drifted back to the window.

"We've got everything ready," he said as he prepared another abalone.

"I know," she replied.

"What did that specialist say was important?"

"Treat them like family," Molla replied. Her focus snapped away from the window with the sound of the second abalone cracking.

"We can do that," Mustellut replied.

"We never have."

"But, we can."

Molla didn't reply. Her eyes floated back to the window, then the ground. The abalones sizzled on the hot stone. The murmur of the shouting protestors droned on in the silence.

CLANG! CLANG! CLANG!

Both of their heads snapped to the door.

"I'll get it," Mustellut said. He pulled the towel from his shoulder to clean his fury hands. He straightened his whiskers as he approached the door. Molla retreated to the shadows of the hallway.

Mustellut looked through the viewing hole. "It's Betra." He slid the locks away and opened the door. "Come in."

The yelling swelled through the open door as an elderly shr-Ossa shuffled in. Her back hunched. The whiskers were sparse on her wrinkled snout. The fur on her outer layer was discolored and matted in a patchwork only long life can weave.

"I'll be glad when those hoolys go away. Kept me up most the night, the idiots."

"Have a seat, Mrs. Johnnos," Mustellut said as he helped the woman into a chair in the sitting room.

"Don't mean to barge in like this," Mrs. Johnnos said as she lowered herself into the chair.

"It's quite alright," Mustellut replied.

"Molla here?"

"She's just waking up. I'm sure she'll be right out."

"Just waking up?" Mrs. Johnnos replied. "When I was your age I worked in the solar energy division at C.H.A.R.O.N. Had to get up three hours before the sunrise to get all the systems up and ready to gobble those sun rays and turn them into power."

"Mmhhm," Mustellut replied, returning to the near-burnt omelets.

"Was late in opening those panels by three minutes one day. Three minutes! Thought I was going to lose my license, I did."

"Did you?"

"I didn't. Just got a warning. Was never late again. Haven't slept in since."

"Morning, Mrs. Johnnos," Molla said as she emerged from the hallway.

"Hard to sleep with all that racket out there," Mrs. Johnnos replied.

"Morning, dear," Mustellut replied, doing his best to act like this was the first time he'd seen his wife this morning.

"When I was your age I worked in the solar energy division at C.H.A.R.O.N.," Mrs. Johnnos shared with Molla the same information she'd just shared with Mustellut. Molla found a seat in the living room across from their guest.

"Did you?" Molla asked, trying to sound like she did not know the answer.

"I didn't," Mrs. Johnnos replied. "Just got a warning. Haven't slept in since." The old woman gestured at Molla.

"I'm afraid I've got some kind of sickness. Didn't sleep much of the night," Molla replied in defense.

"Bet it's the shimms, from being all nervous. Stomach feel all upside down?"

Molla nodded.

"Paws all shaky? Scared to straighten your whiskers for fear of scratching your own eyes out?"

Molla put her paws in her lap and looked down at them.

"Would you like some breakfast, Mrs. Johnnos?" Mustellut said from the kitchen.

"That would be wonderful, dear," Mrs. Betra Johnnos called back to the kitchen. She turned back to Molla, whispering. "Is that husband of yours making you do this?"

"No," she replied, looking Mrs. Johnnos in the eye for the first time.

"Well, I had to ask, dear. You know I did."

Just then, Mustellut entered the living room with three plates. He handed one to Mrs. Johnnos first, then Molla, before sitting down on the long stone couch next to them.

"Doesn't this look lovely?" Mrs. Johnnos said. "When I worked for C.H.A.R.O.N. they had this five-star chef from the West, Nemo Crater, I think. Best omelets I've ever had."

"That's great," Mustellut replied.

"Every morning he'd make us fresh breakfast. I've heard they don't do that anymore. They spend all that money, money from our taxes you know, and on what? Can't even take care of their people anymore."

"You didn't like working there?" Mustellut asked.

"I loved it. Best job in the solar system if you ask me. Got new leadership now, that Doctor Erebos ain't trying hard enough if you ask me. We can travel through the galaxy at blazing speed, harness the power of the sun, but we can't make no babies?"

"It's a different science from what I understand," Mustellut replied.

"That's what all papers say, don't tell me you believe that?"

"I think we better get going, Mrs. Johnnos," Mustellut replied. "We've got an appointment this morning."

"Oh, that's today?" Mrs. Johnnos replied, doing a terrible job faking ignorance.

"Yes," Molla replied. She gathered their plates and made her way to the kitchen. She overheard Mrs. Johnnos in the other room as Mustellut was seeing her out.

"All that money, and still, in two or three generations…" Her voice trailed off before picking back up again. "I hope you know what you're doing young man."

Molla heard the door close a few moments later.

Mustellut came to the kitchen. "That Betra is something else. That can wait, dear," Mustellut said, pointing to the leftovers Molla was scrapping into the disposal. "We should really get going."

"Already?"

"We're running late."

Molla set the plate on the counter and rubbed her hands clean on her fur. She remembered she left a cup in the bedroom from the middle of the night and went to go add it to the pile of dishes. Mustellut followed her into the room. He pulled a jet-black formal hat from the closet and put it on. Molla grabbed the cup.

"Just need to put this away," she said.

"It'll be fine," Mustellut replied. He ushered her back into the living room. She put the cup on the counter. "Let's make our way out."

"I need my bag," Molla said. She made her way back into the bedroom and slid open the closet door. A dirt brown shoulder bag hung from the wall. Sliding the door shut, she caught a glimpse of light through the blinds. The murmurs of protest filled the room. She took a step toward the window.

"You alright?" Mustellut yelled down the hallway.

"Yes," Molla replied. "I'm coming." She gathered herself and left the bedroom.

The mob split in their driveway, giving their vehicle room to exit, just like Mustellut promised her.

"No one wants to get close to the fusion exhaust," he said with his brows raised. "Singe the fur right off your hide, it will."

The protesters yelled with contorted, rage-fueled faces. Molla closed her eyes.

"To Butler Mons," Mustellut said to the vehicle. He took his paw from the steering wheel and placed it over his wife's clenched fist. "They're gone."

Molla opened her eyes.

"I'm nervous, too," he said.

Molla looked at her husband.

He smiled at her, which caused her to let out a little laugh.

"It's hard to take you seriously with that silly hat on," she said.

"This is my business hat," he replied. He adjusted the hat in the mirror.

The smile dropped from Molla's face. "This is business for you?" she asked.

"Molla," he said, disappointed. "I didn't mean it like that. We have a responsibility."

"I know," she repeated.

"If we see an injustice, like this genocide, we have to do something."

"Stop, Mustellut!" She yelled. "I know, okay? I know it. That doesn't make me ready to be a mother." She turned away to look out of the window, so her husband wouldn't see her tears.

"Molla," he said in a gentle voice.

"C.H.A.R.O.N. should find someone else."

The car hummed along the smooth stone road while Molla and Mustellut sat in silence. The tall oglaas from the city shrank in the distance as they sped toward the base of Butler Mons. The sun had risen and the ice planet they orbited was faint against the blue sky.

"We have arrived at Butler Mons," the car said, breaking the long silence.

Mustellut took hold of the steering wheel. There were Ossa dressed in bright colors, directing traffic. Mustellut stopped the car and handed one of the workers an envelope. The worker escorted them off of the main road, into an underground parking garage.

"This is it," Mustellut said as he parked the car.

"You know I want children," Molla said, still looking out the window. "When I was a small pup I would play house and pretend my mother's vegetables were my babies. I loved them."

"I know, dear," Mustellut replied.

"Then, the discovery. I couldn't believe I was affected. I was tested three times."

"Three?"

"Yes," she replied. "I didn't tell you about the other two tests because I was ashamed of my disbelief."

"Molla," Mustellut said gently. He placed his furry paw back on hers. "You did nothing wrong."

"We're too old, now, Mustellut," she replied. "Our bones crack and our fur is splotched. What are we doing?"

"We are giving these earth-species a second chance."

Molla looked up at her husband.

"We're preserving our society." Mustellut wrapped his arm around his wife. "And we're fulfilling our dream."

Molla leaned into his embrace, her anxiety melting away.

Without saying a word, Mustellut kissed her on the forehead and she gave him a nod. They exited their vehicle and Mustellut led them up to the surface level, toward the loading dock.

Protesters, gathered behind security guards, shouted the same obscenities Molla had heard all night at her home. A long line of Ossa stretched down a path ahead. Molla held on tight to her husband's hand as a security guard lead them to the front of the line.

They passed dozens of other Ossa, some coupled together, some standing alone, all in a line leading to a large stone landing pad.

"There will be this many earth-seeds?" Molla asked.

"More, from what I understand," Mustellut replied. "I saw a headline that we'll need thousands more willing to foster."

Molla did not reply. Looking into the faces of the soon-to-be parents, it was like dozens of Ossa shaped mirrors reflecting back at her. She could see her fears, her doubts, in all their faces.

"Mustellut and Molla Bergamo?" a tall, slender shr-Ossa in a white coat asked as they approached the front of the line.

"Yes, doctor," Mustellut replied.

"It's an honor to be the first to welcome the earth-seeds," the doctor began.

"I apologize for our tardiness, the protestors—"

"The C.H.A.R.O.N. ship has been delayed," the doctor interrupted. "But, it should arrive any moment. You are very lucky."

"Yes," Mustellut replied.

"I assume you have completed the training?"

"We have," Mustellut replied.

"And you?" the doctor asked, facing Molla.

"I have," Molla mumbled.

"Excellent," the doctor replied. "If you could place your paw here to acknowledge you have been properly prepared, I've got a few other late-comers who need briefed."

Molla and Mustellut Bergamo placed their paws on the clear sheet of glass until they heard a high-pitched ding.

"Thank you."

"Why are the earth-species disposing of their own seed?" Molla asked, in a moment of bravery. The question had been on her mind since Mustellut first mentioned the possibility of fostering.

"Ah, yes," the doctor replied, reveling in the opportunity to display her expertise. "It seems to be a complicated matter. Some of the earth-seed are with physical defect. But, others seem to be developing without error. In some instances, it appears the earth-mother's health would be in danger if the earth-seed were to continue through the full gestation period. It's impossible to say exactly why so many of the earth-seed are undesired.

"No reason for alarm, though," the doctor continued. "We might not be able to figure out why our reproductive organs are unable to function, but we did figure out how to repair the earth-seed life force and make slight biological modifications to prepare them for our atmosphere. These modifications are happening aboard the C.H.A.R.O.N. ship right now."

"Thank you," was all Molla could reply.

"Very well," the doctor replied. She gave another nod and then continued down the line until she found another Ossa couple.

"There hasn't been much in the news about why the earth-seeds are undesired," Mustellut said. "Glad you asked."

"It's just so strange."

"Very much so," he replied. "If only the earth-species knew it was possible for a whole generation of species to be born sterile…" His voice trailed off.

"Our people have cast many shadows, too, Mustellut," Molla replied.

"It's true," he replied. He grabbed his wife's furry hand.

Just then, a thunderous wave cracked the sky as the C.H.A.R.O.N. ship dropped into the atmosphere. The dirt-brown metallic exterior reflected the sunlight as it descended. Circular windows dotted the upper rim of the massive ship. Fusion exhaust billowed below as it neared the landing pad.

Molla began to weep.

"And now we have a chance to shine some light, too," Mustellut replied, wiping his own eyes.

The massive ship landed on the stone slab in front of Molla and her husband. The entire place had grown silent. Protestors were awestruck at the splendor of the ship and anticipation of what was next. Soon to be fosters were without words as their decision to raise an earth-seed as their own was about to become reality. Molla was among the speechless.

"We can do this," Mustellut whispered to his wife.

The back of the ship dropped open like a drawbridge. The interior was full of some kind of white fog. A stocky shr-Ossa, wearing a black round hat and dressed in a black jumpsuit adorned with small medals, walked down the ramp toward Molla and Mustellut.

Molla closed her eyes and took a deep breath. When she opened them, the shr-Ossa had reached them.

"My name is Captain Santgianna," the shr-Ossa said. She took off her hat and tucked it under her arm. "And I'm glad to report our mission has been completed with one-hundred percent success." The captain smiled. "Do you know what that means?"

Molla and Mustellut shook their heads.

"It means you are going to be parents." Molla noticed a tear streaming down the fur on the captain's face. "It means our intercept and transport of the 3,903 earth-seeds was successful."

Molla could feel the tears welling up in her eyes.

"It means our culture will live on. More importantly, it means that these little earth-seeds will be loved and have a life here on Charon."

Molla couldn't hold it in any longer. The tears flowed freely. She pulled a small handkerchief from her bag.

"Are you ready to meet your little one?"

Molla and Mustellut nodded.

The captain turned to the ship and motioned to a deckhand onboard. Moments later, a middle aged hr-Ossa walked toward them carrying a glass box in his hands. Once he arrived, Molla could see a life pod with a tiny, smooth-skinned living creature inside.

"This is your daughter," the captain said. "Would you like to hold her?"

Before Molla or Mustellut could reply, the captain unlatched the lid of the pod and lifted the precious earth-seed out of the glass box. Captain Santgianna extended her arms and offered the child to Molla.

Her instincts kicked in as she received the earth-seed. She cradled the small being, her child, against her fur. The child nestled into the warmth of Molla's outer coat and continued sleeping. Molla looked up at her husband through wet eyes. His eyes mirrored hers.

"This is your child now," the captain said. "What are you going to name her?"

Molla looked down at the warm, smooth-skinned sleeping child in her arms. Her daughter moved her lips in a sucking motion, dreaming of eating no doubt. Molla thought of the memories that will be made with this little one: sharing laughs, teaching her how to walk, showing her what compassion looks like.

It was so much to take in.

And, still, she knew she wouldn't be able to get enough.

"Well?" the captain asked. Molla came back to that moment with a sense of clarity. She remembered an earth-species story about a mother who loved her daughter the most a mother could ever love a daughter.

"Her name," Molla replied, "is Manuela."

The Dragon Planet

Howard Andrew Jones

"You see here," Dabir said, and pointed to the long curve of charcoal stretching over the dirt floor of the home. "He was trying to draw a circle."

I had seen such circles before, upon the floors of those who cast spells, and apart from one I had seen my friend inscribe they never were intended for good purpose. "He didn't get very far, praise Allah," I said. There was only a little over a quarter of the circle, and above it some strange characters etched also in black charcoal, right beside where the circle was smudged. This was where the body had fallen.

Of the corpse there was no sign, for the son, upon finding it, had gathered it for burial. He had also kept others from the room in which he had found his father, so in some ways the place was undisturbed, although I knew well my friend Dabir would have preferred to have seen everything exactly as it was, including the body.

Clutter of the kind you would expect from scholars filled the room, for there was a desk, and unlit candles and hanging lanterns, also shelves with scrolls and books, and chests that likely held more of the same and were piled high with them besides. A carpet had been rolled up to one side and now butted up against the legs of the desk.

Dabir knelt in silent regard of the characters I could not read.

"Can you tell what magics he hoped to work?" I asked.

I heard the tread of the son stop behind us.

"He was not a sorcerer," he declared with certainty.

At this I traded a swift glance with Dabir and then looked back to the dead man's offspring, whose voice rose in indignation.

"That is not his handwriting!" He was a stocky fellow dressed in browns, and his black beard was well-oiled. Little eyes peered out accusingly at us from a flat face from which a thin nose protruded something like the figure head of a boat, or a crier proceeding the horse of a nobleman, so far did it go in advance of the rest of him. I had not warmed to the fellow, even given his obvious grief over the strange circumstances in which he had found his father.

He had come to us after evening prayers and led us to his well-ordered Mosul home. From some room in the complex close by we still heard the sound of female wailing.

The man looked back and forth and rightly judged that I, at least, was skeptical of his claim, given the evidence at our feet. "I tell you, he was not a sorcerer!"

Dabir stood. In those days he was not yet middle-aged. Marriage meant he was no longer quite so gaunt, for his wife made sure he ate even when troubled by some problem that would have absented food from his consideration in our earlier days. His spade-shaped beard was well-trimmed, as it ever was, and his blue eyes studied the younger man with compassion. You would not have known that we two were so well-favored by the caliph, to look at his clothing. Yes, it was well-made, but there was only a hint of yellow in the brown jubba, no gold, nor was he bedecked with jewelry, apart from the emerald ring he always wore.

"I would that you had brought us here sooner, Hamshid," Dabir said mildly. "There is much that I could have learned by seeing the way that the body lay when you found it. Now I must rely upon your memory, and memory writhes like an eel."

"He was murdered," Hamshid declared, not for the first time. "And it was done with magic. His skin was icy to the touch, and I felt the cold breath of a djinn when I entered this room."

"You saw a djinn?" I asked.

Quickly he shook his head. "I saw nothing, but what else might it have been?"

"There is no knowing, yet," Dabir said with pronounced calm. I knew he meant this to soothe the agitation of Hamshid, but he was not to be mastered.

He pointed at Dabir. "Folk say that you are a slayer of monsters and wizards. One who ferrets secrets! I mean you to find his killer."

"It looks to me," I said, "as though he was overcome by some force as he knelt over this drawing. You say he was old. Perhaps his heart was weak. It is sometimes hard to tell in a man." I pointed at the smudged portion of the circle. "This is where you found him?"

"Yes."

"We do not share everything we do, with our children," Dabir said. "It may be that he had practices of which you were unaware. But—" my friend said quickly, stilling the mouth opened now to offer defense and objection "—a child can often be well acquainted with the character of his parent. Were you and your father close?"

At that Hamshid's open mouth slapped shut and we heard naught from him for the time of nearly a dozen breaths. "He was kindly," Hamshid said at last. "But he was given to musing about stars, and planets, and meaningless things."

"Things that hold no meaning for you, at least," Dabir said, not unkindly.

"Yes."

Dabir nodded once. "It should not surprise you to know that I had met your father, through the library." Here Dabir referred to the Library of Iskander, a small university of Mosul which he sponsored, especially in the allocation of funds for books.

"I did not know that."

"Did Ramshad talk to you of his fascination with the skies?"

"It was hard to get him to stop the talking of it," Hamshid admitted. "Even when he knew I had no interest."

"Some with interest in the stars and planets also consult with fortune tellers."

I could see that Hamshid wished to object. There are many who consult with such folk. The rich and powerful keep company with them and the poor buy their charms. And yet is it not the height of arrogance to claim to know the plans of Allah, the all-knowing?

"He was not one," Hamshid insisted. "But he kept company with many star watchers."

"Had he enemies?"

"Enemies?" It seemed Hamshid was unfamiliar with the word in relation to his father, for he puzzled over it with grave intensity. "Nay, my father was too mild a man for such things. But friends he had, who cricked their old necks by nights staring at the sky."

He had not much more to say than this that did not repeat his earlier words. And all of his expostulations boiled down to three things: his father had not died naturally, supernatural forces were at work, and Dabir must find and destroy them. Also, he mentioned that he would pay an appropriate fee, at which Dabir nodded with only a little interest. I knew my friend would surely turn over any such funds to the library, as was his wont, for the caliph supported us both on a generous stipend.

Dabir ushered Hamshid from the room and inspected the place in silence.

I tried doing this myself, by long study of him seeking to find what might be out of place, or the absence of something that such a man ought to have. Assume nothing, Dabir had once told me.

While I did my best to ape the manner of someone wise, carefully eying the small collection of books and scrolls and gently lifting the number-strewn documents upon the desk, Dabir crouched once more at the half-finished circle. He asked me to bring down the lantern from the hook and this I did.

I felt as useful to him in this place, at that time, as goat horns on a housecat. I was not unused to feeling lost during the early portions of his examinations, when I could only stand about with my sword at my waist and guard against dangers that were not there. I mis-liked even the beginnings of the circle. I had seen blood-curdling things emerge from such places in my time. I spoke low, for I could not be sure that Hamshid wasn't listening on the opposite side of the door. "What does it all mean?"

Dabir's voice was soft as well. "The man did not know his father well. Yet I think he tells the truth as he sees it. The person that drew this circle seems unaccustomed to such work, and if you compare it to the graceful penmanship upon the papers upon his desk, they seem of a different hand."

"If he were dying as he began to craft the circle," I said, "his hand might have been weakened with palsy or the like."

Dabir nodded. "This is true. I should like to have seen Ramshad's hands, to see if there was charcoal upon them, but the son acted too swiftly." Already the body had been ritually washed and readied for burial.

"Hamshid spoke also of the strange way he found the body. With the hands about his own throat."

"This also I should like to have seen."

"Perhaps he was choking on an olive pit," I said, "whilst readying to summon some demon."

Dabir smiled slyly at me. "I don't think it was olives. Even to the end he was about the heavens." He tapped his finger in the air above the unfinished circle, pointing at a strange swirl. "This is unfinished, but I think I see enough. Do you recognize it?"

I stepped to his side and peered down, then shook my head. Who can tell about such things? Besides, to stare too long did not seem wise.

"That," Dabir said with the faintest hint of triumph, "is the sign of the dragon planet."

Now I had heard of such, for I had once served as guard captain to none other than Jaffar, at the time the quadi and later the vizier, and the master of a great house. He had an astronomer in residence and sometimes consulted them upon the street in his journeys through Baghdad. Such men would mention the dragon planet in their predictions if they wished to sound especially ominous and important. "I've heard it mentioned," I said. "But I don't know what it means."

"Astronomers count seven visible planets. The sun, the moon, Mercury, Venus, Mars, Jupiter and Saturn. But some believe that there is an eighth, invisible planet. This is its symbol."

"An invisible planet," I said, and I could not help but sound skeptical. "Could such things be?"

"Who is to say? Allah has presented us a universe rich with secrets to unveil. Now some of the seven are difficult to spot, lest you know precisely where to direct your eyes. But why Allah, the creator, should fashion one completely invisible and then tell of it solely to mountebanks defies my understanding." He held up his hand. "And I know you will tell me I blaspheme to assume—"

"Nay," I said. "It may be that I blaspheme as well, to think to know the mind of Allah, the compassionate, but I doubt he whispered knowledge only to men predisposed to exaggerate and lie." I nodded to the circle. "It seems clear that Hamshid's father believed in this eighth planet, for it was among the final thoughts he had in his lifetime."

"Indeed." Dabir climbed to his feet. "Come, Asim. Let us ask Hamshid for the names of Ramshad's finest friends. It may be that they will guide us from the darkness."

II

Shortly we departed the dead man's home, Dabir now armed with the names and approximate dwelling places of Ramshad's friends. I, myself, was armed only with sword and knife.

By accident or design, the home of one of Ramshad's friends lay only two blocks over, so we stopped there first. It was a sizeable place, with a stable and servant's entrance visible down a side street. As twilight neared we beheld a team of servants unloading a cart heavy with firewood and carrying the lumber through the servant's entrance.

"It seems odd, in the summer, to stock so much wood," I remarked to Dabir. "lest they plan a great quantity of cooking tomorrow."

"A good thought," Dabir said as we stepped to the main door. He knocked upon it.

His summons was answered by a fawning servant in a red turban who apologetically, with many bows, informed us that his master was indisposed and could see no one this evening.

Dabir then insisted, regretfully, and touched the neck chain without producing the small engraved medallion depended from it. He was loath ever to do so, though it gave him license to insist upon nearly everything, by order of the caliph. I had one myself. Dabir simply said: "tell him that Dabir ibn Khalil must consult with him, and that it involves the death of a friend."

The servant bowed before closing the door and scampering away.

We did not have to wait long before the old cedar opened again before us and the servant led us to a little receiving room on the right. It was lit only by a pair of lanterns and a row of candles upon a hanging shelf that the servant hurried to light.

It was a small room, with expansive carpet and wall-hangings of Persian make. It was furnished with cushions, but we did not take our seat, awaiting the arrival of the owner. From somewhere deeper in the house came the unmistakable clatter of wood dropping on stone as the lumber was carried inside, likely to the house's courtyard.

Before very long a short, straight-backed man of middle age appeared in the doorway. He was garbed in a fine, off-white jubbah and turban. Rings shown upon his fingers. It might be that he was a scholar, but judging by his home and appearance such was unlikely to have been the means by which he earned his living.

He raised his fine head to greet us. "Ah, Dabir ibn Khalil, and Captain Asim, no doubt. Peace be upon you."

We responded in kind. Dabir gestured to the fellow and I watched his glittering brown eyes as my friend named him. "Asim, this is Saghir ibn Malik. Forgive us our intrusion. You must be preparing for a party."

"Not so much a party as a gathering. I have little time to speak, Dabir. Perhaps next week?"

"I must regretfully take some of your time this evening. I'm given to understand you are friendly with the astronomer, Ramshad."

"Indeed, he will shortly be attending our little gathering."

Something in our manner apparently alerted him, for his expression grew curious. The servant had, after all, been ordered to tell him a man had died.

"Unless…" He did not finish.

"I regret to inform you that Ramshad has died," Dabir told him.

Saghir's noble head rose and he breathed in sharply. There was surprise in his expression, and also a hint of something else. Alarm, or fear? "How did it happen?"

"He died in his chambers," Dabir said, "passed out over his work."

"You bring terrible news," Saghir said softly. "Tell me, though, why one of Mosul's most famous citizens has come to speak of this, and not some messenger?"

The servant, having finished his work upon the candles, stepped past us. He hesitated at the threshold, probably wondering if Saghir should order refreshments, but the master of the house dismissed him with an impatient wave and he hurried off. I could not help noting that Saghir did not offer us a seat.

"There are certain curiosities involved in his death," Dabir said.

Saghir sounded quite calm. "What manner of curiosities?"

Dabir did not answer. "We've learned he was a member of a small group of fellow scholars and star watchers."

"Yes, yes, we meet twice a week, weather and skies permitting. Sometimes others among us host – but how is this related to a death? We but study the stars and planets and note their movements."

"Has Ramshad ever voiced an interest in the eighth planet?"

Saghir laughed shortly. "Yes. A little folly of his. We used to tease him of it. The Greeks never noted it, and the fortune tellers tell us it is invisible." He shook his head, apparently amused. "An invisible planet."

"The old Greeks knew many things," Dabir said, "but theirs was the beginning of wisdom, not the end. There may yet be other planets, undiscovered. Be sure you do not dismiss the idea too quickly."

Saghir grinned without mirth. "You sound like Ramshad. Poor fellow. May peace be upon him." He sighed.

"Your pardon, but I must see to the arrangements, for my guests will begin to arrive within the hour."

"Yes, of course," Dabir said easily. "But tell me, Saghir. Was Ramsahd ever known to dabble in sorcery?"

"Sorcery?" Saghir asked glibly. He chuckled. "You mean the wearing of lucky amulets and such? Many of us are guilty of such."

"I mean consultation with beings through sorcerous means," Dabir said.

Saghir blinked rapidly, as if trying to remove something from his eye. "Ramshad was no sorcerer," he said. "Of that I am certain. What a peculiar question."

"Yes," Dabir agreed. "Perhaps so. Well, we will bid you farewell and be on our way."

Saghir shadowed us to the door. "Thank you for letting me know of poor Ramshad's fate. We will have to pay our respects to the family." He opened the door onto dusk. "I hope that we shall meet again under more pleasant circumstances."

We made our farewells, then left him. Dabir looked to right and left, then strode suddenly left.

"He hides something," I said.

"Almost certainly. But I'm not sure what. He did not seem as surprised as he should have been to learn of Ramshad's death. If anything, he grew more eager for us to leave. I think the only thing that truly surprised him was the accusation that Ramshad might have been a worker of magics."

"So he expected he might be dead?" I asked.

"It's not that he thought Ramshad would be dead, it's just that he was not entirely surprised by his passing."

"What does it mean?"

"I lack enough information to make an informed decision," Dabir admitted. "So we will keep looking."

III

After that frustrating interview it was time for night prayers. I was all for returning to the home our families shared, for my children liked to hear a bed time tale from my lips each night, and my wife's company hardly displeased me. But Dabir wished to press on, and being his faithful friend, I went with him. For I knew well that he would continue on even without me, and I had been ordered to protect him by none other than the caliph himself.

Thus did we find our way to the third home that evening, one much smaller than the first two, down a side lane. I had stopped to purchase a lantern from a shop near the central markets and Dabir carried this before him, a little amused, I think, by my caution. But I wanted my hand free should some bravo seek to accost us. And he and I were not without enemies, as you may know if you have heard some of our other accounts.

In that gloomy street ours was the only light source. While Dabir rapped knuckles against the weathered door I took in the buildings about us, wondering if anyone watched from the second-floor windows. My eye was drawn higher, to where the stars peered down upon us, bright in the blackness beyond the moon. I have looked upon the stars many times, and in the desert and upon the sea their immensity is truly stunning.

Gazing upon them that night, though, I knew a curious disquiet, and the hairs along the back of my neck stood on end. It might be that Hamshid would have called that the breath of a djinn. I guessed it for nerves.

No one had come to Dabir's knock, so he tried a second time. "I think our man lacks a servant," he said.

"Perhaps both are at a late dinner," I suggested.

"Perhaps." Dabir's eyes went up, too, but not as far as mine, for they stopped at the old enclosed wood balcony that projected over the street to the right of the door. "I'm loathe to ask this of you, Asim," he said, and I sighed.

"You wish me to find us a way in."

"Yes. Do you smell a strange scent in the air?"

I sniffed. "Like eggs have rotted?"

"Yes. And there's a chill."

I had thought I imagined that. I contemplated the struts supporting the balcony. Sensing my thought Dabir shone the lantern there.

Some think that a man who is large and tall must therefore be plodding and slow, and they are fools. In moments I had leapt and caught the struts. The wood creaked somewhat to bear my weight, but in moments I had lifted myself up and by quick stages arrived at the lip of the balcony's shuttered side window. It was barred from within, but I pulled myself level with it, my left arm bent and holding me in place, and bashed with the flat of my right hand. The shutter swung inward.

"Truly you would have made a masterful thief," Dabir said below me. He was mouthing some other jest which escaped me, for I had felt an icy breath in my face. That was not the sole reason the hairs upon my neck and arms stood upright, for I sensed danger.

I pulled myself in through the narrow window and tread across ancient, wood, protesting my weight, until I reached the arched doorway that was but a portal to deeper gloom.

I saw nothing, but I felt a great cold, and that faint odor, as of rotten eggs.

I put hand to sword hilt, and debated my course of action. "The stench is strong, Dabir," I called over my shoulder. "And so is the cold."

"What else can you determine?"

"I have discovered," I said, still peering into the gloom, "that it is impossible to see details in a darkened room when there is no light."

Dabir could be heard muttering something about wit, below me. He then urged me not to advance, lest there be some unforeseen danger. In this I agreed. I then unwound my turban cloth and slung it down through the balcony window towards him. Dabir tied it about the lantern handle and I brought it up, swaying ever so gently, then advanced with it before me, bare-headed, lantern off to my left side, bared steel in my right.

Dabir heard my exclamation upon stepping once more into the chamber beyond.

He called in honest concern. "Asim!"

Struck as I was by horror I did not immediately answer, and his concern for my fate was clear from the tension in his voice. "Asim!"

"I am well," I called back. "But we are too late for this fellow."

This small room was meaner and less well furnished than that to which Hamshid had led us. The rug that had been cast back from the floor was old and patched, and the exposed floorboards were warped. But otherwise they were similar, for there was part of a circle with figures and symbols scored along its surface. The main difference was that in the place where the last circle was smudged a man lay across it. It may be that the graybeard lying there did not look like Ramshad, but his death resembled that told us by his son, for he lay twisted with his fingers about his neck. His face was ghastly, reminding me of a soldier I'd once seen dying from a sling stone that had struck his throat.

His skin had a bluish tint. I did not touch him to see if he was cold; I searched the old cramped room for sign of djinn, or hidden physical enemies, but I saw no sign of them. Since by their nature invisible things are not to be seen, I trusted to smell, hearing, and instinct. There was a faint scent of rotten eggs, but nothing more, and I eased through the room, keeping well clear of anything Dabir might find of interest, and by and by found my way down the stairs, through a cluttered front room, and opened the door for my friend.

Shortly he was bent down beside the corpse, looking without touching, and before long he was pacing along the edge of the circle. He pointed down to a symbol I now recognized.

"The dragon planet," I said.

"Aye. This circle is better finished," he said. "But remains incomplete."

"What was it intended for?"

Dabir frowned as he looked over the symbols.

There are some who claimed Dabir a wizard, but it was not so. Dabir did not always abstain from wine, and might have stood to pray more often, but he was otherwise a good Muslim. Thus it was that while he wielded magics in my presence, it was only ever to counter evil sorceries, or to break them. That may make me sound like a splitter of hairs arguing my case before a quadi, but it is the full truth of the matter.

"I would need to consult my books to be certain," he said after a moment.

"But?" I prompted.

"You have seen such circles in the past."

"Aye. Usually with some terror lingering within them."

"Think of it as a door that opens not onto a physical place nearby, but upon some other place far away. Through these symbols it is rendered far closer than it truly is."

I nodded and then fell still, thinking swiftly. "You mean to say that these were trying to open a door to the dragon planet?"

"I believe so."

"But you yourself said that the circles were unfinished. You would think that these sorcerers would be dead only if the circle had worked."

"Indeed. The circle can't work until it is complete."

I was about to ask him concerning the stench and the coldness in the air when I heard a clatter from below. Swiftly I took the creaking wooden stairs down to the main level and shone my lantern on a man sprawled upon the floor. As to where he had come from, the lid of a chest stood open behind him, against the wall, in a place rather overstuffed with furniture. He looked up to me with panic in his eyes. He proved a paunchy fellow, not quite so old as the one we had found upstairs, and not dead, either. Otherwise there was a similarity in appearance. His wide eyes showed me their whites as I regarded him, then flicked over to Dabir, who stood in the doorway.

"Is it gone?" he asked.

"There's no sign of it," Dabir told him.

"The thing cannot be seen except in the circle," the old man said. "And even then it is hard to glimpse."

"The thing is from the eighth planet," Dabir suggested.

"Yes." And the old man pushed himself up and stood, wobbly, then braced himself against the chest. "My brother. Is he—"

"The man upstairs is dead," Dabir said. Then added, "I am sorry."

The old man nodded, looking suddenly ages older.

"How came you into the chest?" I asked.

"When I knew the thing had come, and that it had seized my brother, I fled. For I had seen what it did with poor Amin."

"Another from your circle is dead?" Dabir asked.

The old man nodded. "Last night."

I frowned. Saghir had made no mention of it. I thought Dabir might say something about Ramshad, but he did not speak.

"Why did you summon it?" Dabir asked.

Now this question puzzled me so that I interrupted him during the questioning, something I but rarely did. "I thought you said that they could not have summoned it," I reminded him. "The circles were unfinished."

Dabir spoke quickly in answer. "This little group summoned this thing, before. Now, when it comes upon them, they're trying to trap it by drawing a circle. But it slays them before the spell can work."

Then the old man shook his head. "Saghir means to trap it, not us. My brother and I want nothing to do with it, now."

"He was working upon a circle upstairs, at his death," I said. Did the man think us fools?

"Are you Waffiy, or Farid?" Dabir asked him. He had learned the names, of course, from Hamshid.

"My name is Wafiyy. And this is not what you think. We thought that if we stayed away from Saghir, that the beast would not find us. But it did. My brother cried out that the monster was within him, and then he began to draw. How he remembered what he did of the circle Saghir's astronomer drew, I do not know. Maybe the monster recalled it. But I was struck with the cold, and feared, and... I ran."

"Why then did it not seek you when it failed with your brother?"

"I cannot say, unless I hid too well."

"Perhaps there are no chests on the eighth planet," I said. To my mind it and a wardrobe were among the two most obvious hiding places in the two rooms of the little place I had so far entered.

"Perhaps you'd best tell us how this matter began," Dabir suggested.

The old fellow sighed, wearily, and his glance passed heavily over the stairs that led to where his brother lay. He then closed the chest and sat upon its edge. "My brother and I, we were booksellers. We sold out stock to our nephews two years ago and had enough for this little place. It was my brother who found the old Greek text by Anaximenes that mentioned the sighting of an eighth planet, and he presented it to Saghir. We thought only that we might be able to locate the planet again, but Saghir had other plans."

"What plans?" Dabir asked.

Waffiy's expression soured. "Ask those who cast with the dragon planet. They say that when it is known to all a new age of calamities will be ushered forth. Wars will sweep the world. There will be great spears that kill many men at a distance; even entire armies and whole cities."

I started to scoff at such nonsense, but I saw the sober look in his eyes.

"You wanted this?" Dabir asked sternly.

He shook his head, no. "Nay – but Saghir said that if such was fated, we could use such knowledge to protect the caliphate from other lands. He convinced us that this wisdom would be a splendid gift to make to Haroun al-Rashid. The Greeks and the Khazars and even the far Chinese would have to bend knee to him!"

"And what a splendid gift he would make to you, no doubt," Dabir suggested.

"Of course," Waffiy admitted without chagrin. "Madness. Oh, we located the planet in the constellation of Capricorn, so dim it but appeared another star, until we saw it moving night after night. But something went awry with the summoning."

"Something always goes wrong with the summoning," I remarked quietly to Dabir, who nodded distractedly.

"Saghir knew a man who knew the way of summoning, passed down from the ancients, and we but altered the formula. We would contact the denizens of the planet, and ask of them these secrets. But this… monster… came through. You could only slightly see it. A kind of snaky thing, radiating the cold of hell, and a stench, and fear. Such fear as turn a man's belly to water. Frightened out of his wits, Ramshad scuffed the circle when he turned to flee, and the circle was broken."

I knew from prior experience than when such a circle is broken, that which dwells within has free rein to leave.

"And it's been roving free ever since." Dabir's words were more a grim pronouncement than a question.

"Why it sought out poor Amin first, I do not know. And now my brother. And it tries to make them draw the circle."

"It killed Ramshad before him."

Wafiyy looked up in surprise at this news.

"Somehow it knows which people were involved in calling it here," Dabir explained. "It has marked you. It will come again."

The old man's yellowing eyes rounded. "Say that it is not so!"

"Saghir at this very moment has called people to him again, purportedly to look at stars. But they were gathering enough wood for a great bonfire. Do you know what he intends?"

Wafiyy only stared.

Dabir stepped closer. "Can he call the thing back, and send it home?" he demanded. "Is that what he wants?"

"I don't know what he can and can't do," Wafiyy said. "There was talk of finding a way to call it back and binding it with magics, so that it would serve us, but my brother and I and Ramshad wanted nothing to do with that. Saghir hopes to win acclaim, not just for sharing with the caliph the finding of a new planet, but with the discovery of great weapons of war."

Dabir frowned. "He may already be at work this very moment. Wafiyy, I think you know that what you did was folly."

He nodded, slowly, and looked away from Dabir's eyes.

"Your brother's body needs care. But before even that, you must act to help undo the dangers you've unleashed."

He raised his hands, protesting. "I'm going nowhere near Saghir's summoning circle."

"I don't intend that," Dabir said. "You are to find Captain Fakhir, of the guard, and tell him to come with a contingent of men to Saghir's home. Make haste."

"What should I tell him?"

"It is enough to say that Dabir and Asim have sent for him," I said. "He will come."

"Hurry," Dabir said.

"I do not think you can stop this thing with swords," Wafiyy warned us as he rose.

I looked to Dabir. "That may be so," he admitted.

"How am I to guard you against such a thing?" I asked him.

"You worry about the men. I will worry about the monster."

IV

Dabir might not have been worrying about the monster, but I surely was. I did not know how I might defend him against a thing that could not be seen, and struck only when it took over your body.

As we hurried back to Saghir's residence I asked again how he expected me to protect him.

"So far it has only attacked those involved in summoning it."

"It is a demon," I pointed out, "summoned from some hell. There is no telling when it will turn its wrath upon others."

"That may be so," Dabir said. "But watch the people. I think they may be the greater threat. For no man likes to see his plans thwarted."

When we neared Saghir's home I thought Dabir would once more direct me to some climbing, but he instead brought us to the door of the adjacent home. To its servant and owner he made polite play with the medallion he wore and the old gentleman in residence gladly gave us access to the stairs that led to the roof. It may be that you are not familiar with the ways of Mosul, so would not know that in the heat of the summer folk sometimes sleep upon their roofs, thus there is always access, sometimes with a ladder, though in this and other well-to-do homes it was with a small set of stairs.

We took those steps, and climbed quietly upon the low wall dividing one roof from another, and climbed over. With quiet Dabir and I advanced through the darkness, illuminated only by the countless pinpoints of the cosmos high above. Our goal was the edge of the roof that looked down upon Saghir's inner courtyard.

Crouching, we soon beheld the rectangular pool in the courtyard's center. To its right lay a complete circle in charcoal, inscribed over the flagstones. Everywhere upon it were strange symbols and sigils, and there was an inner circle as well. About the circle were no less than four blazing bonfires. And yet I tell you that there was a chill in the air above.

Men stood about the fires. I recognized only Saghir, short but proud, head high. There were other star gazers, to judge by their appearance, and one knelt beside the circle, as if making inspection of the symbols there. I counted three others besides, younger folk with sheathed swords. Guardsmen, then, and not well-armed servants, for these were broad, powerful looking men. Even their dim, fire-lit figures suggested competence.

One by one my gaze passed over them, and then settled unwillingly upon the presence I felt rather than saw hovering somehow in the circle's center. I had the vague sense of a being perhaps the size of a lion, but suspended somehow at a height above Saghir's head. Things like snakes writhed beneath it. Also, there was an unpleasant odor, that of stinking eggs.

"They have summoned and recaptured it," Dabir said.

I could not observe the thing's details while peering closely at it: somehow, I seemed to glimpse it better from the corner of my eye. And it was by turning my head that I realized we were not alone on the roof. I pushed Dabir down a heartbeat before a spear transfixed the air where he'd crouched only a moment before.

It clattered onto the roof behind us.

Saghir must have feared his doings could be interrupted.

I lunged to my feet, drawing my sword in the same moment, and just heard Dabir's wish to keep quiet.

He has asked more impossible things, in the past. I would not have shouted a battle cry in such circumstances, but it is difficult to kill a man without having him cry in pain.

The guard slashed out at me as he came in, misjudging my speed. He ducked when I aimed at his throat, and my sword slashed through his turban. It unspooled and fell across his face. While he pushed with one hand to tear the cloth away, I closed and grabbed his sword arm.

He grunted in alarm, and then once in pain as I clouted him with my sword hilt. He dropped the sword, seeking to grapple me until I punched him again. This elicited a third groan and then he slid to the rooftop. I nudged him with the toe of my boot, decided he was unconscious, then followed to where Dabir watched the doings below, right along the roof edge.

He looked back at me, and I crouched bedside him. Then I stared down upon the scene, where Saghir beseeched the strange, colorless thing at the center of the circle, telling it to give over its powers.

A response that was of cold and darkness washed over us, lacking passion, lacking even voice, aye, for I believe I felt the sound rather than heard it, as you might feel a man walking over the floor above, with your hand pressed to the beams, even though he makes no sound. The meaning writhed against my inner ear.

"I know nothing of this war," the voice said. "I know nothing of your secrets. My spirit weakens. Far away my body dies. Return me from this hellish place."

One of Saghir's minions spoke to him then, and I just made him out over the crackle of one of the fires below. "Why don't we just return it?"

Saghir faced the man with a frown. "Don't you see, even if it can't tell us of weapons, the thing is itself a weapon. A silent weapon that can kill at a distance!" He spun to the kneeling graybeard. "You said you truly can bind its spirit? Even when it leaves the circle?"

Though the man's precise words were lost to me, there was no mistaking his assent in the bob of his head.

"Please." Fear emanated from the thing at the center of the circle, and much like a towering column of ocean water strikes at those on shore, the men below first shivered and drew away a little, and then as the wave advanced it hit me so that my hairs stood on end and an unmanning terror urged me to run screaming for some bright place.

One of the old men below us broke and ran.

I understood then that the thing did not mean to inflict terror, but that it somehow shared what it felt itself.

Beside me Dabir shook off his own fear and turned to me. I heard anger in the words he whispered. "Come, Asim."

We found an old stair leading down from the roof to the balcony overlooking the courtyard. From there we simply dropped to the flagstones. By the time we were rising, my blade was already clutched in my hands, and Dabir bore the caliph's medallion in one of his. It shone with reflected firelight.

"Return the creature whence it came," Dabir said, his voice crackling with authority. "By order of the caliph."

Saghir looked unimpressed. "Not the caliph, but you," he said. "I think the governor and the caliph should judge this for themselves, don't you? Think of the power they can command!"

I looked over the three guards and the three astronomers and tried to keep my eyes from the thing that wasn't quite there.

"What you do here is wrong," Dabir said. "You plot to murder using sorcery. You think the caliph will condone this?"

Saghir smiled. "I think he would reward someone who could eliminate problems from a distance. You know I speak truly. And if he lacks the wisdom, other men would see its benefit. The vizier, perhaps."

"I will instruct you only once more. Send it back."

"I shall send it *forth*," Saghir said, then turned to the kneeling graybeard. "Command it to kill them!"

The time for talking was past. I leapt toward Saghir. Immediately two of the guards interposed themselves and Saghir slid away. The pair hesitated as I slashed my blade before them. Another charged Dabir. If he expected a helpless scholar than he was sorely surprised, for my friend was a trained bladesman. It happened that night that he wore only his knife, but he well knew how to ably dodge a blow.

While Dabir was distracted avoiding the warrior, though, Saghir grabbed one of his arms and it might be the warrior would have skewered my friend if I'd not brought my blade smashing down across his and then whipped it up diagonally. I tore out the man's throat. He fell into one of the braziers and scattered coals, writhing in pain from the heat as he died.

The other guards eyed me warily and I paced to the left so that I might watch them as I closed toward Saghir. I leveled my blade. "Release Dabir."

Scowling, Saghir pushed Dabir's arm away. "You're fools, both of you. The caliph will praise me."

The graybeard kneeling at the circle's edge wiped part of the circle away, then rose, his black robe stained gray by charcoal. He pointed to us. "Attack them!"

The thing in the circle's midst flowed out, and as the cold touched me I was reminded again of the great blizzards I had once endured. It might be that this cold was worse still, but I leapt through even as Saghir laughed, exultant.

In a heartbeat I reached the side of the graybeard and forced him down with a sword to his throat, urging him to change the symbols lest my trembling hand injure him. Hastily he bent to work even as Saghir raged.

I spared a glance to Dabir, forced to his knees and shaking in the cold. I sensed the invisible thing draped over him, its mass of tendrils brushing against his shoulders. Then the graybeard beside me finished his shifting. At once the thing swept over to Saghir, who cried out in protest, then walked with strange, stiff legs, to the circle's side and took up the charcoal the gray beard beside me had used. The two of us stepped apart even as Saghir bent to the circle, wiping away two symbols.

I spared an eye to the guard and the other conspirators, but they dared come no closer. One of the guards was backing ever so slowly into the darkness, no doubt to flee.

Saghir's hand shook as it began to write in the space he had erased. His skin blued.

"Nay!" Saghir cried. "Do not make me do it!" But even as he spoke, he scrawled three different symbols.

Once more Saghir spoke, his eyes rolling to face us. His mouth moved, aye, and it was his voice, but the words were not his. "By staying to speak longer this one weakens," he said. "I do not wish that. You must close the circle once I have passed within it. Then I should return."

"I shall," Dabir vowed. He climbed to his feet.

Saghir spoke once more. "I thought this only a place of demons, until I met you."

"It is a place of complexities," Dabir said. "But go now, with God."

The thing left Saghir, gasping and shivering, and floated through to the circle. Dabir then stepped to pry charcoal from Saghir's fingers and finished off the circle. The moment the charcoal lines touched, it vanished, though the cold and the odor lingered a while after.

At almost the same instant Captain Fakhir, his nephew, and a host of guardsman arrived. Dabir then ordered Saghir and the others carted off, though can you believe, Saghir protested the entire time, saying he would show his powers to the governor and the caliph himself.

After their departure Dabir sought through the notes gathered in the courtyard, leafed through two of the books, and then did a thing I would never have thought to witness. He tossed all those papers he carried into the nearest bonfire, where they shriveled and blackened and were consumed.

Moodily he watched them burn. "With those observations," he said, "they would have tried again."

"Were they dark magics?" I asked.

He shook his head, sadly. "Much of it but charted the course of the eighth planet. If it is true that terrible weapons will be given man after the eighth planet is known to all, then it shall not be through the observations of these men. It may be I have delayed that horror for a while longer."

"Let us hope. So it seems the thing did not desire vengeance after all. Even though it was a monster."

He eyed me sharply. "Nay, my friend. It was but trying to return. It had been pulled from its land to a strange and distant place, and was forced against its will to do the bidding of others. I think the monsters we faced came from much closer to home."

ANDROMEDA

Tracey Baptiste

How she had ended up lashed to a rock on the edge of a cliff, was a matter of public discussion. Her mother's big mouth, her father's cowardice, the god's ultimatum. Everyone had something to say about the situation and each of the players' roles. Not behind hands, or in hushed tones, either. Out loud. In the streets of the capital and along the muddy footpaths that connected every surrounding village throughout the hills of Ethiopia.

Andromeda, though, said nothing. She didn't plead for her life when her father succumbed to Poseidon's order. She didn't look in her mother's eyes—to find what? Pity? Remorse? Hardly. She was a princess of the kingdom, and as such, she had been bred from birth to sacrifice. Her nurse had kindly taught her, that with privilege came responsibility. Sometimes royal blood would need to be spilled because it was precious. Enough to buy things. And here she was, hard edges of rock scraping her dark skin, hands and feet bound in a position uncomfortable even to look at, waiting for the moment the creature would emerge from the depths of the sea to take her. Her blood would save every life in the kingdom.

Precious.

Precarious.

Same thing.

The creature was certainly taking its time. So long, in fact, that the entire citizenry had gathered against the craggy cliffs to watch the spectacle.

"How long will it be?" one asked.

"It will surely be quick," hoped another.

"How hideous is the creature?" someone else wondered—with glee.

The guesses rumbled through the crowd. "The creature will be here soon." "It will all be over in a moment." "Even if it is hideous… well, none of us have to look at it for long, anyway… and certainly none of us from the *inside*."

Andromeda breathed deeply. Sea air had always been her favorite. Beneath her feet, the Red Sea writhed as it always did, gleamed as it always did. The morning's sunrise had been particularly spectacular. A gift, perhaps from the gods. Maybe they pitied her when few else did.

"What can we do, Princess?" one of her women had asked that morning. They fed her on wine and beef. She wondered if they considered the irony.

"Nothing. There is nothing to do," Andromeda replied, eating with smaller bites than usual, savoring the salted meat, sipping the fortifying liquor. *For courage* they had told her.

But Andromeda knew courage didn't come at the bottom of a cup. It was another lesson from her nurse, who had driven the point home about her worth one morning as she dragged the young princess across the cliffs and away from her music lessons in the palace, past the grounds with

Cepheus' pet lions, past the growing fields. Andromeda had been happy of the diversion, thrilled to be in the wind, and listen to the sound of the waves crashing against the rocks below them. That was true music. No plucked instrument could compare. It was freedom, that moment. Freedom and bliss. Until it wasn't. Until her father's guards surrounded them with their bows drawn, their spears pointed, their faces resolute.

The nurse. Her nurse. (She had forgotten her name because afterward they all made sure she forgot it.) That nurse had grabbed her then by the neck and pushed her out over the rocks.

"Choose," the woman had said. It was a voice low enough that Andromeda thought for a moment the nurse was speaking only to her. But it was the soldiers who had answered.

A single lancing shot speared one and spared the other. The nurse stood with one end of the shaft coming through her back. The tip glistened with her blood in the sunlight. Dripping. Andromeda was splattered, but the nurse did not let go of her. Not until she started falling, arcing backward toward the sunbathed cliffs. One of the soldiers lurched forward and grabbed Andromeda from the nurse's clutch as the woman tumbled down, spitting blood from her core.

All Andromeda could see were her eyes, and hear what she had said before they had run off: "What are you worth, Princess?" and then, "Royal blood will buy freedom."

But it was the nurse's blood that had spilled. And there was no freedom to be had at the bottom of a cliff.

It was the same cliff (naturally) she was tied to now. The same rocks, the same pink-tinged sunlight, the same unfaltering waves below. But now the water rippled.

The shadowy body of a hulking creature came beneath the rolling waves. It moved steadily. Directly. Sure of its mark. The path it made was the tip of a spear straight toward her.

Her heart fluttered.

The crowd stilled.

Andromeda, fine-tuned to the creature headed for her, had no time to notice wings, even large ones, even ones attached to the body of a white horse, even ones that whipped the air around her and elicit gasps from the crowd. She only noticed the creature in the water looming larger every moment with every heartbeat.

And then there was something. Someone. Somethings next to her. Pressing in.

Andromeda turned her head the little she could, bound as she was. There was a man on a winged horse next to her.

He was tall and muscular, sweaty and intense. Eyes deep blue as the sea below them, and skin the color of sun-kissed sand. The Pegasus he rode flapped its wings and folded them, picking up a breeze that blew back her tangled, kinky hair. He looked at her in such a desperate way that her heart instantly squeezed with pity. He was ocean and land and air at once. A place to swim to stand to soar.

She tried to breathe and couldn't find air.

The crowd crowded.

He asked, "What is going on here? Why is this woman tied to a rock?"

One of Andromeda's handmaids explained. Well, the *whole crowd tried* to explain, but he focused in on the maid, and everyone else shut up.

The story told, Perseus' eyes gleamed. He had had enough of gods and their whims. He assessed the situation quickly. The creature had breached the waves, one giant, barnacled paw clawing at the base of the cliffs. The paw alone was longer than Andromeda was tall. It glistened in the morning light as seawater trickled through every crag, and poured away from it.

"You will not die today," he assured the princess, his voice rough with determination.

Certainly, he could get her off this rock and whisk her away from the monster. He had all the equipment for it: winged horse, rippling muscles, the desire in his eyes to capture the prize for his efforts.

His entire body was infinitely readable. In every chiseled bone beneath his skin, in every tensed muscle, in the intensity of those bright eyes was love and lust and confidence and swagger. This was a man who had faced monsters and won. A man who was undaunted in the face of danger. A man who saw what he wanted and worked for the desired outcome. His mouth was beautiful. His muscles were beautiful. Andromeda parted her lips to say something, but he didn't wait for her to speak. There was no time to wait. The creature was rumbling up the rocks, coming for her. Coming coming coming. Its dark head rising like a craggy city from the water.

Perseus grabbed the Pegasus's mane and in one smooth movement, remounted the creature and untied a sack from its side. He dug his heels into the animal's ribs, and leaned forward. The Pegasus sprang away from the edge of the cliff, and as they hit air, spread its wings wide, then dipped down, hard and fast.

The creature's entire body was out of the water now. It was an impressive beast. Black as any Ethiopian, and immeasurably stronger. Hideous and frightening, and as impossible to look away from as the queen who had started this mess to begin with.

The creature roared. The sound echoed off the rocks, and pierced the ears of every person waiting for the princess's fate. Its teeth were slick with thick yellow mucus. Andromeda was barely a morsel for this creature. Scarcely a swallow. Hardly worth the effort of such a titan rising from the depths.

Andromeda's heart quickened. Her body slicked with sweat.

The clash between Kraken and Man Who Had Fallen in Love at First Sight was inaudible. Perseus pulled something from the sack—Andromeda couldn't see what—and held it up. The creature stilled instantly. The glisten seeped from its skin. What little softness there was in its body hardened further until it was all stone. Man and stone, staring at each other against the cliffs. And then the creature fell, tumbled, end over end back from whence it came.

Triumphant again, Perseus rode Pegasus back to the top of the cliff to untie Andromeda from the rock and feel, finally, the softness of her skin against his own.

"Who is responsible for this?" Perseus asked.

Andromeda, still breathless, was unable to explain. Again, the maid stepped in.

Perseus found Cepheus in the castle. Drunk. Laid low. His wife next to him, the definition of beauty and calm.

"I have killed the kraken," Perseus told them.

Cepheus looked up. Surprised. His eyes went from the man in front of him to his daughter, whose hand was firmly folded into his.

"I will marry your daughter," Perseus said.

"You saved her," Cepheus whispered hoarsely.

"But what of the kingdom?" Cassiopeia asked. "Poseidon will be angry."

Beneath the waves, Poseidon had long turned to other matters.

"The gods are fickle," Perseus shrugged. "And I will always save her. Save you." He squeezed the princess's hand tighter in his own.

Cepheus nodded. Cassiopeia looked about to say something, but the king cut an eye at her, and she shut up. For once.

The couple left the palace, and mounted the Pegasus. Andromeda sat behind Perseus and wound her hands around his waist. Her tightly coiled black hair fell over his shoulders.

She did not say goodbye. She did not mourn the loss of her kingdom or the people she knew in it. She had been bound from birth. Bound to the rules of royalty. Bound to her parents' wishes. Bound to a rock awaiting another binding—via consumption—with a sea monster. And now, she would be bound to Perseus.

In the years after they married and had children and grandchildren she thought often of the rock, the creature, the moment of certain death. She would never be certain of it again. And long after she was gone, leaving behind legacies with her blood like Hercules, they told her love story and painted it in the sky. Outlined in stars, and dark as night, Andromeda fell toward earth, as if Perseus had never saved her, had never whisked her off the cliff. She tumbled toward earth, the sea, the kraken that would consume her.

Because in the end, she was always to fall. It was the only freedom. The nurse had been right all this time. She finally understood the lesson as the beast had emerged from the water. If anyone had asked then how she would like her freedom, in the arms of a man, or the mouth of a creature, she would have chosen the kraken.

It would have been quicker.

SHREWD DEVICES

Emily Munro

Or else flush'd Ganymede, his rosy thigh
Half-buried in the Eagle's down,
Sole as a flying star shot thro' the sky
Above the pillar'd town.
— Tennyson, "The Palace of Art"

And I aver that even in the case of Ganymede, it was not his person but his spiritual character that influenced Zeus to carry him up to Olympus. This is confirmed by his very name. Homer, you remember, has the words, 'He joys to hear;" that is to say, 'he rejoices to hear;' and in another place, "'harbouring shrewd devices in his heart'...
— Xenophon, Symposium. 8.30

As his rover plowed its way across another crater, making its tortuous way across the icy surface of Jupiter's largest moon, Gan wished that he'd listened when they'd warned him just how boring a month-long trek on the surface would be.

But when something had taken down the radio tower at the Nenlil air extraction plant, the lure of a hazard pay job that would wipe out a big chunk of his debt in one go was too much to resist. Besides, he'd thought, at least he'd be able to get some work done.

"Time to next checkpoint, nineteen hours," the rover said.

"Thank you, Touchstone," Gan replied. He sighed and resettled himself sideways in the driver's seat. "Wake me if anything interesting happens, ok?"

He'd been talking back to the rover for days now. Which had been another unpleasant surprise. It was dumb as a toaster and, worse, hardwired so he couldn't even reprogram it to be a better conversational partner. Like a toaster.

"I will wake you in the event of an anomaly," the rover replied.

"Yeah, that too," He sighed and set aside his most recent design. "Play my sleep mix" he told the machine.

The tiny cabin filled with the soothing cacophony of Martian neo-prog, and ice continued to roll past the window outside.

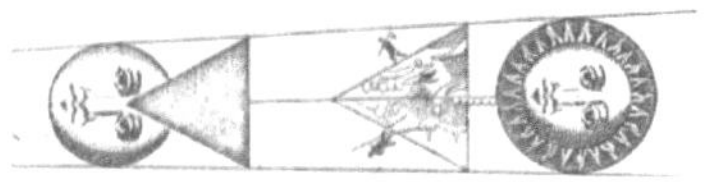

"EMERGENCY, EMERGENCY, EMERGENCY," the alarm blared across the music. Gan jerked awake, hitting his head on the spot on the armrest where the metal had worn through.

"Courier craft Zulu-One-Five, I am hit by unknown assailants and preparing to crash land on Galilean mare. Repeat…"

Gan yanked himself vertical. "Touchstone, plot that signal."

Glancing out the window Gan caught a streak of fire as it cut diagonally across the sky in front of him. No way that was a controlled reentry. And with the radio tower at the Nenlil plant down no one else was going to hear the call either.

"Calculating," the rover replied with its infuriating calm.

The voice on the radio got the message out once more before abruptly cutting off.

"Signal source 5.5 kilometers away," the rover said.

"Reroute course to signal location, maximum speed."

The rover paused a moment as if considering whether that was in fact an option. Finally, it said, "Rerouting will end billable hours and may incur a charge to your account, do you wish to proceed?"

Gan pounded a fist on the control panel. "Ice billable hours, this is clearly an emergency. We're the only other living things for a hundred miles."

The rover paused. "Command not recognized."

Stupid dammed cheapass machine. Gan roared his frustration.

"Command not recognized."

He took a deep, shuddering breath, trying to get his frustration under control. "Yes, billing accepted," he snapped.

The rover paused its forward progress, made a slow right turn, and headed off at a tangent and at higher speed without further comment.

Gan scrambled out of the driver's seat towards the back to check the emergency supplies, and hoped that whoever was out there didn't freeze to death before he arrived.

Cresting the ridge twenty minutes later, Gan spotted the downed craft by the light of the many fires it had left burning across the crater. It had been the kind of ship that wasn't rated for atmosphere at all and was used for ultra-high priority packages like medication or stock reports, designed for pure speed. Entry into even the thin stuff that passed for atmosphere on Ganymede had torn it apart. Still, the pilot had done an excellent job putting it down. While the rear of the ship was in tiny pieces, stretching for a mile across the crater, the front was still intact, barely, and embedded in the wall of the crater like a thorn.

Gan directed the rover up the side of the crater until the tilt warning was screaming at him at full volume, then he had to fight with the rover to take manual control.

"Fire warning, cannot proceed." The rover rolled to a stop.

Gan slammed his foot on the speed control.

Nothing happened.

"What now?"

"Maximum distance is one hundred meters from an active fire. This is for your safety." Touchstone intoned.

More like protecting company assets, he thought. He didn't have time for this. The pilot over there didn't have time for this.

Despite the ice and lack of oxygen to burn, the cockpit was covered in nearly invisible blue flames. He wasn't nearly close enough, but he didn't have time to argue with the damn thing's programming. This would have to do. He pulled the levers to set the stabilizers and went for his exosuit.

Programming aside, whoever had done the physical design for the standard exploration rover had been a damned clever bastard. His going-outside suit docked into the side of the rover like a human shaped glove, with a clever lift to keep it above the surface so its boots didn't drag in the ice when he was driving. In an emergency, he could jump through the inside access, shove his legs and arms in the slots, hit the emergency seal and drop off the side of the rover. During his one company-mandated practice session he'd achieved an acceptable time of twenty seconds. This time he was detached from the rover and running across the ice in less than eight.

He ran a hundred yards to the cockpit, scrambling up the steep slope for the last bit. It was harder in the suit, even with reduced gravity.

When he reached the lock, it was a mess of melting and reforming ice. Fires at the top of the ship caused a rivulet of water which had refrozen right across the emergency handle. It took several strong blows with his emergency case to crack it. He quickly pulled the handle before the ice could reform. The hatch detached in his hand, revealing not an airlock but a nightmare's worth of crumpled hallway and torn paneling.

Damn. Well maybe the pilot had had time to put on his mask.

He cranked his speaker and shortwave radio both to full blast. "Anybody alive in there?"

A thudding sound from the direction of the cockpit.

He hustled towards the sounds of life, clawing his way through dropped wiring relays and a gap that looked empty but his suit insisted was filled with invisible fuel-flame.

He grabbed the fire extinguisher, somehow still in its slot in the wall (*good engineering that*) and grinned slightly as he pulled the pin, aimed, and threw it into the gap. The extinguisher exploded, filling the gap with fire suppression foam. His grin got bigger. He'd always wanted to do that.

He ducked past the last of the hall and got to the cabin door. It was off its hinges, despite being designed as a last-ditch defense against the vacuum of space. He tore it aside to find the cockpit almost intact.

But the pilot in his chair was completely still and the copilot's seat was empty.

"Hello?" he called out from the doorway.

The head whipped around, sterling gray eyes spearing him in place for a fraction of a second before rolling in frantic need.

Gan hustled forward. "I've got extra oxy," he said, "how're you doing?" He glanced at the indicator on the flight board. Low.

The pilot tried to wave him away with one hand. Something was wrong with the other: it hung limp, probably broken.

"It's OK," Gan said, "I'm here to help."

The hand waving grew frantic, interspersed with wheezing.

Gan dodged the ineffectual gestures to pop off the internal oxy-mask and thrust the emergency mask over the pilot's face. He grabbed the waving hand and shoved it against the mask, saying "Hold that. I'll see what's got you trapped."

The pilot's eyes rolled in their sockets as he dragged deep, wheezing breaths through the emergency mask.

"There you go buddy, just keep breathing." He patted the shoulder nearest to him and felt hard muscle beneath the thin sponge of the pilot's suit. Lots of muscle.

Gan shook his head to clear the distraction (adrenaline could make you notice the damnedest things), and hit the release for the pilot's straps. Nothing. He hit it again and tugged hard. Jammed. He pulled out his working knife sheathed at his waist, and the pilot's eyes went huge, thrashing against the restraints.

"Relax buddy, it's for the straps. Let's get you out of here before you freeze to death." Gan could already see frost forming in the man's stubble where the oxy mask didn't quite fit. He had minutes — maybe — before hypothermia started where oxygen deprivation had left off.

He slashed the first of the straps holding the man in his seat.

"Thanks," the pilot wheezed, a little logic returning to his eyes, "You have to go. Leave me. It's not safe."

"You left all your fuel on the other side of the crater," Gan said, tearing at the next strap, "We've got a little time, but not much. Can you stand?"

"No. There's no time, they'll be coming soon." The pilot's eyes were wide with panic and he thrashed again against his restraints.

"Shh," Gan said, patting that muscled shoulder again. "What's your name pilot?"

"Zeus," the man hissed.

"Really?" Gan asked. He'd always suspected that fate had a shitty sense of humor. "You can call me Gan"

"Gan, please, you have to leave." Zeus's breath was getting shorter in the mask. "They'll be here soon for me."

They who? There wasn't another station for a hundred miles and the radio was out. "I'm not leaving without you," Gan persisted, "You can meet your friends when you're safe." His knife slicing through the last of the webbing.

The man shot out of his bucket seat, forcing Gan to back up a step. At least his legs weren't broken, part of Gan's brain babbled, because the pilot was enormous. Zeus's knees buckled as he fell to the floor of the cabin, shivering uncontrollably.

Gan scrambled to open the thermal blanket from the emergency kit using its activating pull tab. Heat radiated from the smart fabric, enough to feel it even through his insulating gloves. He threw the thing around Zeus's shoulders. "Who else is onboard?" Gan asked, getting his arm under Zeus's and levering him to his feet. That trick only worked because of the lower gravity and Gan's earth-grown muscles. It didn't look right and it certainly felt ridiculous.

"Nobody, else," Zeus said, "Piloting solo."

Gan blinked. So, he'd rescued an idiot or a daredevil. Probably for the best, though. He didn't think he was up for a second trip. Earth muscles or no, he'd just spent the last month basically on his butt.

"Let's get you someplace warm," Gan said.

Zeus nodded, allowing himself to be towed towards the door and safety.

Gan hustled him out of the wreckage and across a short stretch of ice as fast as Zeus's tired legs could move. Despite the warmth of the enveloping thermal blanket, he was still shivering uncontrollably. His teeth had joined in by the time they reached the airlock of a bog-standard lunar transport rover, the Aquarius corp logo on its side. That was ok then, his uncle owned Aquarius. Zeus was pretty sure his uncle wanted him alive as a counterweight to his father.

At least he couldn't think of a reason why his uncle would fund the pirates that had ambushed and fired on his ship. No, that was much more his father's style. The pirates had killed a number of Zeus's staff before his guards could stuff him on the courier and force him to launch. Zeus had taunted the pirates from the courier, hoping to draw them off, and he'd been marginally successful. He'd been aiming for the station in orbit around Ganymede when the limpet mines exploded, putting him on a crash course for the opposite side of the moon.

His rescuer rushed Zeus straight to the rover's airlock, practically stuffing him inside the tiny space giving him no time to contemplate any further. The man went so far as to lift him over the edge of the door when Zeus's trembling knees locked at the wrong moment. Strong, for a little guy.

Zeus collapsed against the interior wall of the airlock as it began its hissing and beeping routine. At least his boots were well insulated. He didn't think he'd be losing a toe to this misadventure, though his collar bone was broken for sure. Setting it was going to be a pain.

At that thought, Zeus glanced over at his rescuer. What was he doing out here anyway? Exactly in the right place to rescue him? There just weren't that many people on the surface of Ganymede. Anyone smart was up in the station. So, was he an assassin too? No. He could have just let the cold and lack of oxygen do their work, or killed him with that knife when he was stuck in his seat. What then? If he wasn't here to kill him, what was he doing out here on the wrong side of the moon?

Zeus's limbs had started to tingle like they'd been set on fire by the time the airlock finally finished its routine. The feeling was a welcome distraction from the doubts whirling in his head. The airlock dinged, and the door snapped open: not on the standard rover living space, but on a cave apparently formed entirely of sheets of paper. Paper covered every available surface, overlapping on the walls, hanging from the ceiling, in drifts on the floor.

Every piece of paper was completely covered with drawings, writing, plans and sketches. They weren't print outs. They were all done by hand, with the unmistakable lines of actual graphite and ink on paper, with scribbles and notes in the margins and even lines connecting across the pages.

He'd been rescued by a madman.

On closer inspection, a very talented one.

A section of drawings nearest the airlock were done in vibrant colors, a panoply of places and people and machines. He recognized one as a view of the main street of Ganymede station, but from above, as if the artist was outside the dome looking in. The perspective was better executed than most work he'd seen at the Mars Sojourner academie where he'd done his art year. The sense of longing, of being outside and looking in, was palpable.

Another hissing noise, then a voice, "Welcome back Engineer. Overage charges will begin in one hour." And echoing from the suitlock door as it opened, "What part of emergency don't you understand, you rusted wreck?"

A body wriggled and pushed from the square hatch near the floor until it emerged backwards to flop on the deck of the cabin, spilling a short mop of sweat-curled brunette hair against the silver floor. Long-lashed brown eyes spotted him from across the room. "Oh, you already made it in."

Zeus blinked stupidly. His rescuer was beautiful.

The other man wriggled his legs out of the legs of the suit, which gave Zeus a very good look at his lithe musculature. The protective skinsuit most people wore under clothing and spacesuits alike left absolutely nothing to the imagination, and even so the silvery gray tone of this one seemed to outline the edge of every muscle. It made him want to change the color of his own to match, but gray was so plebeian his didn't even have the color.

His savior blinked at him, "Sorry for the mess," he gestured around the room, "It's been just me for the past month."

Zeus felt like he'd been staring too long. He tried to cover by offering his hand, but that caused a spike of pain to shoot from his shoulder straight down his spine.

"Ah, you're hurt," his savior said. He jumped to his feet in one smooth motion, a frown creasing his sculpted face. "Let's get you over to the med panel."

Zeus shook himself and looked around the rover's cabin for the med unit. The sparse furniture typical to a rover could just be made out underneath drifts of paper. A tiny table bordered an even tinier meal prep unit scattered with partially finished meal packets. The handle to a closet-sized door was just visible on the wall. A single messy sleeping nook filled with a tangled nest of blankets was the only surface devoid of paper, and even it held a drawing pad. There was no sign of a med unit anywhere.

He tried taking a step forward, but his leg filled with pins and needles refused to support his weight and he stumbled and fell.

"Woah there." Strong hands caught him and held him up despite the height difference and his bulk.

His rescuer guided him two steps and a half turn over to sit on the bed, where a med panel was rapidly blinking and beeping to life in the nook's ceiling. Why did the damn machines have to make so much noise? His head and his shoulder were killing him. Strong hands steadied him as he sat on the edge of the bed, then they shielded his head as he eased himself flat.

"Thanks," Zeus muttered, exhaustion sank into his bones like an increase in gravity.

His rescuer sat one hip on the edge of the bed, leaning over Zeus as he fiddled with a panel on the inside wall, elegant hands moving like he was conducting an orchestra.

A sharp pain in Zeus's neck presaged a wash of coolness spreading from his shoulder.

"So what's a man like you doing on an iceball like this?" Zeus asked.

Gan glanced down at him, face and blue eyes highlighted by the light from the panel. "Was that a pickup line?"

Zeus blinked, suddenly feeling exceptionally stupid. "No. Yes? Would you like it to be?"

Gan laughed and patted his knee with the hand that wasn't inputting directions into the panel. "Let's just get you healed up. There'll be plenty of time to talk since you're stuck with me until I get the radio tower fixed."

Zeus smiled back. Something about that sounded wrong but the cessation of pain and the adrenaline leaving his system was making him loopy.

"Besides, you haven't even thanked me for saving your life yet," Gan arched an eyebrow at him. The med panel went into a blinding whir of activity.

Zeus thought he got out a whispered, "Thank you Gan," before the machine's anesthetic field pushed him down the slide into sleep.

Gan contemplated the amazing, impossible form of the man in his bed. What had he been thinking? Piloting alone? He had to be extremely good, or he had a death wish.

He picked up his notebook and pencils from where he'd swept them off the bed and sat at the table, the only other seat in the living area now that the bed was occupied.

The real question was, what next?

Normally he'd call emergency services and they'd send a ship down from the station. But they were out of range from the station now and wouldn't be able to call until he fixed the radio.

Well it wasn't like they'd run out of food, though they'd have to hot bunk it until they could get back if the station didn't send a ship. His mind served him an image of them sharing the bunk instead and he firmly shoved it away. No. No getting involved until he paid off his indenture. That had to be his first and only focus. He wasn't going to live his life like the other engineers at the station. Working forever without any progress to show for it. Old and still as deep in their indenture as they were twenty years ago. Grateful for the bare pittance of free time the company granted them and never dreaming of anything bigger than the next drone race.

The idle sketch he'd started had become the pilot's face as he leaned over him in the bunk. Eyes wide and dreamy, long hair spread in waves across the pillow. What kind of pilot had long hair anyway?

The rover gave a whiny beep, startling him from his reverie. "Overage charges beginning. Please return to scheduled route to end charges."

Crap!

Gan threw himself towards the cabin and the controls.

He got the rover moving again, pulled up the med display and tossed it to a side panel. It looked like Zeus was going to be OK. It was showing a broken collar bone, already under repair, and a good deal of light frostbite from the cold. Nothing the med unit wasn't equipped to handle.

He gazed out at the endless wasteland of ice and stone as the rover moved back towards its programmed route. It might be nice to have somebody else around for a few days.

Gan woke to the impossible smell of pancakes. He blinked his eyes open and peeled his face off the plastic of the armrest. The rover was already parked at the .

How long had he been asleep?

Something thunked behind him, and he almost startled out of his seat.

He glanced around the side of the chair into the cabin, only to see large, blanket-clad hips shimmying back towards him

"Wha?" Yesterday's pilot spun around, turning a thousand-watt smile on Gan.

Woah. That smile was... was something.

"Oh good you're up, finally." Zeus was holding a large plate of genuine looking pancakes, gently steaming: golden brown batter, a pat of butter, they even had syrup on them.

"Morning," Gan replied automatically, then, "How the fuck did you make those pancakes?"

Zeus turned up the wattage on his smile. "It was a challenge, I'll admit. But any guy who saves my life gets pancakes the next morning." Zeus handed him the plate.

Gan's jaw wanted to drop. In the four weeks he'd been in this bucket he'd only ever gotten the meal prepper to produce rubbery eggs, soggy toast and something it claimed was oatmeal that his parents wouldn't have fed their pigs. Speaking of which: definitely no bacon.

Zeus blinked at him, "You've never heard of meal hacking?"

"No?"

Zeus turned that smile on him again. "It's simple. All you have to do is open up the components and put them together yourself." He gestured at the table where a pile of plastic boxes sat in front of a spread of machine parts: his meal prep unit, broken into its individual components. Yep, there was the heating surface, and that bit there had to be the mixer, and that cup-shaped thing was from the dispensing unit.

Gan's sleep fogged brain felt a rush of unease. "You opened the unit?" Why hadn't he ever thought of that?

"What?" Zeus looked confused. "It's simple. Everybody does it." Zeus spun back over to the table and began tossing spoons of powder into the cup.

"Look, the pancakes are simple. You take the protein powder, milk powder, egg powder, and sugar syrup. Add a little water and mix." He took a big dollop of goo and slung it onto the surface of the warming plate. Gan stared fascinated as it began to bubble almost instantly. After a moment, Zeus used a knife to flip the thing over. "Cook it on the warming plate and voila." A few seconds later another pancake landed on Gan's spare plate.

Gan didn't know whether to be impressed that Zeus had gone to the trouble just to make him breakfast or just annoyed with himself for not thinking of it before.

Because it had to be a charge, his backbrain told him. A large one. In fact he'd specifically seen it mentioned in his prep kit for the trip. So why wasn't the rover screaming its head off?

"What happened to the AI?"

"I'd hardly call it that" Zeus scoffed. "It was annoying so I turned it off." He started cooking another round of batter on the hotplate.

Gan's jaw did hang open at that. That was brilliant a part of his mind insisted. The rest of him was calculating in horror. Depending on how long the thing's speakers had been disabled, it was possible he was now *losing money* on this trip. And with that, the rest of his brain caught up and noticed what had been bothering him since he'd woken up:

His papers were gone.

All his work.

How dare he. How *DARE* he.

"Where are my drawings?" Gan demanded.

Zeus took a step back. "Woah, woah. I had to get them out of the way to get to the unit. They're on the bed." He gestured with the spatula.

Gan tossed his plate to the table and rushed to the bed, where a pile of papers was strewn in a disorganized heap.

He rifled through them, panic closing his throat. If they were torn or damaged or anything...

He took a deep, shuddering breath. They were all here. He sniffed. His eyes burned. All safe.

Zeus was looking at him like he was afraid Gan would explode. Zeus took a hesitant step forward, then went down on one knee by his side. "Hey. I'm sorry. I didn't want to get any batter on them and then I got to looking at them." He put a hand on the bed by Gan's knee. "They're amazing by the way. I love your art style."

Gan sucked in a shuddering breath, struggling to get his breathing back under control. "You like my art style?" He blinked at that. Maybe the pilot hadn't spotted what was hidden in them.

"I do. I especially like this one." He held out the pad of paper with last night's rough sketch on it.

Gan's face heated like a small sun. He snatched for it but the pilot held it away out of his grasp.

"You weren't supposed to see that!"

"Why not? I think it's the best portrait anyone's ever done of me." He ducked down so he could look Gan in the eye from where Gan was trying to hide his embarrassment. "You're really talented, and I've seen *a lot* of art so I should know. Why the heck is someone as talented as you are out here instead of working at one of the academies?"

Why wasn't he working as an artist? Like that was ever an option for an indentured farm boy born on Earth.

Maybe he didn't understand. Zeus was a pilot. Which meant he had to have been born free. People who owned their own lives never really understood how it was for the rest of humanity. Like he'd ever had a choice.

"I'm indentured." Gan gulped, and wondered why this was so hard to talk about.

"So? Lots of people are indentured."

Gan's mind stuttered to a stop. This guy really was an idiot then. How could he not understand.

"I mean, it's just money right?"

Just money.

Just money.

Gan laughed and it sounded a little insane even to him. He waved wildly with the pile of papers in his hand. "I'm five years paying off my indenture. If I do that I'll be the first person in my family since forever to break out. I'm. This. Close," he thrust his hand, thumb and pointer fingers almost touching, in front of Zeus's nose. "Do you have any idea how dangerous that is? What they'll do to try to keep me on the hook?"

"Any ideas, ANY IDEAS, I have before I'm paid off belong to the company. Any improvement. Anything that isn't," he made finger quotes, "personal artistic expression. So that there represents the only thing in the entire world I actually own. Not my clothes. Not my toothbrush. Not the air I breathe or the quiet in my own head. Just those papers. And I can't even sell them because then they'd be commodities and the company could claim them too." Gan glanced at the disassembled prep unit. "And now I'm going to get charged for that, and for turning the AI off, and probably for diverting to pick you up, so I'll be adding another six months on my payments and stuck here going stir crazy." The tears started leaking on their own and he hid his face in his hands. "I'm sorry," he sobbed, "I'm not sure why..."

"Shhh," Zeus rose and sat beside him, putting an arm around his shoulders. "Shhh. It'll be ok."

"No it won't. I'm going crazy out here."

"You're not crazy." Zeus told him, he reached out with his other hand, snagged the plate of pancakes, and shoved it under his nose. "Here. Eat something. It will help."

Gan picked up the plate and took a reflexive bite. It was good.

Really good.

He took another bite and another. Zeus handed him a napkin to wipe his mouth and streaming eyes. Their fingers touched and Gan jerked his away as if burned.

"So where are we anyway?" Zeus asked.

"Where are we?" turned out to be a hundred kilometers from where he'd crashed, Zeus discovered, as he carefully fed the engineer more pancakes.

They were in a deep crater called Ninlil that was home to a major atmosphere generation plant. The thing was huge, a giant tower sending up plumes of gasses, increasing the density of Ganymede's atmosphere one one-hundredth of a pascal at a time in an attempt to make the surface habitable by more than robots and crazy engineers.

Zeus had never considered that an engineer out here might be indentured. He could see how it made sense, from the business side, if an indentured worker died out here then they weren't paying death benefits. But what a life. Who the hell charged for peace and quiet? Well, it sounded like something his father would do.

"So what's the plan from here?" Zeus asked casually. He'd had a bit of time to think when he woke up in the med pod-cum-sleeping chamber. If he could just get up to the station, he might still have a chance to meet with his contact at Aquarius corp and recruit their help.

"Well, I have to fix the radio tower here," Gan said, calmer now that they were talking about his work. "Once I do that we can use it to call for a transport for you. That will get you a ship back to the station, and from there you can get on with your life. Or they could ask me to get you home, in which case it'll be about twenty-four days in the rover to the elevator at Tros."

Zeus had an instant's vision of him and the engineer cuddled up in the single bed together. Talking about those amazing drawings, him spilling all his troubles to Gan, and them coming up with some brilliant plan to defeat his father and release him and his siblings from the terror of his plans.

But that wasn't going to happen. He was on his own, his father had made sure of that.

"Station to pilot? Come in Zeus?" Gan said, waving a hand in front of Zeus's face. "Are you OK? The med box didn't say anything about a concussion."

"Sorry," Zeus said, blinking the engineer's face back into focus. "Why don't you clean this up while I take a shower, and then we can get moving."

Gan's jaw slipped open. Why didn't he clean up? Who the hell did this pilot think he was? Gan debated whether it would be worth telling the guy off. Well, no. The faster he got the emergency comm in the station back online, the faster he could get rid of his unexpected guest.

He fumed while he cleaned up the partially used cartons, none of which could go back now that they'd been opened. What was he going to do with a month's worth of egg powder? He'd have to put in completely new boxes ahead of schedule. Which would cost him - almost three days more work.

Cleanup done, he picked up his drawings from the bed and stacked them neatly into his storage envelope. Putting them back in order so he could return to work on the return trip would be a pain in the ass, but it was better than letting Zeus have a closer look at them. He had already noticed too much.

Zeus stepped out of the bathroom, golden hair fuzzed by the dryers into a halo, backlit by the ridiculously bright light. "Do you have an extra - "

"No." Gan interrupted. "Get your boots on. I'm already behind and I'm not leaving you here to get into anything else. You can compose a report to your employer while I deal with whatever is blocking the comms here."

Gan slipped over to the airlock to check that the holding bay had been pressurized for work. If there was one thing the atmosphere plant had in abundance, it was air. At least he wouldn't be charged for gassing the place up to work in comfort. He'd heard rumors from guys who worked for other companies that they had to work completely suited most of the time, because their employers were too cheap to keep their outbuildings at a workable air pressure (let alone with marginally breathable atmosphere and temperature). Aquarius never let them forget that it was a kind and benevolent employer. Hah.

Gan gave Zeus a look as he came to join him at the airlock.

"What?" Zeus asked.

"Uh, grab an airmask?" Gan said, pointedly glancing at the case by the door.

"Why?" Zues peered at the indicators again. "It says we've got air out there."

Gan sighed. "Look, I don't know how it works on a spaceship, but down here when we're about to enter a damaged facility we take emergency equipment. The radio tower, a basic and hardwired function of this installation, is down. We have no idea what caused that. So you'll forgive me if I'm just a little skeptical of anything the software is telling me. Humor me and grab a mask." Gan finished with his breath coming harder. What right did the pilot have to look like a kicked puppy?

Zeus took one of the breather masks from its case.

Passing through the airlock, Gan suppressed a spurt of amusement at Zeus's startled jump as the lights came up on the garage. Row after row of repair-bots stirred, car-sized boxy bodies with six icepick legs, and two smaller manipulator arms below the many-faceted "eye stalk" cameras that let the robot perceive its surroundings.

"Good morning team," Gan said softly. The nearest few bots turned in place, several ton bodies prancing in place and articulated heads cocking at him.

They chirped together in childlike voices, "Hello Gan San!"

One of the bots twirled to face Zeus and exclaimed "Gan San, you brought us a new friend?"

"Yes! Yes, Zeus is a friend. Very friendly." The bot's cutesy act was just that: an act. Each of the bots had lasers and manipulator claws, which could shear through ice as hard as steel.

"Welcome Zeus San!" the crowd chirped together.

Zeus, a little pale, said "Uh, hello." He whispered to Gan, "Are they…?"

"The Aquarius 5c autonomous work unit is a marvel of Japanese engineering." Gan kept his face as straight as possible, but he suspected the suggestion of a smirk leaked through. "I'm sure it's a coincidence that they look like chibi crabs and talk like four-year-olds. At least they're smarter than the rover."

"Uh huh." Zeus looked around. "Why so many?"

About a hundred of the bots filled the garage to capacity in neat rows.

"You know," Gan said, "I have no idea. I mean they built the place, but you'd think the company would have moved most of them elsewhere. Maybe this was the last extraction plant built. Or maybe it was cheaper to just leave them here. They each have a little fusion reactor onboard, so it's not like you want them close to anything important, right?"

Zeus leaned away from the bot that was still inspecting him with it's extended eyestalks. "Yeah, that could be ba—" Zeus eyed the bot and changed mid-sentence "—interesting"

Gan laughed and clapped his hands twice, calling the attention of all the bots in the room. "Let's get started. Who knows what happened to the radio tower?"

A bot on an inside row began dancing in place, with a grinding sound that said joints were out of alignment, "Ohh! I know, I know. I saw it happen Gan San."

Gan scanned the crowd. There were at least three crabs missing from that row, the spaces glaring once he looked for them.

Gan walked through the rows, the bots prancing aside to make room for him, Zeus trailing along and speeding up as they moved back into place. Reaching the bot that had spoken, he sucked in a breath. Two of its legs were crushed to unusability. The others were torn to shreds. The bot's paint job was a mess too, with a huge dent in the body's outer shell.

"What happened to you, my pretty?" he crooned.

"It was awful!" the bot wailed, "It came out of the sky and hit everybody and the tower. And I called and called but nobody could hear me."

"Aww," Gan patted the bot on its shell, "You poor thing. You've really been through the wringer. Come over to the repair station and show me the video." He continued his walk through to the far side of the garage, trailed by Zeus and — joints screeching and wailing with each step — the injured bot.

The controls for the station reproduced his rover almost exactly, courtesy of replaceable parts and company "efficiencies". Instead of the windshield, it had a huge screen and extra software to coordinate the work of all the crabs.

Gan settled into the bucket of the control seat, with Zeus peering over his shoulder. "Let's see what's up. Send the incident file to my screen, buddy?"

The injured crab made a little uploading trill, and a video opened up on the huge screen. An exterior view of the station, with the spire of the radio tower coming up on the right-hand side. As they watched, the pseudo greyscale of the snowscape gained a yellow tinge. As the bot turned to examine the new light source, it crashed into the tower, exploding in a huge yellow fireball that raced towards the camera before knocking the bot end over end and blacking out the video.

"Wow, there's some bad luck," Gan mused. His fingers flew, starting to pull up a parts list. "What are the chances of a direct hit by a meteor? At least—" he started, but a glance at Zeus showed he'd gone as gray as the ice outside. "What's wrong?"

Zeus let out a huge breath, like he'd been holding it since they'd seen the video. "I don't think that was a meteor."

"Well what the hell was it then?"

"I think—" Zeus started.

A buzzer on the console interrupted him. The radar?

"Huh, someone's on a landing path for the station," Gan said, pulling up the radar image. "We haven't sent out a signal yet. Was someone else around to see you crash?"

"They're not here to help," Zeus said, voice resigned.

"And how do you know that?"

Zeus sighed, reaching over to back up the video still on the screen. "Because that's a missile, not a meteor. My dad sent them. They're here to kill me."

A small screen flicked to life, covering half of the windshield view. It showed a man in a dark gray exosuit without markings, his helmet held under his arm and a nasty looking gun slung on a strap over his shoulder. His face looked surprisingly urbane, lacking the expected villainous eye scar, or villainous beard, or moustache. He looked like somebody you could pass in a station and not blink twice. Forgettable.

"What do we have here?" The man said. "Have you called to beg for your life? Or are you perhaps calling to keep us from killing the nice engineer that picked you up? Ganymede, was it? Ironic that."

Ganymede, huh? So that was Gan's full name. Zeus pulled his attention back to the man proposing to kill him.

"Give yourself up, come quietly, and we'll make it a nice 'recovery' facility instead of the dumps they keep your brother Mars at."

Zeus exaggerated his sigh for the camera. "Just how many of us does Dad think he can use this trick on?"

The man laughed. There was the evil. It was a laugh like a trickle of ice water down the back of your suit.

"As many as needed, I think. He's already got a better plan for your sister. She's got that so convenient weak heart, you know."

Red closed in from the edges of his vision, and his voice dropped half a register. "You leave her out of this."

The man laughed again, and propped his head on a hand. "What are you going to do about it, pretty boy? You're trapped in that little ice cave. One missile and — Boom! — you're toast. So why don't you just skip the threats, and beg for your life?"

Gan sat astounded as the whole story tumbled out of Zeus. His real name was Zeus Josephson. Heir to Olympian Industries, Zeus Josephson. Olympian Industries, who ran half the industrial works in the solar system, with a few hundred other offerings on the side. They owned half of Jupiter and almost all of Saturn. His infuriating pilot had probably never had to clean anything in his life. Which explained a bit.

What it didn't explain was why his father had sent assassins in the first place.

"Yeah, that's a long story," Zeus said. "Basically, my father pissed off my grandpa by trying to have him declared incompetent. So grandpa got back by willing the company to dad's kids. All of us. Dad only controls the company in a trust for us. Except my two older siblings both had 'accidents' before they could reach their majorities. Now one's in a mental institution on Earth, and the other is permanently bouncing between rehab centers."

"That's fucked up," Gan said.

Zeus rolled his eyes and swept his hair back out of his eyes. "That's my family. Dad stopped having kids when Gramps died, but there're still eight of us."

Gan considered it. It jived with the rumors he'd heard about the crazy and reclusive family that controlled half of everything between here and Earth

"And so your dad's sending assassins to kill you so that you don't reach your majority and take over the entirety of Olympus industries, basically becoming the richest man in the solar system."

"Not the richest. I'd hold a lot of the company in trust for my younger siblings."

And didn't that bit sound rehearsed. So he'd only be nearly the richest. Like it made a difference.

"How can I help?" Gan asked.

Zeus froze. Shook himself.

"What do you mean help?" His voice rose to a squeak. "You stay out of the way, I don't want anybody else getting hurt over this." He stalked to edge of the repair area and stalked back.

Gan considered it, "Nah. That's not gonna fly. How are you going to beat him? Your dad I mean."

"Beat him?" Zeus said it slowly, like he'd never really considered it. "He's got trillions of dollars and a system wide industrial base to draw from. You don't beat that."

"Yeah, but you can't just roll over for him. At least make him fight for it. Think of all the good you could do with that kind of money."

Zeus started pacing the room, the crab bot's eyes following him back and forth. Gan looked at the bot, then at the garage where line after line of bots waited patiently on his word.

"If…" Gan said, a thought slowly accreting weight like an asteroid, "If I could think of a way to get you — get us — out of this…" he said, drawing out each word, "you're rich enough to buy my indenture right? Hell, you could probably buy it with your pocket money right now."

Zeus's head snapped up, his eyes wild. He huffed out a breath.

"I only have money if I inherit," he glanced at the radar on the screen, the dot blinking closer and closer, "and right now it looks like that's never gonna happen."

"But if you inherit? If you actually beat his ass? What then?"

"You figure that out and I'll buy out your indenture, sure."

Gan raised an eyebrow. "Buy out my indenture and get me an engineering workshop. Or set me up in your R&D department."

Zeus raised an eyebrow at him, "You good enough for that?"

Gan gave him a smile like a little boy hellbent on mischief. "Consider this my interview." Gan held out his hand. "Shake on it?"

Zeus eyed the hand. "You really think you can?"

Gan gave him a savage grin. "Shake and find out."

Zeus grinned back, and slapped his hand into Gan's. "You bet."

Gan looked at the battered crab bot, who was watching them with obvious interest. "Did you record that?"

"Yes Gan San," the bot said, "I'm streaming a record to your rover."

Spinning around, Gan started wildly tapping commands into the console, then spun back to look at the astonished Zeus.

"We've got still got twenty minutes. Tell me everything you know about these bastards."

The sound of crabs warming up their joints echoed through the cavern.

Zeus's grin grew wider. Then he started talking.

Zeus sat at the table of the rover, wondering how it had only been three hours since they'd been sitting here having pancakes. Gan had asked him to pick up only one thing from the rover before the plan kicked off. The sheaf of paper drawings he'd shoved into a bag on the bed. Now they were spread out over the table, a panoply of people and places and random scribbled lines.

He reached for the one showing him in the bed, and his fingers brushed one sheet with a streetlamp over another with a person's face. The brushy lines on the edges briefly overlapped, creating a third image visible through the thin pages. Well damn. He looked closer.

The only thing he really owned.

The rover screeched at him. A screen popped on showing the last crab bot disappearing over the ridge.

Showtime.

He swept all the papers into a stack and back into the bag.

On another screen the assassin's ship screamed in on its final approach, at an angle where the rover's ridiculously underpowered radio could reach it without the signal boost from a tower.

He wiped the grin off his face and ordered the stupid AI to make a connection.

"Well, little boy," the pirate said, sneering at the screen, "Are you ready to beg me for your life?"

Zeus smiled a little. "Funny you should say that. I was just about to say the same thing."

The humor went out of the man on the other end of the line. "What?"

Zeus calmly hit a button on his console. A recording sent itself across the field, to the assassin's ship.

The man looked away from the camera, a flash of confusion crossing his face.

"The dots you're watching," Zeus said, "are a radar recording of ten Aquarius 5c maintenance robots on randomly programmed courses to the five nearest broadcast centers, where they'll shout your plans to anyone who will hear them, including—" the dots changed their trajectories from straight lines to random jogs, "—a recording of our conversation, which I've just sent them."

The man's eyes widened, then narrowed. "Nobody will believe you."

Zeus smiled. "They don't have to believe me. I've added financial records, and other bits and pieces. Including records of Dad's payments to you for what you did to my brother." He shook a data stick at the camera. "You really should have asked for more. I got more than that for pocket money in college."

The man's face went apoplectic before he abruptly severed the connection.

"Well I think that's well and truly pissed him off," Zeus muttered. As he watched, eight figures in black and white boiled out of the rear of the ship. Quickly, they ran across the frozen landing field towards the dig site and the garage.

"Good," Gan said in his ear. "We need them pissed off, not thinking. Get moving, I'm starting step two."

Lights flashed on the outside of the installation. The figures in gray kept running, but they unlimbered long matte-black weapons from their backs. One of the doors to the garage began to rise, and out poured a flood of the crab-bots.

Zeus savored the surprised reactions of the mercenaries for half a second, then grabbed the small bag from where he'd dropped it at his feet and scrambled for the suit built into the side of the rover.

The fit was *tight* but the suits were designed to accommodate different occupants in case one suit broke or someone got injured, or any number of other problems. It also had a healthy dose of deeply funky living-in-a-gym-sock smell, which all such suits acquired over time, no matter how effective the cleaning system. Still, it was simple to operate. Overboots constricted to fit his feet, gloves tightened on his hands, and constricting bands cinched the whole thing close to him to start the movements that would augment his skinsuit's ability to help his circulation. Not that he needed help at the moment. His heart was racing.

With a final hiss, the back lock closed and popped him free from the rover. A single crab bot was waiting for him, bowed low so he could climb on.

This has to be the stupidest thing in the long list of stupid things I've done, Zeus thought as he clung to the leading edge of the crab's cargo deck.

"You're behind," Gan muttered in his ear. "All secure?"

"Yeah," Zeus said. He took a deep breath, "Punch it."

The crab took off at full speed, sending a shooting pain through his recently healed shoulder. They popped around the rover to see the dig field scattered with downed bots, but the majority still advanced on the group of mercenaries.

The crab he was on sped up until everything nearby became a blur.

Zeus watched. At least two of the mercenaries ran out of bullets, most of which bounced off the tough construction robots. The other six mercenaries were retreating, but not faster than the bots could advance. As his bot got closer, the line of mercenaries braced for impact. The advancing line of bots swarmed closer, until just before they made contact...

They split.

Half the line went right, half the line went left, thundering past the little squad and straight for their ship.

Hah! Suckers.

In their astonishment they almost missed him, as his bot joined the tail end of the swarm thundering past. He longed to give them a mocking wave, but his fingers were starting to cramp.

The vanguard of the swarm got to the ship just as the engines were starting back up. As they reached the ship they jumped, landing on the fuselage, causing the whole thing to rock on its landing struts.

The pilots ought to have been shitting themselves right now, which was his cue. "Put me through," he said.

He heard a chime, Gan's signal that he was now broadcasting.

"Attention pirates," he said, "I am impounding your ship. Surrender and throw down your weapons if you ever want to leave this ice ball again."

Silence.

Then, over his earpiece a voice more annoyed than scared, "Why the hell should we do that?"

The bots began working at the engine hatches. Not ideal, but they had the equipment and — surprisingly — the programming to disassemble the entire thing, if they had to.

He put as much confidence as he could muster into his voice.

"Well first, the bots just began disassembling your main engine hatch. You're not going anywhere if they get to your fuel line."

One of the Crabs waved a claw in triumph, holding the part he'd singled out for them to acquire first.

"Second," he said, looking back at the mercenaries tearing their way back towards their ship, "Each of these robots with me carries a mini fusion reactor with enough fuel to blow us all to kingdom come. And my friend back in the base is an engineer with all the override codes. He's probably feeling pretty desperate, since you threatened to kill him too. And he did say that he'd always wanted to make one of these explode. You know how engineers get right?"

A line of eight of the remaining robots advanced back towards the mercenaries. Looking small on the ice field, they threw down their weapons.

The crabs accelerated and snatched them up.

The pilot emerged from the ship with his hands up.

Zeus cracked a smile. He was going to buy Gan the biggest most beautiful workshop ever.

The ambush was sprung just inside the pirate ship's airlock.

Huge arms swept Gan up into a giant bear hug and whirled him around like a rag doll. "You beautiful, glorious, brilliant man." Zeus was shouting in his ear as he struggled to breathe through crushed ribs despite his respirator.

"Lemme go!" he wheezed. The arms released and he dropped to the floor. He stood panting and looking up at Zeus.

"Did everything go well with the pirates?" Zeus asked.

"Yep. They're all packed into the rover and headed back to the station via the slow route."

Zeus laughed, his face lit up. "I wish them joy trying to fiddle with the AI."

"Knowing Aquarius they'll probably try to charge them for the trip," Gan said with a twist to his mouth.

"Here are your drawings." Zeus held out the satchel to him.

"You saved them." Gan took it and clutched it to his chest.

"Well we wouldn't want you to lose your best ideas," Zeus said.

"You noticed then." Gan clutched the satchel closer.

"Yeah I noticed. How the hell did you come up with that drawing technique to hide the blueprints? It's brilliant."

"Boredom mostly." Gan said. "You'd be amazed what you can come up with when you're locked in with nowhere to go."

"Well, I'm a man of my word." Zeus said, "I've got the money for your indenture in my account. It's the least I can do."

"No it isn't," Gan said. "You promised me an R7D position. Besides, I think you're gonna need help with your dad."

"That's not your—"

Gan would blame his next move on an excess of adrenaline. He stepped closer, stretched up on his tiptoes and tipped his head at Zeus, quirking his eyebrow in challenge.

Zeus stopped, then blinked at him uncomprehending for half a second before raising his eyebrows and leaning down to complete the kiss.

Warmth swept Gan from mouth to toes, heat dissipating the last of the chill from the planet outside.

"Thank you for saving me," Gan said, breaking the kiss before they toppled into the wall.

"You saved me first." Zeus said, breathless.

"Do you think the prep unit on this tub will make pancakes?" Gan asked, leaning in for a second kiss.

"Mmmm, if it doesn't I know how to make them from scratch." Zeus said. He swept Gan off his feet and up into his arms, laughing. "Let's go find out."

ON THE PRINCIPAL OF DISORDER

Alex Sirkman

Whoever thought the radio alarm clock was a good idea?[1] Finn rolled over the pile of blankets and clothes on his bed, over again, and a half rotation more before realizing he'd overshot. His dorm bed was lofted unnecessarily high, leaving time to thank the deity of disorder for the overflowing laundry that would cushion his fall.[2] Somewhat. The radio alarm, devoid of sympathy, kept squawking.

---

1 At the borders of consciousness, neurons fired at will, analog electrons surging in the currents of Finn's mind. A lucky few landed on subconscious shores as fleeting thoughts like this. At least, he imagined they did, while approaching that state commonly misnamed "full consciousness."

2 The clean and dirty piles merged into a state of quantum cleanliness,* generated by the chaos of grad student life. Accumulated pants and shirts stretched towards each other on Finn's floor; stained sweatshirts and fresh button-downs became a grand column, meeting on his bed. Laundry is a job for

Every time we think we're reaching consensus, somebody says something to prove that we're not. The IAU[3] *has been a hotbed of discord since its discovery among the frozen asteroids of the Kuiper Belt: Eris.*

A voice called out, "Hail Eris," muffled and muddled by blankets and waking. A mass of questionably clean t-shirts, arms, jeans, and legs wrestled itself up into full consciousness from the floor of a dorm in the East Village, Lower East Side, New York City, etc.[4] It resolved into a pale, lanky, grad student of a man, just over six feet, ropy muscles barely retained from an abandoned rock-climbing addiction. Bright, shaggy ginger hair hinted at the Gaelic ancestry of Finnegan MacHowth, a student of language in a city that speaks – or invents – them all. During the fight for verticality, he'd grabbed an outfit of black jeans and white Clash t-shirt, cleanliness averaging out to "acceptable."

In a linguistically accurate but nonsensical manner, the alarm clock continued to speak:

Intoxicated Finn, a manic gift to his future, hung-over, self. Nobody knows who sorts it all.

*What if washed clothes end up in the dirty pile? What if clean clothes are washed doubly, entering a state of hyper-cleanliness? Cleanliness and dirtiness (and hyper-cleanliness (and godliness)) exist in superposition. Only a good sniff can collapse the possibilities: Schrodinger's scent.

[3] The International Astronomical Union, i.e an excuse to argue about very, very big rocks very, very far away while very, very, *very* drunk.

[4] State of New York, the (ostensibly) United States of America, United Nations of the Planet Earth, the egocentrically named "Solar System" (as if no other stars mattered), all within The Universe, where we keep our stuff.

After a year, the IAU is no closer to a resolution. The dilemma was a dark cloud over the General Assembly; researchers endured eight days of contentious arguments, with four proposals being offered, two fistfights breaking out, and over 43 bottles of liquor consumed.

Last night was an impression of flashing lights and blaring klaxons. The apple stamp on his left hand and the residue of cheap drinks suggested he'd been clubbing,[5] not arrested. A few scraps of memory queasily agreed.

One controversial suggestion would bring the total planets to 12, including Ceres, the largest asteroid, and Pluto's moon Charon.

An unexpected image snagged on Finn's awareness and he froze, half-crouched, reaching for his messenger bag.[6] Golden sequins and a whiff of apple blossom perfume floated through his cerebellum; Finn said it out loud, in case reality popped the bubble of fantasy. "Did I meet a woman last night?" he asked the piles of his room. They did not answer. Finn's grip on the memory was loose: he could almost picture her face, leaning in, whispering words that were perfectly clear, telling him she wanted—

This is absurd; a "complete mess," as Eris' discoverer told reporters, the snarky radio blared. Its clock face read "9:30 a.m." in baleful red.

Shit. The library opened at 7:30 a.m., and the best nooks were gone by nine, even on a sunny summer Saturday like today. Finn rushed out past security, into the unremitting glare of Third Ave. Through six years of graduate life, he'd approached and evaded degrees in history, cultural anthropology, sociology, and philosophy, reaching a

---

[5] Of the liquid, not solid, variety.

[6] It was black, well worn, and creatively patched and pinned; Finn hoped it expressed his ideology and sense of humor. It could have been one of a hundred bags in a five-block radius.

personal best with the linguistics department. The itch for novelty was growing, however, spurred by fear of leaving the academic cocoon. Finn pumped his long legs towards Washington Square Park, enjoying the relative quiet, but three blocks in it was too much. He reached for his phone, feeling a scrap of card stuck on it, then stopped when he noticed the screen.

The phone read "6:30 a.m.," right on its smug little face. It made no sense. The radio alarm must have had its numbers reversed, or its time zone changed. The library didn't open until 7:30, and it was just fifteen minutes away. Finn felt betrayed by electronics on every level. He blindly shoved everything back into his pocket, and took a deep breath.

"Fuuuuuuuu..." he began, growing to a visceral howl which recalled the primal battle cry of his ancestors, braving the English clad only in woad and personal flair. "AGH", he continued, walking onwards. At Ninth he turned on a rare diagonal street — rebellion against the grid, however minor, appealed to him. Finn's ratty Converse All-Stars (cherry red, dirty) carried him on towards Alphabet City. He caught a promising whiff, and aimlessness became laser-targeted hunger: bacon in its sights.

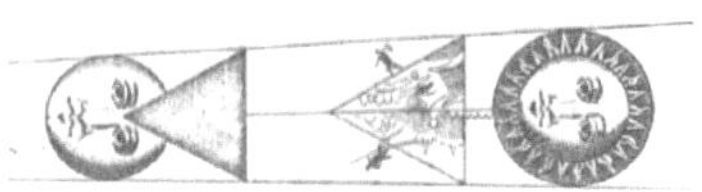

A bodega with two and a half small tables looked over the north side of Thompkins Square Park, its cluttered window taking in the haze of dawn over the grass before it burned away. Finn entered to the customary *ding*, door swinging behind him, disrupting the bodega's reverie.

"A bacon, egg, and cheese, please," Finn ordered from the man behind the counter.

The man nodded mutely, his moustache having consumed his jaw in some tragic accident. His expressive eyes inquired about a beverage to match Finn's repast.

"A tea, too, with cream and sugar."

The moustache approved, and accepted Finn's money.

Finn grabbed three ketchup packets and a handful of napkins, settling by the window. He lodged his bag beneath the table, and took in the view the window had admired before his interruption.[7]

A student of history, Finn appreciated the peaceful trees and plasticized fences of the park; he was reminded of the distant nineties, when he'd been just "a wee bairn," as Gammer always said.[8] The metal-lattice trashcans were still the same, and he imagined the graffiti was too, as well as the human rainbow of youths playing an eternal pick-up game on the public court. Down the street, skater kids period-appropriate to Finn's nostalgia were clad in ripped jeans and vintage t-shirts. One lanky child with long blond hair could have been in Hanson, a band none of them would recognize. They were trying to grind on an old bike rack,

---

[7] Finn readjusted himself to see between a miniature ATM and a rack of plantain chips, above a miscellany of plastic-bagged pastries, and below a neon sign announcing popular cheap beer was sold inside.

[8] Abaigeal MacHowth, mother of Finn's mother, born on the Lower East Side with the spirit of the old country. She loved tall tales and whiskey; when one flowed, the other would soon follow. Her masters in cultural anthropology (plus degrees in Gaelic and Irish Folklore) meant she never ran out of stories to ensorcell Finn's impressionable young mind. He could thank her for his love of knowledge, and mischief.

abandoned by the city by a bagel shop which had occupied the street for decades, and beyond them some men in tan fedoras and trench coats hid in an alley, which was classic… Get Smart?

Something was off. Finn enjoyed that spy spoof, but he couldn't imagine why those three men were huddled, talking into their blocky wristwatches. All Finn could tell was that they were intensely focused in his direction. Maybe they smelled the bacon frying in back?

On a whim, Finn retrieved the unexpected card from his pocket. It was thick stock, in cream, or eggshell, or some other expensive shade of white; one side was embossed with a stylized apple. On the other, he found handwriting, his own. "Mind the book, Profit!" was scrawled in smudged blue pen.

Looking up from the unwanted mystery, Finn saw that the three men had exited the alley, towards the bodega. This did not bode well.

Finn was not a bad person, morally speaking. From years of practice and natural inclination, he was quite good at being a person. Gammer's gift of education (and anti-authoritarian gusto) had shaped Finn into a deeply moral person, with a nuanced perspective on human vice and virtue. From a banal and strictly legal *weltanschauung, however, Finn's rap sheet was real, eccentric, and extensive.*[9]

[9] Possession, possession with intent to distribute (and how did they know what he intended?), a handful of drunk and disorderlies, a few disturbing the peaces, some quite specific citations for questionably legal pharmacology, an ongoing prosecution for the alleged sale of casu marzu, and one charge of nautical barratry.*

Accordingly, Finn was uncomfortable with the sudden approach of three caricatures of 1950s G-men, armored in soul-stifling beige. They approached in a straight line, rigid frames obscured by flapping trench coats left loose in the heat of the day. The men on the flanks drew smooth gunmetal grey objects from their coat pockets, which lurked unreflective and obscure in their hands. They entered the street, and Finn experienced a dilemma shared by a handful of New Yorkers at exactly the same time:

Dashawn worked in finance, and he'd been up since 6 a.m., on Friday. Desperate for food and sleep, he'd ordered an Uber to the corner of his favorite food cart. But the damned car showed up too quickly.

Alice was rushing to the gym to work the bags, but made a pit stop for breakfast at the all-purpose deli. Unfortunately, Jen (her evilest ex) descended from the tables upstairs just after she'd ordered.

Phil had hopped the turnstile on the M train in drunken pursuit of a rare subterranean food stop, when he heard the heavy thud of police boots approaching.

Dashawn, Alice, Phil, and Finn experienced an absolutely un-provable but true empathic bond at that moment, expressing identical poignant words of love and loss. *Shit,* they collectively realized, *I have to ditch my bacon, egg, and cheese and get the fuck out of here.*

---

* Entered in a junior regatta against his will, Finn intentionally ran his crew of polo-clad teens aground in a rocky cove. He'd claimed they had to swerve to avoid hitting a naiad.°

°Briefly thereafter the crew looked up "naiads," and Finn had his first disturbing the peace. That was the last time Finn's parents committed a regatta under duress.

Finn shoved the napkins into his pocket and snatched his bag. The rough swing over his shoulder knocked the plantain chips askew, but he thrust the dinging door open and rushed frantically for an avenue of escape.

The suits were momentarily stymied by the skater kids, bless their rebellious hearts. The tall blonde child (not even a decade younger than Finn) was grinding along the bike rack, taming the narrow tube of metal with impeccable balance. They'd lined their friends up across the street, in just the spot the suits were marching through, and the kids weren't moving until their friend was quite done.

Finn's heart went out to them. Their gender-non-specific spirit of adventure reminded him of his checkered past. Finn briefly put aside his customary nostalgic bitterness,[10] and he could have cheered as the suits were crowded back by the wild pack of street-puppies. Instead, he kept walking away.

The biggest pup wore a black undershirt and cut-off jeans. Only his vape pen, polluting the air with cotton candy chemicals, marked him as a son of the aughts, not the seventies. From a block and a half away, Finn caught only the shape of his conversation with the leftmost suit, in tone and volume: an exchange of insincere pleasantries. A rising stand-off of "alpha male" growling. An unexpected high-pitched whining. Finn whipped his head around, feet stumbling to a stop.

Ozone was in the air. The boy was a full-body rictus; his friends scattered as he collapsed on the cracked asphalt. Finn sincerely hoped the boy was merely unconscious. The

---

[10] Which he'd cultivated for TAing at the University.

suit brushed off the front of the oblong grey device in his hand, and took an action Finn thought of as "re-cocking."

The suits continued their approach, directly at Finn.

Surely, Finn thought, *I have no reason to fear three upstanding*[11] *gentlemen in this city where I have no outstanding warrants, where I have had only three very bad breakups in the past six years, and where I help raise the young and (mostly) privileged to respect (or at least fear) the power of language.*

A man's voice, with the deep assurance of authority and the commanding timbre of a former cop, echoed down the street: "Finnegan MacHowth! Stop!"

Finn felt like a delinquent caught in a non-specific but clearly guilty act. Abruptly, he decided to pretend he was someone else. He turned his head to match his feet, and scanned the area to see which "away" looked most promising.

The imposing suit bellowed as he and his men approached, "We just want to talk, on behalf of the Deputy Mayor for Economic Development! We know you have the book! Let's just do this the easy way, right?"

The problem with "the easy way" is that it's often only easy for the one proposing "the easy way." Finn had no idea what a Deputy Mayor might want from him. What did a Deputy Mayor even do? He didn't have overdue books, not that the collection of scholastic texts fell under "Economic Development" (as far as he knew). Finn might have asked

---

[11] They were well dressed; their dreadful beige suits were well-fitted, and their shoes matched their outfits. Finn could recognize fashionable attire through exposure to donors at fancy alumni dinners. Wealthy citizens are always upstanding, because they can afford to have someone place them upright on their marble stands. And dust said marble and charge admission.

the suits for a primer on city government, but he chose instead to power-walk into a nearby alleyway, hoping for a shortcut. He dodged past an indignant rat perched on a freshly painted dumpster, and rationalized strenuously at himself. *There must be some confusion. Maybe I should let them catch up, and see what they want.* A kicked can skittered across paving stones: *flee first, determine why later.* Finn increased from a frenetic walk to a loping bound, like the great extinct Irish elk. Double-checking his simile, he ran faster.

Another problem with the easy way: you never know how hard it is until you try. As Finn approached the other end of the alley, he encountered three blocky forms interested in his apprehension. He skidded to a halt, rubber soles slipping on trash and old take out menus, and was entriangled by the three suits. The suits on either side grabbed Finn's arms, and the man in the middle slowly raised his head. An unexpected voice greeted him in charming tones, which brooked no dissent.

A woman's face looked out from beneath the central fedora. An iPad was ingeniously attached to the front of the man's face, transmitting the voice and presence of a stunning redhead with a million-dollar hairdo. She began to introduce herself, but Finn realized immediately that the Deputy Mayor of Economic Development for the City of New York was Carrie Thornley, financial celebrity, and contender for richest woman in the world. The cover of *Forbes* knew her as "The Rose of Wall Street."

She elaborated her numerous titles and accolades, which encouraged Finn to relax; couldn't this be some legal snafu, or an overeager attempt to offer him a grant? *No*, he decided, *this is not a good thing.* Predators smile when they corner prey. A ringing in his ears quieted just as he noticed it. He finally focused on the Rose when the suits appropriated his bag.

"You're clearly an intelligent young man, Mr. MacHowth," said the woman who'd built her tech portfolio into the engine of a burgeoning economy, who looked younger and healthier than Finn had since high school. "You've studied history, and linguistics; you know that language shapes thought, that the victors write history, and the reality of the world is what those with power say it is, *heehee*, isn't that so?"

Heehee? It must have been a giggle, but it didn't come across as whimsical or girlish. Instead of being endearing, Finn could only imagine her practicing that laugh in front of a mirror, a sea of yes men reassuring her that she'd accomplished a perfectly normal human laugh, which perfectly normal humans would consider a basis for perfectly normal human connection.

Thornley purred as she broached her favorite topic, "Money, Finnegan. Power, control, mastery of this world; it all comes from money. The definitions of our society are in the hands of those who publish dictionaries. I control the sources that Wikipedia cites!" She was revving up into a full villain speech, which Finn found more comforting than her attempt at a giggle. "*Heehee.* With the information hidden in that book, my FinTech[12] geeks will be real wizards! A visionary algorithm that can predict the future of complex financial markets? I'd never have believed it if I hadn't seen the evidence myself. Turn over the Principia, Finn!"

---

[12] Finn was flattered by her apparent obsession with him: despite his over-education, he wasn't aware "FinTech" stood for "Financial Technology."

"The.... Principia?" Finn turned the words over, tasting them as he spoke, and the pieces did not fall into place. He tried to get his mental bearings, but he spoke before he thought: "The *Philosophiæ Naturalis Principia Mathematica*? I don't... I've never even read it. You think Isaac Newton knew how to predict the future? Moons of madness!" Finn might have gone too far with his exclamation, but a career in linguistics is like a bad birthmark: embarrassing and hard to hide.

Thornley giggled terribly again, "*Heeheehee*," through the pristine speakers of the iPad-faced man. Finn couldn't think of any queen or warlord in the world right now with more material wealth than the woman telecommuting into his mugging. "Now is not the time for obfuscation, my dear. My men have had you under surveillance for longer than you must have expected. Now is the time for you to relinquish the *Principia Discordia*."

"THE WHAT?"[13] Finn asked Ms. Thornley, the thugs, and the universe at large. "I have the 4th edition, but that's free to download. It's thought-provoking, I love the humor, but... WHAT? It's a parodic religio-philosophical text written by psychedelic aficionados, about relative truth, how chaos and order are a matter of perspective, and radical social pranks. Is this... are you pranking me?"

There was no giggle this time, right when he'd needed it. "Finn, my dear boy, this is a simple economic exchange.

---

[13] The Principia Discordia, or How I Found Goddess & What I Did To Her When I Found Her, Being a Beginning Introduction to The Erisian Mysteries, Which is Most Interesting, as Divinely Revealed to My High Reverence Malaclypse The Younger, KSC Omnibenevolent Polyfather Of Virginity In Gold And High Priest Of The Paratheo-Anametamystikhood Of Eris Esoteric (POEE) – 4th ed.

Don't worry about my men," she purred again, and leaned forwards conspiratorially.

She'd wanted to make him feel as if they were sharing an intimate moment. Instead, her face loomed on the screen, obscenely enlarged, lipstick wet and thick like clotted blood. Finn realized her voice modulated but never really changed, like a digital assistant who'd made it all the way to the top.

"My men are loyal, and they will not mistreat you, not if you comply. Don't assume the worst." She leaned back, smiling brightly, and continued, "You'll be handsomely compensated for providing me the keys to the kingdom. You can have a place in my organization, if you help decipher the algorithm; I could buy you a kingdom, if you'd like. Wouldn't that be nice?" She smiled like the cat that owned the dairy and bought canaries wholesale.

Having his debts paid off would be nice, Finn mused. A kingdom sounded like trouble. He maintained his expression of dumbfounded shock, which had worked great so far.

During his silence, the suited thugs shook his bag onto the pavement: out fell a 3-ring binder full of flapping papers, a textbook on Victorian corsetry, a single tampon, the latest Nicholas Sparks novel, and an ancient e-reader.[14] The thug on the left looked down at the pile, then held his gunmetal grey device up to Finn's neck.

Finn did not recognize the device, but if he had, he'd have known it was the latest in high-end personal self-defense products; an over-engineered high-capacity taser. It

---

[14] The e-reader was an antiquated two-year-old model, under recall for overheating problems. It lay on the sidewalk, blinking its low-batt light in shame, hoping to avoid notice by the top of the line model currently threatening Finn.

came in gunmetal grey, porcelain white, and rich mahogany, with a standard and deluxe model.[15] Despite his ignorance, Finn felt duly threatened.

"Where's the book, Finn?" the thug drawled, sounding bored. "We know you had the book in your bag. Where did you hide it? Back at the bodega?"

"Nope!" Finn assured the men, in a more strangled tone than he'd tried for, "That's my bag, that's all there is in it, you can check my apartment or the bodega or anything, no Principia here."

The thug frowned. "You know, we're licensed to use non-lethal force, and I'm sure you wouldn't like the feel of one of these" he said, shaking the taser menacingly, and finished, "in the neck."

"I'm very sure," Finn told the thug on the left, the thug on the right, the man in the middle, the woman through her electronic screen and anyone else who would listen.

The authoritative former cop spoke from behind Thornley's now grim visage. "So, this is your bag, and you don't have the book. You just have… this stuff. And a tampon." Thornley was tight-lipped and silent.

"I get nosebleeds." Finn would be proud of that, later.

The thugs looked at each other, and the two on either side looked at the iPad, and the iPad went blank. The thugs released his arms, and the faceless suit came up close, handing him his emptied bag.

---

[15] This was, of course, the deluxe version. Thomas A. Swift would have drooled over the extra features on this Electric Rifle, including leather grip, wi-fi compatibility, and a calorie-counter you could download from the App store. As it turns out, trigger pulling burns a remarkably high number of calories, particularly on the receiving end.

“Our apologies for the inconvenience, Mr. MacHowth. If we find that you’ve lied, we will hunt you down and torture the truth out of you. Do not follow us, do not ask about us, and do not tell anyone anything that occurred here.” The man punched Finn in the stomach, hard, doubling him over.

Finn clutched his gut, and tried not to lose the few sips of tea he’d gotten down. “Have a nice day,” the man finished, and the three suits walked away.

Finn gathered “his” things up and relaxed into the bath of confusion the day had drawn for him. One thing was clear: he’d switched his bag with someone else, and the objects he’d gathered off the floor of the alley gave him a good idea who. A whiff of apple blossom floated through the trash, presumably lost on its way out of the park. Finn slung her bag over his shoulder and made his way downtown, to Silver’s Gym and Juice.

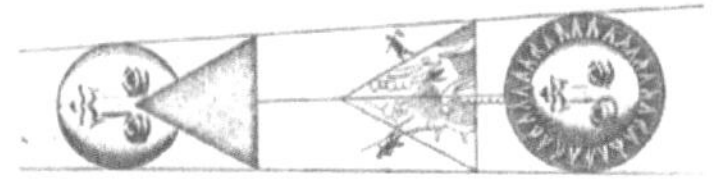

Alice made it to the gym without emotional turbulence, but her stomach resented the lonely green juice roiling inside it. Her little Chinese grandmother would have insisted on feeding her congee and *youtiao*. Her little Jewish father would have agreed, and he would have thrown a century egg on top. She missed him, but she was glad he wasn’t around; just the thought of translucent amber eggs and blue-grey yolks made her queasy. Alice Finkel was six foot even, long-limbed and strong, with more substantial fare than color juice, gruel, and really odd eggs to thank for her robust figure.

For a long breath in, and out, Alice and her grey sweat suit lay mostly flat on the blue puzzle-piece mats lining the workout area; her auburn bun was too low to rest her head properly. She sat up, she sat down, she pushed the earth away, and she welcomed it again. After testing her customary range of motion, she took a great many steps without going anywhere. Alice enjoyed the routine, those parts full of green notwithstanding, but she didn't come to the gym for light exercise and a juice bar.

With maintenance complete, Alice could get to the meat and potatoes. Beneath a poster of Muhammad Ali (with authentically printed signature), she wrapped her hands in shiny gold cotton from her gym bag and considered her abandoned sandwich. Some grease was needed for breakfast, to protect from acid during the day. Acid was inevitable. It could be brought on by toxic patriarchy, academic backbiting, or coffee. Usually all three. But always coffee. She'd been humming "London Calling" while looking for her boxing gloves, then inspiration's right hook struck. Thinking about the Victorian fashion text she'd found at the library, Alice was struck by inspiration. She had the perfect metaphor for the sociological implications of corsetry aesthetics, framed by period coffee house culture. She'd found her gloves, but she paused before donning them to grab her messenger bag; she needed her loyal e-reader, Ol' Smokey, repository of her thesis notes. Suddenly, her name echoed through the gym (and attached juice bar). She knew the voice.

"Alice!" Finn shouted unnecessarily loudly, as he rushed breathlessly between tiny tables and a pyramid of fresh oranges. "I need you… your… d'you have my bag?" Panting, Finn held a black messenger bag too close to her face, with all her familiar patches and buttons.

Alice looked at the bag she held, which she hadn't opened since going clubbing[16] last night. It had been a new club and a hell of a party, full of bright lights and rank smells, pounding bass and shouts of "appletinis for all!" The front of the bag held a Celtic knot patch. Finn had ironically purchased it at a Hot Topic, when he'd visited to meet her parents; she'd been seeing it all day without knowing it. That had been a good trip. Things had been good for them, then, and then they weren't, and they'd broken up over a sorrowful autumn semester. Finn was her least evil ex, but she did NOT find this whole bag swap thing endearing.

Alice punched Finn in the shoulder, hard, and shouted, "You butt! Why did you take my bag? Do you have my corsetry book?" She hoped Finn hadn't noticed she'd kept the pin from their third date: a bearded and robed deity poking his head out of a box (á la Schrodinger). It was a good gift for an atheist from an agnostic, who'd met as TAs for "Theological Ontology and Quantum Semantics" with Professor Haggbard. Her grey eyes began to clear from their academic haze, and she asked, "What are you even doing here?"

Hushed, Finn said, "I've been accosted in an alley by a man with an electronic face."

His pupils weren't dilated, and Alice couldn't smell anything on him. Concern and irritation roiled inside her along with green juice. She remembered the feeling well.

Finn gazed at the bag she was holding, then met her eyes, sharing a hopeful and earnest smile. She'd always said he had pretty eyes, but he never believed her. Alice sighed, and they exchanged bags. "Finn, you can't just barge in here…"

---

16 Of the solid, not liquid, variety. Then followed shortly by going clubbing of Finn's liquid variety.

she trailed off, and considered his current state: sweaty, out of breath, disheveled, all beyond status quo, and it was just ten past seven in the morning. Timing alone indicated something was wrong.

Finn sensed an opening and went for it. “Can you grab some coffee with me?”

Alice tried to be tough, to ignore the endearing humor in his eyes, his tousled Raggedy Andy locks, and how badly she wanted a cappuccino.

Finn mustered a weak smile, and glanced up at Ali. He tried to channel the greatest, the man who shook up the world, and added, “I’m the prettiest” with a wry grin.

How could she say no?

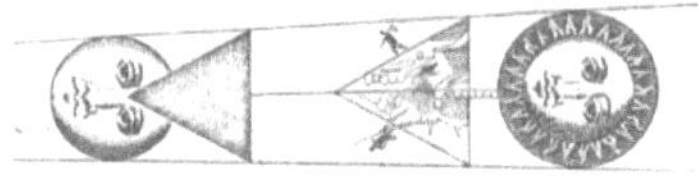

Coffee was fine.

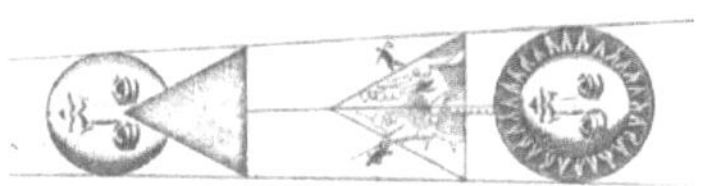

Four men and a rabbit with expressive grey eyes sat around a very small table. One man looked like an aging longshoreman[17] with a tampon in his nose. He faced a weaselly fellow in a dingy gray suit, similarly past his prime, with a bandaged left hand. Finn sat facing an impressively overstuffed hunter green armchair, around which piles of

[17] This assessment, while accurate, was deeply anachronistic and moderately anatopistic.

books held eons of dust. The esoteric tomes towered, buttressed by each other, the chair, and an ancient Brit perched at the center of it all. Remove him, and the wisdom of ages might tumble down. He looked like Nosferatu on a good hair day, wearing a freshly laundered burial suit. His manicured nails tapped on the object occupying the tiny tabletop. It was a black plastic binder, holding greying pages from some bronze-age printer, proclaiming itself a first edition copy of the Principia Discordia.[18]

To Finn, this seemed dubious: how could it know it was a first edition?

The old man didn't identify himself, but his goons called him "Bookman." Finn hoped it was an occupational surname, like Butcher, Baker, or Chandler. He was hoping many things. He clutched the rabbit tightly and stroked its fur, not sure if he was soothing her or himself.

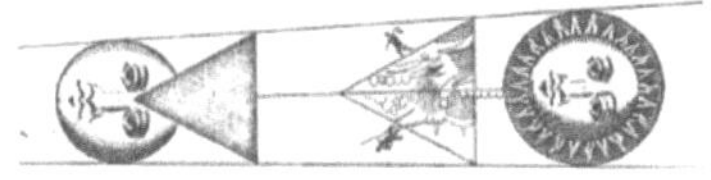

While returning from coffee, the big goon had dragged Finn into an alley by main force. Finn had obliged; it was an alley-centric day. The thin goon had been lurking in the shadows, knife in hand. For a fleeting moment Finn had been relieved. It was just a normal mugging, he assumed, the classic exchange of violence for money. Their antiquated style was unusual below Houston Street,[19] but Finn was just

[18] Technically, "*The Principia Discordia, or How The West Was Lost - 1st Ed.*"

[19] No, don't pronounce it like that. This is (fictional) New York City, and we say "Houston" here.

grateful they weren't rocking spiked leather or rainbow-colored dreads.

Alice took the unceremonious assault as an invitation for a nose-breaking jab. This encouraged the big goon to loosen his grip as bright red showered his tan sweater.[20] Finn stumbled back from the fracas, and Alice did something slick; crouching low, she entered the big man's personal space and flicked a hand at his bleeding face. He flinched and knocked her hand away but she was already standing, knee planted as a fulcrum behind his thighs, elbow jamming into his stomach. The goon went down hard, to his and Finn's surprise. Alice landed on his chest, knees first. Finn winced in empathy.

Finn had given up on making sense of life years ago: today was deemed a lost cause in that alley. Inspired by Gammer, Finn had studied chants, curses, and invocations from across the globe, but he'd never truly believed.[21] He'd had moments of magical taboo thinking, evading sidewalk cracks or praising a big beard in the sky, but he'd never imagined real proof existed. He should have grasped the danger of the knife. The thin goon had drawn the naked blade over his palm, chanting something Finn didn't understand in a language he couldn't identify. The goon had

---

[20] He donned a clean olive sweater after settling Finn in the sanctum. His preference for Holy Land colors was a holdover from seminary. He'd been kicked out for romancing a Franciscan postulant, but his familiarity with dead languages was essential in his new career. Still, he'd always regret the nun who got away.

[21] In full disclosure, he hadn't known not to believe as a child, and there'd been moments involving substances (under ongoing investigation) when he'd seen things that couldn't be real. Those were just hallucinations, though. They must have been. Unless corporate hallucination is impossible… which it is…

flung out his hand in an unsanitary gesture, and… Finn wished it *had been* all an acid flashback. It would have been a comfort. Unfortunately, his pharmacological know-how suggested this was no hallucination. Magic, some magic, was absolutely real, and Finn felt elated and nauseated.

And then… he'd been dragged down skewed stairs near the amorphous border of Little Italy and Chinatown, entering a musty bookshop crammed with used classics, untouched self-help books, and scattered cheap fiction paperbacks. The sign said *Ravenhurst Booksellers*, and the dust said nobody had been through these aisles in months. The goons had led Finn behind a secret door in a bookshelf, which would have been exciting on a different day. Finn took in shelves crammed with fascinating texts, mysterious bottles, and eldritch statuettes; the air was dry, and he caught the hum of a powerful ventilation system. This was the true pearl of wisdom, hidden from the world inside a clam of obscurity.

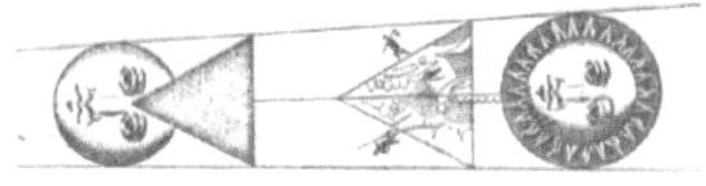

Presently perched on his overstuffed throne, the Bookman leered, self-satisfaction overflowing sallow cheeks. His feet dangled off the ground, kicking with repressed excitement like a kid in a candy store.[22] He opened with unexpected gentility: "Johnny Vellum, I presume?"

Everyone looked at Finn, including the rabbit.

---

[22] It would have been a gothic candy shoppe, decked in black lace and stuffed crows, serving spice drops, sherbet and similarly soapy sweets favored by grandparents losing their sense of smell.

Finn stared blankly back. He hadn't caught the names of the goons, but the Bookman was looking right at him. Taking a deep breath, he risked the truth, just in case it worked.

"Not me," he replied, "I'm Finnegan MacHowth, NYU grad student, Linguistics Department. My friend was too." Finn's hand, stroking the bunny's ears, jerked like a needle skipping its groove. "Could I charge her e-reader? She keeps her thesis notes in it, and she, Alice..." he trailed off, and hugged the bunny tightly to his chest.

The goons were honestly impressed. A cavalcade of habitual criminals, hard-boiled detectives, and half-mad occultists had been sat on that chair.[23] Not one had been comfortable with their bunny, and they'd usually known why the Bookman had invited them to his "sanctum sanctorum."[24] The goons weren't sure what he wanted with an overgrown punk like Finn, but he'd looked them right in

---

[23] It was not a good chair, and it knew it: poorly-fitted particle board bound with rusting staples and resentment, with nary a cushion. It weighed half as much as the other, better seats at the table, and harbored unspoken resentment for the green monstrosity it faced each day. The sunless confines of the sanctum were unmitigated torture: only unwelcome guests were relegated to its uncomfortable support, and both were routinely manhandled. Such mistreatment left the chair scuffed, splintered, and battered. It had been abandoned, upended and alone, for days on end. The great green beast lurked across the table, smugly superior in its fashionable upholstery, decadently pillow-laden despite its plush stuffing. The particle board chair's thoughts focused solely on revenge, cold as an ass on its bare seat: *the green armchair must die.*

[24] The Bookman believed women couldn't have the knowledge or importance to demand kidnapping. It felt misogynistic to the goons that they never kidnapped women, but they weren't sure how to convey their concerns to their employer.

their goon eyes and asked a favor for his friend. They shared sympathetic goon glances,[25] and the big goon gave his boss a beseeching look.

The Bookman responded with cursory assent, and the e-reader was plugged in behind a nearby bookcase. Magnanimous in presumed victory, he smirked, and pressed on. "Finnegan? MacHowth? A laughable pseudonym. 'Finnegan,' from Joyce's Finnegan's Wake, and 'MacHowth,' from the first line thereof: 'rivverun through swerve of shore, and bend of bay,' etc. Quite droll. Did you think I wouldn't see through such petty obfuscations?"

Sticking with what had failed so far, Finn babbled on. "It was MacHeath, originally, but it got misspelled on a registry in Connecticut when we left the tenements. I've never read through Finnegan's Wake." The Bookman's eyes narrowed, seeking a trap, but Finn ploughed on, "I hit the 'baba'… 'bababadal'…'bababadalgharaghtakamminarronnkonnbron ntonnerronntuonnthunntrovarrhounawnskawntoohoohoo rdenenthurnuk' line and I give up. I memorized that part, though, to prove the point."

The Bookman's face tightened through each nonsense syllable as his grand confrontation slipped away, but he wouldn't give up the narrative without a fight. Flexing his fingers in deep thought, he mused with growing vigor, "MacHeath… you couldn't believe a Brecht reference would slip me by, could you? Mackie Messer, the Threepenny Opera? Oh, Mr. Vellum, cease your pointless efforts. Whatever chicanery you employ," and here, his eyes

---

25 Like your normal sympathy, but thicker and with more scars. This is why some faces that only a mother could ever love are loved by other mothers, whereas some faces are only loved by the only mother that can ever love them.

ignited with purple phosphorescence, "know you sit before one who has tasted true power!"

Bellowing now in full villainous swing, the Bookman enthusiastically thrust an outstretched finger in Finn's direction, then shifted his arm for better accuracy. He over-corrected, adjusted again for precision, then continued his diatribe.

"HAH!" the Bookman barked, and the rabbit fled from Finn's lap. The rabbit, unwatched, dashed around the closest bookshelf. Hidden from view, it noticed the dangling cord of a time-ravaged e-reader plugged into the wall. Out of some lapine instinct, perhaps, it hopped upon a convenient stack of papers and began gnawing.

The Bookman's laugh was so harsh, Finn expected dust to puff out of the old man's thin lips. "This game has covered eight continents and three decades, but here we sit, with the Principia in my grasp. Your devious father taught you well; you must have some tricks up your sleeve, but I'm prepared for every eventuality."

Finn, whose father was an orthodontist in Connecticut, hoped the Bookman was right. He didn't know what dental hygiene could do in the face of the truly supernatural,[26] but hoping was all he had left.

The Bookman continued in full swing, saying, "I have dangerous men working for me, but nothing is more dangerous than knowledge. I am a spider in a hidden web, and you are a child lost in the woods who has unwittingly walked directly INTO IT!" He rose to a fever pitch, pleased with his half-baked simile. "I've gathered rare tomes, studied ancient rituals; I hold secrets that cannot be bought

---

[26] To be honest, he didn't know what dental hygiene could do in the face.

with coin. In Hecate's name, I've summoned spirits at a crossroads. I know words to animate lifeless life, signs to blind men's eyes, gestures that cloud the minds of the weak-willed.[27] If you aid me in unlocking the secrets of this… three-ring binder… I will teach you. You will be a master of the hidden light, an initiate of true rituals. We will shape the future of the world!" The Bookman ended his (clearly rehearsed) exhortation on the edge of his looming armchair, baleful purple gaze locked on Finn's eyes of shock.

Finn's thoughts, unmoored, drifted to Alice. She wanted to believe the universe was rational, that it would all make sense if people just thought hard enough. Finn didn't know what he believed, and he liked it that way. He'd never met a god, or a platypus, but the world was more interesting if he allowed for the possibility they existed.[28] The most important things didn't really exist; truth, beauty, justice, love, all stories we tell about how the world can be better. If believing in gods, or dragons, or little green men makes the world more virtuous, richer and more interesting, why be stingy with faith? Finn didn't want a mundane truth, he wanted a beautiful mystery, a beautific vision. Alice could explain why the light flared when the sun set just right, but she couldn't explain why Finn smiled and wept to see it. Alice, who he couldn't get off his mind, a muffled screaming beneath his consciousness rising fast: he had to address the

---

[27] He would not admit, at his moment of triumph, that comprehensive NLP training works more reliably than magic. Moreover, a well-trained agent doesn't need to know exotic dead languages, or which part of the tiger is the "chaudron."

[28] He could be wrong, but if he had met a god (or platypus) in disguise, he'd forgotten. Especially if it had been a god disguised as a platypus. Or vice versa: Hypocritiplatytheism.

lagomorph in the room. "Before we talk about the book, as a sign of good will…" he laughed nervously, and held up the rabbit, "could you please turn her back?"

It had been good to see Alice, but now he feared he'd lost her entirely. Finn contemplated prayer: he'd been raised lapsed Catholic, and Gammer had essentially been pagan, but Finn would have accepted aid from the Morrigan,[29] Buddha, or even Tom Cruise.

The Bookman chortled at Finn's humbled request, but the thick goon brushed the feminine hygiene product in his nose and winced. Ignoring his warning look, the Bookman nodded approvingly. "Go ahead, Reg. Remove the curse of Astaroth from the girl. But know this," he continued, with a nasty glint in his eye, "I've seen men who would not break from torture reduced to catatonia when released from this spell. Do you think your lady friend will thank you?"

Will she thank me for any of this? Finn wondered.

He wasn't hopeful.

"She can do what she wants, when she's human again," Finn responded, locating spare backbone under the seat cushions of his consciousness. Avoiding the Bookman's indigo glare, he scanned the shelves for a sign. He noticed a yellowed journal with "Abraham Joshua Norton" on its spine; he'd been the first and last Emperor of the United States, and a Discordian Saint, Second Class; but that wouldn't help now.[30] Distracting himself was fruitless, and

---

[29] Finn's last prayer had been a half-hearted entreaty to the Morrigan before a pick-up game of rugby. His team won, but he'd accidentally broken a friend's wrist, so he'd decided to leave exploratory invocations behind him.

[30] Finn was a Discordian Pope, if that mattered. Technically, every man, woman, and child on Earth is a Discordian Pope. Sainthood

Finn plead, "She has nothing to do with this mess. Please, she's almost done with her thesis!"

The Bookman relented, saying "Very well." Reg leaned across the table and pulled a black iron nail from his pocket. He offered the head of the nail, and tapped the rabbit's foot. Finn must have blinked, because Alice now sat on his lap, overwhelming the structural integrity of the uncomfortable chair. It shattered under an abruptly doubled load, flinging vicious splinters into the nearby shelves. The Bookman and his goons were lucky to evade perforation.[31]

Alice blinked rapidly and appeared to burst into tears, hiding her face in Finn's shoulder. He made soothing noises, and shifted so she wasn't sitting on a nerve. The Bookman, satisfied with the pathos of the display, continued exhorting Finn to join him.

"Johnny, you have no secrets from me. We have the book. You are the key. A new age is upon us. Pluck the fruits of mankind's next great spiritual evolution, or be the tree that is plucked. You do not have o'erlong to decide!"

Finn could feel the excessive apostrophe, and it was the last straw. He asked himself a series of questions, beginning with "Why?" and ending with "WHY?!" He had no

---

is more exclusive; real human beings can be Second Class Saints, but higher classes are strictly reserved for fictional beings.

[31] The longest and sharpest splinter flew true, lodging in the heart of the great green beast and tearing at its insides, causing a rip that would grow to disembowel the overstuffed monstrosity. Shattered, the particleboard chair (a dramatic sort) yelled its dying lines: "Towards thee I roll! Thou all-destroying but unconquering beast! To the last I grapple with thee! From hell's heart I stab at thee! For hate's sake I spit my last breath at thee! Thus, I give up the spear!" The rest of the room hesitated a moment, shocked at the inanimate outburst, before continuing.

satisfactory answers, and his attention wandered in the increasingly uncomfortable silence. Saints, Popes, Eris… well, she was a planet now, or a dwarf planet, or Pluto wasn't even a planet and the word didn't even mean anything anymore. Finn absently patted Alice's back; she hadn't been prone to crying in the past. Finn had always cried easily. Gammer had sung to him then, when he was scared, sad, or just lonely; she had a saint for every season, each tied to a deity of the old emerald isle. A wisp of tune bubbled between his lips, but he faltered. He couldn't think of a saint for a time like this.

Kicking restlessly, the Bookman whipped his angry purple glare around the room. Whatever came out of the cockney corpse-keeper's mouth next would be an escalation of threats, and not by a half-step. Finn took a deep breath, smelling burnt lo mein sneaking in through dry, climate-controlled shelves. Suddenly, thought and memory coalesced, ravens dancing on the wing; Finn realized he already had a saint in mind. The Bookman prepared to pronounce further doom, but Finn absently held up his index finger behind Alice's back, forestalling further threat.[32]

Picture San Francisco, in the late 1800s, anti-Chinese sentiment ravaging Norton's home. A group of Chinese people stood, blocked by angry rioters and fearing for their lives, until Saint Norton appeared. He stood resolute between them, reciting the Lord's Prayer over and over until everyone safely dispersed. Finn wanted desperately to feel safe: he remembered feeling protected and warmed by

---

[32] The Bookman was selfish, arrogant, and power mad, but he was British, thus incapable of ignoring the traditional sign for "One moment, please."

Gammer's shawl, nestled in the pews of an old church with brick walls held up by creeping ivy. Its strange books held power, in Finn's fresh eyes. He hadn't felt something that true for years, and then he began to sing.

"I arise today through a mighty strength, through a belief in the threeness, through confession of the oneness of the Creator of creation." Finn arose into an endless moment from the remains of the broken chair, trying to help Alice find her footing.[33] He sang St. Patrick's Lorica for the first time since Gammer had been laid to (acceptably insincere) rest, in a Catholic cemetery along I-95. "I arise today, through the strength of heaven; light of the sun, splendor of fire, speed of lightning, swiftness of the wind, depth of the sea, stability of the earth, firmness of the rock." The Bookman and his goons were taken aback, as if they expected sudden heavenly retribution. "I arise today, through God's strength to pilot me; God's might to uphold me, God's wisdom to guide me... God's shield to protect me." He was losing the words, but it still felt right; meaningful, powerful, comforting. He felt her there again, in the great cavern of the church, prayers echoing and candles burning, holy smoke rising all the way to heaven. Finn's eyes stung from the strength of his emotions.

Finn's eyes also began to sting in the thick smoke gathering overhead. He left Alice and hopped around the nearest bookcase, where he found the e-reader had arisen along with sacred smoke and holy words. It had flamed out in sufficient glory to ignite a stack of papers, cheerfully self-immolating; the blaze had already jumped to several nearby

---

33 Alice needed no help, however, and had been breathing evenly into his collarbone the whole time.

shelves. Finn, dismayed at the burning books, shouted "Fire!"

Alice was already turning, grabbing the Principia Discordia. Before anyone could react, she kicked the small table into the Bookman's face.

The goons had a problem. They were caught in a strange loop of priorities, unable to choose between their master, his sanctum, and the culmination of his life's work in Alice's hands.

Finn might have stayed to put the fire out if Alice hadn't grabbed his hand. She chambered her right leg and side-kicked the big goon in the face, just as he made up his mind to chase them. He went down and they went out, up, and onto the relatively normal streets of New York City. Alice shoved the binder into her bag, which she'd grabbed in the chaos, and handed Finn his bag, which he'd forgotten. Leaning on each other, laughing in relief, they found the hot garbage smell of the streets sweet.[34] Curls of smoke meandered up the steps, and a fire alarm blared from behind the false storefront. Familiar emergency interrupted their preternatural calm, and they broke into a panicked run.

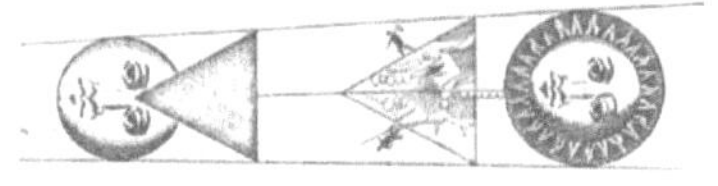

Green signs with white lettering whipped by as they ran, paused briefly to huff and power-walk for a block, then ran onward until collapsing on a bench in Washington Square Park. Children of all ages frolicked in the basin of the great central fountain, in bathing suits, rolled-up pants, or no

[34] It was a familiar smell, but not usually appreciated.

pants at all. Some wore tie-dye, or tiaras, or great bushy beards, but they were all vibrant and noisy and absolutely normal (for the city).[35] Alice and Finn supported each other against the gentle slats of the bench as they finally caught their breath. An eternal moment passed, fountain spray and half-dappled sunlight through sparse trees, and the fragrance of blooming apple blossom comforted them.

An older woman, straight blonde hair fading to white, joined the bench. She wore a comfortable white linen pantsuit and an iridescent tie-dyed shawl. They knew her: Professor Selena Haggbard, head of the smallest and most esoteric sub-department at NYU, Applied Philosophy. Her smile was warm and crooked, and a Nordic lilt danced as she said, "I suppose you have the Principia, Finn. I'd love to see it, if you don't mind."

Finn couldn't muster the energy for shock, not without lunch. Putting his thoughts in disorder, he tried to ask everything at once. It didn't work.[36]

Alice responded first. "Professor Haggbard, do you have ANY idea what's been going on? It's been… Today… we were assaulted, and… I was a rabbit." She looked over the fountain, and further out, to the unknowable ends of existence. Her nose twitched, and she finished quietly, "Please help us understand."

---

[35] A handful wore all three, and silken fairy wings to complete the ensemble.

[36] Nothing came out but disjoint sputtering, and Finn swore he'd sprained his tongue.

The Professor patted Alice's cheek, and murmured something softly.[37] "Go to the fountain, sweetie," she suggested, "Let the day wash off of you. You'll feel better."

Alice, unsure of things she hadn't known she could be unsure of, looked to Finn. He had no answers, and wasn't sure of the questions. She squeezed his hand and entered waters that once flowed through the forest of the Ashokan reservoir; she was immediately soaked, but her smile was broad as she splashed with a gaggle of fairy-winged children.

Professor Haggbard sighed, "It's a cruel thing to take a person's sense of self. I've done what I can. She might not care to remember today's particulars. You two have been through too much. Threatened with violence familiar and strange, offered mastery of the world, seen and unseen. You're in an uncomfortable position, and I'd like to help." She patted Finn's knee.

Tears of relief overflowed his clear blue eyes. His tongue felt swollen, and he couldn't express a tenth of what he wanted. The professor's manicured hand proffered a benediction.

"Sweet boy… you've witnessed the powers of the world, wrestling for dominance. They threaten, cajole, offer more and less than you'll ever need. Pah!" She spat, then waved an expansive hand over the park, shawl slipping down her shoulder. "I can't offer you great wealth, Finn, although I hope I can offer you tenure, if you stay with our department. I'd like to invite you to join a non-profit I've formed, with some friends: Professors Wilson and Shea, a handful of big donors, and some names you might be surprised to hear."

---

[37] Finn caught part of it, in an ancient dialect of Greek: "be cleansed", though the verb could mean "purify" or "purge", or even "prune."

Her smile was enigmatic, but it hinted at a comfortable mystery, in the comfortable context of Finn's comfortable life. "We call it 'Illuminatus Inc.,' which is our little joke. Our directors and tax filings are public record, and we pride ourselves on being open and accessible. That's why we'd like the Principia, an authentic first edition! We have later editions, but that would be a real gem. I can't wait to show you our library, open to the public every day, excellent security, complimentary coffee pods. Everyone who wants to study the book could do so, safely."

Finn had been worn down by each mystifying and wondrous moment of the day, and he felt abandoned by normality. The professor's offer, at the cost of freeing him from the problematic text, was a way back to the path he'd applied for at NYU. No obscene wealth, no occult mastery, just pure academic inquiry.

Professor Haggbard beamed as Finn worried at the future, continuing, "I'd like to invite Ms. Finkel too. You both have a head for… esoteric studies. I know you'd like to spend more time with her, and I believe there's something there to rekindle. I can help." Finn blanched, eliciting a good-natured laugh. "There's nothing supernatural about it, Finn. I keep my eyes open. I was there for you both, during the break-up; I know I can offer guidance.[38] What do you say, sweet boy?"

The Professor's snowball of promises rolled down the slope of Finn's subconscious, accreting unspoken dreams

---

[38] The professor had laid two husbands to rest, one she'd grown to love, and one she'd learned to hate; she was now happily partnered with a mustachioed carpenter, and an erudite lass with bright pink locks. They shared two cats and one true love between them.

abandoned through ages on the academic path, careening abruptly towards the present. It was a pure white wrecking ball crashing through his core, offering him what he hadn't known he'd always wanted. As Finn sat happy in the wreckage of anxieties unspoken, he saw Alice sunning by the rim of the fountain. He knew she was a part of the future the Professor had offered, the future he'd worked so hard for, survived the madness of this day to obtain. Finn knew, as you must know reading this now, that he accept—

"No, thank you, professor. Really, thank you, but no."

She was nonplussed. Her smile thinned as she straightened her shawl - positively misused, it seemed. Disappointment was in her eyes, and Finn caught a rough inhalation from her coral lips. "Are you sure you want to answer so categorically, and so quickly? We can talk about this…" she trailed off. She must have seen something in his eyes; she stood, brushing nothing off of her lap and patting him on the head. "We'll talk later, perhaps. Make the right choice."

Professor Haggbard walked away.

Finn wasn't sure what choice he'd made, or if he was still making it. There was someone else he needed to talk to, someone who had been missing all day.

She plopped onto the bench in a gold-sequined jumper. Her nails were a light blue at which she'd been picking, and her thick curly black hair was barely restrained in a scrunchied bun. With the delicacy of apple blossom embracing him, Finn realized the apple trees were not in bloom. She seemed Mediterranean, Greek or Italian, until he really saw her. The jumper could have been a toga, or sackcloth and ashes; her essence would have shown through. Finn could not have told you how he knew the music he liked best, or the most beautiful painting in a gallery of masterpieces; knowing more languages than most people could name, he had no words for what he saw in her face. Certitude was insufficient. Recognition, of something intangible and irreducible. She was a goddess; to disagree would be a cerebral tantrum, like insisting dark was light or up was down.

"Yo," said the goddess. Maybe "Ya."

Finn was awestruck, slightly. The indisputable reality of divinity should be beyond the pale to a committed agnostic, but something about this goddess had been missing all day.

"Well..." spaketh divinity. She stared, awaiting response.

Dumbfounded, Finn said nothing. He watched her raise a hand, wondering if she would bless, or curse. She watched herself make a fist, then pressed her thumb into the second knuckle of her index finger. She wiggled her thumb up and down, and spoke to it. A fist puppet.

"Hello Eris, nice to see you," she alternated with her hand. "It's nice to see you too, Finn, how's the sacred charge going?" "I was going to take it seriously, like you commanded, but instead I ignored everyone you sent me to and I kept the book for myself." "Wow, thanks for accepting my divine mission, then deciding you know better. I need a prophet, but you do you Finn." "You can't get good help these days, Eris. Thanks for the appletinis, by the way, which you personally created from nothingness."

Finn remained dumbfounded, for new reasons. Eris, exasperated, leaned in to flick his forehead and say "remember" in ancient Greek. The previous night crept back into Finn's awareness like a hungover teen, mumping home past his disappointed parents. This was his second, far clearer moment of theophany: *he'd met Eris last night at the club.*

She gave him a look.

Finn knew this was the most important sober conversation of his life. He'd studied spiritual traditions across six continents. He could describe a hundred approaches to welcoming a god. He knew the right honorifics, the ritual syntax, and he opened his mouth only for the wrong thing to come out.

"Sass isn't helpful," Finn complained, to his immediate despair. Lightning must be imminent, but his mouth kept moving. "I wish you'd sent a text, or written it down. I barely remember any details from last night, even after your holy flick; we spoke about a book, but… you wandered off to dance with Alice. Who I'd JUST been talking about, how we broke up, and—"

Eris coughed, artificially. She looked divinely abashed.

Finn glared.

Eris looked over at Alice, stretching her arms in the sun as her sweats dried.

Eyes narrow, he asked, "Did you even get to the prophet thing, before wandering off?"

She opened mouth. Then she closed it. "I don't remember," Eris griped. "This is all new to me! My star hasn't been on the rise in eons. I trusted my family the first time, which sucked. They're jerks. I'm open to any suggestions you've got."

Finn tried to help a goddess in search of a savior. "The Bookman was a real bastard. You don't want him. Thornley is way too self-important, she'd sell advertising space in your holy book. Wait, do you have a holy book?" Finn considered, way too late, what he was getting into.

"Is that mandatory?" Eris asked. "In the old days, it was all about most praise, fanciest incense, lambs sacrificed per worshipper… Oh! What about that?" She flapped her hand at the Principia. "I like it. They made me important. And it's funny. What do they believe?"

Finn was stymied. "It's complicated. Don't you have laws, or commandments? How are you running this cult, or whatever, once your revelation occurs?"

Eris was irritated by the questions.

Finn was finally in a familiar context.

"I hadn't decided, Finn, thank you very much. If SOMEONE could pick a prophet, we could answer your questions." Thunder rumbled in a cloudless sky, and the echo lingered.

Finn reassured himself that this was perfectly normal summer weather. Gulping, he continued, "Professor Haggbard would be a good choice. She knows everything about contemporary philosophy. You could craft a radical modern ethics with her, based on cutting edge moral theory."

Eris looked hopeful, and the sky was brighter.

Finn frowned, caressing gray pages. "She can be… difficult, though. She's brilliant, but too abstract for most people without two semesters of introductory courses. She's kind though, that has to matter."

"Does it?" Eris mused.

Finn's jaw dropped.

"How could it NOT? You must have some humanitarian message, or meaning or… What is the point of you, if you don't do good for people?" Finn caught himself, once again sure that lightning was coming, any second.

Aaaaaany second.

Eris began to cry.

Finn was relieved, for a long sigh. Then he felt awful. He offered Eris a spare bodega napkin.

She blew her nose volubly and said, "You don't know what it's like! There's so much pressure, but you can't just smite people who aren't doing the right thing. Not that we're told what 'right' is, or wrong. We're just supposed to be, to express meaning, or something. There's no guide. Barely any humans know me, but it's 'my time again.' Why should they know me? What have I done, except ruin a wedding?"

Finn's mouth moved frantically, saying, "You? Because of you, Paris and Helen got together! We can thank you for the Illiad, and the Odyssey, the foundations of the western canon. By extension, for every great work from Europe, which includes these United States![39] You're responsible…Don Quixote, uh, The Hobbit, Oh Brother Where Art Thou, the list goes on. Your name echoes through the centuries. You're practically responsible for epic fantasy, most sci-fi, and the works of Borges. Without Eris, we couldn't have Pierre Menard, Author of the Quixote!"

Eris, cheerful again, replied, "That's wonderful! Who is Pierre Menard?"

Finn realized he'd gone too far. "He isn't actually real."

"Who is these days?" Eris laughed, confident again. Finn fumbled for the thread of his argument, but he was thrown off by Alice's approach. She just wiggled her nose at him, and gave a little laugh, then leaned in over Eris. Alice whispered in Eris' ear and slipped her number into the goddesses' pocket. With a hint of a grin, Alice sauntered away to hunt wild cupcakes with the fairies.

---

[39] This is a reductive and euro-centric point of view, but Eris clearly felt better to hear it.

Finn ignored the scrape of sequins on wood until Eris laid her head on his shoulder. He'd almost caught the thread, but it might have just snapped.

"You're not bad, Finn," Eris assured his tense shoulders.[40] "Once I handle this revelation, maybe… I thought you could worship me?"

Finn relaxed at her request. If you tabled her distressing divinity, and gave her a pass on the torments of the day, Eris wasn't too bad herself. He leaned back, watching the sky go by, and finally said, "I'm conflicted. On the one hand, it'd be nice to pray to a goddess that I know exists. On the other, how can I worship something real and tangible? I could worship the sun as a symbol: Apollo, Ra, Amaterasu. Why worship a big ball of gas? I appreciate its power, but I'm illuminated and enlivened by its energy whether I worship it or not. Is… is that what gods are? Actually, are there other gods? There must be, at least the Greeks, but what about others? What about the big Abrahamic beard in the sky?"[41] Finn lost composure as he pondered, achieving an anxious squawk.

Eris shifted just enough to punch Finn in the side, hard, then returned to her resting state. "That's for calling me a ball of gas, you jerk."

He argued that he'd done no such thing, but she spoke over him mercilessly.

"If you want to be anal about this, you can be my high priest, or… what do you call'em?"

---

[40] What did Eris know, though? Finn had taken far more classes in moral philosophy.

[41] Or wasn't Abraham supposed to have a bosom? And if so, did that mean he wore a corset in heaven?

Finn tried to respond, but she absently punched him again.

"That was a rhetorical whatchamacallit. Pope! You'll be my Pope, uh… what the Principia says, you'll be an Erisian Pope!" She smiled at Finn, the matter settled, and the day shone warm and bright.

Finn's instincts did not fail him. He responded, "Actually, every man, woman, and child is an Erisian Pope, according to the book."

"Oh, I like that!" Eris replied with unexpected positivity. "So everyone worships me already? Good work, Finn!"

"They don't, though," he hesitantly responded.

Eris gazed thoughtfully skywards, and said, "I guess that's fair. Wouldn't be much need for this prophet business if I'm already worshipped worldwide." She took a deep breath; the noise of the park faded away, and the bench was its own private world. She exhaled, and said, "You've got a handle on this stuff, Finn, even if you can be a jerk. You'll do."

Finn thought that was unfair. "A jerk?" he replied, "After what you've put me through, and Alice, and then you punched me, and…" then his ears caught up to his mouth. Tentatively, he asked, "I'll do for what?"

Eris beamed, and Finn felt radiant. "You'll make a great prophet!" she proclaimed, "You think too much about all the right things. Plus, you're fun to mess with. That'll help. You'll definitely be messed with, by the world. And probably me."

Finn once again cursed the inventor of the radio alarm clock.

Eris continued, with growing excitement, "I'll make you a saint too, the best type. Highest class? I only skimmed the book, plus I looked at the pictures. I added some doodles."

Finn tried to focus. "The highest class of Discordian saint is solely for fictional people, like St. Quixote, or St. Bokonon; the Five Star saints are supposedly your apostles, but they're all made up for the Principia, and they come across as a bit silly."

Eris yawned hugely, mouth uncovered, and their private tranquility dissipated like morning mist as the bustle of the park returned. She laid down upon the bench and rested her head on his lap.[42] Eris looked up and patted Finn's cheek with minor condescension, saying, "It's all a bit silly down here, but you can be fictional if you really want to. I'm glad we settled this, Finn. I need a nap while it's sunny; we'll figure out the details later." Yawning once more, languidly stretching her arms and flopping them over Finn, Eris fell asleep.

Finn leaned back, careful not to shift his goddess. He admired the infinite blue of the sky. In the clarity of that perfect moment, he made himself a promise: tomorrow, he would be sleeping in.

---

[42] Future theologians might mark this bench as a holy place, of critical importance to a burgeoning religious movement. They would almost certainly be missing the point.

FOR THE LOVE OF VENUS

Andrea Obaez

Thunder Moon

Anamaria Delgado lived a simple, predictable life of her own making. Compared to the chaos of her childhood, the rigorous process of pursuing a PhD, and the soul-crushing search for a tenured position in academia, a life of quiet, simple comforts felt like the height of privilege.

Ana taught in the mornings and ran errands in the afternoons. When she drove, she would listen to podcasts or her favorite music. In the evenings, she'd either binge watched bad TV with her long-time best friend and roommate, Kristen Sanchez, or relaxed alone, catching up on her never ending reading log. Every moment of her adult life was pleasantly predictable, until the day she dropped her phone in a faculty bathroom sink.

"Crap!" She hissed, and reached out a split second too late. The old trusty Nokia, which had survived worse drops in mud and against the hardest concrete, activated the motion detector on the way down, coming into direct contact with water, and that's all it took. The phone was bricked.

Ana mumbled a stream of profanities, trying to get the phone to restart to no avail. It was just a phone, she tried to tell herself, but it was the same cell phone she'd had for over ten years, and it felt like she was losing a part of herself.

Someone flushed in the last stall, alerting Ana of an audience. Faculty members and staff were often bigger gossips than students, and it took very little for them to start whispering, their words dripping with false concern over so-and-so's ability to hack it in the hardcore world of academia. Ana didn't want to give anyone the satisfaction of seeing her distraught over a damp phone, so she quickly snatched too-short sections of paper towels from the automatic dispenser, and hurried out of the bathroom.

Ana walked across campus angry at the phone for dying on her, and at herself for caring so much. She had students to teach, she told herself. She knew what life was like before cell phones. She should function without one. And yet, she lasted less than three hours, distracted to pieces throughout the day, before she found herself at the mall - pitifully looking for a new phone.

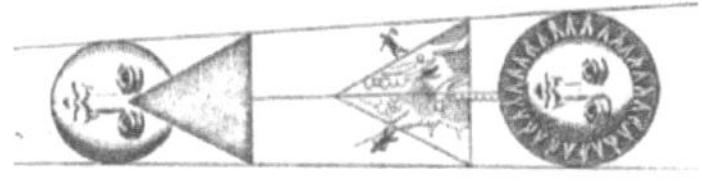

"What do you mean, they don't make that model anymore?" Ana asked a little too loudly. She was standing in the middle of the wireless phone store, and remembered a split second later that she was not exactly alone.

She glanced around nervously, but no one seemed to notice her behavior, let alone her. Stranger things happened at the mall regularly, and Ana was hardly the strangest thing that had happened in that store on that very same day. But Ana couldn't help feeling self-conscious for acting so out of character in such a public space.

The salesgirl, whose name tag simply read, "Sue," was unbothered and unimpressed.

"Miss, that phone is old," She sassed back. "I would've dropped it in the toilet myself if I'd known you were still rocking that," Sue continued, giving the dead phone a poke for good measure.

Ana was taken aback. "I didn't—"

Sue shot her a look that suggested Ana needn't bother to finish that sentence.

For a second, Sue looked pensively, like she could read Ana with a look. Her features were striking. She had dark hair and eyes like Ana herself, but while Ana would often describe herself as mousy and bookish, often hiding her sometimes problem skin behind oversized glasses, Sue's smooth skin and features were firmly classic.

"Why are you so attached to this phone?" She asked, her tone and body language suddenly heavy with familiarity, and the first word Ana could think to describe it was, "Effective." The fluorescent lighting and the no-makeup look failed diminish the magnetic pull of Sue's gaze, and Ana suddenly found herself reconsidering where she landed on the Kinsey scale.

The words were battling their way out of her mouth. "It was a gift," Ana wanted to say. "Someone I miss dearly gave it to me," she wanted to blurt out, but she fought the words back through sheer force of practice. Instead, Ana shook her head, fighting back the blanket of euphoria that had suddenly engulfed her.

I don't remember dropping molly on the way here, she thought to herself.

Sue waited with coy patience for a response.

"I—," Ana stammered. "That was my first cell phone. It was my first phone number. I don't want people that I care about having trouble finding me."

"Oh," Sue simply replied, her tone heavy with implication. "Well, I can make sure that doesn't happen," she reassured, and turned to stare at her screen.

Ana had the vague feeling that she was missing something obvious. Sue's familiar approach felt too intimate for your run of the mill sales person. Still, she reminded herself, she met new people at the university every day. Many who knew who she was before she met them. Sue could easily be an old student she'd forgotten.

Ana tried to refocus, and started again. "I don't I really need—"

"Yes you do," Sue cut her off with a side eye. "You simply don't know the experiences, access and convenience you're missing out on simply because you haven't let yourself."

"My life is fine," Ana responded, defensive, but Sue wasn't buying it.

"And there's nothing you want beyond that?" she asked, tilting her head. Ana fought back another tumble of words, feeling her face redden.

"I'm not sure," she offered.

Sue smiled back but said nothing, returning to the safer subject.

"Look," she pointed at the screen. "You've never used any of your upgrade options. I can easily grandfather your rate into the unlimited data plan and convert your unused upgrades." she clicked a few times. "There. You can pretty much pick any phone in the store."

Ana let out a pitiful sound, too overwhelmed to respond.

Sue took the moment of hesitation as an opportunity. "Hold on," she stepped into the stockroom and returned almost instantaneously. "Here," Sue continued, showing Ana a chrome phone inside sleek packaging that looked like it had just fallen out of the sky. "This is the best phone in the company. It's only supposed to be available for early access, but you have enough credits to buy it."

"You don't have to—"

But Sue continued. "It's user-friendly, shatterproof, has a solid 300GB of internal memory and all the basic social media apps pre-installed."

Ana felt cornered, and she was sure that was Sue's exact intention. "It's just a phone!" She wanted to shout, but that was the point. If it was just a phone, why was she so attached to her old one? And why did touching this new sleek, shiny thing feel like she was being offered a drink of water from a forbidden spring?

"I can literally transfer your contacts and set up social media profiles in fifteen minutes," Sue added with a smirk. "And will be able to keep your phone number."

Defeated, Ana nodded.

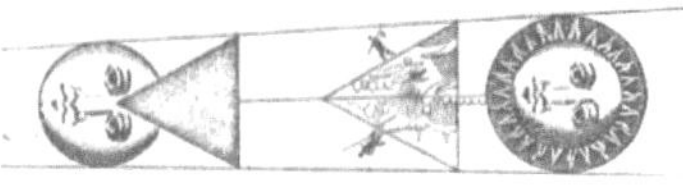

True to her word, within fifteen minutes Sue gave Ana a new phone set up with profiles on Instagram, Twitter, Facebook, Tumblr, and a few more. And within those fifteen minutes, it felt like everyone Ana had ever met found her. Friends, family, students and casual acquaintances from all corners of the internet wanted to link up in some way, so that another fifteen minutes later Ana was sitting in her driver's seat, setting the phone on silent as the many, "Welcome to _____!" and "How have you been?!?" notifications accumulated.

Ana stared at the phone, feeling like it wasn't quite hers yet. Even the lock screen photo had been Sue's choice: a highly stylized photo of a beautiful woman, hair flared out in a halo, against an aquamarine and gold background, with just the slightest hint of pink. It was an artist's rendering of a goddess, but Ana hadn't caught which one.

It was a beautiful photo, one Ana wouldn't have picked out herself. For the first time, she wondered if her reluctance was keeping her from experiencing something wonderful and new, even as it terrified her.

Sue had assured her: once Ana had a better idea of what she wanted, she could change things around. Still, the continued stream of welcome messages didn't help ease her anxiety. Nothing seemed more daunting than spending chunks of her free time interacting with people she knew out of obligation. Or worse: with people she didn't know. She had enough of that at work.

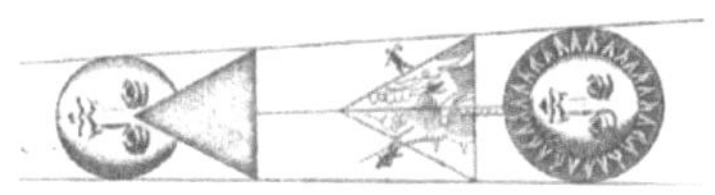

"You got a new phone!" Kristen shouted as she burst into their shared apartment.

Jarred from deep thought, Ana looked up from the papers she'd been grading and blinked rapidly, trying to remember if there was a conversation she'd missed.

New phone, right. She had almost convinced herself that the rest of the day could go on as usual, but she'd underestimated how excited Kristen would be for her. Weighed down with grocery bags running up and down her forearms, Kristen somehow managed to bounce around like a kid on Christmas morning in front of the open door.

"How?" Ana asked, sitting upright on the couch. Kristen managed to raise an arm high enough to lock the door and wobbled across the room, placing the bags by Ana's feet. She shoved her own phone in Ana's face, pointing to Ana's status update: "New phone, who dis?" signed with the name and make of her new phone.

Ana sighed. That update was 100% Sue. "You know, for someone who's known me for like, ever, you'd think you'd be able to tell when I've been hacked."

"Were you hacked?" Kristen asked, raising an eyebrow.

"No," Ana deadpanned.

"Then get over it and let me see," Kristen scolded, putting a hand out. "That model isn't supposed to come out for another three months."

"Bitch, hi to you too," Ana replied, indignant.

"Oh, my gods," Kristen exclaimed. She bent over to rummage through one of the bags.

"Here, a trade" She handed Ana a small pot of baby pink and white roses, with small bits of rose and clear quartz in the soil. "These were on sale, and I just couldn't leave the store without them."

"Aww, you should have," Ana exclaimed, handing the phone over. She got up from the couch and grabbed a couple of the bags with her free hand, bringing them to the kitchen across the room. The apartment wasn't small by any means, but the open layout that made it too easy for two latinas to shout at each other from their bedrooms at opposite ends of the apartment. Their professional friends swore they'd gotten lucky, but they just happened to move into South Whitney Street before it was gentrified, far enough from South Marshall Street that it felt like a different world, and close enough that they could witness its fall and rebirth in real time.

Ana emptied the two bags full of produce and went to grab more. Kristen stood in the same spot, fiddling with the smartphone with almost childlike wonder. Now it was her turn to ask: "How? Did your old phone finally put itself out of its misery?"

"Something like that," Ana replied, taking cold cuts and cheeses out of a new bag. Ana reiterated her entire interaction with Sue to Kristen, down to tone and mannerisms.

"Thank the gods," Kristen mumble, handing the phone back. "You kept that thing for too long."

"Be nice," Ana replied, filling a cup with lukewarm water. "I've kept you around far longer." She didn't want to have another conversation about how she needed to move on and experience new things, so she took the roses to her bedroom and placed them on her nightstand, watering them just enough to moisten the soil. Then she plugged her new phone to charge and placed it next to the roses as well.

Kristen got the hint. When Ana returned to the living room Kristen casually talked about her day and asked Ana about the rest of hers. Ana arranged a platter of cold cuts and vegetables while Kristen poured some wine, sneakily adding some dark chocolate to the plate. They browsed through the Netflix queue and settled on Sweet Home Alabama, a movie they'd both seen before and could watch a million more times.

When the movie was over, Ana announced that she still had papers to grade, so she poured herself a final glass and went to her bedroom, placing the wine by the phone. The words *Makeshift Altar* flashed in her head, but she just shrugged it off, moving on to the next thought.

Ana got comfortable between the covers and grabbed her favorite type of pen, returning to her stack of essays. But soon, much too soon, the wine took effect, and Ana fell asleep.

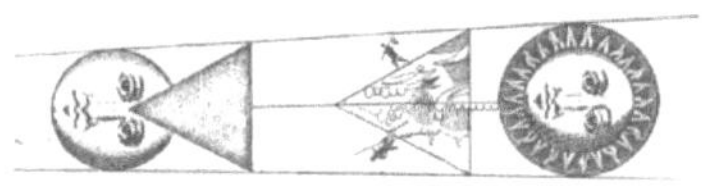

That Friday morning started like any other. Ana recognized the scent of roses before she opened her eyes, and it was wonderful. She hadn't finished her wine before she'd fallen asleep, and almost knocked over the glass as she reached out to silence the phone alarm. That was enough to wake her up. Eyes wide open, she steadied the glass, then eased the phone off the nightstand. Analyzing the lock screen image once again, Ana set the phone to snooze, letting out a sigh of relief.

A lone notification waited for her attention. It seemed that the barrage had ended and she could go back to her life. She exhaled in relief as she stumbled across the apartment towards the bathroom, leaving the phone on the kitchen island — away from the wine — and started her morning routine. When she came back out from the bathroom, there was coffee waiting for her.

"You know, maybe it's not so bad," Ana offered.

Kristen looked up from what she'd been reading without moving her head, and raised an eyebrow in anticipation.

Ana tried to explain. "I worried that getting a new phone would hijack my time, but it's not such a bad thing. I'm the one who decides how much time I spend using it." To illustrate her point, she picked up the phone and, with barely a glance, dropped it in her bag.

"Wait." Something caught her eye. "What the hell?" She snatched the phone back.

Kristen stood to read over Ana's shoulder. "You have three messages on Love Goddess Dating." She whipped her head to look directly at Ana. "You signed up for a dating website?"

"No, I did not," Ana replied, tapping furiously. "I would never. Did you?"

Kristen shook her head. "I wish I thought of it though."

Ana groaned in frustration as she opened the app. Somehow, she had a profile on a dating app she'd never heard of before, complete with pictures and taglines from her social media accounts, so that it looked as official as everything else. "Sue. It had to be Sue," she mumbled furiously, searching frantically through the settings for a Deactivate Account option. *I'm going to give that girl such a bad review,* Ana thought, knowing full well that she'd never.

"Maybe it's in beta testing since it's a new phone?" Kristen offered, but Ana wasn't interested.

"I need to uninstall this."

"Wait, why?" Kristen asked, snatching the phone away.

Ana gaped. "What the f—"

"Ana," Kristen snapped, "I'm saying this because I love you. You haven't been on a date since undergrad."

"That's not the poi—"

"Yes, it is," Kristen interrupted. "And we both know why." She softened her tone. "Don't you think it's time?"

Ana dropped her hands. She was furious. "Shouldn't that be my decision?" She snarled. Too many people, Kristen included, had a lot of opinions about how she should live her life, when she was living it just fine.

"It is your decision, one you've been avoiding to make for over ten years."

Ana was practically seeing red.

Kristen stepped forward. "You can grow to love someone the way you loved Henry, but you have to at least try."

"And you'd know?" Ana snapped back, regretting it the moment she saw the hurt on Kristen's face. It was a low blow, and they both knew it. "I'm sorry…" she started, but Kristen engulfed her in a hug.

"Just because I'm aromantic doesn't mean I don't understand what it means to you," Kristen reminded her calmly. She pulled away to look at Ana in the face, but Ana tried to cover her face, and tears, in shame.

"You're lonely. People can see it if they know what to look for, and I think hanging out with me makes it too easy for you to ignore it. Don't, okay? You deserve the love you've always wanted. Please try? Give it at least a week."

Ana nodded, once again feeling like she didn't have much of a choice.

"I guess," she replied. "I guess."

Sturgeon Moon

The phone was determined to make an honest woman out of her. There was a traffic jam on her way home from work that evening, and she suddenly got a notification for a discount hair cut straight ahead, all she had to do was turn right. Traffic was going nowhere, so she figured why not.

Two hours later, after a life changing scalp massage, shampoo and deep conditioning treatment, Ana had the best haircut she'd had in years. The salon specialized in curly hair and she bought one of each of their products, happy to share with Kristen, who had even curlier hair than her. They were both practically in tears at this new discovery, and wondered why Ana had never heard of that salon before.

Ana also started to check out the guys that messaged her on Love Goddess Dating, and whenever they seemed promising, the phone would give her local suggestions that seemed tailor-made for no pressure dates: cooking classes, movies, plays and comedy shows, so that "I guess," turned into dinner with Matt, a first-grade teacher who loved every moment of his job. Comedy shows with Luis, a programmer so funny that she had to beg him to let her breathe. Workouts with Tony, a personal trainer who'd woken her competitive streak. And on and on until the phone became an extension of herself. Or until she became an extension of the phone.

After her initial hesitation wore off, Ana learned she enjoyed having so much information at her fingertips. In her down time, she watched the interactions on different social media platforms with fascination, chiming in with her two-cents when it felt right. When it didn't, she moved on to the next thing without a second thought.

In a matter of weeks, her lifestyle went through a complete makeover, so that her entire world slowly stopped revolving around work. It felt difficult to remember what her life looked like a few weeks before. Almost. People noticed and asked questions that she didn't want to answer in depth:

Are you seeing someone new?

Yes, several someones, thank you, she thought.

Why are you smiling so wide at nothing at all?

Because I'm happy, and I don't think I knew what that was like.

Harvest Moon

So what would a perfect Saturday look like to you? Matt asked in a text message. Ana thought for a second. It was a Wednesday afternoon, and she was deep in a conversation about likes and dislikes with Matthew Ferrante.

Matt was the first guy Ana went out with on Love Goddess Dating, and while she would never admit to it aloud, she'd been smitten from the moment they'd met in person. Not only was he incredibly good looking in a California boy kind of way, there was just something deeply uncomplicated about Matt. He had an inner peace that radiated off him in waves, and Ana could tell, almost immediately, that he was both comfortable with who he was, and open to learn new things about himself. She found the combination incredibly attractive.

During dinner, she mentioned that *His Girl Friday* was one of her favorite movies and they fell into a mischievously friendly banter after that had her in stitches. And as he was dropping her off at home that same evening, he gave her a soft kiss on the lips that made her shiver from head to toe.

Ana liked his style. She also thought he had the patience of a saint. The youngest after three sisters and two brothers, Matt had an age gap of six years from his closest sibling, and had the stories to prove it. There was little that could get under adult Matt's skin. He seemed to understand, deeply, just how easily people could complicate their own lives, and he had no interest in doing the same. Anna thought there was a lot she could learn from his laid-back approach to life.

Farmer's market. Ana replied, finally. *Making brunch together with friends. Pastries and mimosas.*

A reply came in a few seconds later. Ana went to look, only to realize the message wasn't from Matt. Her heart thudded harder in her chest. It was a message on Love Goddess Dating from Henry.

Henry.

Henry was her past and Henry had been her everything. Even in her darkest hours, when no one was around to see or hear how she was really feeling, Ana adamantly refused to admit how much she missed him still, even now, years later. Henry had been all she'd ever wished for, and here he was, messaging her on a dating app, like it was the most natural thing, like he hadn't destroyed her world the last time they spoke.

I'm so happy to see your face again, his message read.

She immediately forgot about the conversation with Matt. She wanted nothing more than to talk to Henry again. But where could she even begin?

He messaged her again: *Can we talk?*

Ana was crumbling under wave after wave of emotion. They'd grown up shouting distance from each other — Ana, Kristen and Henry — in the kind of neighborhood you grow up wishing to escape, and only a few manage to do so. For as long as she could remember, Ana had a crush on Henry that was difficult to hide. The kind of crush that had a young girl taking chain letters seriously, twisting apple stems and breaking them off when she came to the first letter of his name, dreaming of escaping together.

Henry seemed interested in the obvious ways. He was her first kiss, her first love, but he'd kept her at arm's length in many little ways, ways that mattered. Physically, he was there. Emotionally, he was so hard to pin down: he refused to label whatever relationship they had. As much as she *believed* that he loved her back, he avoided giving her any kind of clarity, and whenever she tried to push the subject, he'd react by pulling away.

Once, after whispering that she loved him, she didn't see him for weeks. She thought it was her fault. She came on too strong. She wanted him too much. They were too young. She should be focusing on school anyways. She had a life of her own to lead. She'd convinced herself to never push again, and things were okay as long as she knew where to stay.

And then she saw him chatting up another girl. She'd stood there, part frozen, and the other part not wanting to make a scene. He saw her too, and when he came to her later, trying to pretend like nothing was wrong, she'd simply asked: *What about me?*

"Do you really think you're the only one?" he spat. And there it was. He'd been so quick to break their connection, so brutal, that her only choice was to walk away. It was easy, even if it hurt more than anything else. She enrolled for grad

school at an all girl's university two avenues across town, far enough from South Marshall Street that it felt like a different world, and she rarely came home. She fell into a world of books only, anchored by Kristen and little else, and it was fine, even if she felt half alive.

He messaged her again. *I'd like the opportunity to apologize to you.*

She sat down and stared. She took forever to type out three characters:

Oh?

A few seconds later: *I was stupid and self-absorbed, and when you tried to talk to me about it I remember just thinking that you were trying to lock me down. Like you were trying to claim me even before I had a chance to decide. I got so defensive. I wouldn't listen and I'm so sorry for that. It was one of the stupidest things I've ever done and I'm still kicking myself for it.*

Ana stared at her phone. She could swear she lost her eyesight and hearing. She realized her mouth was hanging open and she quickly closed it. She blinked a few times, but the words were still there, every single word she had wanted to hear for almost ten years.

Can you call me so you can actually hear me say it? He added his phone number.

She was shaking so much she dropped her phone. It was the same number, she noticed. She'd almost forgotten it, and some part of her wanted to count that as a triumph, but as she dialed, she wondered if he'd kept it so she'd find him again, like she'd hoped he'd find her.

"Ana," he breathed her name, a sigh of delight and melancholia mixed together, and she melted.

She was so nervous that she couldn't will herself to speak, and it was as if he knew (of course he would know, she thought later, he knew everything there was to know about her) so he spoke for both of them until she could.

He apologized. He apologized some more. He went over all the minutiae of their last conversation and all he did wrong. When she was able to speak again she asked him about his life, about how'd it been since they last spoke. He wanted to know about hers, and what teaching was like, and they talked until Ana could hear the birds chirping at sunrise. She didn't want to hang up. She didn't want to let go, and he knew too, and promised to stay on the line. She placed the hot phone on her pillow and fell asleep, and when she woke up hours later, he was still there.

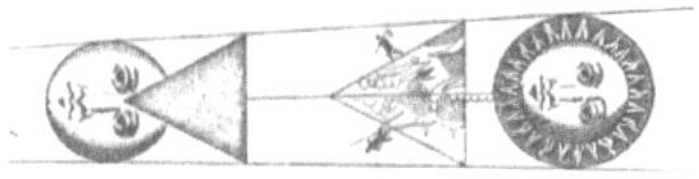

They met for brunch at *Tisane's* that Saturday afternoon. Ana barely slept the night before, and she spent the better part of that morning trying to pick out an outfit that was a combination of casual, sexy, flattering, and appropriate. It'd been a nerve-wracking experience, and as she made her way to *Tisane's,* she was still wondering if she was wearing too much makeup.

And then she saw him. He'd aged in the past ten years, that much was certain. His hair was darker, and she wondered if he'd dyed it. His face was lined, but he was the same man: Tall and broad-shouldered, with a smile that said he was up to no good. The feeling of love and nostalgia that she felt for him hit her as strongly as the first time. He smiled at her, and she wondered in that split second if he could see everything she was feeling written all over her face.

It was like no time had passed. He kissed her hand and then her lips. And it was good. So so good. "You missed me, haven't you?" he asked.

She nodded quietly, not sure how to respond. The question didn't sit right, like he was curious about what power over her he still had. She tried to brush it off. They went inside.

"Welcome to *Tisane*. Please have a seat anywhere you like."

Ana blinked. "Wait, Sue? You work here too?"

Sue shrugged. She was wearing a different uniform but it was Sue alright, only her name tag had her full name: Suada.

"I'll find us seats," Henry offered.

Ana couldn't respond. Sue followed Ana's gaze and rolled her eyes.

"Yeah, they're really strict about using legal names around here," She shrugged. "A job is a job, I guess. How's the phone working for you?" she asked with an eye-wiggle.

Ana was aghast. She looked at the phone in her hand and back at Sue, and something clicked in her mind.

"Why are you so attached to this phone?"

"That was my first cell phone," she'd responded, but the real answer, the one she'd fought back was: because it was a gift from Henry, and she was still holding on.

She felt faint. "Did- did you do this? Did you know?" Ana asked a little too loudly, once again shouting in a public space because of this girl.

Sue shook her head with a smirk. "Nope, I just asked my manager for a special exception, and she agreed."

"You're lonely. People can see it if they know what to look for."

"You deserve the love you've always wanted."

Sue glanced in Henry's direction and looked back at Ana, eyebrow raised, like she could read Henry with a look. "But.. him?"

"You don't understand..." Ana began, but she realized that she didn't want Sue to understand, not really. How could she want that for anyone, craving someone your entire life?

Once again, Sue took Ana's silence as an opportunity to plow forward.

"Just because he desires you doesn't mean he loves you," she offered a little too knowingly.

The words hit a raw nerve. "You don't know him." Ana snapped back, the heat of humiliation starting to radiate off her cheeks.

But Sue did not back down, "He knows *you*." She responded softly, leaving Ana reeling. She had no response. The exchange stung the same way eyes hurt after turning on the lights after hours of staring out into the dark, only the pain was in her lungs, so that every breath burned.

Ana walked away under Sue's gaze, her words still clinging on Ana like bad perfume. Ana tried to push them out of her thoughts, but as she and Henry talked, they pulled her back. *He knows you.*

Henry barely noted how off center she'd felt, how distracted she was, how her mood had shifted from one moment to the next, and while part of her was relieved, she wanted nothing more than to talk about the root of that pain, the things that made her wonder if she could trust him. The things they needed to cover before they could move on.

"You've apologized, but how have you really changed?" She wanted to ask. She wanted him to list examples and truths and reassure her with clear promises to never fall back on bad behavior, but it wasn't exactly first date appropriate conversation. Before she knew it, the deepest thing they talked about was *Love Goddess Dating,* and how they'd miraculously reconnected again because of a drowned phone.

She went home with him that night, and everything felt like the good parts from before. He touched her and it was like coming home.

Just like before, every physical thing he offered her felt right, but it wasn't enough. It never was. The feeling stuck with Ana, and she was afraid that once Henry believed she was within his grasp, he'd feel free to take her for granted. She wouldn't let that happen. She couldn't let that happen again.

Dying Moon

Even on her deathbed, even if she were forced to put her hand on a stack of bibles and promise to tell the truth, Anamaria Delgado, professor of English and American Literature, would never admit that she didn't like to read Emily Dickinson.

It wasn't *just* Ana's policy of never speaking ill of the dead. It was the way Dickinson's poems were constructed, so restricted, with the absolute minimal amount of words to convey a thought… Ana felt claustrophobic just reading them. She knew that was the point. Dickinson used one of the only mediums available to her to convey the repression of her reality. Many of Dickinson's well-known poems had been procured from private letters and friends, and that form of voyeurism also made Ana uncomfortable. She often wondered what kind of art Dickinson would have been able to produce had she had lived in an age where women were encouraged to fulfill their full potential. Ana didn't know what that age was, but she was curious all the same.

Ana understood what it was like to grow up in an environment designed to limit you. She understood it for Dickinson, and she understood it for Henry. They'd grown up in the kind of environment where a "Love 'em and Leave 'em" mentality was expected of boys; *Caring* and *Compromise* were slurs, and girls were expected to be grateful because male attention meant social validation, even as they were punished for seeking it out.

Ten years before, Henry had used every bit of his intimate knowledge of her to keep her off balance and submissive. He'd dismissed most of that knowledge past what he wanted or needed, and she'd ignored the feeling that she was being manipulated because she was in love. She'd believed it was the only way he knew how to communicate with women, and told herself he was insecure.

But now they were adults. She didn't want to be handled in her own relationship. She didn't want to wait for explanations that always seemed designed to make her feel at fault, always arriving after the fact and never when she needed it. The difference between Henry and Dickinson was that Henry was a man alive in contemporary times, and he had a choice. She just wanted him to see it. She believed that he could.

Henry started implementing his strategy almost immediately after their first date, and Ana was sure he didn't think she'd notice, like before. It was a sneaky process, sprinkled throughout their interactions, delivered so deftly, just enough for her to notice but still not worth pointing out.

It was:

"Sorry, I missed your texts, I've been super busy the last couple of days," when she could see him active on the very dating app she was desperately trying to erase.

It was:

"Nah, I don't feel like going out, just come over," when she tried to set a date.

It was:

"You know Kristen hates me," when Kristen, bless her soul, bit her tongue and said nothing, noting that she was ill-equipped to judge this very thing.

It was her, silently begging, *Please. Please do the right thing. Please don't do this.*

They say that when you have rose colored glasses on, red flags just look like flags. But this was worse, this was being challenged to find flags wearing smudged glasses through gaslight. It wasn't love, at least, not the kind of love that makes you wish the best for the other person. It was manipulation of the most vulnerable, taking advantage of a person simply because they unwise enough to care for you, and she told him so. *You're doing that thing,* she said, *like you've already decided how this is going to go and you'll only tell me when I guess wrong.*

He responded quickly: *It's not like that. I'm busy.*

She thought for a moment. *There's an Of Gods and Globes exhibit at the museum next month, and I really want to check it out with you.*

Nice, he replied.

Not a real response, she thought.

Please, let's go, you and me. We can make a night of it. And then: *This is important to me.*

Sure, he replied, after a few beats. Not good enough.

So you'll go with me?

I said sure.

"*I said sure, not yes.*" She replied quickly, quoting his words back to him from long ago. *You've pulled that shit before.*

Finally: *Yes, I'll go.* And she almost believed it.

The night before the exhibit he didn't text her, even as she reminded him. The familiar urge to bombard him with apologies overwhelmed her. Ten years ago, she wouldn't have hesitated.

It was a dumb idea anyway, She would have said. *It's stupid of me. What do you want to do instead?*

She didn't want another ten years of wondering if she'd overreacted or if she'd been handled. She didn't want to leave any room for plausible deniability. She was adamant on seeing this through. So she held back the urge and went to sleep. Then the day came, and he was late. She went to the museum anyway, and she waited. *Hey, I'm here,* she texted once she'd arrived, and waited.

He knows you.

You deserve the love you've always wanted. But what she wanted was him.

Ana sat outside, telling herself that she loved the crisp night air. After fifteen minutes of waiting she texted again. *Are you on your way?*

For an hour and a half there was no response. She walked the exhibit alone, slowly, deliberately, hoping even then that he'd show up. She found the bar. She drank some wine. She was truly drunk, and then:

Sorry, I got caught up. I suck. And then, *Why don't you come to my place?*

And there it was.

Caught up doing what?

No answer, again. She waited some more. She paid for her drinks but just as she realized that she was in no shape to drive, someone walked up behind her.

"C'mon," She heard a voice, and before she could look up, she knew it was Sue. "I'll drive you home."

The look of concern on her face was too much. "Dear gods, you drive Uber too?" Ana snapped.

"No," Sue replied softly, "this one's free."

Ana held back the tears until she got in the car, and then she couldn't stop. She covered her face with her hands. She was humiliated. She looked at her phone.

He'd ignored her question and continued texting her, an apology first, some self-berating, and again: *Just come over when you're done. I still want to see you.*

Sue watched her from the corner of her eye, but Ana had been here before. The apologies were new but the outcome was the same. Her full of longing, never knowing anything for sure, elated for the few scraps he could spare.

And he knew, he knew that deep down she wanted to believe it, the unspoken promise he was dangling in front of her: that if she was patient, if she'd just wait and not push, he'd finally love her the way that she deserved.

But she'd already done that. For years, she'd waited. She stayed in her invisible fence, and the first time she'd asked him to consider her feelings, he broke her.

Do you really think you're the only one?

She couldn't risk that again. She pushed anyway.

You never planned to meet me tonight, did you? She replied, and she stared at the screen. And when he didn't reply she wasn't surprised. This is just who he is, she told herself.

This is who he chooses to be.

Henry hadn't replied by the time Sue dropped her off at home. He hadn't replied by the time Kristen coaxed her into getting some sleep, and in the morning when he still hadn't replied, through eyes nearly swollen shut from the tears, Ana blocked his number for the last time and went back to sleep.

Frost Moon

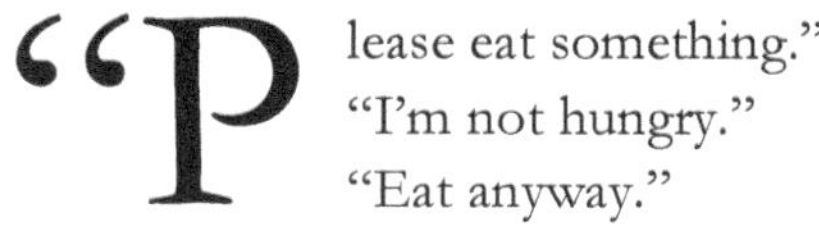

lease eat something."

"I'm not hungry."

"Eat anyway."

Long Night's Moon

"Do you have any plans for New Year's Eve?"

"No, I'd rather stay home."

"Ok, I'll stay home with you."

"You don't have to do that."

"I know."

Spirit Moon

"I had hoped…"

"I know. There is nothing wrong with having hope."

Hunger Moon

Sugar Moon

Pink Moon

Strawberry Moon

"Why is it so bright out here?" Ana asked, shielding her eyes.

"That's the sun, sweetheart," Kristen responded by her side.

"Can't it like, cut it out?"

"Write a letter."

Ana looked at her friend and gave her a knowing smile. They were finally, somehow, at the farmer's market. Ana had spent the past few months in hibernation, only looking up to go to work and go back home, a routine that was easy to fall back into even as she felt she'd fundamentally changed. Ana had been mourning what could have been and coping with what was. She admitted to herself that, deep down, she had always hoped to end up with Henry, and she'd been okay with submerging herself in her work, hoping that someday she'd look up and he'd be there, ready to build something together.

She'd never said so out loud. Not in ten years, even though it was the only wish she had. It was the wish that she'd held deep within her heart, but the Henry she wished for was not the man Henry was, and she had to accept that. What Ana felt went deeper than heartbreak. It was the death of a potential reality she'd deeply longed to make true.

Kristen squeezed Ana's hand, as if she sensed her thoughts wandering off. Ana squeezed back in reassurance. Kristen had been her rock this entire time, and Ana was eternally grateful. She'd always wanted to share her life with someone who knew everything about her. She had that, she realized. She had that now. She looped her arm around her friend's and kissed her softly on her cheek.

"Thank you," Ana said, "for everything."

"You're my sister," Kristen replied simply, and that was that.

"Ana?" she turned around quickly at the mention of her name. A really hot guy was watering greens and waving at her. She didn't recognize him at first. He was tanned and he'd grown a beard, but it was him. "Matt, what are you doing here?"

"Well, you told me about your perfect Saturday," He explained while simultaneously misting a batch of romaine. Taking a silent cue, Kristen strolled away, leaving them to talk.

"I came down here to check it out. One thing led to another, and…." He waved an arm over the greenery to illustrate his point. "I kind of work here some weekends now. I texted you about it."

Ana was embarrassed. She still hadn't managed to uninstall *Love Goddess Dating* from her phone, and had only succeeded in muting the app. But Matt had her phone number. She'd read a few of his messages trying to make sure she was alright. She just couldn't bring herself to reply.

"I'm sorry," Ana offered. Matt looked unfazed. There was that inner peace radiating off him again, and she could feel it taking effect. After a bit of hesitation, Ana tried to explain.

"Someone from my past popped back into my life and I thought…" She couldn't bring herself to finish that thought without breaking down into fresh tears. "I'm sorry for disappearing on you like that, but I haven't been in the best shape."

Matt nodded, patient, saintlike. He handed the hose to a girl standing nearby and stood closer. "I've been there. I think everyone has a person like that, the one that still makes you wonder, *what if?*"

"You had someone like that?" she asked her softly.

"Kind of. From afar. I was a lanky kid," he explained. "And I projected this massive crush on this girl named Madeline. Everything I achieved, I did it thinking it would impress her. I started working out in college, getting all this attention…" he shrugged. "I finally got the nerve to talk to her during a friend's pool party one summer break, and we had absolutely nothing in common. Nothing, it was bizarre. I don't think we were speaking the same version of English."

Ana smiled a little, tilting her head, questioning.

"I'm serious!" he insisted. "She was sweet about it, but I learned a lot that day. I'm really sorry you didn't get the answers you wanted," he said. "Did you learn anything new?"

Ana thought about that. "I think I did."

"Mind if I copy your homework?" Matt asked. Ana smiled, really smiled, feeling a warm glow when he looked at her again. It wasn't the same nostalgic ache she'd felt for Henry, but that wasn't a bad thing. It was something new and uncomplicated, like the life she'd always wanted. She knew, deep in her core, that she would never have to wonder where she stood with Matt. And still, she wasn't sure if she was ready to start dating again after spending so much time actively mourning.

He noticed her hesitation. "You can say no. It's your choice, at your pace. But I do have a confession to make," Matt added, shyly, showing her his phone. "This app keeps telling whenever you're close by..."

But Ana wasn't listening. She was staring at a spot past Matt's shoulder. Nothing happened, but a sense of déjà vu washed over, telling her to wait.

A split second later, Sue sauntered by, pink and white roses in hand. Sue held the roses close to her nose and winked in Ana's direction, disappearing into the crowd.

Just then, Ana's phone started to go off, loudly. "What the hell…" she mumbled. She was sure she'd set it on silent before she left the house, but the notification on the screen made her stop: *Love Goddess Dating ready to uninstall.*

Matt showed her the same notification on his and, wordlessly, they both clicked *delete.*

A DAY IN THE LIFE OF THE MOON

Ken Altabef

Alakrasina was the most beautiful girl in her village. Everyone told her so. She was quite clever and a terrific seamstress — she could sew rings around all the married women and most of the old women too. The seams in any pair of sealskin boots she made always held watertight, even when dripping wet or frozen solid. So, as you might suppose, many men wanted her for their wife. Many suitors came to her father's house, and none ever left without offering a formal proposition, but the girl was hard to please.

For example, Aqioq was young and handsome, all furtive glances and shy smiles, but Alakrasina refused. What use was a man who was merely good-looking? Ivariak was well-established, a supreme hunter with a hundred sled dogs and a mountain of fresh skins, but still Alakrasina refused. What good were all those material things? Migalluq was the most well-liked man in the village and by all accounts would have been a devoted husband and an excellent father to her children, but again Alakrasina said, "No."

To her father, this was maddening. On several occasions frustrated suitors tried to carry her away, and the frustrated father would have let them, but she fought them off. She was a strong woman.

Her poor beleaguered father worried she'd never marry. He berated her night and day, saying he hadn't raised her to be so haughty, thinking herself too good for all of the men in the village.

In fact, there was only one creature in all the world good enough in her eyes — and it happened to be the Moon. At night she would gaze up at it, marveling at its size and splendor. She saw a face in its shadows, a face both kind and beautiful, and she imagined it smiling down at her. She lay naked on the frozen beach, turning herself so that she might always face its silvery light. She imagined what it would be like to make love to the Moon. At last she went around the village claiming the Moon as her husband, and the people thought her mad and possessed of demons. Her father, in great distress, brought her to the shaman.

The shaman could find nothing wrong with Alakrasina except perhaps a case of extreme conceit, and quickly dismissed the case. The girl took the opportunity to ask him for advice. Since he had taken flight to the Moon on several occasions, she asked how he did it. Of course the shaman was not about to reveal his secrets to her, but Alakrasina gathered it had something to do with the Moon mask he kept in his tent, which bore a large, round, white face.

She asked what the Moon was like and the shaman described the Moon-Man, saying, "He is an ancient and kindly spirit, most wonderful and bright. He is humble too, for he is powerful enough to lift the weight of the oceans, but doesn't use his power except to shift the tides twice a day. He is benign and generous, for he lights the way for the people to see at night and in the winter, asking nothing in return. These are all good things he does." Alakrasina knew at that moment that she was truly in love, for she found these feats much more impressive than a man bringing down a caribou with the bow, or spearing a whale.

So, she decided to assay a flight up to the Moon. One night she stole the shaman's Moon mask and put it on; she sat cross-legged in the snow as she had seen him do. She gazed skyward, concentrating all her desire on the Moon; she wanted it so badly.

And then she took flight. Oh, the exhilaration she felt as she sailed up through the night sky. Her soul rose higher and higher, leaving the careworn world behind. The higher she went, the lighter her spirit felt. The air, the clouds, the sky — all were hers.

Alakrasina arrived at the great, shining *iglu* of the Moon-Man. He was not entirely surprised by her visit, for he had noticed her devotions on clear nights, looking down upon the world below. When she lifted the Moon mask half of it stuck to her face and wouldn't come off, but it was alright — he still thought her beautiful. And she found in him all the wonders the shaman had foretold.

When her father found her lifeless body still lying on the ice floe he buried it, thinking her a very beautiful but very foolish girl indeed. But Alakrasina was unaware of all earthly worries or cares. She and the Moon-Man were very happy together, living in the gigantic *iglu* and in time she brought forth a daughter, Tatqeq, whom people call the Moon Maid. A beautiful girl with skin like ivory glittering with moonbeams at play. Such a lovely girl.

Alakrasina should have been well satisfied, but she wasn't. From her new vantage point on the Moon she had an even closer look at the sky and she found her gaze lingering upon the stars above, especially the Never Moves. The Moon-Man was out working most of the night, and she stared longingly at the Never Moves, so distant, so unreachable. If her husband was so great and wonderful, she thought, just imagine the power and majesty of the mighty north star. She was sure the star would love her just as well. Eventually she made up her mind to take another soul flight.

Her husband caught her at it of course, and when she told him of her intentions he was deeply sorrowed. He pleaded with her to stay, for the Moon-Man was a level-headed sort and knew he would never find another woman like Alakrasina.

It was no use. She was determined to go. She spread her arms and pointed her beautiful face up toward the star. The half-Moon mask dropped from her cheek. And nothing happened.

At last the Moon-Man revealed to her that she had never been able to fly at all. She had not flown up to him: rather it was the Moon, seeing how she loved and admired him, who had reached down and brought her soul up. She couldn't fly to the Never Moves or anywhere else. She was only a ghost.

Of course, he sent her away after that. He banished her to the Upperworld, where she lives to this day. She sits on the rooftop balcony of her little house on the cloud shelf gazing from her lofty porch across the blue skies of day. Now people call her the Morning Dawn because she paints the sky red twice every day. At sunrise she's red with rage when the sun comes up and her beloved Moon must go away, and at sunset she glows with happiness that she may see him once again. Some say it's happiness, anyway. Some say it's shame.

Annigan the Moon-Man awoke with a start. His first thought, which was always his first thought upon awakening, was 'Is it time?'

Is it time?

He rose from his pillow of cloudstuff and forced sleepy eyes awake. Through a convenient peep-hole cut into the wall of his gigantic celestial *iglu*, he peered down at the sky below. Indeed, the fiery glow of sunset had already laid its first stripe across the Northlands.

He jumped out of bed and crawled through the entrance tunnel. He had slept late again. His Moon-dogs whined for their breakfast as he passed, but he paid them no heed. He strode across the frozen wastes of the Moon, admiring its supreme desolation, a cratered expanse of milky white crust and flaked ivory dust. He paused to peer down at the blue-green orb below.

Sunset, which was born of the passion of his ex-wife Alakrasina, was a spectacle he did not ever miss. Its fiery glow wrapped half the planet as she raged at her estranged husband in the sky. At him. Yes, Alakrasina had always been a very passionate woman.

Annigan smiled.

He remembered his young bride as she had first appeared on the Moon, her long raven hair, the high, proud cheekbones, her face partly obscured by half of the shaman's Moon mask. At last a companion to walk the empty sands of the Moon. A soul-mate. He'd never felt such excitement. He remembered their first embrace during the long, empty hours of the night, beneath the starry sky. She'd looked back at him with a passion that matched his own.

Yes, he remembered the intensity of her tender devotions as she lavished them upon him, and also the love she showered upon their beautiful daughter Tatqeq. A loving bride, a beautiful family. Annigan had felt such exuberance in those times; he beamed down from the sky with a blaze of ethereal light, swollen with pride as he drove the tides to boisterous extremes.

All gone now. Blown away, with the wind.

He stood there for a long while after sunset, shining down at the world below, although admittedly his light was not as bright as before. His moonbeam eyes watched carefully, witnessing all that transpired among the softening crests of melting snow and the spinning jumble of icy floes. It was a very short night, so far into summer, and most of the people were asleep, exhausted from their many labors of the long day. Some few were still about, thankful for his glow. One man glanced gratefully upward, lost out on the flats and trying to find his way home. And the beasts of the field were also thankful for his light as they walked the plains — wolves stalking their prey, snow hares and foxes in search of mates, caribou picking for a late-night snack of moss or lichens.

As he presided over the solitary creatures of the night-time world, the sleeping world, Annigan felt so very alone.

The Moon recalled the dark times, that long stretch of loneliness before there was love. He recalled the fevered yearnings of Alakrasina as she called up to him from the world below. How she had loved him, gazing endlessly up at the sky, how she had adored him. He, who was privy to all the dreams of men drifting up from the night-time world, had never witnessed such a marvel. She was like a mirror. All his own hopes and desires were embodied in the soul of that one woman.

No more. Betrayed. And gone.

Her taste no longer tingled on his tongue, a glory forsaken, a paradise lost. Lonely? In those days, the days before Alakrasina, he hadn't even known the meaning of the word.

Sunset was now long over and she had retired to her sleep among her gulls and owls in the dark night of the Upperworld.

Annigan cast one long look out at the stars above and turned away. Time to feed the dogs. He plodded back to his gigantic *iglu*. His team of three waited there, milling excitedly around the kennel. He never bothered to tie them up. Where could they go? They were as trapped as their master.

The gigantic huskies circled, tails wagging gaily, great gouts of Moon mist clouding their faces as they panted and yapped at him. Their shimmering fur, made of moonbeams and star dust, glowed silver-white. The Moon-dogs were not strictly real, merely a trick of his own light. What companionship could they offer? But still he must keep them fed and fit. He lashed them to his sledge, which was made from the massive jawbone of a blue whale. He ran them around and around, taking the team through their paces, calling out commands which echoed back to him in the night.

After a while he unhitched his team and tossed them some tidbits of moonstuff to eat. This celestial food satisfied dogs who were made, unknowingly, of moonbeams themselves. Did it satisfy him? How could it? What was there for him? These long years there had been only one thing, one woman — so long gone.

He walked on. The short night was already drawing to a close. Perhaps, thought the Moon-Man, he might yet have some company. Maybe a shaman would visit. He sat atop the glittering dome of his celestial *iglu* and waited. He waited and waited but no one came. It was a rare thing for a shaman to make such a spirit flight, to project their soul all the way up to the Moon. It hardly ever happened any more.

He stared absently again at the night-time world. All asleep now, deep in the night. Peaceful. Lonely.

Oh, he thought suddenly, he had almost forgotten to raise the tide. He was getting so old and forgetful.

Annigan climbed down from his high perch and walked to the edge of the Moon. He was late, but hoped nobody would notice. He gazed down on the vast blue ocean below, marshaling once again his great force of will. The beach must be scrubbed clean, the sea beds raised, the fish brought close to the fishermen's nets along the shore. He took a deep breath, gathering strength from whatever deep reserve he had left, and pulled. He raised the vast bulk of the sea as if he were pulling a blanket across a swaddling baby, an awesome show of power which was not even hard work for him. But he was weary of doing it, deep down in his bones. Weary.

As he tugged, he noticed a pale white beluga whale swimming toward the rising surface. As it breached, Annigan looked deep into the whale's eye.

Could the whale see him, he wondered. No, he was much too far away. But it did notice the moonbeams glittering atop the sea-foam.

"I see you," Annigan whispered.

So then, alone, the Moon-Man composed a poem:

Beluga, beluga,
Beneath the vast water's sea,
Look up, look up,
Cast your floating shadow over me.

He imagined a storm at sea and added:

Through wind and through gale,
Turn and spread your weathered eye,
To my lonely roost here,
At center of a cold, darkened sky.

He spent a long while debating whether he should replace 'center of a darkened sky' with 'amid the darkened sky' but decided at length to stick with his first inclination.

Annigan smiled, thinking the rhyme not all that bad. He had written thousands of such poems during his lonely vigils in the night. No one would ever hear them. No man would ever sing them.

Having lost track of time, sunrise surprised him as it broke over the world below. The fiery ribbon rose across the horizon, painting the tundra red, setting the world aflame. Alakrasina.

"She misses you," said a warm, soft voice.

"She regrets nothing," he said.

An alabaster hand pulled his shoulder gently backward and Annigan beheld the lovely face of his daughter Tatqeq, the Moon Maid. A young woman whose smooth, milky skin shone with his glittering moonlight. Her face was round and plump with playful cheeks, a small dainty nose and pale, smiling lips. Wet with light, her long white hair shimmered and sparkled.

"She burns with shame," she said. "Can't you see that?"

"No," said Annigan.

"Let me speak for my mother."

Why not, thought Annigan? His daughter was, after all, the living embodiment of the spirit of romance.

Tatqeq held a sad, sincere look in her silver-gray eyes. "She made a mistake. Can't you forgive her?"

"She said this to you?"

"Not in words, but I know her heart."

"I knew her heart once also. But it proved false."

"Can't you forgive her?"

"No," he said. "I cannot."

Tatqeq puffed out a frustrated sigh. "A harsh judgment."

Annigan looked away. "It's daytime soon," he said. "I'm tired. I would go to sleep."

He leaned forward to kiss his daughter on the cheek.

"Good night, my love," he said.

"Good night, Father."

The Moon-Man began his slow walk back to the *iglu*. A harsh judgment. Perhaps. But what else was there to do? The Moon-Man must have his pride. Without that, how would he ever be bright and full again? How would he ever be able to raise the tides?

Asteria

Vonnie Winslow Crist

Asteria Dawn McClaran didn't know some of the blue-white ice of Western Antarctica had melted, though she'd heard about the Dwayyo who walked on two feet like a man, but was really a wolf. While the rest of the world scrambled to resettle millions of coast-dwellers as oceans rose and swallowed vast swaths of land, Asteria, Mom, and Nan lived their regular lives in the same wooded hollow where generation after generation of the McClarans had eked out a living. But even in a coal mining town nestled between the ancient Appalachian peaks, global warming had consequences. Unbeknownst to the miners and their families, an extraterrestrial sentient and former resident of an eon-dead Antarctica city had taken up residence.

Though only seven, Asteria knew if you selected five letters from her first name, they spelled: *a star*—so she loved stars and only wore shirts with stars on them. Five-pointed stars to be exact. On June fifteenth, three days after school closed for summer vacation, she wore her favorite *You are a*

Star tee-shirt where the word *Star* had been replaced with a glittering silver star. She waved to Nan, who was busy shelling a bucketful of peas on the porch of their ramshackle house, and skipped out the door.

"Stay out of the water and mind the snakes," warned her grandmother.

"Okay!" called Asteria over her shoulder as she danced across the yard, past the chicken coop, and down a grassy path to the fishing pond at the foot of the hill upon which her ancestors had built their log cabin hundreds of years earlier.

Asteria loved to draw pictures of what she saw in her dreams while sprawled on the dock that jutted into the pond like a fallen barn door. And though Nan and Mom didn't like to talk about it—some of those pictures came true. Asteria flopped down on the rough boards, opened up her paper pad, and looked around as she twirled a pencil between her fingers. As the morning sunbeams streamed between the mockernut hickory and locust trees, dragonflies zipped by, and little wavelets slapped against the dock's pilings, her eyes spotted a dark shape hovering just below the surface.

She leaned over the dock's edge. "Hi, there. Don't be afraid. I won't hurt you."

The thing didn't swim away—instead it gazed up at her with its many green eyes.

Asteria had watched tadpoles, minnows, frogs, fish, turtles, and even snakes swim in the murky water of the fishing pond, but she'd never spotted this creature before.

"I can't see you very well. The water is dark because of the hemlock needles and oak leaves that steep in it like teabags," explained the girl. She grabbed a piling and inched farther out over the water. "You've got to come closer," she said. As she gazed at the creature, she noticed the glittering star on her shirt reflected by the water.

With a series of burbling, slurping sounds, a black blob of slime covered with iridescent eyes bubbled above the water.

Asteria wrinkled her nose. The glob of jam smelled worse than skunk roadkill on a summer afternoon—but she'd been told dozens of times: *If you can't say anything nice, don't say nothing at all.* Before she could think of something pleasant to say, her ears rang with a cacophony of whistles and piping that sounded worse than the howls of a Snarly Yow. "Stop it!" she yelled.

The putrid-scented ooze fell silent.

"If you can't talk, then just think things really hard or sign the words out with your hands."

Two arm-like appendages of gelatinous blackness reached towards Asteria.

She hesitated a moment, whispered to herself, "Be as brave as a Titan goddess," and then extended her right hand toward a gooey arm. When slime touched flesh, the girl suddenly had images of a ship sailing by stars and planets. Next, the ship plummeted from beyond the moon toward earth. It dove through burning air, plowed into snow and rock, then plunged into water as cold as ice cubes. Finally, she saw huge buildings and towers of stone rising from mountains of snow as her head seemed to fill with a whirlwind and her skin goose-bumped.

"It must be freezing there."

In the center of its mass, the puddle of gel formed a bump which appeared to nod.

"I'm Asteria—it is a place on the planet Venus. People call Venus the morning star." She tried to imagine a star shape in her mind.

The stinking muck quivered when she said the word, *star*. Then, it extended one of its pseudo-arms and touched the five-pointed shape on the girl's shirt.

"That's right! That's a star! So what's your name?"

The many-eyed glob formed, then curled and uncurled a third tentacle-like arm. Finally, it placed the tentacle on Asteria's flesh.

"Goth!" she said. There had been more words and syllables whispered in her brain, but *Goth* was what she picked from the slurring muddle of sound. "Nice to meet you."

Goth's tentacle stretched into a thinner version of itself, wrapped around Asteria's forearm, and pulled up and down several times in a weird version of a handshake. Then, the foul mucus retracted its arms.

"Are you hungry? I got chips." The girl opened a plastic bag and dumped more than half of its contents to one side of Goth.

While the semi-liquid creature surrounded, then absorbed the potato chips, Asteria ate the rest. "We can be friends."

"Asteria. Asteria."

"Coming," she replied. "Nan's calling, so I've got to go—but I'll be back after lunch and read you a book. I'll bring something else to eat, too."

Goth's silence seemed acquiescence, so the girl raced up the hill toward the McClaran cabin.

"What you been doing down the pond this morning?" asked Nan when Asteria hopped onto the back porch.

"I made a new friend who flew by stars, the sun, and Venus to get here."

Nan smiled. She'd had an imaginary friend when she was a girl, so a new friend when there was nobody about seemed a perfectly natural thing.

"What's her name?"

"Goth," replied the seven-year-old. "Though, I don't think it's a girl. And Goth kind of smells like roadkill."

"Well," said Nan as she set a peanut butter and jelly sandwich in front of Asteria, "I don't suppose a name or body odor matters as long as you're friends." The woman smiled as her granddaughter ate.

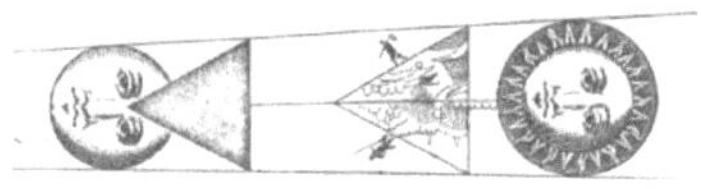

As she'd promised, after lunch Asteria returned to the fishing pond with several books and a plastic bag of crusts and stale bread Nan had been saving for the chickens. "The biddies will have to share with you," said the girl as she dropped a handful of bread into the water near the waiting clump of odoriferous ick.

Goth floated on the pond's surface beside the dock as Asteria read. She'd brought a book about pond life, a picture-book about friendship, a booklet about a penguin she'd gotten free in a box of cereal, and a hard-backed book that was missing its cover about a visit to a beach. She'd found the last book beside a dumpster in the parking lot of the soft ice cream shop on Main Street.

With each book, Asteria read a page, then showed the pictures to Goth. Her friend seemed interested in the first two books, but formed and waved four tentacle-like arms when it saw the pictures of the penguin in the third book.

"You like penguins," said Asteria as she watched her friend's tentacles flutter. Images of eyeless white penguins popped into her thoughts. "But you like all white ones that only live in the dark." The girl paused, thought about the evening star rising over the mountains, then added, "I like the dark, too."

When she got to the fourth book, Goth seemed mildly interested in the seashore visit until there was a photograph of a starfish. Again, the tentacle-arms formed. Again, the foul-smelling ooze stared with all of his fern-green eyes at the page.

"You like starfish, too," observed the girl. "Wait," she said as she remembered Goth's reaction to her tee-shirt, "you like stars. And that's why you like me, because I'm named Asteria—and long ago, Asteria was the goddess of falling stars."

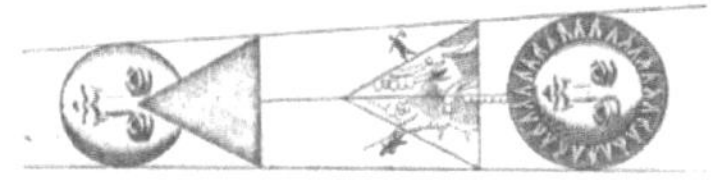

The odd friendship between the girl and the rancid jellification continued all summer. Asteria found some old paint in the barn and painted stars on all of the dock pilings so Goth could look at stars falling—even in the daytime. She also painted stars on the surface of some of the boulders between which water tumbled into the pond. Everyday, she drew pictures of her dreams to show Goth, played games with him, and read books, told stories, and sang songs to her friend. And everyday, she fed him.

Beginning in late August, five days a week, Asteria rode to school with her grandmother who worked in the school's cafeteria. After lunch was served, Nan drove home. Asteria rode the school bus home a few hours later. Once her homework was complete, the girl hurried down to the dock to spend time with Goth. She'd walk up the path to the cabin for supper just about the time Mom got home from her job at the nursing home. On the weekends, when the weather was nice, Asteria spent as much time as possible with her friend.

When Mom complained about all of the hours she was spending with her imaginary buddy, Nan said, "She's got quite the imagination, but she's happy. You did name her after the Greek goddess of oracles and falling stars—what did you expect?"

"I named her after an area on Venus—so she'd be a loving child," answered Mom.

"She's loving, lovely, *and* has her head in the stars," said Nan with a wink.

An exhausted single parent, Mom didn't argue.

One warm fall day when the crickets were chirping so loudly it almost hurt her ears, Asteria was walking beside the pond with Goth floating near the shore. She was telling him about the panther who lived in the hidden places of Appalachia. "He's blacker than coal with terrible claws and a long tail," explained the girl. "When your hear his growls, it can scare you to death. Nan says he's got teeth so sharp that they'll..." Whatever Asteria was going to say next was lost in a scream. Curled on the ground at her feet was a copperhead. The girl had been taught about the venomous snakes that lived in the mountains, and identified the leaf-patterned reptile at first glance.

"Help! Snake! Help!" she hollered.

"Coming," yelled her grandmother from the cabin.

Before the animal could strike, Goth slurped from the pond, engulfed the copperhead, and with a terrible squashing sound, he decapitated the snake then swallowed its head. By the time Nan reached the pond, all that was visible in front of Asteria was a slimy, headless snake.

"Lordy, it's a copperhead," exclaimed Nan "What did you kill it with?" she asked as she lifted the scaly body with a stick.

"I didn't. Goth killed it. He saved me."

"Well then, Goth is a brave fellow," Nan replied as she tossed the snake's carcass into the water. "We'll let some critter in the fish pond snack on the snake." The woman brushed her granddaughter's curls away from her face and smiled. "Well, my beautiful-faced goddess, why don't you come on up to the house and have an apple dumpling?"

Asteria agreed. But before she followed her grandmother to the cabin, she said to the still pond, "Thank you, Goth. If you want, you can eat all the snakes around here."

Though Nan was already half way up the path and missed seeing it, Asteria observed a crow-black tentacle of jelly wave above the surface of the tannin-stained, murky-as-the-night-sky water.

Winter swooped in like a Snallygaster. The wind clawed at Asteria's skin, the plummeting temperatures gnawed at her fingers and toes, and the knit hat Nan had made for Asteria didn't seem thick enough to keep her head warm. Before the pond froze solid, the girl tramped down to the dock and called Goth.

The ebony slime that was her friend blurbled to the surface. Goth had morphed from a gooey puddle into a rug-sized ovoid of sludge.

"You look like you're still growing," observed Asteria. Though the stench of her friend had likewise increased in strength, the girl chose not to mention that talking to Goth smelled like she was conversing with the dead.

"Winter is almost here," began Asteria, "and you need to swim to the bottom of the pond where you won't freeze. I'll visit when I can, but..."

The girl stopped speaking as her mind filled with images relayed to her by Goth. First, she saw the same towering buildings of a frozen city she'd seen on the first day she'd met her mucousy friend. In her mind's eye, she walked into a building, then traveled with Goth down long tunnels that ended in frigid water, slid into the liquid, swam deeper, and explored an undersea world of strange plants and animals. Next, with dizzying speed, Goth and she swam through churning water as the land above them trembled and folded. Then, they floated to the surface inside a huge cave with many branches. The cave was filled with all of the glistening stone shapes Asteria remembered from her visit to Luray Caverns: stalactites, rock straws, curtains of limestone as thin as bacon, columns like you see on the front of rich people's houses, stalagmites, and other shapes.

That's when Goth grabbed her wrist with one of his pseudo-tentacles and pointed with another tentacle at the waterfalls which fed the fish pond.

Asteria gasped as she realized the cool, but not too cold cave with the beautiful stone formations her friend was trying to show her was inside the mountain behind the waterfalls.

"That's where you need to go when it's freezing outside. Go inside the mountain."

Goth caressed her right cheek with a clammy finger of gelatin.

"I'll miss you, too," said the girl as she patted his tentacle-arm. "But spring isn't too far away."

Several of Goth's eyes slid up his tentacle, starred at her for a moment, then slid down to his main lump of jelly. Sending a final image of her face surrounded by stars to Asteria, the sludgy slop that was Goth, sloshed beneath the pond's surface.

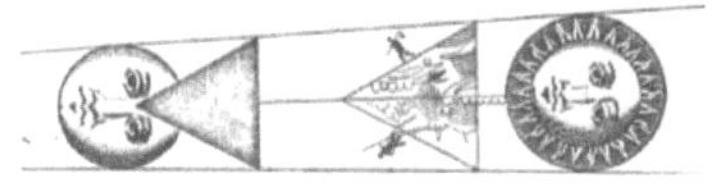

Though it was a bitter winter, spring came early. Snowdrops bloomed by mid-February and skunk cabbages poked their folded leaves up by the first of March. The piping of spring-peepers signaled to Asteria that is was time to look for her friend.

Down the path to the fish pond she ran. Before she could walk out onto the dock, an inky pool of slush awash with moss-green eyes lifted a half dozen tentacle-like appendages from its bulk and waved to the girl.

"Goth!"

Once on the dock, Asteria held onto the largest of Goth's tentacles as he wrapped several smaller armlets around the girl. "I missed you," she said before giving the tentacle a final hug.

Asteria and Goth shared their winters. She'd turned eight and had taken a school trip to the planetarium where she'd seen a picture of the Asteria Region on Venus. He had consumed fish from the bottom of the pond and cave creatures. She had learned to read much better; he'd moved a few big, flat rocks to the pond's edge so they'd have more places to play. She'd brought him a starfish she'd found at the local Buy Things Cheap Store, he had brought her a small stalagmite from his cave.

"Thank you," said Asteria as she held the crystal-encrusted cone of rock from the cavern. "It's the most amazing thing I've ever seen."

Goth wrapped himself around his starfish. His bulk quaked and the girl had sudden visions of huge starfish-headed anemone.

"I'm glad you like it," she said. "I've got to go up and do my homework, but I'll come back to visit after school tomorrow."

Goth waved as she ran back to the cabin, then sank into the pond.

"Where in heavens' name did you find that?" asked Nan when Asteria showed her the stalagmite fragment.

"Goth gave it to me. He found it in the mountain where the pond's water comes from."

"Really? Well, Goth must have sharp eyes to spot that chunk of rock in the pond."

"No, Nan, he didn't find it in the pond—he found it *inside* the mountain."

"What an imagination you have, my little goddess!" laughed her grandmother.

Homework done, supper eaten, an hour spent with Mom, and Asteria went to sleep that night thinking about how much she loved Goth and what fun it would be to explore crystal-filled caverns with her best friend.

The next morning, she rode to school with Nan, then showed the other students and her teacher the stalagmite. Morning classes were easy, Asteria said hello to Nan at lunch, and afternoon classes went by with nary a hitch. The end of the day came quickly, and all Asteria could think about as she clambered onto the school bus with the other children was seeing Goth again.

About halfway through the bus route, the driver stopped the school bus at the end of the lane which led to the McClaran home. The lights on the bus blinked as Asteria climbed down the steps and crossed the road. She was smiling and thinking about Goth when the dump truck's fender hit her.

She flew into the air, then plunged downward like a falling star, and landed on the gravelly road in a rag doll heap of clothing and limbs.

Nan and Mom held Asteria's funeral service in her school's gymnasium. All of the children in her class came to the funeral as well as hundreds of other mourners. She was buried in the family plot—a flat spot on the side of the hill above the pond. The elementary school, the Buy Things Cheap Store, the ice cream shop, the nursing home, and a couple of other businesses collected donations to pay for her funeral expenses and to purchase a beautiful headstone which read: *Asteria Dawn McClaran, A star who graced us with her beauty and love for eight years*. Below the words, her birth and death dates and a five-pointed star were chiseled into the granite.

With a star missing from their sky, Nan and Mom found their lives less bright. Each blamed themselves for Asteria's death—as did the bus driver and the truck driver who ignored the flashing lights. Still, life returned to a new normal for all, save one.

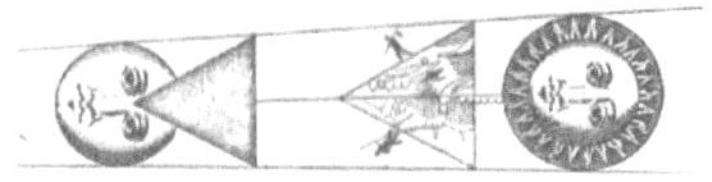

One Sunday morning near the end of summer when Nan made her daily visit to Asteria's grave, she dropped the zinnias she was carrying and cried out. She cried out loud and long enough that Asteria's mother rushed down from the cabin to see what was wrong. Arms wrapped around each other, the women stood by Asteria's grave, gazing at a strange memorial.

The night before, during the dark of the moon when the heavens were ablaze with stars and Venus shone like the bright queen of the sky, someone had meticulously arranged fist-sized chunks of cave crystals in a star-shape atop Asteria's grave. Around the crystalline rocks, five rows of smaller, round stones spaced half an inch apart repeated the star outline. On the outermost row of pebbles at each of the star's points, a four-foot tall stalactite was embedded in the ground. In the center of the innermost star, a split geode with a diameter of about thirteen inches sparkled brighter than the tears on the women's cheeks. And fittingly, the crystals in the center of the geode were the same brilliant vermilion of the scorching area of Venus known as Asteria.

Enthralled with the beautiful tribute to their fallen star, Nan and Asteria's mother didn't notice the somber jellied blob that slurped, along with the pond's excess water, down a tumble of rocks and into a creek—a creek that wound its way through the Appalachians to the verdant foot hills of the Piedmont and finally into the Atlantic.

Had they spied the shadow that was Goth, from Asteria's graveside they would have never spotted the starfish enveloped in slime like a falling star in the night, floating among the dozens of emerald eyes in the very heart of the shoggoth.

THE KING OF THE SEAS ALSO WEEPS

LANCELOT SCHAUBERT

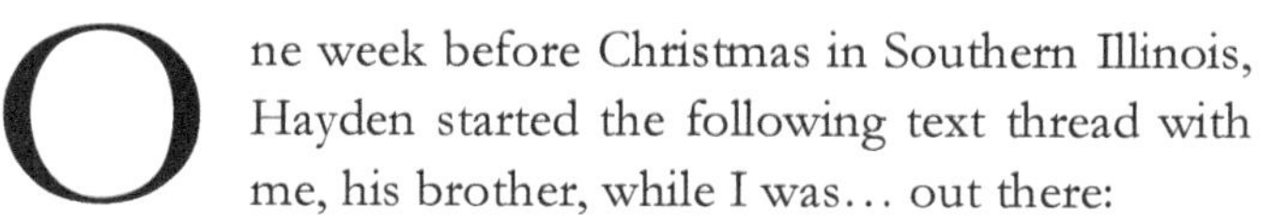

One week before Christmas in Southern Illinois, Hayden started the following text thread with me, his brother, while I was… out there:

[Hayden's texts.]
[My — Toby's — texts.]

Hey.
Yo.
You busy?
A bit.
How busy?
Up to my arms in mermaid shit.
Like the shit shoveling I did for Serve Pro?
Worse, in a way.

No way dude. You see my pics of how deep it was?

Yeah, but mermaid shit's way worse. Like cleaning out a turtle cage.

Come on, man, that ain't bad.

Try me. They eat their shit like turtles and rabbits cause their stomachs

Too small?

Yeah and immature. It's like a cow's cud chewing, only they have one gut so

When you tell jokes, they give shit-eating grins.

Nailed it.

I win. But it smelled so bad in my basement.

And?

Four feet of shit.

And?

Bad enough I puked on top and still kept it sucking.

Exactly. We don't have those vacuums here.

Wait, what? What about the dehumes?

Tech don't work the same way here.

You're texting me.

That's different.

I still don't understand how that works.

I'm allowed certain things as the world maker. I don't just speak Narrative. But it'd change the whole course of this planet's history if I introduced giant firetruck sized vacuums. Or dehumidifiers, especially because it's an aquatic environment.

How you keep all that straight?

Notes. Trial and error. Also being willing to get shot or excoriated or stabbed.

Excoriated?

Flayed. Hulled. Laid bare. Flensed.

Pared? Scalped?

Skinned.

You'd make a nice rug. Coming home Christmas?

Depends if the work camp lets me out.

Work camp?

I pissed off a mermaid king. Technically a mermaid duke.

Dude. You have GOT to stop pranking people.

I know. You try.

Don't wanna. Come home for Christmas.

***Sigh* I'll do my derndest.**

Do judo or something. Call down fire.

You could always come get me.

Hate traveling to big cities.

Smaller than New York.

Bigger than St. Louis?

It's… less sprawly. No cars or trains. This one doesn't have smog.

Sounds underwater.

It's… moist… ish.

They let you have a phone?

I told them it's a medical device that keeps me alive.

Some truth there.

Yup. Gotta go, bub. Foreman's eyeing me.

Don't get stabbed with a trident.

Too late.

Then don't get shanked with a trident AGAIN.

Too late.

Don't die.

See you at Christmas?

I'll make you moonshine!

…

Bubba?

…

I was just shitting you, you know.

[Hayden's texts.]

[My — Toby's — texts.]

Hayden, earlier that week:

How many times did he have to tell this lady to stop flushing her goddamned tampons? How many times? He tried putting up signs like you might do in a girl's dorm or in a bathroom at a diner where you could barely fit between the walls without hitting your knees. She was ninety, Maybel. How did tampons even make sense? How's that work? Lived at home, still getting it done without live-in help and still getting it done *wrong*. He'd explained it to her like corks. (Why'd it have to be *him* explaining it to *her*?) He'd butchered a flannelgraph from his wife's Sunday School class to try a dramatize a diagram. He'd looked in a couple spellbooks to see if there was anything magical that would get another person to understand a foreign concept but, like normal, all that elitist magical bullshit had no practical value for his life in

Southern Illinois. He'd drawn on fridge art for her and had even staged a field trip lesson by getting her to come downstairs and pick up a shovel when the whole floor for the ninth time flooded knee-high with shit smelling about as well as you can imagine:

"You know, when I was your age—"

"Don't," Hayden said.

"Don't what, honey?" Maybel asked.

"Don't do the thing where we're doing this *gross thing*, hand in hand, and you say the *condescending thing* I expect some rando old women to say while we're doing that aforementioned gross thing together as if I'm supposed to feel weak or dirty or whatever compared to the hypothetical version of you I'll never meet, lady." The shovel made a squishing, bubbling sound.

Well she didn't have much to say to that so she harrumphed and went on shoveling. Hers had rust spots. "I just don't get it," she said.

"What's to get, lady?" Hayden asked.

"Well I just don't get how it keeps on clogging like this. What did they make the house wrong or something?"

It felt tight. Enclosed. Claustro-freaking-phobic. Hayden stewed. He stewed enough that he pulled back his shovel like old Hector of Troy and threw it, spear-like, into the wall, holder of houses. It sounded a loud crack, thunder of thunderers. It stuck. It must have hit some precious pocket. A great boil'd been lanced. An underground reservoir of shit burst open and added another foot of sewage to them both. Meant they'd need to fix the wall too. He puked on top. Sour plus rotting. He pulled out a green plastic nose clip from his pockets, but there was still the heat of the mangle.

The old lady swore in a way old ladies seldom swear as she tried to get her balance back. Swore in the way that *only* old ladies can swear.

He brought the giant vacuum hose down and inserted it and start suction again, redirecting towards the sewer main, hoping for the best. Hayden let Maybel go to it and went to the bathroom and pulled out his phone whilst on the pot. "Hey," he texted and then, "You busy?"

"A bit," I, his older brother, texted back.

"How busy?"

A three-day delay followed before Hayden received a response from me…

Why I was delayed:

I'd come out of a tunnel in the great reef and started drowning immediately: blurry burning eyes, pressure collapsing skin, water in lungs, ear drums rupturing. Hurt like hell, hell on all sides. Dying would set me back a bit, you know, as it does, so I wove gills into my neck, wove pressure and cold resistance into my skin, adjusted the pressure in my inner ear, extra lens and lubrication on the eyes, underwater hearing, etc. Then I swam hat and three-piece and hairy bare feet, into the great turquoise of The Blazing World. Before me corralled a great series of live-in stalagmites, slimy and writhing with squirming tubules, the Citadel of Sirens, great and green and glowing as if backlit by the Mother of all mother of pearl.

Before we get to my texts to my brother about why I got delayed, stabbed with a trident, and so on, you need to know three things: a first thing about how I can get hurt, even as a narrator, a second thing about the Narrative tongue and why I'm talking directly to you, and a third thing about how worldmaking and narrative magic works. I'll tell you about them as they come up, but first thing, regarding the who: don't make the mistake folks normally make and assume that just because I'm the one telling the story in the first person that everything ends up okay. I made that mistake reading *CivilWarLand in Bad Decline* by George Saunders, a first-person perspective story in which the narrator dies. Complain about spoilers later, we have work to do, and I — the narrator — might die or worse. That's how this works. In fact, getting stabbed hurts twice as much when you know it's coming and you accept it anyways: once for the blade, once for worrying about it and resigning to your fate.

I had opened a threshold with a coral compass and travelled to The Blazing World in search of the best fishing rod in the world. My bride had done all of the Christmas shopping and I'd needed a present for Hayden. Hayden had texted me earlier that month with a photo of a massive catfish he'd caught out on Kinmundy lake without a fishing license, cleaned and fried (sweet caramelized flour). She'd been pregnant. He'd gone on Papa Bren's new fishing boat — the boat that Bren had always wanted growing up, the one he'd salivated after once the long line of black trucks and hand-decaled Pontiac firebirds tired him out, an old Ranger with a new motor and a leaky hull and some of the worst outdoor carpet imaginable. Hayden had gotten the fish and lost the rod, his only rod.

So I wanted the best. For him.

What better place to look than a world of water and fish?

"Just how I remember you," I said. I really needed to dream up some places like this back home for Hayden to enjoy. He'd probably prefer a Rural King gift card...

Great trains of folk passed through now-dormant lava dikes and sills and secondary vents like parasites in the hardened arteries of a fallen giant. People flowed into the subaquan city from all angles, but in more or less flows or currents and schools of fish that weren't quite fish, shimmering and shining, the fragrance of wet seaweed all around. Swap the coral for a futuristic city and the swimming lanes for air lanes and it's basically the same feel.

On the great oceanic floor, I saw all sorts of folk, sentient and otherwise, selling wares from booths cut into coral and stone and built up from the silt. He swam that way, towards hippie curtains made of large seaweed (less rattley, scratchier like fine sandpaper) and amoebas strung out on driftwood (literally, not psychedelically), towards sellers of seashell necklaces, salves and butters for cracked scales and torn fins, deep pressure glasses and pressure-steeped fragrances for gasses, strands of pearls, sponge pillows, kelpsicles, ugly ass rocks.

And one very loud and obnoxious merman with a shark's tail yelling in the Narrative tongue. Good thing he spoke Narrative cause common tongue wasn't so common anymore, what with how my stories are translated these days. That's the second thing, the what, specifically the Narrative tongue: as hinted in the transcript earlier of mine and my brother's texts to one another, I'm a world-maker. It complicates things. Vonnegut, King, Lewis, Dante, and a whole slew of other authors show up in their work but none of them really thought through the consequences such a phenomenon has upon the author, the characters, the narrative, and the reader. Except for Lewis in an obscure article long after he wrote his *Dark Tower*, but no one reads that and he died before he could finish the story, so it doesn't count. Typically, fiction authors just do it and move on. Or don't. They don't realize that, for instance, no matter if the characters speak Sindarin or Klingon or Esperanto, they're ultimately speaking Narrative that will get translated into all the languages of the worlds — and we who keep the Archive carefully tend to the Narrative mothertongue. It's called Narrative because, for better or worse, translated or otherwise, *these* are the characters who will be translated into all the tongues in The Vale (the universe… s). It's something like an angelic tongue: the tongue of the authors, makers, and artists. The Meta tongue. The Tongue of those who know the tongues. Some who speak it know they're in a story. Most don't. But we can understand them and that's what matters. He yelled, "Gear for anglers! Fisherman's first choice!"

A couple walking by him cussed him out.

"Just trying to make a living, salty," he said.

"Worthless," a lady muttered.

"It's a scalable business! All means for catching and eating fish! All means of—"

I swam up and said, "You got fishing rods?"

"Hey there, young man, you look like quite the catch for the ladies."

"Okay yeah, yeah. Fishing rods?"

"All means of catching fish, salty."

"Where are your rods?" I asked.

"We've got all kinds of nets. We've got bottom trawls, cast nets, coracles, dragnets, drifts, drives, fixed gill—"

"I want a fishing rod," I said. "It's not like I want folks to call me Ishmael."

"Even without white whale hunting, it's still a good harpoon. Folks from earth—"

"You know Moby Dick?" I asked. "You've seen Earth?"

"Never heart of Dick, but I speak Narrative enough to know the tale of Ishmael and the White Whale Madness. And of course I've been to Earth, being a trader. It's one of the thirteen tors. Why wouldn't I?" He looked up to the waves above him and squinted as if he could see the stars above the atmosphere above the waters overhead.

"Oh wow," I said. "Okay good. So in SOiLL—"

"So ill?"

"Southern Illinois?"

"Never heard of the northern version," he said.

"It's a state."

"Of being?" he asked.

"United States," I said.

"Didn't know there were divided kinds. A divided state of being sounds deadly. Want a net to gather these states up?"

"Nevermind," I said.

"Or how about an air-powered harpoon gun? We have enfarted and sansfart—"

But I'd already left and followed the Narrative path of the schools and swarms and pods into the heart of the merfolk kingdom inside the city gates, made of great shells of some long-dead stylet-shaped sea creature, stretching such great heights in a narrow and tall way, slender spirals like turbulence or thermals incarnate. You could almost feel the water swirling up them. I could barely see the tops and knew it would take me hours to swim that high, taller than the city itself was broad. I asked around to see if someone was interested in finding a fishing rod, stopping the stragglers in the unending stream of fishy folk into the city. A ten-foot lobster with a face like a scarred-up plumber shouted some Blazing cusswords. A clam tried to eat me in response to me asking for a fishing rod. Many, many merfolk started shoving, pushing, tossing me into some of the dirtier fishing lanes.

I said, "Come on, now, surely *someone* has heard of requests for fishing rods before."

"Sure," a mermerchant said in clean Narrative tongue, "but it's not like people walk around your New York asking everyone they see for heroin or firearms."

Hadn't thought of it like that, I suppose. "Well still, do you got any?"

The merchant scoffed and signaled the city guard.

I asked *them* for a fishing rod.

They shackled me.

"Hey guys, where are your tridents?"

One of them hissed. "You think we're barbarians? Demons?" They had some kind of harpoon pistols.

"I think you're aquatic Andy Griffiths."

"Are you an idiot? Gryphons couldn't live here."

"My mistake. As your maker, I want you to know that I really like you both."

Then dragged me before their centurion. He was a crusty old carbuncle, once stabbed with ship boards that now festered in his flesh — a large, unintended body modification. "What do you seek?" he asked.

"Just trying to get a new fishing rod for my brother for Christmas."

"Condemned by his own words," he said. "Throw him in the stocks."

"I appeal."

"To whom?" he asked.

"Whoever's higher than you, I guess," I said.

"That would be the duke of this sector. You'll find him less welcoming."

The merduke was a tumorous old boil of a merman, parts of him seeding and sprouting off of other parts of him. Lumpy. Like a wet, old biscuit that somehow secreted coagulated floor dirt. "What'd you bring me, Jack?"

"My name is Arno, sir."

"Yeah, but you're every mer Jack to me. Who's this?"

"He appealed."

"What did he do?" the merduke asked.

Jack said, "He—"

I said, "I'm Lancelot Tobias Aurelius, your excellency, good to meet you."

"Oooh," the merduke said. "Good to meet you as well. You sound American."

"You know Earth?"

"Of course I know Earth, I speak Narrative, don't I?"

"Yes, but speaking and knowing are two things, sir. I met an albino kitty girl that spoke fluent Narrative and hadn't heard of thresholds before. I'm also friends with several folks on Earth who don't read fiction, so…"

"Don't tell me that, I know that, don't I know that? You have a hint of Missouri in you."

"Missourah, I'm told."

"But you don't talk like that," the merduke said.

"Yeah, well, my friends do."

"Tell me: do you know Current River?"

"Canoed there some as a teen."

"Next time you go, you *have* to say 'hi' to my cousin Mark. He has a little shack near the Blue Spring. You have to tell him I said, 'Hi.' He's trout-tailed." The merduke flapped his tumorous tail. It swished enough to make air. "Obviously I have a bit more blowfish in me. Or maybe some flounder."

"Of course," I said.

"Well a Missouri boy, how wonderful."

I didn't tell him I was from Illinois. It didn't matter, did it?

"So, what did this poor little Mark Twain do on his trip to the Blazing World? Wreck a steamboat? We don't have many boats on The Blazing World, I'll have you know."

"Sir," said the guard.

"Yes Jack."

"Arno."

"What is it Jack?"

"He tried to purchase a fishing rod."

The merduke's face darkened with shadows, but his pustules and tumors darkened with a purpling blood, veins bulging and barging. "You did what?"

"Trying to buy a fishing rod," I said. "For my brother's Christmas present."

"Condemned by his own words," Arno merJack said.

"Condemned by his own words," the merduke said. "Why oh why, Tobias Missourius?"

"Aurelius. Mean's gold. It's a Narra—"

"Why you think that's a wise choice?"

I said, "Because my brother's hard to buy for, he likes fishing—"

Their tails and scales flexed tensely.

"—And I have access to the best aquarium in the thirteen tors, six mounds, and seven suns," I said.

"Aquarium."

"Sure!"

"The Blazing World," he said.

"Why not?" I asked.

"Did I call your planet a terrarium?"

"Well no, but—"

"Did I call Mars a herpetarium?"

"Of course not, mainly because reptiles haven't—"

"Then why do you treat us like fish? Fish to be *eaten*?"

Dadgum. I didn't have no answer for that.

"Did you know I'm a vegetarian, Tobias?"

"No your excellency," I said. "I am happy to submit to your culinary—"

"A vegetarian. And you want to buy a *fishing rod* on *my* planet."

I said, "Some of the vegetarians I know still eat fish on Fridays."

He was in my face. The speed at which the bulbous, tumorous form had moved from lounging twenty feet away in a general's perch to *in my face* rocked me back on my heels a bit. He hissed like a fish gasping for water. "*Some of the vegetarians I know still eat man on Mondays.*"

"I mean, only farm-certified organic man," ArnoJack said. "No offense, I just… I mean… your people *are* tasty."

"None taken," I said. "Don't you guys eat fish?"

"Maybe he's not so bad, boss, he—"

The merduke said, "We hunt mammals and reptiles and birds and drag them into the water," he said. "When we're omnivores. *I'm* a vegetarian."

Arno rolled his eyes and fins.

I didn't comment on how vegetarianism *obviously* helped the merduke's girlish figure.

"Mermen do not digest meat all that well. You're about to see why. Take him to the brig."

"But I didn't do anything wrong."

"Legally. Morally I find you reprehensible. And morals lie at the heart of the law. I send you to the brig not as a prisoner, Tobias from Missouri. I send you as a *student*." His teeth clacked on the "t" of student.

They threw me in the brig with a shovel. My bones hit metal and bruises simmered. I could feel either my bones beneath my muscle getting in the way of a soft landing. I wished then that I was as big and tough as my brother. I'd need to work on that soon. Soon I would. I'd do it tomorrow. I looked around. The brig was really a glorified sewer with a net where the prison bars should go. I landed in a pile of mermaid shit that smelled of spoiled cabbage and jellied krill. I mean, jellied krill goes nice on everything bagels if you can get it back to NYC unspoiled, but still…

Around that time, I noticed Hayden's text. "How busy?"

I sighed and texted back. "Up to my arms in mermaid shit."

What Hayden saw:

In the three days since Hayden sent his text, he had successfully gutted a house that had been blitzed by fire — assessing damage for the Illinois-based insurer — and had set up a ton of déhus for a realty that had flooded. On the third day, after checking the burnt house and the flooded realty, Hayden got a call.

"Hey sugar."

"Goddammit, Maybel."

"Language, hon."

"Goddammit."

"Don't use the Good Lord's name in vain, sugar, I just—"

"No, Maybel, no. I want God to damn your goddamn sewage lines."

"I don't know what happened."

"I do. I think I do. I think *you* do."

"It wasn't my tampon if that's what you're thinking."

"No, it's not what I'm thinking. Because why would you do that? Why would you flush tampons at this age, Maybel? I gotta know because a ninety-year-old shouldn't have a period, period."

"Sarah did."

"Sarah laughed at God for telling her she'd get pregnant."

"I flushed them."

"You flushed them."

"My tampons."

"*Your* tampons."

"Unused."

"Goddammit. Goddammit, Maybel. Why? Good God in Heaven, why would you do that?"

"Cause I like seeing you, cutie."

Hayden had nothing to say to that. He mouthed for air like a fish out of water.

"See you soon." She hung up on him.

He didn't know what else to do so he turned on *Crazy Train* in the van and got a text back from me. "Up to my arms in mermaid shit."

Heirs of a cold war,
that's what we've become,
inheriting troubles,
I'm mentally numb

Hayden was so sick of me complaining about my cush job while he had to stay back in the riverland and shovel shit. He rage-texted back. "Like the shit shoveling I did for Serve Pro?" Did. Why did he text *did* when Maybel had just summoned him?

He got my response. "Worse, in a way."

"No way dude. You see my pics of how deep it was?" He resent the pics.

"Yeah," came my response, "but mermaid shit's way worse. Like cleaning out a turtle cage."

"Come on, man, that ain't bad."

"Try me. They eat their shit like turtles and rabbits cause their stomach—"

"Too small?" Hayden texted.

"Yeah and immature. It's like a cow's cud chewing, only they have one gut so"

"When you tell jokes they give shit-eating grins," he texted.

"Nailed it," came my response.

Hayden set aside his phone and got out his roto rooter, which had an in-need-of-degreaser feel on the grip. He marched up the old limestone steps, grabbing hold of the black metal railing — which wobbled, giving him vertigo, so he released it and moved slower up — then knocked on the door. Then rang the doorbell without waiting for a response. Then kicked the door repeatedly until—

"What in God's?! Oh hi, sugar."

"Don't use his name in vain," Hayden said. "Where's the clog?"

"Bathroom," Maybel said and giggled.

Hayden went in, took what could be took apart, apart, roto rooted it, went out back, didn't even have to worry about digging for line access in the loamy soil (spongy underfoot) because of how often he'd done this same house over and over again, roto rooted that. Checked the basement and thank God he'd gotten here quick enough it hadn't flooded with shit again. Looks like he got off easy, his brother got off hard today.

"Shucky dern," Maybel said from the top of the green-fishboat-carpeted stairs.

Hayden looked up. His neck hurt. He could feel either his curls or his muscle or some fat getting in the way of neck and back. He wished he was as thin and scrappy as his brother. He'd need to work on that soon. Soon he would. He'd do it tomorrow. "Maybel, I'mo tell you once: now I know you're doing it on purpose, this is the only one I'll file for insurance. After that, I'm filing malicious intent and you're gonna have to pay for it."

"I have money."

"Maybel, I'll make you a deal."

"Really?"

"Sure. My father-in-law Bubba has everyone over for lunch after mass every Sunday. Every Sunday. If you swear to me you won't flood this basement ever again, you can come with us — every Sunday — to have lunch."

Maybel cried.

"Maybel?"

Maybel sobbed. "Always knew you loved me." She rained kisses all over Hayden's cheeks.

"Good God, lady, just bring some sandwiches or—"

"I'll bring you them deviled eggs you like."

"How you know I like them deviled eggs?" Hayden asked.

"Cause I heard you talking to your lady friend."

"My wife."

"No difference."

"Bigass difference, Maybel, Good Lord."

"See you Sunday."

"That's Christmas," Hayden said.

"Exactly," Maybel said.

Back in the truck, Hayden texted. "I win. But it smelled so bad in my basement."

"And?" came my response.

"Four feet of shit."

My context while texting:

When my brother texted *four feet of shit,* I was suspended in a hammock above just that much mermaid shit, rocking. I hadn't kidded about the whole turtle cage thing, rabbits and whatnot. Vegetarian mermaids, it turned out, had a sort of reverse-vomitorium which is where their brig was: hammock, large cube-shaped room hemmed by rough netting, the sort that gives you twenty-seven splinters if you grip it too hard and get yanked around. The floor had about four feet of sludge — the mermaid shit — and nets the walls for that prison, big thick rope like the sort you see on ship anchors, tied up tight enough they might as well have been bridge cable. I texted back, "And?"

He texted, "Bad enough I puked on top and still kept it sucking."

"Exactly," I texted. "We don't have those vacuums here."

"Wait, what? What about the dehumes?"

I jumped down into the sludge. The phone floated down and almost landed in the shitsludge were it not for the fluid resistance that made it sink in slow swoops like a dying bird.

I caught my phone, pocketed it, took up the shovel they'd left me and started shoveling it all towards a corner in the netting where I thought I could get most of it through. It was barely chewed, barely digested. When I said they're like turtles and rabbits, I half-expected them to suction this stuff up and serve it as a second course so that they could eat it again and get the real nutrients out of it. And no. We couldn't use dehumes underwater. Plus tech lag on this world was far, far worse than on Gergia. "Tech don't work the same way here," I texted.

"You're texting me."

"That's different."

"Still don't understand how that works."

"I'm allowed certain things as the world maker. I don't just speak Narrative. But it'd change the whole course of this planet's history if I introduced giant firetruck sized vacuums. Or dehumidifiers, especially because it's an aquatic environment."

"How you keep all that straight?"

"Notes. Trial and error. Also being willing to get shot or excoriated or stabbed."

"Excoriated?"

I thought of the tridents they didn't have and thought of fillet knives. I wondered still if these particular mermaids flayed humans. "Flayed. Hulled. Laid bare. Flensed."

"Pared? Scalped?"

"Skinned."

"You'd make a nice rug. Coming home Christmas?"

I shoveled some more for a while, then texted, "Depends if the work camp lets me out."

"Work camp?"

I looked around me. Wasn't really a chain gang like that time in No'ad, but still. "I pissed off a mermaid king. Technically a mermaid duke."

"Dude. You have GOT to stop pranking people," he texted.

"I know. You try." I hadn't pranked anyone. And I *was* searching for a gift for Hayden. But he didn't know that.

"Don't wanna. Come home for Christmas."

I laughed there in my cell. The sound carried weird in the water and the sludge, but it carried. "°Sigh° I'll do my derndest."

"Do judo or something. Call down fire."

He really thought I could do anything. I mean, I *could* do *most* anything, but that kind of defeats the purpose of an author showing up in his own work: you're either a character or you're not. To be a character, you have to yield to the rules of characterization. Besides, when was the last time he ventured off-planet? When we were kids? Maybe this was the time. "You could always come get me."

"Hate traveling to big cities."

"Smaller than New York."

"Bigger than St. Louis?"

"It's… less sprawly. No cars or trains. This one doesn't have smog."

"Sounds underwater."

"It's… moist… ish."

"They let you have a phone?"

"I told them it's a medical device that keeps me alive," I texted.

"Some truth there."

One of the guards came through to check to see if I was still shoveling. Still learning my lesson. "Yup. Gotta go, bub. Foreman's eyeing me."

I put down the phone and started shoveling a ton. The things I saw mixed in the sludge: tiny shells, bits of rusted metal, ratty seaweed, the wiry remains of an old timey telephone, golf balls. I kicked at it to dislodge it and it kludged into a sort of found-art piece, sliding and slipping in the muck. A large thunk and clank up the channel cavern behind the foreman. The scent of fragrances stirred in the water.

He turned.

Another merguard brought down that hawker from outside the city gate.

"You're krilling me, mermaid, for God's hake."

"Shut up." She opened the gate and threw him in.

"Well?" he asked. "Did ya get it?"

"Me?" I asked.

He treaded water in a slow circle, hands outturned. "Sorry, was there someone else?"

"Man," I said, "I really don't want to talk. I have my lessons to attend to." I shoveled some more shit.

"Oh. You didn't commit a crime?"

"What, you did?" I asked.

"I didn't have a license."

"What happened to scalable business?" I asked.

"First to the fishmarket, man, that's how it goes."

"I think fish market means something else to me," I said.

"I'll say. You find your fishing rod?"

"No," accenting the word with a stroke of the shovel, the sound of the slop.

"You want to settle for a net?"

"No."

"You gonna leave empty-handed from The Blazing World?"

"Probably," I said, throwing hard again, wishing he'd shut up.

"You don't have to."

I turned and looked at him. He had yellow eyes like what you'd expect on a centaur or a gryphon. The sort that hid some wisdom. Wisdom I did not impart to him. It was beyond me. Literally. I returned to my shoveling, didn't want to stare. "You telling me you found a rod and reel? And some line? I'm just — really, honestly, man—"

"Merman."

"Honestly, merman, I'm just trying to find a Christmas present for my brother."

"What's Christmas?"

"It's a long story."

"I have time."

"It's sixty-six books long plus some oral traditions plus a really weird economic system overlaid on top that sort of co-opted the whole thing. Plus a lot of conflicting emotions because of that and other competing philosophies. It'd take days to explain."

"Where am I going?" He pointed to the bars.

"It's a holiday."

The foreman threw another shovel at him.

He caught it poorly and started shoveling. "I tell you what. You explain this Christmas to me and I'll tell you where you can get a rod." He threw some of his sludge into the net.

I spent the next three days trying to get to the point where it made sense why I wanted to give a rod to my brother. We'd shovel for ten hours or so and then we'd sit up in the hammock and he'd fiddle with the giant ropes netting us into the brig. It was actually difficult on multiple fronts because of his insatiable curiosity. I'd get going on something and then use a phrase like "Christmas tree," and then I'd have to backtrack a few thousand years and work forward through about nine different cultures and timelines. Or "wrapping paper," that was fun to explain to an eco-conscious aquatic mammalfish. Or "post office" or any number of things that had no direct parallel in The Blazing World. Everything connected in some weird way to this one fishing rod. I suppose any given thing in creation can do that: the Wikipedia problem.

By the start of the fourth day, I had finished my tale and we had almost finished the sludge.

The Netter said, "I actually understand why you want a rod. I get it. But you really won't find any good ones on The Blazing World — they banned them centuries ago. Sorry."

Time for the third thing: as a worldmaker making and sustaining my subcreated worlds, I could make mindless automatons who do my bidding, but that's a bit disinteresting and it amounts to little more than talking to one's self. I could do the full-blown deistic demiurge thing, make the gun how I want, pull the trigger blindfolded, and walk away without assessing the damage. But seat-of-your-pants writing seldom ends well or even seldom ends satisfying when it ends poorly. (No offense if you write that way.)

But there's a third option between employing fatalism or deism in my worlds:

I could resolve that *though* I can take any bad scenario and work it towards the good for the sake of my characters, *even still* there's a point at which I stop acting like a true character in my own story and more like a removed narrator or demiurge (such as now), violating the very nature of the world, the very nature of the story, the very nature of characters being *themselves* anymore. As imaginative wills know the five senses and bring them together in images, so rational wills like mine assemble the totality of senses and imaginations in order to know — at once — what they mean without removing their agency as imaginative wills. If I break that? It's not just the death of the author and authorial intent you ought to worry about: it's the death of the living and breathing work of art.

Ultimately, I made that mistake hunting for a Christmas present. I violated their Narrative.

Thus the trident.

I was so sick of submitting to the rules of the world. I could change them. I'm the narrator, aren't I? I can do whatever I want. "You know what? No. This *is* a world where I could find a fishing rod." At the word *is*, I heard a great groan like a grave careening shiphull in a squall, cedars clicking and waiting to break, colossal coffin on the waters.

His eyes darkened, yellow flecks went black. He said, "You're right. Tonight, tell more of your story, but tell it louder. I will not be listening. Do what I do and follow me and I'll take you to your rod."

I nodded.

We shoveled for another ten hours, switching to brooms and squeegees mid-day and got the place pretty clean by evening.

"All done?" the foreman asked.

"How's it look to you?" I asked.

He said, "Cleanest vegetarian poo repository I've seen."

"Ummm," I said. "Did you just—"

"Good work." He went to push a large green button covered in a mother-of-pearl casing.

We climbed up in the hammock. The net salesman went and started fiddling with the net that made the wall above the hammock and nodded for me to join him in the process. I did the best I could to keep untwining, unraveling what he'd worked on but this guy knew his nets and knots and stitches and braids. It's like he looked at the whole thing and saw exactly what would unravel the whole work.

The sludge had piled up around the outside of our netted cage for the past few days. The foreman, oblivious of us, pressed the big green button and a foghorn echoed somewhere in the great conch shell of a castle. A crowd of thirty or seventy (hard to tell with writhing and tumbling fins and tails) came and opened mouths wide — fangs — and devoured the shit.

As they scrambled like coy in a kiddie pool, the netter said, "Come through *now*." He half pulled me, half shoved me through the opening in the net he'd unraveled slowly over the workdays.

I fell out and floated down onto the writhing mess of mermaids and said, "Aahhh! Ach!" as I slid down their slime, as I scaled their scales and swam towards the edge of the fight for the half-digested food.

The Netter just swam quick out and had hold of my hand as the crowd of mermen and mermaids worked one another over and over, wringing hands, twisted rubber bands, well-oiled snakeskin boots falling out the closet in a sewage-flooded basement. He pulled me not up the main cavern where the foreman — where had he gone? Into the fray? — had originally brought us along with his cronies, but rather down into their main rest area and the pipes there, some for aeration and some for tertiary sewage after such feeding frenzy, it turned out later, and some pipes for second-hand sludge and others similar to bank teller pneumatic tubes, a whole capsule pipeline system of bivalve shells that hid little secrets. One of them was larger. The Netter pointed to the larger one. "Climb in," he said, pointing to a large bivalve shell.

"No," I said.

"Yes, climb in."

"I'm not Nascita di Venere."

"I only speak Narrative, I'm sorry. I don't know even what language that is," he said.

"Venus being born."

"We don't have time to debate mythology, especially on a planet governed by her namesake, a planet currently against us. Get in."

"Fine," I said. I climbed in the mollusk. It was strangely cozy, kind of like some weird midcentury modern furniture: lots of pillows (made of a tongue), lots of walls, not a lot of back support.

He climbed in with me.

"Oh this is NOT a two-seater," I said. "Give me room."

"Shut up, human."

"If you knew the gift of the author and who it is saying to you, 'Give me room,' you would have asked him for room and he would have given you a whole freaking underground safe room."

"Dude, you have no room and this pipe is air-tight, where are you gonna get a room? Shut up and slide in."

I sighed. They never get it.

He hit a small lever, typed in a series of codes, and the shell closed, a giant sucking sound vibrated the edges of the shell and then it sucked us back and into the capsule pipeline system. Then I lost my sense of direction: up and down, yaw and pitch, left and right, fore and aft, everything went haywire and my stomach threatened to reverse.

"Don't you dare throw up," The Netter said.

"You guys did."

"That's because we can't digest things. Human puke is disgusting: you can't eat it again."

"That… yeah that might be the grossest thing I've *hu*—" I had to cover my mouth to keep it all in as we spun and flipped and… were we going lower?

Then the thing slowed easily, spun less, came to a halt with a click and a clatter and then… almost sighed open as if in coitus. What's a mollusk after coitus?

A cuddlefish.

We climbed out of the shell, which had dumped us into something like a room of doors if the doors were sewer grates and the room was a main intersection for various pipes unconnected to the capsule pipeline system. He said, "Come follow." And swam through the undercurrent of the great mermaid city, the tertiary sewer system of the twice-eaten. We swam past great boiler rooms that held hot air and stirred up a tumult in the air currents around them, past grey market shops selling things they ought not (no fishing rods that I saw, but plenty of pirate treasure and other stolen goods), beyond small forests of bad kelp, through the bones of some long-forgotten seamonster retrofitted into a hip nightclub, and large expanses of deep sea deserts: sand and sand and black sand and dead white coral and the busted hull of some great tanker.

Then we came to an airlock door in a massive, retired submarine that you could barely see for the chromatophores. Changing color, subtly. Cause outside, two GIGANTIC squids stood guard. They stretched the full length of the hull on either side so that if someone tried to attack the thing, they'd have to kill two massive sea monsters first and then literally have to get through to the sub over their dead bodies. Quite the excavating feat.

"Need in, Lotan. Got quite the catch."

"It's just Lots, Magellan. I told you that."

"Magellan like the Portuguese explorer?" I asked.

The Netter named Magellan turned to me. "I don't know much about portly geese, but if Cloud Cuckooland has a fat goose that explored the ocean depths, then sure, that's me." Then to the nearest squid eye, "Can you let us in, Lotan?"

Some of the giant tentacles nearest me coiled and roiled, suckers the size of the spoons it would take to eat bridge cable noodles, folding and opening like the foraminated petals of my mother's steam basket insert — the one she uses at Christmas time. "Do not call me Lotan. Do not invoke the name again. I am not he. I am only one of a great line who carries his name. Lots is fine."

"Well that's great since there's lots and lots of you," I said.

The squid shot its full eye on me, focused, and stilled.

The other squid's parallel eye did the same.

Magellan the portly geese netter looked at me, full on. "Honestly."

"What?" I asked. "Great big squid like him ought to know he's really—"

"She's," Magellan said.

"*She's* really quite greater than others."

"Stop," Magellan said. "I need in Lots."

"No one sees Tak."

"Not even me?"

"Not even you."

"Not even when I have quite the catch looking for a rod?"

The squid suckers billowed on both.

We waited.

A bale of turtles swam by on a quick current that came and went.

"Come in," Lots said.

"Who's Tak?" I asked.

"The Angler King," Magellan replied.

We went through a small crowd of fishy folk, their arms and armor, modern and ancient and weird and alien alike, and then went through a dearth of folk until the room opened up into a domed room, a perfect sphere perched atop a perfect cube like the Pantheon in Rome (Caesar's personal one that's now a Catholic church) It perfectly sustained sound, acoustics like amphitheaters donated from the four winds and smashed together in all directions. The top of that dome had an open-water oculus that led out of the dome and the sub. Some strings or something caught the light there in the hole and I should have better paid attention to those, in retrospect. But there on the floor in the middle sat a great halved redwood on two great marble blocks. Beside one of the blocks, something great had turned the dirt beneath it into a spawning bench. A bass nest with wee fishies.

But the bass was not wee.

A largemouth bass the size of a New York City MTA bus. No, it's not that kind of fishing story: I'm not talking about something I caught. I'm talking about the prototypical fish from all of the stories that have ever been told by all of the fishermen ever. The one from all of the story books, The Fish That Got Away. Always got away. The one that had pulled directly against — and won out over — both trolling and outboard motors. The one that had eaten every favorite lure ever. The one that kept getting longer with every one-upmanship of a new fishing story. Behind him in a great semicircle hung the greatest rods and reels I have ever or will ever set eyes on.

The Angler King.

His mouth had been torn twenty ways and mended sloppily as if he'd splashed on that orc draught that Merry and Pippin had once drank, splashed it on like bad musk and aftershave. The Heidelberg dueling scar: I'd never seen one on a fish. One of his gills had been mutilated with the world's largest needlenose pliers. One of his eyes had been punctured with some anchor or some large hook, larger than Captain Hook's — up through the roof of his mouth, through the backside of the eye socket so that the eye permanently looked up and out, bulged, hung a bit outside of the socket, twitching now and again. White stripes of scars where gills should go. One fin slow in growing back, something like a baby's arm on a grownass man. But the largemouth version.

I was staring. Meditating on it, even.

"Okay that's enough, shank him," The Angler King said.

A twice-jumbo shrimp with a trident stabbed me. Rest easy: it hurt like hell. Blood in the water, blood in the grates. Some lesser sharks stirred in the shadows, chained.

My phone buzzed. Hayden had texted.

Sinking down on the sub floor on the ocean floor and bleeding, I checked it.

"Don't get stabbed with a trident."

"Too late," I texted back.

"Are you unheeding?" The Angler King asked from the comfort of his spawning bench.

"Then don't get shanked with a trident AGAIN," Hayden texted.

They shanked me again.

"Too late," I texted.

"The name?" The Angler King asked. "What in *the name* are you doing?"

"Medical device. Keeps me alive on a place like this. I'm unacclimated to the pressure and quantity of water, all due respect. I'm not from here."

"Don't die," Hayden texted.

"See you at Christmas?" I texted.

"You are using a diving bell?" The Angler King asked.

"Like that, only smaller and more efficient and less cumbersome."

"I'll make you moonshine!" Hayden texted.

The Angler King said, "Are you done? Are you done. Are you done? Because I find it disrespectful to do… *that*… while your elder talks."

"Bubba?" Haden texted.

I didn't answer. I put it away.

It vibrated again.

I left it alone. "I've calibrated it for the moment."

"Good," he said. "You are bleeding, you see?"

"I see."

He looked over at the sharks. "And they can smell, hrmmm."

"I'm told you like fishing rods."

His good eye flashed and focused. His dead eye twitched wildly, almost enough to go back into the socket. "Yessssss." He sounded like a catfish out of water. "You enjoy the rod and the reel? You feel enjoyment hook, line, and sinker?" His tongue fondled his lip scars at the word *hook*.

"I'm shopping."

"Shopping." He grinned. His teeth flexed in a way I'd never seen on a bass. Normally it's a row of pesky, velcro-like barbs. His looked like a row of mangled alligator fangs, as if the barbs had mutated slowly over time, drawing on his bitterness and vitriol for the men who had caught him, drawing to grow into ever climbing: the deathspires danced at night.

"Dude," I said. "How are you even alive? I mean, no offense and all — I'm a hard guy to offend, but aren't largemouth bass freshwater fish?"

"Is my personality not salty enough for your taste?"

"Touché," I said.

"Come and see my lures," the Angler King said.

"No thanks, just the rods and reels."

"Of course," he said, moving the same way, "that's what I meant."

They looked gorgeous: tons of flecks of reds and golds and silvers. The variegated beauty of the best angler craftsman, the best hook heads. I thought of how my dad'd been called Captain Hook on the job site for union jobs and part of me wondered if—

"Enlighten me," the Angler King said.

"Yes?"

"You have an interesting accent, though you speak the most fluent Narrative I've ever heard. And I've been around for many a good fishing story. One might say *all* fishing stories. Terran?"

"Earth, yeah."

"American?"

"They claim me. I don't really claim them. Claiming things in America seems historically… bad."

"But you were born there, Son of Adam?"

"Sure thing. And most people there don't really believe in Adam, but I—"

He whipped round and flared fins. "It is but a turn of phrase."

"I was going to say I accept the phrase gladly for what it means to you: I am a man from the line of men, born of woman and not cloned or artificially inseminated into the womb of another, untethered from the powers of science and the dominion of governments and the machinations of men, a true man of earth and not a man born off-planet nor am I centaur or mermaid or faun or sphynx or what have you."

He lowered his voice. "Middle West?"

"Illinois."

"Southern?"

"Yeah. Land of Lincoln. Rivervalley."

"Little Egypt."

"You know it?" I asked.

"Tell me — was your father a Redman?"

"The… oh those lake-based fishing tournaments?"

His tongue licked up and touched his dangling eyeball. That moment another man came in — some familiar Gergian, not a storyweaver or other kind of magician, though he spoke Narrative well and breathed without a mask — escorted by the squid and then the twice-jumbo shrimp. Magellan the portly geese netter said, "Sir…?"

The human said, "I have searched over six Tors to meet you, your highness."

Clearly flattered, the Angler King said, "Excuse me, *friend*." They held parley and the man couldn't stop talking about the names and makes of the rods and reels and their various lineages as if they'd come from sword maker lines like Excalibur and Hatori Hanzo and Folly and whatnot. He talked and he talked and he talked and he talked and I just listened to him make an ass out himself. The Angler King said, "Try your *favorite*. Try it well."

The man reached out for a long, bright, red, corkhandled rod and reel. He opened his hand wide, grabbed hold.

And screamed.

The Angler King was singing, "*I will make you fishers of men, fishers of men, fishers of men.*"

The rod fused to his hand in a molten array, blood shot out as hooks pierced his whole forearm parallel to the handle and the hooks set deeper, bending his arm so that some set in his stomach as well. Then the nearly-invisible bridge cable suspending the rod caught the light as it yanked him up through the oculus in the dome, screaming the whole way, keeping a—

You know.

I really don't stay around for detailed descriptions of moments like that when all I'm looking for is a last-minute Christmas gift.

I'm gonna be honest here: I booked it for the door. Door was sealed. And my brother's right, I suppose: when there's enough magic in the room, I can justify using a bit, especially when it's my fault the rods and reels existed in the first place. So I did indeed call down a teensy bit of fire: it shot out a burning plume of liquid oxygen out my boots as it might on one of those old chemical burn rockets. As that happened, I wove the steel of the room into a drill bit helmet and stuck one leg rocket at an angle so that I spiraled. Something grabbed my arm, but I didn't pay any attention to it because I plowed clean through that steel airlock and the two giant squids got so scared that they doused the whole shooting match in ink. The man who'd grabbed the rod was suspended in air, slowly getting shredded with a ball full of needles. I dropped the drill bit helmet as I climbed and noticed the thing on my arm was Magellan. "Aww man, come—"

"You come on," he said. "I warned you about fishing rods."

"You did," I said. "You did that." I checked my phone.

Hayden had texted, "I was just shitting you, you know."

Christmas Eve Gift Exchange:

"So that's why I didn't get you a rod this year," I said.

"Sure. You totally waited until the last minute," Hayden said.

"Nah uh," I said.

"Dude you were texting me last week."

Our mom sipped her apple cider moonshine that she thought was just apple cider. Hayden'd given it to her.

"Well open it anyways," I said. "Magellan gave it to me."

He opened it. "It's a net," he said. "A cast net."

"You know the difference?"

"No," he said and held up the tag. "Tag says *cast net: for personal fishermen.*"

"Ah," I said. "I guess it's *legal.*"

"Well what's the fun if I can't fish all the fish out of Kinmundy pond using dragnets and dynamite?"

"You know what the great philosopher Stephen Wright says," Papa Bren.

We all recite: "*There's a fine line between fishing and standing on the shore like an idiot.*"

Hayden asked, "Don't cast nets work with harpoons?"

I shrugged. "Guess we need to go carve some spears at Bryant Park or something."

Papa Bren looked at me. Eyed me, really. "Angler King, huh?"

"Angler King," I said. I lifted my shirt to show the trident scar…s in my side.

"Told you I caught the biggest fish ever," Papa Bren said.

Hayden said, "Yeah, well, doesn't count if you don't get him in the boat, now does it pop?"

"How's Maybel?" I asked.

She walked in carrying three plates: tuna salad, fish sticks, crab rangoon. "You'll love this stuff, Toby. I make it cause your brother likes it."

"You got anything vegetarian?"

Hayden said, "Yeah, my brother prefers to eat shit and die."

Everyone stopped and stared at my brother.

"Hayden!" Maybel shrieked.

But I laughed and laughed and laughed.

"Good cider," mom said, oblivious as only a teetotaler can be. "Good, good, good cider. Mmmm mmm."

"Hey," said Hayden, "Don't drink all that! I made the moonshine for Toby's present."

"Moonshine?!" mom shrieked, staring at the jar. She fell off her chair and landed on the floor hard enough to belch.

I said, "All you last-minute Christmas shoppers are the worst."

Hayden cast the net on my head and pulled the drawstring.

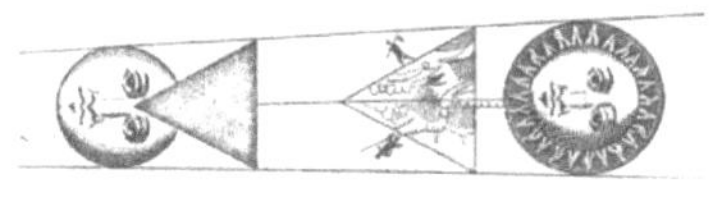

BIOS.

(which, mind you, is a Greek myth for "life")

Kaaron Warren is an Australian author of horror, science fiction, and fantasy short stories and novels. She is the author of the short story collections Through Splintered Walls, The Grinding House, and Dead Sea Fruit. Her short stories have won Australian Shadows Awards, Ditmar Awards and Aurealis Awards.

Howard Andrew Jones is the author of the Ring-Sworn heroic fantasy trilogy from St. Martin's, starting with *For the Killing of Kings*, as well as the critically acclaimed Arabian fantasy series starring Dabir and Asim, and four Pathfinder novels. He's the editor of the print magazine *Tales From the Magician's Skull*, among other things, and can be found lurking at www.howardandrewjones.com, where he blogs about writing craft, gaming, fantasy and adventure fiction, and assorted nerdery.

Alex Sirkman is a form of couch infestation common in New York City. Alex Sirkman will not remove those tough, greasy stains. Alex Sirkman may be applied directly to the forehead; massage thoroughly for best effect. Alex Sirkman is no miracle cure, just a cutting edge application of high-tech algorithmic gimcrackery. Alex Sirkman - Not even once.

Brandon Ketchum is a speculative fiction writer from Pittsburgh, PA who enjoys putting a weird spin or strange vibe into every story, dark or light. He is a member of the Horror Writers Association, his work has won Writers of the Future Contest honorable mentions, he leads the Pittsburgh Writers Meetup Group, and coordinated the 2019 PARSEC Short Story Contest.

Brandon McNulty is an author of supernatural thrillers and horror. His novel *Bad Parts* won both Pitch Wars and RevPit, and his short fiction has been published in Spinetingler Magazine, NewMyths.com, and Digital Horror Fiction. He offers weekly writing advice on his YouTube channel Writer Brandon McNulty.

J. T. Glover has short fiction in *Best New Horror*, *Pseudopod*, and *Nightscript*, among other venues. He's published nonfiction in *Postscripts to Darkness*, *The Silent Garden*, and *Thinking Horror*. A librarian by day, he lives in Virginia and can be found online at www.jtglover.com.

Anthony G. Cirilla is an Assistant Professor of English at College of the Ozarks. He writes fantasy and science fiction, inspired by C.S. Lewis, J.R.R. Tolkien, George MacDonald, and The Legend of Zelda. He blogs as The Boethian Acolyte at theboethianacolyte.wordpress.com, in honor of his favorite philosopher, Boethius, author of the Consolation of Philosophy. He lives with his beautiful and talented wife, Camarie, in Branson, MO.

Carole McDonnell is a writer of Christian, sword-and-soul, fantasy, and ethnic stories. Her writings appear in various anthologies, including *So Long Been Dreaming: Postcolonialism in Science Fiction*, edited by Nalo Hopkinson and published by Arsenal Pulp Press; *Jigsaw Nation*, published by Spyre Books; *Steamfunk*, *Griots*, and others. Her story collections are *Spirit Fruit:*

Collected Speculative Fiction by Carole McDonnell and *Turn Back O Time*. Her novels are *Wind Follower, My Life as an Onion, The Constant Tower, The Daughters of Men, The Charcoal Bride*. Her Bible studies include: *Seeds of Bible Study, Blogging the Psalms, A Fool's Journey Through Proverbs, Great Sufferers of the Bible, Christian Laws of Attraction.* She lives in New York with her family.

F.C. Shultz is the author of three middle grade books, and writes stories and poems about dragons and sea people and honor and family. He loves Ray Bradbury and peanut butter, and lives in Missouri with his wife, son, and cat.

Tracey Baptiste is the New York Times bestselling author of MINECRAFT: THE CRASH. She is also the author of the popular JUMBIES series including THE JUMBIES, RISE OF THE JUMBIES, and THE JUMBIE GOD'S REVENGE. She has written several other fiction and nonfiction books for children. Find Tracey online at www.traceybaptiste.com and connect on Twitter @traceybaptiste and on Instagram @traceybaptistewrites.

Ken Altabef's short fiction has appeared in fantasy magazines such as F&SF, Interzone, Daily Science Fiction, Intergalactic Medicine Show, BuzzyMag, Abyss & Apex, Perihelion etc. His stories have received honorable mention in Years Best SF and Best Horror of the Year. He is the author of eleven fantasy novels, noted for vivid characters and powerful emotion. He is best known for popularizing Inuit culture with his ALAANA'S WAY series which takes place in a unique fantasy world based on Inuit mythology. His critically acclaimed LADY CHANGELING TRILOGY features shapeshifting faeries, action, intrigue, and romance. Visit his website at www.KenAltabef.com

Andrea Obaez is a once aspiring journalist with bylines in her hometown newspapers The Hartford Courant, The Hartford News, and each of Central Connecticut State University's student publications. Now armed with a sociology degree and years of experience in social and customer service, Andrea is working on exploring gender dynamics, social expectations, and what it means to be happy, healthy and whole through fiction. She is working on her first erotic pulp novel set in her hometown. You can read most of her previous works and social observations on her blog, www.andreaobaez.com.

Emily Munro is a writer and educator living and working in New York city.

She currently creates content full time as the Social Media and Communications Specialist for the Children's Museum of Manhattan. Visit them useum's Website, Facebook, Instagram, or Twitter to see some of Emily's work. She also reads anything that will sit still long enough, knits socks, and drinks far too much tea. She can be found scribbling away in Brooklyn. Random updates are occasionally available at Emilymunro.blog

Vonnie Winslow Crist, SFWA, HWA, is author of The Enchanted Dagger, Owl Light, The Greener Forest, and other award-winning books. Her stories appear in Cast of Wonders, Amazing Stories, Chilling Ghost Short Stories, and elsewhere. A cloverhand who has found so many four-leafed clovers she keeps them in jars, Vonnie strives to celebrate the power of myth in her writing. For more info: http://www.vonniewinslowcrist.com

About Lancelot Schaubert

Two excerpts of Lancelot's debut novel BELL HAMMERS have sold to *The New Haven Review* (Yale's Institute Library) and *The Misty Review*, while a third excerpt was selected as a finalist for the **last** *Glimmer Train Fiction Open* in history. He has also sold poetry, fiction, and nonfiction to *TOR (MacMillan), The Anglican Theological Review, McSweeney's, Poker Pro's World Series Edition, The Poet's Market, Writer's Digest*, and many similar markets.

Spark + Echo just chose me for their 2019 artist in residency, commissioning me to write four short stories.

I have published work in anthologies like *Author in Progress, Harry Potter for Nerds*, and *Of Gods and Globes I & II* — the last of which I edited and featured stories by Juliet Marillier (whose story was nominated for an Aurealis award), Anne Greenwood Brown, Dr. Anthony Cirilla, LJ Cohen, FC Shultz, and Emily Munro. My work *Cold Brewed* reinvented the photonovel for the digital age and caught the attention of the Missouri Tourism Board who commissioned me to write and direct a second photonovel, *The Joplin Undercurrent*, in partnership with my friend and photographer, Mark.

Born and raised in Southern Illinois amid four generations of carpenters (and named either after Lancelot the knight or Lancelot the soap opera character, depending on which parent you ask), I moved to Joplin, Missouri for college where I did internships in San Diego among young artists and in Detroit — Dearborn — where I taught English and citizenship to Arab immigrants. I auditioned for some TV shows, helped internationals feel at home, and started an artist support group with Mark Neuenschwander, the photographer.

In college, I majored in rhetoric and minored in mythology and ancient literature. Somewhere in there, I fumbled along trying to woo the grooviest girl in the world to marry me. She was from Ferguson, Missouri.

Now, we live in New York City. In addition to writing and producing, I work for ACT International helping artists in the city think cleverer, feel deeper, and act truer. Sometimes I give them grants to jumpstart their careers. Most of the time I just cook them food, let them crash at my place, and hold them when NBC rejects their screenplay or only five of their paintings sell at their gallery. If that's you, I'm in your corner. By now, I've written hundreds of articles and stories and poems (maybe thousands?) and I've spoken for various conferences on writing, culture creating, neighborhood development, and virtue ethics.

also by Lancelot Schaubert

- *Of Gods and Globes I: A Cosmic Anthology*
- *Writing Rules, Revised*

From *The Vale* universe:

- *Bell Hammers: The True Folk Tale of Little Egypt* (debut novel)
- *All Who Wander* (album)
- *Wombrovers**
- *That Wooed the Slimy Bottom of the Deep*
- *Carry Cannons by Our Side**
- *Wilderness**
- *The Blissful Dreams of Long Ago*
- *Earth Swallowed*
- *The Blimps of Venus*
- *∞ Falls 1 Stand*
- *Portrait of the Nonartist*
- *Inconveniences, Rightly Considered* (poetry)
- *The Elevator Out* (picture book)
- *Cold Brewed* (photonovel)
- *The Joplin Undercurrent* (photonovel)

---

* Audiobook available

www.ingramcontent.com/pod-product-compliance
Lightning Source LLC
Chambersburg PA
CBHW030525310726
48979CB00010B/1798/J

* 9 7 8 1 9 4 9 5 4 7 0 5 4 *